Praise for Lilith S

"Incredibly timely, well written and important....A testament to Saintcrow's skill."
—*Los Angeles Times* on *Afterwar*

"Vivid prose highlights the immediacy of battle, and the war-fractured landscape and the emotional and physical toll of fighting are realistically drawn....An unsettling vision."
—*Publishers Weekly* on *Afterwar*

"So refreshing and original....With non-stop action, you won't be able to put down *Cormorant Run!*"
—*RT Book Reviews*

Praise for Gallow and Ragged

"Saintcrow deftly mixes high-minded fantasy magic with rough, real-world rust using prose that veers between the beautiful and the bloodcurdling."
—Chuck Wendig, *New York Times* bestselling author

"Painfully honest, beautifully strange, and absolutely worth your time. Lilith Saintcrow is at the top of her game. Don't miss this."
—Seanan McGuire, *New York Times* bestselling author

"Saintcrow's urban fantasy series launch is expertly crafted with heartbreak and mistrust, far darker and lovelier than the title suggests.... Saintcrow's artful, poignant descriptions remain with the reader long after the tale's end, as does the persistent sense of dark, unsettling unease."
—*Publishers Weekly* (starred review)

Praise for Bannon & Clare

"Sensual writing, intricate plotting, and sympathetically quirky, satisfyingly competent characters make this series one to watch."
—*Publishers Weekly* (starred review)

"Saintcrow scores a hit with this terrific steampunk series that rockets through a Britain-that-wasn't with magic and industrial mayhem with a firm nod to Holmes. Genius and a rocking good time."
—Patricia Briggs, *New York Times* bestselling author

"Innovative world building, powerful steampunk, master storyteller at her best. Don't miss this one. She's fabulous."
—Christine Feehan, *New York Times* bestselling author

Praise for Romances of Arquitaine

"The richness of the story and character interactions will have you finishing this book in one sitting....If you find yourself falling for knights and feathered hats, for politics and court intrigue, for consorts and love that lasts years—and we mustn't forget violence and pain—you will love this book." —*USA Today*'s *Happily Ever After* blog

Praise for Jill Kismet

"Jill Kismet is, above all else, a survivor, and it is her story that will haunt readers long after the blood, gore and demons have faded into memory." —*RT Book Reviews*

"Loaded with action and starring a kick-butt heroine who from the opening scene until the final climax is donkey kicking seemingly every character in sight." —Harriet Klausner

Praise for Dante Valentine

As Lilith Saintcrow

BLACK LAND'S BANE

A Flame in the North

DANTE VALENTINE

Working for the Devil
Dead Man Rising
The Devil's Right Hand
Saint City Sinners
To Hell and Back
Dante Valentine: The Complete Series

JILL KISMET

Night Shift
Hunter's Prayer
Redemption Alley
Flesh Circus
Heaven's Spite
Angel Town
Jill Kismet: The Complete Series

ROMANCES OF ARQUITAINE

The Hedgewitch Queen
The Bandit King

BANNON & CLARE

The Iron Wyrm Affair
The Damnation Affair
The Red Plague Affair
The Ripper Affair
The Collected Adventures of Bannon & Clare

GALLOW AND RAGGED

Trailer Park Fae
Roadside Magic
Wasteland King

Cormorant Run
Afterwar

As S. C. Emmett

HOSTAGE OF EMPIRE

The Throne of the Five Winds
The Poison Prince
The Bloody Throne

A
FLAME
IN THE
NORTH

BLACK LAND'S BANE:
BOOK ONE

LILITH
SAINTCROW

orbitbooks.net

Copyright © 2024 by Lilith Saintcrow
Excerpt from *The Fall of Waterstone* copyright © 2024 by Lilith Saintcrow
Excerpt from *Shield Maiden* copyright © 2023 by Sharon Emmerichs

Cover design by Lisa Marie Pompilio
Cover art by Michael Heath | Magnus Creative and Shutterstock
Cover copyright © 2024 by Hachette Book Group, Inc.
Map by Tim Paul

Orbit
Hachette Book Group
1290 Avenue of the Americas
New York, NY 10104
orbitbooks.net

First Edition: February 2024

Orbit is an imprint of Hachette Book Group.
The Orbit name and logo are registered trademarks of
Little, Brown Book Group Limited.

Library of Congress Cataloging-in-Publication Data
Names: Saintcrow, Lilith, author.
Title: A flame in the North / Lilith Saintcrow.
Description: First edition. | New York : Orbit, 2024. |
Series: Black Land's Bane ; book 1
Identifiers: LCCN 2023025338 | ISBN 9780316440332 (trade paperback) |
ISBN 9780316440431 (ebook)
Subjects: LCGFT: Fantasy fiction. | Epic fiction. | Novels.
Classification: LCC PS3619.A3984 F53 2024 | DDC 892.8—dc23/eng/202306012
LC record available at https://lccn.loc.gov/2023025338

ISBNs: 9780316440332 (trade paperback), 9780316440431 (ebook)

Printed in the United States of America

LSC-C

Printing 2, 2024

For those who must leave home.

When there passed us a woman with the West in her eyes,
And a man with his back to the East.

—Mary Elizabeth Coleridge

Several problems have tormented the translator of this tale; many a term in the Old Tongue or southron dialects holds nuance not easily explained in other languages. The reader's patience is humbly solicited. Any error is unintentional, any inaccuracy likewise.

May the Blessed smile upon both reader and scholar alike, knowing neither insult nor injury are meant.

PART ONE

JOURNEY NORTH

Hastily Done

For seidhr *is a tree, and some branches wider than others.
Those gifted with its touch may bend one of the great forces
of nature to their will, and those with any of the weirding may call a spark. The most blessed among them we call*
elementalist, *and they perform not mere kindling but hold
actual flame…*

—Navros, First Scholar of Naras in the
days of King Edresil

By solstice day the great Althing at Dun Rithell was almost over.
Our father took Astrid and Bjorn to the last day of the riverside fair but I did not accompany them; I was already thinking upon
the fire.

Mother was abed with winter ague and Bjorn her firstborn useless
when it came to organizing, both by temperament and upon account
of maleness. If you wished something heavy lifted, something bulky
heaved a great distance, something stabbed, slashed, or thumped into
submission, he was not only willing to oblige but also an expert of
such endeavors, but should you wish for aught else disappointment
was the result. Astrid had already done her part with the great feast
upon the penultimate day; many a toast was drunk to her health and
Ithrik the Stout had already gifted our hall with a great gem-crusted
plate as a sign of earnest.

My sister liked the sheep-lord's middle son Edrik well enough; he was a fine fighter and careful with his father's great flocks. Astrid's marriage, while not final by any means, at least was assured in *some* direction. Come spring Bjorn might be married as well, if any of the visiting girls and their kin liked the look of him. Both prospects pleased me like they should any good sister, but did not mean I wished to go a-fairing that day.

Besides, crowds are always…difficult. Though the quality of my cloth and the marks upon my wrists grant me space and there is always Arneior, I did not cherish the thought of being called to render a summary judgment between drunken warriors *or* perform some small trick to please a wide-eyed child among a press of visitors and jostling neighbors. Arn might have wished to go upon her own account, but I did not think of that until Father had already left with my siblings and my shieldmaid gazed longingly down the road, her ruddy hair a beacon in the strengthening dawn. Twin hornbraids crested on either side of her head, their tails dangling behind her shoulders wrapped into clubs with leather thongs, and the stripe of blue woad down the left side of her face shouted *One of the Black-Wingéd's own, do not touch.*

If she had not the woad, her very carriage and steady glare would serve as warning enough. It is known the battlefield maidens of Odynn's elect choose those of quick tempers, not to mention swift spears.

"Oh, fishguts," I said, spreading my hands; the last band upon my left wrist—ink forced under skin with a sharp point—twitched. The scab was almost off, but I had to refrain from scratching or drawing the pain aside to heal it more quickly. One does not use *seidhr* upon such marks. "I did not think, small one."

One coppery eyebrow shot up, and Arn scowled at me. Which is usually a cheerful sign; I have called her *small one* since she was sworn to me at Fryja's great festival during my sixth springtime—and my shieldmaid's ninth, for she is older, though I am supposed to be the wiser of our partnership.

"I do not wish to go," my shieldmaid said, her generous mouth pulled tight. The scales and rings sewn onto her daily hauberk glittered fiercely as the sun's first limb reached above the horizon, frost and thin metal both gilding the roof of our home. *When the sun rises, Eril's hall echoes it*, our men said, and one or two might even lift a drinking horn to the eldest daughter when they did.

One born with *seidhr* is considered lucky, even if 'tis best to be cautious of a *volva*'s temper. What is the sun but the largest bonfire of all, and if I could produce flame to hold back the night who knew what I could darken? It was a logical enough assumption, though the trepidation somewhat misplaced.

I did not think it wise to dispel such caution wholesale, though. Nor had my teacher Idra.

"You do not wish to attend the fair?" I mimicked astonishment, letting my eyes widen and the words lilt. There was a snapping, growling, baying explosion in the direction of the kennels; the houndmaster Yvin would be taking his shaggy, nose-drunk charges upon their traditional run through the South Moor soon. When they returned there would be scraps for both dogs and pigs, and both groups might be exhausted into reasonable behavior for the rest of the day. "Not even after the bonfire is laid?"

"It will take all day to stack," Arneior replied stiffly, and I laughed, taking her left arm. The other, of course, was not to be touched even by her charge. Her longhead spear—well upon its way to earning a name in its own way—occupied her right hand, its butt resting easily upon swept cobbles.

Soon the tables would be brought out for the Fools' Feast before the great evening celebration to mark the Althing's ending—though not the end of legal cases and other matters to be decided—and I would be very busy indeed.

For the moment, though, I could tease my Arn. "Not if I hurry things along. *A volva is hard to please.*" The proverb used to pain me; I watched as Father's golden head sank into the crowd passing down the road, just outside our courtyard's great timbered gates—ajar to show hospitality during the Althing, as was the custom. Astrid, as she only reached Bjorn's shoulder, was already lost to view; my brother, though he had his final growth upon him, would not quite match our father's height. Still, both of them were well-named, a big good-natured bear and a shimmering star.

I oft considered my own naming a great jest, for I am dark-haired as my mother and my father's mother. For all that, I have my mother's eyes; they said there was some of the Elder in Gwendelint of Dun Rithell's line, but I know not the truth of such a tale.

Despite a dark head my temper is much like Eril the Battle-Mad's, and those who see us together are unable to think me anything but his get. I have his nose, and my chin, while rather more pointed, is also shaped just as his, though my mouth and cheekbones belong to Gwendelint. More than that, Father and I share the same quality of gaze—the word is *piercing*, as an awl will go through thick leather, and when applied to a pair of eyes it means we see much more than we wish to, though Father's are dark and mine clear pale blue.

A steady stream of freedmen, bondsmen, servants, and thralls carted wood from every household and camp to the great green across the ancient stone-paved trade-road; the large flat outcropping of greyish rock in the midst of vast grassy space was black-topped from other burnings and bore a stubby crown of stacked logs already. Hopfoot my mother's steward, his reedy tenor aquiver with age, had been fussily directing the laying of the base since the grey mist before a winter dawn. The wicker cages along one side of the Stone would be quiet at this hour, though—they were small and relatively few, holding only promised sacrifices of fowl and rabbits.

There had been no war or raiding to bring excess livestock lately. Perhaps that accounted for my unease. I could even say I sensed somewhat amiss, but it would be a lie. That morning neither the blessèd gods—Aesyr, Vanyr, foreign—nor any other passing spirit gave no indication of the future, not even to me.

I was merely nervous in anticipation of what I had to do that evening.

My skirts touched Arn's knee as we slipped back through the gate; the green-and-white winter festival dress was last year's, true, but I had grown no more and would not reach even Astrid's height. Small am I, *little Solveig like a paring knife*, Father had crowed more than once, lifting child-me in his brawny arms.

As I grew older he became uneasy with my strangeness, but that was only to be expected.

"Hastily done is ill done." Arneior rolled her shoulders precisely once, a sign she was ready for the day's labors, whatever they might be. "And where is your mantle, my weirdling? Your mother will scold."

I shrugged in return. Mother would not glimpse me from her bedroom window; I had mixed her morning medicine with a sedative so she could not fret overmuch at being unable to oversee the feasts. My great fur-hooded green mantle was warm, yes, but I had merely stepped into the courtyard to bid Astrid good hunting in the market and also bring Bjorn the blundering his new beard-pin, forgotten at table. The night's frost was already turning to steam, lifting from our greathall's gilded roof just as the weary sun hauled itself above the black-timbered breast of white-hooded Tarnarya for the last time that year.

Our great mother-mountain would be renewed with dawn, like the entire world.

Tonight was the Long Dark; the bonfire would burn throughout, holding vigil. I would not sleep much either, making certain the flame kept steady, but at least it was dry weather. I did not taste much snow or ice upon the wind. Our river kept much of winter's worst excesses away, and we thanked her each spring for the blessing.

Even if it did include cold mud to the knee, and more than one shoe lost in quagmire.

"My lady! My lady Solveig!" Albeig, holding her cheerful blue festival skirt high so the embroidered hem did not touch the ground, waved from the top of the great stairs. She did not like to leave the inner fastness; our housekeeper hated disorder and there would be naught else in every corner, begging to be set aright. "The tables? Shall we?"

And thus it begins. There was no use in sighing; Albeig knew I wished to order the household myself, if only to show Mother she need not worry. "Make it so, then," I called up the stairs. "But do not set out the meat just yet."

She knew that as well, but Albeig's fair round face eased at proof that *I* was thinking with more than one finger, as the saying goes. She bobbed gently, a tiny wooden boat upon a disturbed puddle, and hurried back inside through the big black carven doors.

"They have not brought the pillars yet." Arn did not move. No doubt she would prefer chivvying those building the bonfire to the thankless work of setting out board for fortunate beggars and any of my father's men who wished a mouthful before going to the fair's colorful, hurrying sprawl.

Each oiled wooden pillar upon the Stone in the green bore a great rune-carving and would sink into prepared holes, ready to keep the lower mass of the bonfire from tipping. Come morning, having done their duty, whatever survived of their guard-watch would be given to the flames as well.

The old must be sacrificed before the new is brought in. So my people believed, and I have not found them wrong. "Then make certain they are placed properly for my first lighting, and return for the nooning." I rose upon my slippered tiptoes, pressing my lips to her cheek as if we were sisters; she gave an aggrieved sigh. "What? I promise not to stir a step past the gate without my Arn. Go."

Even a year before she would have refused, but the bands upon my left wrist were seven in number just as the ones upon my right were five, thin dark double-lines of ink and ash forced under the skin, angular runes dancing within their confines. Not only that, but my hair was braided in the complex fashion of a full *volva* by Astrid just that morn, red coral beads at special junctures, and Father himself had gifted me his mother's silver torc, the bees of her house and lineage resting heavy and comforting below my collarbone.

In short, none would dare offer violence, jostling, or even a light word to a woman so attired inside a riverlord's walls. Why risk exile, or a curse taking the flavor from your mead as the old saying warns? There are stories of weirdlings running hot lead into a warrior's marrow to answer an insult, too.

Every child knows those tales, and is taught to keep a civil tongue when speaking to those with even the weakest *seidhr*.

Arn gave in after a few moments of token resistance, and glared at me afresh from her relatively imposing height. Even her freckles glowed in thin golden winterlight, and her breath was a fine silver plume. "Not a single step past the gate, Sol."

"Then don't be late. Or I might find myself walking alone,

riverside-bound to find Astrid." It was an empty threat delivered only to make her bristle, since I would not willingly stir from the hall's safety until sunset. "And mind you don't make Hopfoot stammer; he is very afraid of you."

"As well he should be." She hefted her spear, its long bright blade winking conspiratorially. "I go, then. Put your mantle on, daughter of Gwendelint."

I dropped her arm and stuck my tongue out, making a battle-face; she laughed and set off with springing steps. I climbed my father's great wide stairs, their grain worn to satin smoothness by many visiting feet, and plunged into the dimness of the entryway, an explosion of hurry and babble enveloping me from slipper-toe to the top of my braided head. The tables were to be dragged out into the courtyard and hung with roughcloth; the feeding of fortunate fools should always begin at midmorn.

Questions leapt for me from every side—where should this be settled, how many dishes should be taken forth, where were the extra trenchers, Father's huntsman Yngold was drunk among the pigs and who should drag him forth—oh, I did not mind even *that* occurrence, for I could set his friends Tar and Jittl upon his track and they would take him to the fair for a sobering fight or summat else. There was Mother's noontide medicine to mix in the stillroom while I was interrupted every few moments for another decision, and the kitchen's smoky clangor to brave for shouted conference with Nisman and Ilveig, the latter furiously calm while the former wielded knife, ladle, or whisk with a warrior's grim determination. There were the great casks to order tapped or set aside, yet more tankards and trenchers to be found, children to be collared and sent to their duties with a tug upon their ear to remind them a *volva*'s request is not a negotiable matter.

Of such things were the last festival I spent with my family made. I would like to think I remember everything about that busy day.

But if I am to be honest, I do not.

Simple, Easy

Even the Sun must be renewed each year. All that is given must be paid for, and all fires need fuel.
                          —Idra the Farsighted, of Dun Rithell

My lady Solveig?" Albeig swiped at her forehead with the back of one almost-limp hand; her hazel eyes were very bright. The great feasting hall was all a-clamor, from its rush-strewn floor to its great roof-timbers. "The sun is going down."

I knew as much, of course—three people had told me in the last few moments, each anxiously expecting praise for the reminder. It was enough to make me almost regret being presented for Idra's training so many years ago.

Almost, but not quite. Uncontrolled weirding is worse than none at all, and though the elder *volva* of Dun Rithell was a harsh teacher she had also been scrupulously just, as any with the burden of *seidhr* are expected to be.

It is an expectation not many fulfill, to hear the songs and sagas tell. But Idra did, and demanded as much from me as well. What I once considered her cruelty was in fact merely discipline, and I am glad I learned the distinction before she breathed her last.

I gave a nod, gesturing directions at the two thralls wrestling the last table—its legs knocked free of mud outside, a chore nobody likes but which saves a great deal of future trouble—into position. More of the household were bearing away the roughcloth from the Fools' Feast and bringing fresh hangings and tapestries; very soon the mighty among Father's warriors and any important guests would begin arriving. Naturally the hall would be ready well before the first merrymaker stamped through the door for wassail, and the great iron cauldron with leaping figures upon its sides was bubbling already.

But the preparation of a great feast is filled with small disasters those who partake of its bounty rarely recognize; the only ones aware of such things are those who must smooth, tidy, and arrange so a great revel seems effortless.

"Settle it there," I said, rubbing my damp palms upon a scrap of wastecloth before folding and tucking it back into a small house-pouch at my belt. "Many thanks; now go swallow summat, both of you. Hurry." With that done and the thralls hastening kitchenward before the evening's work I could turn my attention to our house-keeper, who leaned against the returned table to give me a wan smile, a roughcloth apron shielding her festival gown. "And you should have a mouthful too, Albeig. Don't argue."

"Indeed, I would never." She glanced nervously at the great tim-bered arch through which Father was due any moment. Bjorn and Astrid would greet guests in the entry amid the carvings of gods and ancestors while Father took his place upon the dais, under the large beam with names of battles and other achievements carved into its length and breadth, but they were not returned just yet.

At the time I felt only weary unsurprise. Of course the crowning achievement of my training would pass unremarked by my family; it was the way of such things.

"Solveig!" Arneior appeared in the arch's throat, her hauberk glittering; her left arm was full of heavy green wool and her woad was freshly applied. "Sunset."

Fryja grant me patience; I need a triple measure today. "Yes, my shieldmaid. I know." A stray strand of dark hair was attempting to work free of my braids; I tucked it back in and made another ges-ture, shooing Albeig upon her way. My feet ached, but that was to be expected; I had doubled socks from Astrid's needles, slid my heaviest slippers over them, and stolen a few moments after luncheon to lace up my winter buskins. Albeig could send my overboots up to the Stone as night's cold began to mount, if I did not falter at the lighting. "Albeig, I go, the house is yours."

"My lady." The housekeeper nodded, her shoulders stiffening; perhaps Nisman would send her a cup of batter, knowing her likely to drive herself into foundering under the responsibility of arranging Dun Rithell's hospitality upon this busiest of days. Mother would rest comfortably tonight, though, double-sedated and free of any worry.

I hurried past my shieldmaid, who rolled her eyes and caught my arm. "What did I tell you? Wear your mantle." She settled a thin undercloak and then the deep green woolen prize-mantle over me, the pelt at its shoulders tickling as it brushed my nape and cheeks. Astrid's needlework at the cloak's hem was bright and fine, and Arn herself had hunted the wolf. "There. Now my weirdling will not catch the ague."

"I would not anyway." I settled the wide heavy sleeves, and though my lower back immediately prickled with sweat I was glad of both cloakweights after Arn hurried me through the hall and into the courtyard, sweeping her own dun overmantle across mailed shoulders.

Tarnarya's snow-hood was dyed with brief scarlet sunset. Her timbered bulk was black beneath; I shivered as my father's hall caught the last hint of sunlight and flamed. I would have thought it an intimation of doom, but it was simply that I never liked when the grand peak dipped her head in blood. She is sacred to a crow-goddess, our mother-mountain of Dun Rithell, and when *that* lady is in sanguinary mood even seasoned warriors might well flinch before turning to the business of battle.

Arn kept her left hand upon my elbow, steady and comforting; I was glad of her foresight, as usual. A clot of the curious or those wishing for a change in their luck lingered at the great gate, and the two warriors upon guard duty set up the cry as soon as they noticed Arn's ruddiness upon the great steps.

I pulled my great furred hood into position, settling it with a twitch and dropping my gaze. Everything splashed upon the paving had frozen, and the press of bodies in the space where our house's gate-apron met the road might have buffeted me from my feet if not for Arn's care.

"*Back, back,*" the gate-guards shouted, their axes crossed with staves of office. There should have been another double handful of men to take me to the Stone, but perhaps Father had thought Arn and me well capable without such a luxury. "*Back, for the burning cometh!*"

Arn's grasp upon my elbow did not gentle. Surefoot is a shield-maid, as the saying goes, and I walked where she placed me. My breath was a cloud, drifting to catch in the mantle's wolf-fur, and it was the first time since I rolled from our bed before dawn that I could catch a full lung-draft.

I had deliberately done all I could for the last and greatest feast of the old year myself, to keep hands and head occupied before this moment. Now I had to face the fire.

The thought that it might have been better had I spent some time in quiet meditation was unhelpful indeed.

I watched frozen mud veining across old, worn stone laid well before our people had settled this riverbank, Arn's boots keeping time with my smaller but no less well-wrapped feet, and when we stepped onto the green at the far end it might as well have been more rock beneath us, for the ground was icebound indeed. Winter-yellowed grass crunched uneasily, and there was singing in the distance with a glimmer of lamps and torches.

They were coming uphill from the riverside fair to see the wonder of the longest night. My heart beat thin and fast within my wrists, thumping in my ribcage and generally making a fool of itself.

It was a fair way to the tabletop Stone, but two greens-marshals with curved ram horns hurried to wind them and the crowd parted before those deep sonorous cries. There should have been yet another cadre of warriors from our house to manage the crowd as well, but none had returned from the fair as yet; it was the first real wrongness in a festival day that had, so far, passed like any other. A few warriors of other folds, halls, or steadings hurried to take the place of an honor-guard, a fortunate accident for them.

Accompanying a full-made *volva* upon this duty would grant them luck and strength for an entire year. Whoever among Eril's men had not returned when they should would miss the blessing, but that was not my concern. More warriors joined the cortege, keeping the curious at bay with their size, but Arn did not greet any of them as she would those of my father's hall. Instead, she observed a cold silence, and I exhaled shakily as a faint trace of green showed through dried clumps of grass.

A good omen, clinging to life in the midst of ice. Or so I hoped.

Cart tracks, a drover's trail, and two footpaths bisected our route; Arn all but lifted me across the last. She still said nothing, and I slowed. The fury of a shieldmaid is almost a living thing, pressing invisibly against heart and lungs; I did not wish to feel it scraping my nerves all night.

"Please," I murmured. "Don't brood upon it."

She leaned close as if I were prophesying. A shieldmaid with a weirdling charge is to weigh every utterance, plumbing for the will of the gods; those without some measure of faith do not last upon their particular path.

Or upon mine.

"The least he could do," Arn muttered in reply, and shook her head. "And your very first."

Perhaps Father knows I would be nervous, were he looming here to watch me. "Hopfoot built it, I shall have no trouble lighting it."

"What says the *volva*?" someone wished to know, calling from outside a hard knot of tall, crest-haired warriors in hauberks not nearly so fine as my Arn's. A few of the guards would no doubt ask Father for a place at his board now, granted a fine opportunity by this protective deed.

"Naught you need worry for," a harsh male voice replied, a traditionalist scolding the irreligious, and there was a shout of laughter. Upon the far edge of the green, coming from the river, the misty line of bobbing lights doubled back and forth, a snake with gemmed sides. Faint singing rode the cold wind; we were not a moment too soon.

"Mayhap she asks for flint and steel," someone else called, and my jaw tightened. There was the sound of a blow; it was ill luck to jape so even when a *volva* in question had not lit her first bonfire.

Especially when she was held to have more than average power, being capable of calling flame instead of mere spark. Most with *seidhr* may touch only one of the great natural elements—water, air, earth, wood, metal, and the like—their entire lives. Those who may summon and befriend them all are rare, and their mark is fire itself.

I had lit Idra's cottage-fire many a time, even with wet fuel. This would be no different, except for the weight of expectation standing ready to crush me. Arn said nothing, simply waited until I moved again. The Stone loomed nearer, nearer; she turned us along its stack-lined face so we could properly climb the stairs cut into its westron side.

All jesting ceased, and everyone who owed a god some service or thanksgiving fell silent as I put my foot to the first step. I did glance at Arn then; I could not help myself.

My shieldmaid's head was proudly lifted, her spear-tip catching a last bloody sungleam; she did not look to me, her attention upon the crowd wending from the river's far, slow glitter. A muscle in her pale cheek flickered. Smoke from the trading palisade rose, and normally upon a winter's eve that pall would be underlit with lamp- and torch-light, not to mention the glow of cooking fires.

Yet while I had been sunk in feast preparations, too busy to think about what awaited me past dark, the houses clinging to the riverside had extinguished hearth, lamp, and candle. Soon my father's house would quench its fires, too.

The rekindling of Dun Rithell's heat—and life itself—would be mine alone.

Hush deepened, enfolding both Stone and green as Arn's fingers loosened. Her dark gaze roved far afield, searching for physical danger and leaving me to handle aught else, from weirding to negotiation— that is the compact between shieldmaid and *volva*, and well have we come to know it. Though I did not need her strength at that particular moment, it was pleasant to see her certainty.

She, at least, did not doubt me.

My shieldmaid's fingers gave a last squeeze; I gathered my skirts and the mantle. Slipping upon the steps would be a bad omen, but they had been brushed and sanded well. I climbed one at a time, Arn following close, and as I mounted the Stone, the silence became absolute except for far singing upon the cold breeze.

A bulk of oiled wood crouched over me, a wave frozen by Lokji's kenning or Hel's amused glance, and the wicker sacrifice-cages were now part of its towering. The mountain's snowy head paled as I pushed my hood slightly back, and yet a third procession approached from the ancient standing stones at the eastron edge of safe pasturage, their ring full of chill murmuring even during midsummer. Frestis led that cortege, the flint knife at his belt unsheathed and still damp-smeared.

The wind freshened, tugging at my skirts, threatening to slip a blade-edge through the mantle's folds. I settled my chin in wolf-fur and watched Mother Tarnarya fall under night's shadow, stars glimmering through veils both of cloud and dusk. The last dregs of the old sun swirled in the west; the air bore an entire smithy's worth of iron-taste to my tongue, now clearly speaking since the sun had ceased to pull at its laces.

Snow within a fiveday. Anyone raised near Dun Rithell could tell as much; we know the winter as one of our own families. Sheltered by the two mothers of peak and shore, we were blessèd children even in hard years. What our own efforts could not wring from field or flock the river brought to us in trade or fish, news or coin.

A shape swelled in the failing dusk, climbing the stairs I had used. Frestis's white robe glowed; his grey head nodded. His stave tapped at the Stone's floor, for his right leg dragged worse each winter. Still, his beard was full and apprentices reported his grasp was iron yet. And he wielded the flint knife so adroitly as to cause no pain at the standing stones.

Corag—the most senior of his apprentices—carried the yellow lantern. His dark eyebrows were raised and he studied me curiously in its swinging, fitful glow. I turned my chin slightly, counting the stars as they strengthened.

Idra should have been here, but she had loosened her grasp upon life at the dark of the first harvest moon. *When I am no longer here,* she said often enough, but I had not truly thought such a time would come any more than I could compass Mother's illness or that soon Bjorn would be married and leave the hall.

Or even that Astrid would bring a husband in to take up Father's greataxe, if he could.

There were other shapes in unbleached robes over their winter festival dresses and bulky undercloaks—Molveig, Isolca, Kolle, and Yannei, all crowned with glossy green spike-leaf holly and their lips reddened as blood-fed spirits'. Kolle, her matron-hipped solidity comforting, carried the other lantern, the one said to be of Elder make. It was a fine, beautiful thing, its decorative metal so thin and well-wrought it seemed spring vines had been dipped in steel to make it.

Kolle was the senior *seidhr* now, carrying the ancient distaff, but she did not have much of the weirding. Her bandings were only three upon her right wrist and the one upon her left. The rest bore one upon the right wrist and one upon the left, even young Isolca. Of course anyone who had discharged their first debt to a god had a single bracelet, and there would be many a banding tomorrow as those who had taken a year-vow last winter solstice could consider it fulfilled.

Last year, Idra's torch—the only fire remaining that night, and blessed by her keening song as we watched its flicker, willing the flame to stay—had lit the holy fire.

Kolle took her place upon my right, barely glancing at me. The crowd at the Stone began to hum as the first walkers from the riverside arrived, torches quenched and other lights doused as they halted upon the green.

It took a long while for the crowd to reach its proper size, but I did not shiver, using the deepest of warming breaths to fan the body's inner flame. I stared at the stars as if I could hear their high crystalline singing, to avoid any possible pitying looks from Isolca or Molveig. *Don't worry*, Isolca had confided once. *I'm sure someone will marry you eventually.*

She meant it kindly. I could have answered that a *volva* seldom weds even if one with less *seidhr* might, but had merely smiled instead. True, the expression was somewhat pained, but Idra had labored long and hard to teach me that a sharp tongue, while often *useful*, is not always *best*.

Night had truly fallen by the time Corag stepped forward. A susurration went through the assembly, their breath rising as white vapor and no few among them stamping to force warmer blood into feet and legs. Kolle paused, but only to glance at me as she had each year at Idra.

Just like Idra, I nodded. *I wish you were here*, I thought, and had I heard my teacher's familiar, pained cackle-laugh riding the wind, I would not have been surprised.

Though I might have flinched at the sound. I do not deny it; my courage has only ever been barely equal to circumstances.

Kolle glided forward too, and the two lifted their lanterns high. The stragglers coming up the long slope to the green would notice the twin lights like eyes upon the Stone, one wavering candle-gold and the other a hard bluish glitter because the flame was held in an Elder-crafted cage.

A mismatched gaze, but it served its purpose. Those it fell upon hurried to snuff or at least muffle their lights. The wind gained fresh strength, tugging at my hood and attempting to lift my skirts. The mantle did its work, though, and I was chilled only by the enormity of what I was about to attempt.

Corag lifted his lantern. His face was turned into an ill spirit's by the shadows; his cheeks puffed as he blew, and the light went out.

A small child began to cry, deep in the crowd. More restless mutters raced through the assembly; Kolle lifted the Elder lantern. There was a trick to handling it, and I hoped she would teach Isolca before much longer.

The blue light guttered, dying slowly. Starshine limned flying clouds; a bright festival day means a cold night. Yet many would be the children born ten moons from now, lucky infants blessed with the return of sunlight.

Find warmth where you can, Odynn says; *even the Allmother knows what a misery cold is.*

I had to face the dark wooden pile, my hands aching because they were fists inside fur-edged sleeves. Spending an entire day too busy to dread this meant I did not have even a moment to brace my shield, as the saying goes.

My gaze unfocused. I tried to imagine Idra's voice. *You know what to do, Solveig.*

From the dark breast of Tarnarya, a single voice lifted. It was a wolf-cry, and my mantle-hood turned heavier. Perhaps beast or spirit was singing the tale of how a brightspear shieldmaid had hunted a beast to end depredations upon a river people's livestock, and brought the pelt home to adorn a young *volva*'s mantle.

Idra would be singing over one last remaining torch before she swung it skyward to purge the old year. I merely had to call the flame from where it lived when unsummoned, that was all.

Sounds simple, does it not, daughter of Gwendelint?

Simple, yes. Not *easy*, and how Idra used to laugh while teaching me the distinction.

I stared into the darkness, the fear nipping at my fingers, my toes. It brushed the tip of my nose as the wind moaned amid bracken on the green's edges, kindled a great soughing in the forest cradling the greathall of Dun Rithell, the settlement and outlying steadings sharing its name.

What, in all that blackness, would raise its misshapen head and come for us, should the bonfire not light?

My left hand rose, naked fingers thrust into the wind's jaws. My breath halted, a familiar pressure mounting behind eyes and breastbone.

Of course nobody truly thought the sun would refuse to rise if the fire remained unlit, and many suspect much of *seidhr* is misdirection or chicanery, a cunning of hand and eye still worthy of respect even should it not approach true weirding. At the same time, all know the gods both Aesyr and Vanyr, Black-Wingéd *valkyra*, the hosts of the dead, and passing spirits only occasionally meddle with mortals. Divinities and spirits are usually more than busy with their own affairs; still, a practical, prudent person does their best not to offend even distant neighbors.

For a moment, I was blackly, bleakly convinced that all my practice had been unavailing, all my training a vast prank, and all my marks were going to vanish because I would fail this final test.

A vast hiss filled my skull. A small, still orange point lit in the heart of the big black tower raising before me—or not quite the heart, somewhere around the ankles instead. My concentration almost wavered, but Idra was a thorough teacher, and the fear of a stinging slap to the back of my head before a weary *Again, my lady, and do it correctly* meant my focus returned, and the bright orange dot widened.

There was a *wump* as tinder exploded into flame, and a gasp went through those closest to the Stone. I finished exhaling, sharply, and willed the fire to spread. It did not quite hurt, yet it was an effort and my nape was damp by the time the blooming light was no longer in danger of wind-snuffing.

The bonfire was now a yellow-orange star, visible even in the camps across the river. I did not sway, but I did draw my hood further, shadowing my face. Corag and Kolle relit their lanterns with tapers from the blaze and the women began to climb the steps to file past, lighting torch or twist to take home. The new light would go from house to house; a runner was no doubt standing by to bring ceremonial heat and life to my father's hall.

When the wicker cages burst into flame nothing inside made a sound, though another wolf-howl across the river sounded under a babble of singing, excited chatter, warriors swearing oaths either permanent or yearlong, men and women announcing a god-debt as they climbed down the other side of the Stone upon the wider stairs worked along the rock's lee.

My pulse returned to its usual pace. I kept my hood high, though many who passed bowed or kissed their fingers in my direction. The wind tore at the flames, but could not kidnap them. After some while Arn reappeared from the head of the stairs, stepping to her usual spot behind my shoulder, for now there were travelers from both downriver and up among the neighbors passing by to gain the new, cleansed light; no few of them studied me critically in the bonfire's glow.

Yet still, my father did not show himself, nor Bjorn, nor even Astrid.

Ill News

Nothing good comes from the North, especially in winter.
　　　　　　　　　　　　　—Southron proverb

Even the laggards had come to collect their new-year light and all others were at table, so there were few indeed treading to the bonfire atop the Stone. Once the drinking was truly underway and the riddles began moving from one bench to the next there would be more visitors, and in the very deepest reaches of night there would be constant traffic bearing fuel for the burning and gifts for the gods, not to mention food and drink brought to those who must hold sworn vigil upon the solstice.

It is a cold duty though an honorable one, and I was glad of the mantle. Arn's dun overcloak was thick and furred as well; she paced to keep warm, never very far from me. The bonfire's heat was shredded by rising wind, though I did not have to steady the flame overmuch.

Normally Idra and I would watch together; had Dun Rithell not possessed a wisewoman and apprentice, those with any small *seidhr* would have taken turns at the bonfire's side. Though the flame had returned watch must still be kept, and one with weirding on hand to make certain nothing misshapen from the night's depths—or elsewhere—crept forth to extinguish hope. Once the sun rose the wisewoman could take her ease, not before.

Except Idra was with the Blessed, feasting in a great god-hall or enjoying some amusement she would like better, being of a decidedly solitary bent during her lifetime. Either way, she would pay little attention to mortal problems. Or so I hoped; she had spent her life serving her people, and mine was to be a similar lot.

It was well past feast-time though not yet midnight when a familiar shape slipped up the stairs and made directly for me, weaving between the chance-brought guards like a minnow. Ulfrica daughter of Harrick from over the river was with her, of course, and looked miserably cold in her very fine though not heavy yellow cloak; my sister wore a very sensible hooded and buttoned mantle with her furred boots, and carried my gloves and a hand-pouch as well as a heavy green woolen scarf.

"I brought you bread," Astrid said, breathlessly. "And news. Oh, I'm so sorry to miss it. Was it terribly difficult?" She peered from her hood, a bright pretty star-maiden with a luminous face, and as usual, I felt a faint weary surprise that I could be related to such a sprite.

"Just difficult enough." It was the manner of answer Idra might have made; I wrapped the muffler about my neck and pulled my hood up again. It was a distinct improvement, and I could not wait to bury my hands in both gloves and sleeves. *Your sister is indeed wondrous fair*, Idra had said when I complained of how everyone was 'mazed by Astrid, *but she cannot do what you can, and well it behooves you to remember as much.* "How many dresses shall we be making with your spoils today?"

But for once, mention of sewing enough to keep us occupied until midsummer failed to brighten her. Astrid's dark-golden eyebrows had drawn toward each other and Ulfrica pressed close, slipping an arm over my sister's shoulders, giving me a reproachful look.

"I…I don't know." Astrid rubbed at one of her braids, red ribbon threaded through golden hair. "Solveig, listen. Something awful has happened."

Of course. "I cannot be everywhere at once," I muttered. "What now?"

"Well, if you *had* been there, I don't know how it could have helped." Astrid shook her head, and her large dark eyes shimmered with incipient tears. She was made of water, Gwendelint's youngest child. "It was Bjorn. Some man hailed Father, another laughed in my direction, there were words, Bjorn hit one of them, and then—"

Oh, by Hel, I am so sick of this. "And Father owes someone a cup?" Bjorn was always causing some damage, and Father paying restitution. Still, what did everyone expect? Our sire was battle-mad; it was now bred into the line. Astrid's sons might even gain a double share of the gift.

Dun Rithell was glad enough of Eril's madness when brigands came, or when petty warlords cast envious looks upon our small prosperity. It could even be said his violent rage upon the field was a gift from Odynn, brought by ravens to an infant's cradle, or from Uellar the Hunter, who roamed the world before the first sunrise.

"Worse." Astrid was pale, and her lower lip quivered. I took a closer look at her in the flickering light before glancing at the thin straggling line of latecomers. None of those jostling to relight their hearths whispered, elbowed each other, or cast meaningful glances in our direction. It was almost too chilly for gossip, and that is cold indeed. "Solveig…"

My heart, wiser than me, plunged into my empty belly. "He killed someone." It wasn't a far-fetched guess at all, but the instant I said it Astrid blanched afresh.

"Oh, aye." And there it was, the shadow of fear in her dark gaze as if I had some sooth-knowledge and not simply a working head upon my shoulders. Even those who love a weirdling hold them in caution, as the proverb goes. "A son of a great House in the north. Bjorn hit him, he fell and struck his head upon a stone. There was nothing to be done."

The bonfire staggered, or maybe I had simply closed my eyes because the disaster was, while not exactly what I had surmised, absolutely within the bounds of possibility and I should have expected it. "Which house?" Owing weregild is not a comfortable thing, and did I know who now required it I could make some guess as to what would be asked for.

"Father knows them, or so I think." Astrid's hands were busy at her belt; she drew forth a small package. "Bread and cheese; I toasted it myself. Ulfrica has a skin of ale and Albeig will send much more in some short while. There are guards coming as well; I told Father I would hasten here beforehand. I think Bjorn regrets his rashness, but what else could he do?"

It was the same song I had heard since birth: *What else could Bjorn do?*

I had a list of things which might have served him better, but it was useless. I gave Astrid the kindest smile I could manage, beckoning Arn close. My shieldmaid, of course, was very interested in the aleskin, and Ulfrica quaked as Arn snatched that coveted object.

"My lady Astrid." My shieldmaid greeted my sister with a single chin-tip. "I was beginning to think we'd been forgotten."

I did not quite wince. "A few swallows only, small one, then you must have some bread. Which design do the Northerners bear, Astrid? Not the ones with the rune-mark upon their armor, I hope." *That* captain—Uldfang—had a hungry look. Father did not like him either, despite the courteous words exchanged when the black-clad men arrived at the greathall to lay themselves under pax-law for the festival.

A pax Bjorn had broken.

"The...the wolf-ones." Astrid, her delivery of news and food complete, shivered and drew her cloak closer. "They are very grim, and the one Bjorn...well, he was the younger son of their great lord."

That is not a pleasant tale. I had seen all the high-ranking travelers both North and South last night at the great welcoming feast, of course—who could not? The wolf-marked ones were dark, though a few bore gazes as clear as my mother's, and all three groups were tall in plain but high-quality armor. They were upon some pressing business; rumor had not quite provided any believable information about what it entailed.

Father would have given me at least some intimation upon his return from the last of the Althing's formalities, had not this disaster intervened.

"What of the Northerners? The wolf-ones?" Arn capped the aleskin with a quick motion, then accepted half the cold bread with cheese toasted onto its side. "I did not hear their House's name, but they are from far away indeed. Almost to the Black Land."

I suppressed a flare of irritation; the Black Land was either ancient history or a myth. Still, mentioning that blasted, cursèd place was ill done, especially so close to the newborn fire.

Astrid swayed, her eyelids half-dropping as she shivered, and I shook my head. "Take her home, Ulfrica." Bjorn and I had scared our youngest sibling ruthlessly with tales of the far North's monsters and the long-dead Great Enemy; she was still young enough to shudder at such amusements. "Don't let Father send her out again tonight, though we'll take our dinners as soon as Albeig has time and hands to send them, thank you."

"They're sending guards too," Ulfrica squeaked, and hurried my sister away past the bonfire, stopping only to bob in front of its glow as if she suspected she'd need all the luck she could gain for the rest of the evening, not to mention the year.

"Guards," Arn muttered, tearing into her bread. I watched my sister reel away in Ulfrica's care. Astrid, for all her fineness, was not the type to swoon or pretend some ill; she must have been overwhelmed indeed. "Finally. After you had to walk here alone."

"I am not alone." At least Father hadn't sent Bjorn. I might have tipped him *into* the fire for adding yet another tangle to the festival, one I would no doubt be called upon to sort in some unpleasant fashion. We would have to strip all the roof's gilding for this. "I have my Arneior. Try to chew instead of just swallowing it."

"Look to your own dinner, weirdling." She laughed, turning her head slightly to gaze at the thickening line. Many had now satisfied the first bite of hunger and were coming to make god-offerings; Frestis, Kolle, and their apprentices were at their own feasting, and would not return until just before dawn. "And do not drink all the ale."

"You were not listening." I shivered, took a giant mouthful of bread and cheese. It tasted as fine as Fryja's own baking, for my hunger was sharp.

"What need have I to listen, especially to their babble? You'll tell me what it means." She licked at her fingertips, motioning for the aleskin again. "What of the Northerners?"

"Bjorn killed one of them." I surrendered the ale, knowing she'd leave me at least a swallow, and set myself to the rest of my bread and cheese.

My shieldmaid halted, staring at me as if she suspected some manner of jest. But though I am fond of sharp words and she had been known to make a riddle or two, neither of us prize lightsome speech. "Well," she said, finally. "What does that *mean*?"

"Some manner of weregild." I bent to my own work, for I was hungry. The flame always needs fuel.

I was not wrong. Yet I did not guess how steep the price would be.

Arguments

The gods gave us light and the Enemy gave us war. But we mortals invented the pax, and well we did or we might be crushed between gods and the Allmother's firstborn. Weregild is a smaller price than death, after all, and many is the marriage made in that fashion.

—Arjeson the Riddler

A good double-hand of my father's men arrived not long after my sister's visit, all fully armed and armored despite the festival's pax. All ten were all old veterans, too, none of the boys I'd grown up with. Perhaps Father meant it as some manner of signal, but I was too cold to care and the bonfire needed more supper, too. Every household had contributed to the blaze, and there were stocks enough to keep it fed until morn.

Or so we hoped. I stared at a heap of sullen coals near the fire's foot, the scent of roasting and burnt feathers whisked away downwind. Young boys chest-puffed with the importance of their mission brought more wood, arguing good-naturedly about where to place each load.

"My lady." Flokin was the eldest warrior of my father's hall, slump-shouldered like a bear and possessed of a great grey beard braided with beads of carven horn. The men took up formation about us, breaking the force of the wind's winter wailing; Arn stiffened, though none came closer than they should. Thus released, those who had guarded a *volva* by chance filed past the fire, and would present themselves to Eril for lordly thanks. "Your father would have come to celebrate, but…there is summat unforeseen."

There might have been an implied insult in the observation; what good was a *volva* who couldn't foretell dire woe? Yet the songs, chants, tales, and sagas were brimming-full of idiots like my brother doing things no reasonable *seidhr* would speak of even if they did foresee, or so it seemed to me that night. "My brother killed a man from the North." Unease spilled down my back; the mantle's thickness was little proof against that manner of chill.

It is not uncommon to hear wolves in the hills. To hear them twice upon a winter evening is to be expected. And yet, a wolf-sigil house demanding weregild of my father while their cousins howled?

It did not bode well.

"Aye." Flokin eyed me in the bonfire's fitful glow. A short distance away, spindle-legged Asjel the miller's son had tripped while bringing wood up, and was being mocked by other boys. "He swears he heard the Northerner say summat of your sister. Your lord father, well…"

He should have left Bjorn with me. But I could not play nursemaid to my grown brother, nor could Astrid. Even Mother could not anymore. "What are they demanding?"

Flokin coughed. Perhaps he did not expect me to be quite so direct, but I had just called the winter bonfire. None could now say I hadn't earned each of the blue bandings about my wrists, or the ancient runes living under the skin.

Every pinprick with ink forced into my flesh, every terrible test, every deep lonely night was worth it. I had brought flame from empty air upon the darkest night of the year. Idra, for all her wisdom, would not have been able to do so.

Seidhr is uncommon, though every house has its own cunning, as the saying goes. Only two ancient, half-unintelligible sagas speak of elementalists, though they do not name specific ones. Still, there are many marvels among *seidhr*'s many-branching ways, and Idra had never betrayed any surprise or shock at finding one among her students.

I waited, but the bearded man said nothing. Arn made a short, displeased noise. "Come now, Flokin. Say what you must."

At least he had a healthy respect for her temper; especially during the dark of the longest night. "I dare not speak upon it, my lady Solveig. 'Tis for your father to do." He would say no more, nor would any of his companions.

Put that way, though, 'twas simple enough to guess. The Northerners kept to old ways; some said their proximity to the ruins of the Black Land kept them faithful. The most ancient weregild is a child for a child, and Father must have suspected they might demand as much. He would draw out negotiations until I could leave the green, cross the road, and re-enter the hall; no doubt *seidhr* by his side would help in dawn's cold light, especially after demanding Northerners had spent a night drinking at a fine table.

A wisewoman's strength is not just in weirding but in negotiation. A cunning mind, a quick hand, and a wise tongue are necessary. Besides, before I could even speak I was upon my mother's knee when cases were decided; an eldest daughter is often called upon to give advice to even the haughtiest lord.

Father couldn't lose Astrid; it was unthinkable. If Bjorn were betrothed it could have been a compelling argument to keep him, but perhaps some time with Northerners would hammer some elementary caution into his thick head. The only question would be how long, and that was why Father wished me there before negotiations truly started.

A year and a day is traditional, but I could mayhap shorten the duration.

The bonfire strengthened, and as I turned the matter over inside my head Asjel also turned upon his tormentors with rhyming couplets. Flyting is an ancient game; even those lacking a strong arm may use its sting. A bright light upon his young freckled face, he likened the other boys to a pack of running sores, and his tormenters stepped back, giving way.

I could not help but smile; the gods love those with quick wits, especially upon a festival night. The other boys, taught once more to respect a stream of insults as much as a bared blade, hoisted the young spindle-legged stumbler upon their shoulders before setting off toward the wood stores, singing a few of his choice couplets no doubt inspired by a passing divinity.

It was a night of strange occurrences. A pair of latecomers wrapped well against the cold hurried past to enclose lights in horn keepfires. I shivered, wishing for something a little more substantial to eat; it wasn't like Albeig to leave us unfed.

Sudden dark shapes loomed over Flokin's shoulder, and for a moment I thought the shadows of the stairway had come to life, ill spirits about to throw themselves upon the fire. Arn handed me the aleskin, cocking her head as she regarded the new arrivals, and the men of my father's household stiffened almost in unison.

It was the Northerners, come to visit the flames.

They are tall as Father, those of the North, but mostly dark-haired as Mother's people. Their eyes are often dark too, but even so there is a terrible glow to their gaze, and they are held to be sparing of words as a whole, though courteous enough when necessary. They often do not wear beards, and sometimes it is said there is Elder blood in their high houses that makes it less likely for them to grow such proud appurtenances. Not many of them favor the axe, being instead enamored of heavy swords; it was said they did not have the battle-rage, but a cold calculation in attack or retreat made them dangerous indeed.

There were a half-dozen of them that night, and three had eyes pale as my mother's or my own. They filed past, most watching me sidelong before passing the fire. Their leader—or the one I suspected was their leader, by the colorless gem winking in the pommel of his heavy pax-knotted sword—paused before the bonfire, studying at leisure as if he suspected some trick. Then, he turned and appraised me again, despite my father's guards.

The men of Eril's hall did not move. Arn stepped before me, though, her chin raised. I kept my hood pulled high, because I *felt* the Northerner's glance. Idra's long-ago searching look, while enough to make child-me quail, was not so strong.

So, the Northern lord had some weirding of his own, or one of his lieutenants did. I saw no wolf upon them; they had come to the fire without sigil, bearing no weapon but their captain's sword bound with thin leather strips to make it near impossible to draw.

Respecting pax in the old way; we used yellow thread or cloth at Althings, but had not forgotten the original material.

Flokin cursed when they vanished into the dark past the bonfire, a term of surpassing vulgarity. 'Twas no shock to me—I had, after all, grown up with Bjorn—but I never expected anyone else to utter anything like it near one of my father's daughters.

I spent the rest of that night eating what Albeig sent from the hall, drinking weak wassail, and watching the bright fire of the new year while my head whirled, my hands clenching and releasing inside gloves and sleeves. The question was how to keep them from taking Bjorn for too long, or so it appeared to me then, and I caught myself in the very dead of night muttering bits of logical argument while those around me cast each other uneasy looks and the bonfire had to be fed yet again.

It never occurred to me that the Northerners would demand another of Eril's children.

A Warm Hall

The Blessed themselves respect those granted a touch of seidhr, for it is a gift of the Allmother. Even Odynn while hanging has not plumbed its depths; even Ulimo the lord of the sea cannot guess at its currents. All are threads upon the loom, and weirding the pattern itself.
    —Melair the Cloak-Weaver, Queen of Dorael

Idra said an occasional sleepless night is a whetstone for a sharp mind; I certainly hoped as much. I was cold clear through, though the bonfire had kept any of us from freezing to death, and very grateful that Albeig had sent my overboots and plenty of wassail up to the Stone.

By the time the east lightened, all I·could think of was going home. No doubt the guards regretted leaving the greathall's shelter, but it is lucky to see the dawn with a *volva*—or so all the songs and stories say. In some places a wisewoman may tap any man upon the shoulder, married or not, and take him home for a single night.

We did not do such things in Dun Rithell, though once or twice Flokin had jested with Idra about it.

Even the deep warming breaths my teacher made me practice endlessly were not perfect proof against ice; one can only keep the body's fire high enough to combat winter for so long. Arn was better at it, but then again she had more time to practice during shieldmaid training.

Much, much more.

Walking home was a relief, because it brought us out of the wind to some degree. Even Arn looked a bit pinched, and a shieldmaid loves the cold as others prize summer nights.

When entering a warm hall from a night spent in vigil, 'tis important to remove what layers one can so the chill is not held close to the body. So it was I pulled my aching hands free of pouch and gloves, leaning upon Arn while Sarica and Finduil bent to help with my overboots. Ulfrica took the green mantle and undercloak with a relieved, tremulous smile and a brisk shake to free them of ice; Albeig brought me the great cup. I took it with a will, and the warmth of what it contained filled both my stomach and head. "I could sit in the sauna until spring," I muttered, and Albeig's answering smile was tight and pained. "Where is my father?"

"Still in the hall." Finduil shook ice from my overboots with a slight clucking noise; she would have to brush them hard when they dried. "The Northerners have not slept, and neither has he."

Nor have I. For all that, I was not as weary as I had been after some of Idra's greater tests. "Has he at least…" I swallowed the rest of the question when Albeig gave me an agonized look. It was not her place to discuss such matters, especially after being left alongside Astrid to deal with the great feast. "Never mind. My mother's medicine. Has it been taken up?"

"You have not heard?" Albeig straightened, taking the great cup from my shaking hands. "One of the Northerners—the young one— gave your mother a draught he mixed himself, and the ague has fled her."

Oh. Well, that's fortunate. Still, it pinched; I had been using Idra's best recipe to combat Mother's shaking. "They keep to the old ways in the North," I muttered, a formulaic thanks. "Perhaps he will teach me the recipe for such medicine."

Ulfrica gasped and hurried away, clutching my mantle; I was too cold to care for her dramatics and sorry to lose the protection of fur-lined wool. Still, my festival dress was not draggled, due to Arn's care with her *volva*'s footing, and when the buskins were unlaced my cramped feet gave a sigh of relief I echoed. My slippers were still dry—one piece of good luck among the ill, at least.

Sarica and Finduil left, exchanging dark glances, but I caught Albeig's arm. "Ulfrica did not chatter about who glanced at her during the riddles, and 'tis not like Sarica to risk a defeat upon that field." I cleared my throat, a bit of the cold still caught there, and tried to soften the observations with a smile. "What is wrong, Albeig? Does my father not think I can negotiate these strangers to—"

"There you are." A big basso booming filled the entryway, and as usual, my father's voice robbed all around of him of the air to speak. Big, capped and bearded with blond, and wearing his great bearskin, Eril the Battle-Mad stuck his thumbs in his belt and regarded his eldest daughter with bloodshot dark eyes as if I had been caught returning from a lover's hall after dawn. His cheeks were ruddy with ale, and the gleam in his gaze was troubling indeed. "My *seidhr* daughter, welcome."

"My father." I straightened; Albeig bobbed and offered the cup to Arn, who drank deep, one hand still upon her spear. "I am told my brother did some ill." *And now you wish me to repair it. Well, such is my lot, and I do not shirk it.*

I never had. Bjorn was firstborn, but 'tis the eldest daughter who holds any hall, and we do not forget it.

"I should have been upon the Stone." My father stepped further into the entryway, glancing over his massive shoulder as if he expected pursuit. Not for the first time, I wondered how he and my mother had fit together to produce children, though I had little desire to even imagine such an event. "Your very first, my daughter, and it seems ill to miss it."

It was surprising that he would even mention a dark omen, and my unease grew. "There is always next year." I rubbed my hands together; Arn thanked Albeig with a nod as she handed back the cup. "None will tell me how bad it is, and I think that is upon your orders."

He winced slightly. "You see much," he muttered. "I did wish to tell you this myself, and said so."

Even worse. I glanced at Arn, who tossed a leather-wrapped braid over her shoulder. Her knuckles were white upon the spear haft; a shieldmaid guards her charge even against kin. Not that Father ever lifted a hand to me or Astrid—he saved such things for Bjorn, who sorely needed them—but still, he was a man, and a large one. She had been cautious of him since childhood. "The news must be ill indeed."

That was when I learned the Northerners, upon being told the roll of Eril the Battle-Mad's children, had not asked for the young warrior to serve in the North, nor for Astrid the fair to visit their halls in payment for the one struck down. No, in return for the death of the younger son of their lord, laid out by a southron man's fist and dying headstruck upon a stone, they required a different weregild. And nobody dared to tell me, for such news brought to one with *seidhr* might well gain a curse in return.

In other words, the Northerners wished to take the Battle-Mad's eldest daughter, who had just proved her worth as full *volva* and elementalist both by lighting the darkest night of the year with will alone.

Blessing Morn

The Elder say they taught us of sacred hospitality, but how can that be believed? For they are proof against nearly all mortal illnesses and accident, and may survive even deep winter with scant clothing. No, the laws which render a guest inviolate we gained from the gods on our own account, in the time before we even knew of the Firstborn. In those dark days when the Blessed had left the world to the Enemy, despite the risk of traitors among us we still had to hold a guest sacred. For otherwise, even the mighty among us could perish in a snowstorm, or by misadventure...
　　　　　—Maduilda the Wise, *volva* of Dun Thirion

There were many strangenesses that morn.

For one, Mother was out of bed and at the high dais-table, her bright blue gaze free of fever though she was fearfully wan. She wore her best grey dress and a fine-woven mantle to match, the green-gem-and-silver brooch at her breast flickering with lamplight. Astrid sat beside her, anxiously watching each movement; Bjorn, at the far end of the table, bore a blackened eye and a bandaged hand. I would have glared at him, promising trouble later, had he not been wearing a quite uncharacteristic air of seriousness while he stared at the great stone hearth, his profile at rest very much like Father's.

For another, the dogs were either taken to the woods or a-kennel. No hounds patrolled the passages, stretched out under the tables, watched our guests, or leaned against Mother's chair while regarding her with open adoration. Also, many of my father's men had not sought their beds, probably because the Northerners were still at the guest tables. The group of men in dark armor again wore their three different sigils—bear, wolf, a strange rune with some resemblance to the ancient form of a torch—and the hush when I appeared in the great door at my father's side spread from them to infect the entire hall.

There were other visitors, of course, neighbors and travelers from up- and downriver, not to mention the Barrowhills much farther south. Some were somnolent at table; face in puddle of ale is how many prefer to end a festival feast. Those who were awake, though, caught the silence from the Northerners and rose awkwardly when the dark-clad men did. No few elbowed their resting compatriots into some manner of wakefulness as well.

A considerable number—three full tables—of Northern men eyed me as they stood; my father's hand was heavy upon my shoulder. My mother rose from her great chair, too, with little evidence of how the movement must cost her—but then, she was accustomed to hiding such things.

Astrid and I bear *her* pride.

My sister's eyes were reddened. Evidence of weeping inflamed her nose and brought a blush to her fair cheeks; she wore yesterday's fairgoing dress and pulled one of Albeig's fine knitted shawls close about her tense, delicate shoulders. The hall's quiet was unnatural indeed, and I glanced at Arn.

My shieldmaid studied the Northerners, taking her time. When her gaze turned to me, she looked troubled, but anyone in her position might.

"My daughter." At least Mother's voice was clear, without the betraying shake of ague. "The sun has risen."

"Once more, and may it ever," I replied, automatically. Idra would have been pleased; she held Mother in some awe even though the lady of Dun Rithell had no weirding in her. But formal manners and a high standard were both kept in Eril's hall, and that would make any elderly bearer of *seidhr* happy indeed. "My mother, you have risen as well."

"Our guest Lord Aeredh was kind enough to treat my ailment, though he said your medicine is by far the better course." My mother Lady Gwendelint inclined her dark head; Astrid had rebraided her hair. My own work to give Mother a sleep-braid yesterday morn, our dam propped upon pillows and coughing miserably, would not have survived a feast. It should not have bothered me. "I was not surprised to hear as much."

Well, I am. But nobody minds what surprises me. "I am in the lord's debt, both for the treatment and the compliment." Another formulaic phrase, uttered with all the grace I could muster; a few of the household men at the nearest table elbowed each other. Whispers rose, perhaps passing our words to those in the far table-ranks, perhaps only commenting upon my appearance and carriage.

The weirding-girl, they called me; *Gwendelint's witch-daughter, the one with the* seidhr.

There was a scrape of chairs and bench feet; the wolf-sigiled Northerners moved as a pack of those beasts, detaching from their standing fellows. The one with the gem winking at his sword-pommel was there, a pale face under a shock of dark hair, and his dark gaze did indeed have weight. I felt it afresh as I stood in the door, the great cup's warmth fleeing me and even Arn's presence—at the shoulder my father was not holding—providing little solace. Father did not squeeze to warn me of danger; instead, his hand fell away as if he disliked the touch.

I held my ground. There was a youth among them, granted pride of place at the leader's side; he must have been who they called "the young one," for his features were unlined and his pale eyes, blue as a frosty winter sky, were bright. In fact, his glance held weight as well and his step was very soft, even among theirs.

It was the youth who continued when they halted before me; he was tall enough our heads were level though I stood upon the third step. Massive timbers creaked, the building waking as sunweight touched its bright roof; the great blaze in the hearth—relit from the very bonfire I had spent the night guarding—sang its own crackle-hiss saga of consumption and warmth.

"My lady Solveig," the boy said, a light, pleasant voice. No doubt he sang well, probably even with some *granr*; still, I almost started at being addressed so by a stranger. His accent was very old-fashioned, but then, they spoke differently in the North. "Well-named are you, child of the Vanyr. I am Aeredh; it is a blessing to meet you this morn."

"Lord Aeredh." I could not return any blessing, but I could at least be polite. "I thank you for your care of my mother, though I am told you have cause to grieve here in Dun Rithell." *There.* It was mannerly, though the message was that I liked not dancing about a subject when it could be met directly as my shieldmaid's strikes.

Father coughed, and at least this Aeredh had the grace to look a trifle taken aback.

The man with the gem in his sword-pommel made a short sound, very much like a strangled laugh. When he spoke it was not in our southron language but in the Old Tongue, with a very strange accent. I caught summat about rumor flying like a particular bird even in wintertime, and the boy before me gave his companion a rueful look. A shadow lingered in that rue, though he looked younger even than Astrid.

The Old Tongue is what the Elder learned in the home of the Blessed, or so Mother and Idra taught me; its rhythm runs through *seidhr* like an underground river. It is said the Children of the Star taught mortals to speak it when they arrived upon our shores to make war upon the Black Land, and that our own tongue is descended from it in many branchings like our mother-river as it wends south into the Barrowhills. Mother and Idra alone spoke it in Dun Rithell, having both learned as girls, and my teacher insisted I follow suit.

I did not mind, for a wisewoman must know such things. Even more than that, I fiercely, secretly liked sharing something special and secret with Mother. Bjorn was her son and Astrid her joy, but I?

I was her pride, deep as her bones. We were always of the same temper, as two daggers born of the same forging.

"My friend Eol is unused to the southron language." Aeredh's smile, though merry enough upon its surface, was pained. "My lady, I must ask you directly: Did you light the fire upon the great stone in yonder green?"

"I was seen to do so," I replied, somewhat stiffly. Arn was

absolutely silent at my shoulder, a rare instance of her complete attention resting upon some danger. My father sucked in a deep breath, whether of pain or caution I could not tell. "By witnesses of Dun Rithell's *seidhr*, and others. If you wished to observe the ceremony, perhaps you should have attended it."

"Indeed," he agreed, brightening somewhat. "Yet there is no need. I see its cousin in you, well-named one." His gaze rose past me to fasten upon my father. "We shall return tomorrow, my lord Eril. She will not need much; we travel lightly, yet still in enough comfort for any noble daughter of the Vanyr."

With that, the youth mounted the steps, passing us like a cool breeze. All the Northerners streamed forth, not merely the wolf-sigiled but those at table, too. The man with the gem in his swordhilt lingered only to examine me from top to toe one final time before he followed, and the other wolf-sigiled Northerners attended him. Those with the bear upon them hurried to do the same, and last of all the rune-sigiled ones with Uldfang their lord, one or two performing a curious salute— the knuckles of their right hand to their left breast, then to their lips, finishing at the forehead as they nodded, like a shieldmaid's salute to a woman they respect. Strangely, they did not direct it at Father but at me, almost lost in the protective shadow of Eril's bulk.

A mutter raced through my father's hall. The Northerners were gone, the chill of their presence draining away, and Father's hand descended upon my shoulder again.

" 'Tis only for a year and a day," he said, heavily.

I had thought to negotiate a much-shortened duration, being full *volva* now. But though I had lit the bonfire and proved myself, I was still Eril the Battle-Mad's daughter, and clearly in this situation he would not be forsworn or do a jot less than custom or hospitality demanded. To him I was a child still, weirdling or not, and while Northmen are dour they are also held to guard their women closely. I was what was demanded, thus I would be sent—though it is always grievous to lose one with *seidhr*, no matter how short the time.

Traveling north was not even truly dangerous save for the weather. The Black Land the Northerners bordered upon was only a mythical ruin since the Day of Dust back in a many-greats-grandfather's

time when Dun Rithell bore a different name; there was no longer
any menace there. Even upon that day we held it as true, for we had
all my great-grandfather's life, my grandfather's life, my lord father
Eril's life, and my own.

You should have sent Bjorn. But of course, I thought bitterly, he
would not. Dun Rithell would next be known for Astrid's husband,
though as Gwendelint's eldest daughter I would hold the highest
honor in the hall no matter who she wed. Still, she was the shining
star-maid, Father's favorite, and Bjorn, the vaunted copy of his sire,
would marry into another clan to bring them the gift of battle-rage.

I had never thought it likely I would marry, and yet. I tasted smoke
from the great hearth, my nose filling with the breath of meats and
other piled delicacies as well as a tang of yeast on a hot draft from an
open archway, since the kitchens were finishing the new-winter bread.
None of the other guests—some of the chance-guards from last night
were at the tables for new warriors, one or two still steadily consuming
bits and crusts—had moved, and many avid gazes rested upon me.

"Solveig." Father's fingers tightened, but his tone was oddly
pleading, for once. Did he expect me to protest, and make the situation even worse? "Only a year and a day."

In other words, I would tidy yet another of Bjorn's messes. My
brother would not meet my gaze. He stared at the hearth, almost as
pale as Astrid.

"Sol." Arn took my elbow, and her affectionate shortening of my
name could have been an oblique comment upon my father's bluff-
ness. Or perhaps it was a measure of gentleness, a shieldmaid's care
for her charge. "I think your lady mother requires you."

Of course she would not deign to chide Eril directly, even if one
taken by the Black-Wingéd speaks as she wills. Or perhaps she simply
did not consider him worth the effort at the moment, for I swayed and
might have fallen. The walk to the great stone dais where my family's great oaken table rested seemed much longer than usual, not least
because the hall was packed close with feasters who did not want to
miss whatever spectacle the paying of weregild would give rise to.

The gossips on either side of the river would have many a mouthful to chew as the days lengthened.

My mother Gwendelint stood very straight, her thighs braced against the table-edge. Astrid, frozen next to her, stared at me as if I were a new creature, a misshapen thing come from blackest night and deep snows. A hectic glitter had kindled in Mother's bright, pale gaze, and this close I saw high color in her cheeks. Whatever draught the boy had given her provided at least some short-term strength; I could not even teach Astrid how to mix Idra's more subtle ague-medicine, for it required *seidhr* to work properly.

Mother hurried from the great table, meeting me upon the dais steps with an embrace I fell gratefully into; Astrid moved woodenly to do so as well. Some of the feasting throng, male and female alike, began to drift for the doors where my father stood as if dazed. He bid each farewell courteously enough, though, and Dun Rithell would be held safe and lucky for another year since a *seidhr*-lit bonfire had survived the night. Trade negotiations and legal cases would commence in earnest upon the morrow, when men and women headsore or stomach-sour from feasting had recovered enough to argue for remedy, prosecution, or profit.

It would have been my task to arbitrate no few of the agreements, had I not been bargained away to the Northerners. As it was, I shut my eyes, my face buried in my mother's shoulder, and she did not shake with the ague but held me as if I were young again and she a statue of Fryja brought to warm bounteous life. "My Solveig," she whispered into my braids, still full of smoke and the wind-scent of the year's longest night. "Good fortune to our house, and for you most of all."

It was unlike her to be superstitious, but I could attribute it to whatever potion she had swallowed. My senses could find naught amiss in her breath or pulse, and were the boy's draught poison I did not think the Northerners would promise a return. *I lit the fire, Mother. Tell me you noticed; tell me someone did.*

Then I was chastised for my pride, for Astrid's embrace tightened, her arms woven with my mother's and mine, the three of us standing and breathing as a single pillar. No man, not even Bjorn who had been born of our mother's body, could intrude upon that. Hot water welled behind my lashes.

I swallowed a heavy weight that tasted of tears, and I could tell myself the trembling was Astrid's.

"The winter fire itself," Mother continued, her arms tightening. "My little weirdling; I should have been there to see it. Well done."

"Year and a day," Astrid breathed, ever more concerned with what would be than what had been. "They would not take Bjorn, though Father pressed them. I even offered to go, since I was the cause of the matter. But no. They wanted our Solveig."

At least someone does. But my heart eased, for Mother had noticed my achievement and as long as she did, the rest of the world did not matter so much. "I was afraid I could not do it," I admitted into my dam's shoulder, covered with fine grey woolen cloth. "But Arn was there, and it was like lighting Idra's cooking fire." I inhaled sharply, and hated that I sounded so forlorn. "Must I go?"

It was unworthy of a *volva*. But in the circle of a mother's arms we are all, and ever, children.

"I am so sorry," Astrid continued, fair to bursting with her apologies. She always had the more tender heart, between us. "I was afraid, Solveig. I would go in your stead, if they would but let me."

"It could not be, Astrid. Let us fasten upon what we must do *now*." Mother patted at the back of my head, and she took over the weight of organizing and commanding once more so I did not have to. "Albeig, bring breakfast for my eldest daughter. Astrid, go fetch the recipe Lord Aeredh left; 'tis upon my nightstand. Come, Solveig, sit. Arn, mighty daughter, there is much meat, and you shall have ale from my own cup."

It was as if she had never been ill, and though I was glad my pride also writhed a fraction or two, sensing that the boy Aeredh, whoever he was and despite carrying a sword, had some *seidhr* that I had not studied deeply enough to bring to my mother's aid.

Perhaps he would teach it, then. A small recompense, but one I set myself to wrest from the Northerners if they would insist upon carrying me away.

For after all, a thin worm of excitement had begun to twist at the prospect of travel, down in the most secret chambers of my heart.

Never Fear

If a man is foolish enough to enter the women's quarters, a
spindle-crack upon his skull is the least he may expect.
—Saying of the southron Riverfolk

The rest of that day was a blur, except for when Bjorn caught
me at the door to the women's hall. He had lingered for some
while to do so, his expression suggested, and he did not even flyte
with Arn as he was often wont to do. "Solveig."

"Bjorn." I leaned against the wooden wall, my arms full of folded
textiles; Astrid had indeed found some fine cloth a-market before
doom had fallen. "What under the fishgutting stars were you thinking? Don't answer that, we both know you weren't thinking at all."

"I know I am to blame, you need not harry me further." He
hunched uncomfortably as Ulfrica hurried past, hissing in his direction like a disturbed granary cat. Ever he is childlike, my brother,
when he is not possessed by a battle-god or prodded by a passing
valkyra—the Wingéd Ones have little use for men before they are
dead, but they like battle well enough and those with some facility in
it are often under their gaze. "I did not even mean to do it, I swear."

Arn, with merely a single contemptuous glance, took herself a
few strides in the opposite direction and leaned against the wall,
pointedly ignoring both of us.

"Well, if one of them made a jest in Astrid's direction, of course you had to respond." My legs were not quite steady, but at least I could sleep in my own bed that night. All other matters, consequential or not, would have to wait until I had endured this day and secured that modest blessing. "I am told a cobblestone had the slaying of the Northern lord's son, and you largely blameless indeed."

"Do not mock me, sister." He rubbed under his blond beard, not nearly so full as Father's. But Bjorn had time to grow one, or so we all said. His warrior's crest was freshly oiled, and the braids under it carefully redone. "Though if you ever stopped, I should think you one of Odynn's wicker dolls substituting for my own Sol."

"And if you passed a day without needing my mockery, I might well think *you* substituted." An unwilling smile touched my lips, though a man was dead. Bjorn was, after all, Mother's firstborn and my brother—any breath of disrespect to his two sisters earned enough ire from him to make every warrior in Dun Rithell, not to mention many upriver or down, think twice before uttering lightsome words. "At least you only struck the one insulting Astrid. I can hardly fault you for that."

"Well..." He glanced over his shoulder, as if afraid the entire household would hear. I remembered stitching his shirt, content to do the dray-work while Astrid's fine touch embroidered sleeves and hem; at least he had not forgotten his new belt or beard-pin, and wore both proudly. Even his felted indoor boots were familiar, and a sign he did not perhaps think it quite wise to leave the hall for some short while. "Actually...that is to say..."

Oh, for the love of Fryja. I stepped closer, my arm-cargo bumping his broad chest. "Spit it forth, my brother. What happened?"

Even though I was half his size and younger to boot, Bjorn ever retreated before me. "I do not know." His breath bore precious little cargo of fermentation; he had not been at the mead in his usual way. Who was this fellow, and what had he done to my brother? "Astrid and I saw the Northerners outside the Althing hall just as the last sacrifices were done. They made some sort of announcement inside, but only to the elders and *they* will not say aught, even Father himself, and he was silent for a while. Then, a little later we passed them at the palisade, upon the row where the fine weavers and smiths sell wares from south-over-sea, and one of them looked at Astrid and said summat. Father looked sour, for he knows a very little of their Old Tongue, and Astrid asked what he had said, and—"

My head ached, attempting to imagine the scene with only this halting explanation. "So you struck him for...?"

"Another fellow said summat else in that strange talk of theirs, to take him to task by the tone, and the first one laughed. *You* know the manner of laughter I mean. So I hit him, the laughing fool."

Without even knowing what was said? Still, I did indeed know the manner of laughter Bjorn meant.

Every woman does.

"An ill deed." I studied his face in ruddy hornlight; inside the women's hall someone raised their voice in a midwinter song. Several others followed suit, Astrid's tone a clear silver bell. Something was missing from my brother's story. "Then they required weregild of Father, and...?"

"Well, at first he said he'd give me to them in bond." Bjorn's expression suggested a certain discomfort with the notion, which showed he was not entirely brainless. "Astrid cried, and the Northerners were discussing when the boy-one passed by with the wolf-leader."

"The one with the decorated hilt?" I did not like the one they named Eol, but he perhaps did not like the weight of my glance either. Sometimes *seidhr* presses certain others who possess it away with invisible force, like a lodestone turned against its fellow—yet he wore a blade, so he could not have the weirding. "You slew *his* son?" He did not seem of an age to have a child old enough to leer at a girl, but it was said those in the North wore their years lightly, and perhaps they married young as well.

"No, their great lord is still in the North. Eol has the leading of the wolves and the others have their own captains, though 'tis the boy Aeredh who seems to have the guiding toss." Bjorn glanced over my shoulder as a trio of thralls bustled past, each giving him a dark look. Or perhaps they were merely anxious. "I can only guess they told him what occurred in their own tongue, and the boy said to Father, *We shall take the daughter who lights the fire tonight, my lord.*" He did not quite have the lightness of lilt to mimic the youth's voice, but it was a good attempt. "And nothing Father said or offered would shake them."

"They do not seem easily shaken," I agreed. I did not know the noble houses of the North beyond that certain of them acknowledged one named Aenarian's overlordship, probably as some outlying halls and steadings nominally acknowledged Father. "But perhaps they will forget me by tomorrow; I hear Northerners are great travelers." Ever looking for the next horizon, they are said to be, though we had not seen many come through Dun Rithell.

We were too small to bother with, though fine enough in our own way.

"Whatever they told the elders is being kept from other ears." Bjorn's gold torc—my father's bear-heads upon its ends instead of my paternal grandmother's bees—glistered as he shifted, and the runes embroidered upon his shift-cuffs throbbed for a moment as my exhaustion mounted another notch. He did not wear a small-axe as usual, probably wisest for all concerned at the moment. "If 'tis war…"

My weariness acquired fresh depth. "And against just whom would we be warring, then? Even the Robed Ones and their strange god pestering the Barrowhills are more occupied with each other than with us, and that Dagnar fellow in the east died without heir." I shook my head, glad of a fresh set of braids after the sauna's delicious heat. Healthful cleanliness works wonders against exhaustion. Still, I was weary, and longed to set my burden of cloth down. "There's nobody to fight except other petty riverlords or greathalls wanting tribute." Which was the problem; if Bjorn could have plunged into a real battle or two, he might have learned a little restraint for peaceable life. I took a deep, smoke-tinged breath; the afternoon's bread was still baking. There would be more wassail tonight, though I might not drink quite so much of it. I ached all over, but this late in the afternoon I could only grit my teeth and wait for dusk.

The sooner I could climb into my own bed, the better.

"Well, there's some talk old Dagnar *had* an heir, but summat strange happened." Bjorn's golden-wire eyebrows lifted significantly. If not for his nose and my own, an onlooker might have held us to be from two different families entirely, but in that moment he looked very much like Mother—and hence, me—indeed. His black eye was puffing closed, and I knew without having to ask it was Father's work.

It would be difficult for Bjorn with me gone. Astrid was too gentle to keep an old bullock and a young one from touching horns. It takes a stubbornness greater than either to build that fence; in Dun Rithell, only Mother and I possessed that deep a measure.

Ulfrica passed again, hissing at Bjorn once more. He made a face, and had I been younger I might have taken her to task for such behavior even if she was a freedwoman performing honorable service in a lord's hall. Now, however...well, brother or not, he deserved some discomfort. Arn's scornful laugh was soft, but still clearly audible.

I freed a hand from the folded cloth; we would be sewing until Midsummer. Or Astrid would; she would have to forgo some embroidery in order to repair and make afresh what I was no longer available to. Naked indeed is the house without a woman at the needle, as the saying goes.

It did not seem possible I would be sent forth as weregild—not bondswoman and not thrall, certainly, but not quite free either. Frankly, I hoped I would wake the next day and find the entire matter simply a vivid dream, like glimpses of the past or future seen through pungent smoke and spinning disorientation. One who has *seidhr*, empty of stomach and skull, may stare through drug, hunger, and time itself to find an answer to the deeper riddles, stave off god-anger, or to turn aside disaster.

"Lean down." A deep sigh rose unbidden from the very pit of my belly. "And be still, or it won't work."

"You shouldn't," he muttered, but bent close anyway. His beard-oil was scented with pungent purple laventeli, a reminder of summer. "I deserved it."

Yes, you did. "Who will comfort Astrid and Mother while I'm gone? It will have to be you, Bjorn; Father has other work." My fingertips rested upon his warm brow; my palm cramping from proximity to bruise-pain. "Hold *still*."

"It feels odd." But he froze, ox-patient now that I had given him a task. "I'll look after them, Solveig. Never fear."

You'd better. I drew out the swelling, my face a mask as my own left eye smarted. Spreading the pain up my arm, exhaling hard to drive it away, imagining a starlit glow to eat whatever discomfort remained—there are several ways to treat any wound, and I ever thought it best to combine a few for safety. Idra held that one way fully followed was better than two or three mixed, but every *seidhr* has their own preference. "I wish I could put a halter upon your temper, like Lokji was put to plow." Mentioning that son of the All-mother was not the best luck, but it fit the situation.

"I try," Bjorn said mournfully, nothing but his mouth moving. He was very big, my brother, but he did not strike women or children. If the Northern lord's son had been a daughter, my brother would have borne any laughter or gibe from that quarter with good grace. "You know I do."

Oh, 'tis Bjorn, what can be done? I drew my hand away before the wound was fully healed; I would help, but not fully erase. "You must save your gift for the battlefield, brother mine. Even if there are no wars to be had."

"I am sorry, Solveig." He must have truly been so, for he regarded me with the most penitent of his looks, lower lip pushed slightly out and his big dark thick-lashed eyes mournfully wide. "I will keep my temper until you return."

They will probably leave me here, content to have made their point. Even the bare thought of travel, interesting though it was, wearied me further that day. "I might not depart at all, to save you the trouble. Go find summat to do. Help Father."

"I doubt he wishes to see me at the moment." My brother straightened, subtracting cloth from my trembling arms. "Where is this bound?"

"The storerooms, where else? Tell Albeig to salt them well, some of the fabric will have to wait for next Midwinter. Oh, and do not hit anyone." I could not resist an ill-tempered farewell.

"I won't." He glowered at me, but I stuck my tongue out and he laughed, performing a sharp turn before setting off upon what had been my errand.

"Too kind by far," Arn muttered, stepping close and eyeing me. "You're pale, my weirdling. Ale and an early dinner?" The music from within altered, becoming Vanya's plaintive reply to the fisherman, with Astrid once again taking the higher melody.

She did so love to sing.

I surprised myself with another deep sigh. I sounded, in fact, very much like Mother. "If I sot myself before dusk I shall not sleep past moonrise." I pressed my knuckles into my back, stretching catlike, and nodded as Rigertha passed. The thrallgirl squeaked and hurried along, still overwhelmed at being given to a greathall. "Perhaps they will ask for gilt instead at the last moment. Father might have to strip the roof."

"Small price if it keeps his eldest daughter home." Arn's spear leaned against the wall, her fingertips but lightly upon it. No shieldmaid ever lets her weapon roam truly free. "*I am hungry.*"

"Then go to the kitchens and beg something of Ilveig, small one." Albeig's under-captain was much easier to win a mouthful between tables from. I remained leaning against the wall, now rubbing at my forehead with my fingertips. The headache would not leave me, and I had made it worse by taking Bjorn's pain. "I must see to the candles."

"Let someone else. Come." She beckoned, picking up her spear. "We have not spoken yet, and we must."

I had been dreading just this. "You do not have to come with me."

"Oh, I do not?" Her dark gaze kindled; Arneior still had not changed out of her hauberk. A shieldmaid is ever ready, and perhaps she hoped for a battle of some kind today. Few were those of Dun Rithell who would meet her in the training-yard, but strangers arriving for trade-fairs and great festivals were not nearly so reluctant. Even when she bested them all. "You are my charge, Solveig. And what would I do with my weirdling gone, my lady? I think you seek to keep all the adventure for yourself."

"As if I have ever wanted any adventure beyond a new couplet or two." Which was not quite the truth; when younger I had oft chafed at Dun Rithell's borders, longing for the horizon as Northerners or those with the sea-longing are said to. I pushed myself upright, letting go of the wall. "I should have made *you* carry cloth to the storerooms."

"Praise to the Wingéd Ones, that is no task for a shieldmaid." Her smile was as ready as ever, though her forehead wrinkled. The blue woad-stripe upon her face had been refreshed yet again.

I had to admit it made some manner of sense for me to be the one; Arn was good protection for a traveling lord's daughter and was sworn to me besides. Yet if Bjorn had not struck a man I would be at leisure to bask in some small inner glow, knowing I had done well and could sleep without care for at least one night.

We might have had this conversation somewhere more private, but Arn did not care to. Besides, seeking any seclusion in a large hall is a fool's game. There are always eyes watching and tongues ready to wag.

I wondered if it would be the same in the North. If the black-clad men returned, and if they were not simply after the roof-gilding, I might yet see what lay over distant hills and have my fill of travel.

It still did not seem possible, even that afternoon. Certainly the old ways said *a child for a child*, but...these were modern times.

"I should have foreseen this," I said quietly, and Arn's face changed.

My shieldmaid looked stern indeed, instead of simply amused at the world's many follies and the weakness of those unblessed by guidance from the Wingéd Ones. "Idra would tell you not to doubt the *seidhr*."

"Idra is gone." My shoulders sought to hunch, very like Bjorn's. "And in this case there was no *seidhr* to doubt. The Northerners have their own; perhaps it overmatched mine."

"Or perhaps 'tis fate." So easily, Arn consigned such questions to the realm of *uninteresting to pursue*. "In either case, I go with you, and that is final. But for this afternoon I have an empty belly, and you must sit for a moment. Will you come, or shall I drag you?"

"Let me simply catch a glimpse of Mother—"

But Arn took my arm, and in this one case, she was serious about dragging where I would not walk.

I did not gainsay her, for in those days my shieldmaid rarely sounded so worried, and this novelty disturbed me as much as the other new things crowding upon Dun Rithell.

Stripping the Roof

Many crafts hath the Elder perfected, for their lives are long and the Blessed themselves their tutors. And yet it is mortals who hold the Allmother's greatest gifts—or so it is said by the Elder themselves.
—Scroll of Naethron One-hand, *seidhr* of
Ancisus in the Barrowhills

The Northern youth who had mixed Mother such a powerful draught left his recipe inscribed on a piece of fine-woven bark, southron runes carefully inked though many were joined in odd places. The bark was rolled and slid into a cunningly carved scent-wood tube; the scrap even held a notation for the specific word to be chanted into the liquid. Even a warrior could use such a formula and not suffer any loss of virtue from handling weirding instead of his proper weapons.

It was a simple enough medicine, and I could not argue with its effects. Mother was weak but upright, and there was a fire to her summersky glance I had not seen in some while.

Still, she retired early, and so did I, still mulling upon the boy and his craft—I could not bear to think upon the next morning. Which meant my shieldmaid was abed early as well, though she might not have felt much weariness.

Sleepless nights are common among those the Wingéd Ones

breathe upon, and her excitement at the prospect of a journey was well-banked but still glowing evident. And though I would not have admitted it aloud I felt the same, except for the exhaustion of an all-night vigil; I bore such things less easily despite my youth.

Arn freed herself of hauberk and jerkin, padded shirt and linen with swift impatient movements. Her ringmail trousers were likewise set aside upon a large chest bearing the sign of Dun Rithell, my father's bear and mother's stag both proudly represented. Muscle flickered in Arn's limbs as she stretched, then hurried into loose sleeveless nightwear. I was already in my shift and under the covers, every part of me twitching with the leftover day. Normally a single sleepless night is a small matter, but I had lit the bonfire, held it steady, and also taken pain from my brother.

Such things wear upon a *volva*. Even one with an elementalist's gift might well feel the weight; it is vital force we spend to work such craft, and mortal things must replenish that stock, albeit imperfectly, with deep rest.

In the women's sleeping-room, the unmarried girls and thralls settled upon their pallets or spoke in low voices, braiding each other's hair; soon they would be a murmuring sea of night-breathing, shifting, and other soft noises. One of the younglings was overtired and cried with the peculiar note meaning a child is vexed rather than pained, and I was glad to have some small private space. My closet was not very large, but it was bigger than Astrid's—maybe only because Arn shared it with me.

We had shared everything since I was ten winters old, and it was familiar as my own breath. Or hers.

Arneior swept the door almost closed; the only light was a stripe from the lamplit hall. A hound passed by with nails clicking, probably brindle Britha, one of Father's favorites and much given to patrolling the halls at night. Albeig's youngest lieutenants would be along to douse the horn lanterns as soon as all were settled, before hastening to their own beds, dreaming safely beside a parent or elder sibling.

"The Northerners will certainly return," Arn finally said, grimly. I arranged my pillow, too tired to care. "Maybe your father should start stripping the roof tonight."

And appear weak? I made a soft, disparaging noise. "I wonder if they're camping near the river." I wondered about that youth, too, and the recipe. Had he been sent forth with it? Was he carrying more rolled bark; was it his hand upon the runes? The small cylinder smelled powerfully sweet and spicy at once; everyone marveled over the delicate details of the carving. It showed a hunt, but the hind which horsed harriers chased was far in the distance with a good chance of escape.

Perhaps that was to be my fate. I yawned hugely; I could not seem to stop. I had not fallen into slumber over my dinner, which was a blessing indeed.

"They are probably wandering the night, making plans to steal some other daughter." Arn thrust back the covers and clambered in. Then it was time to warm her, so I clasped her close though I was the smaller. "May the snows take them, I say."

"Traveling in new winter." I shuddered, my sleeping-braid scratching herb-fragrant pillow. Bjorn could have stayed his hand until better weather, but he was never one to put off an inconvenience to his weirdling sister. "Well, they are Northmen, they must know a trick or two for such conditions."

"But any worth learning? That is the question." She rested her chilled hands against my stomach; I quelled the wriggling. When we were younger a wrestling-match would warm us both, but nowadays it was simply easier to let her use me as a hearth-heated brick. "I could challenge them. All of them, at once."

"Oh, yes, that would be helpful." I snuggled into the mattress, ready to push her hands away after a decent interval. "I wonder why I did not think of that before."

"Because you are not a shieldmaid." She gave up warming her hands and turned upon her other side, the better to do battle with her own pillow. "If one of them touches you, I shall chop his fingers off." Clearly, she meant to be comforting.

"And no weregild for that." I turned my back to her as well. Sometimes we fell asleep in each other's arms, but lately I wanted to spend the few moments after I closed my eyes with myself alone. There was hot water welling traitorously behind my lids again, as there had been at odd moments during the day.

I never have liked weeping. Since Idra's passing the urge had come upon me more frequently, and weariness will make water, as the proverb says.

The Northerners were simply pressuring my father for some reason; he would take down a portion of roof-gilding and send it forth with them to pay for one war or another. It would take a few more good years of trading downriver to regild, but with two marriages and a *seidhr* daughter, that was not an insurmountable challenge. He might even take Bjorn a-trading and marry my brother off somewhere the battle-rage would find an easier outlet.

So I comforted myself, the night after the longest dark of winter. I would not quite call it a lie, for some part of me honestly believed. But the *seidhr* in my bones knew different and my dreams were restless, as Arn told me later; I did not wake from their heavy anxiety.

The next morning the Northerners appeared again, riding from the west to the door of my father's hall.

A Fate in This

On the Day of Ash the Black Land's creatures boiled forth and slew all before them. Much lamentation arose that morn, and the smoke of the fires veiled the Sun. The Elder stood against the onslaught with the Secondborn who loved them, yet not by battle could the Enemy be overcome. Mere defense was all that was achieved, until Lithielle and Bjornwulf braved that far land...
— Arnan the Bard, *The Saga of Bjornwulf*

My mother's second-largest trunk held a faint good scent of pine; I left packing to Albeig and Astrid, who enjoyed such things. Many gifts were brought to Dun Rithell early the previous afternoon, for the double pleasure of gawking at a fully proven *volva* with the elementalist's gift and also at a lord's daughter surrendered as weregild. Mother's health continued to wax, and it appeared she would not need another dose of the Northern youth's ague potion.

I had mixed more just in case, though its potency would linger in a wax-sealed bottle for only about a moon's turn. Still, it would take her through the worst of new winter's cold; I could not do more. One of the other *seidhr* of Dun Rithell would have to be paid to perform—probably Frestis, who would also earn a handsome fee blessing everyone's flocks.

Good fortune for him.

The air was softening, the sky had turned grey; Tarnarya's top was lost in cloud and her black shoulders bore a dusting of snow like scattered lime upon a battle-grave or sacrifice pit. And as the first edge of dawn crept over the river and hills, the Northerners arrived at Dun Rithell's gate. Flokin, at the end of a cold night-duty there, grumbled to all who would listen that they had simply *appeared*, their large white steeds melding with cold fog and their tack oddly quiet.

For now they were mounted, the men of the North, on long-limbed steeds. Only the wolf-marked ones showed, the rest having some other business farther south in the Barrowhills. Eol's men passed some words with my father, who was at his morning practice in the sparring rounds; soon after, he left with two of his men for Frestis's house. He and the elderly *seidhr* would sing a lament for my temporary loss and make sacrifice for both my safety and theirs during my absence—and Father would not return to Dun Rithell until certain the Northerners were safely gone, for a weregild must be "stolen" to balance the initial theft of a life.

Such was the custom, and even Eril the Battle-Mad obeyed it. Soon after his hurried departure we were shaken awake by a whey-pale Albeig, who narrowly avoided a clout from Arneior for her pains.

My shieldmaid's temper is fierce indeed when her rest is disturbed.

My mother, however, was arisen and fully dressed, and it was she who greeted the Northerners formally in the greathall while Astrid hurriedly braided my hair and Bjorn, half-dressed and wild-rumpled, burst into the women's quarters to find me. Ulfrica was too busy to hiss at first, though he garnered a fair share of slaps and kicks, not to mention a sharp couplet upon his incompetence from Albeig herself, which must have stung since *she* is a mistress of insulting the parts of a man he most hopes are without compare.

Even my mother laughed helplessly at Albeig's rhymes, whenever the housekeeper was in a mood to give them.

Finally Astrid put her skirt over Bjorn's shoulders as he went hands-and-knees upon the cold floor, and then the women let him be—except Ulfrica, who made a threatening motion with a heavy distaff each time she passed.

If a man intrudes upon noblewomen's quarters he is made a foot-rest for his pains; not many dare or brook the loss of pride.

"White horses, like the Elder are said to have ridden." My brother could finally give his news in a breathless jumble, shifting uneasily beneath Astrid's skirt—which threatened to slide from his broad shoulders. " 'Tis the boy and the wolf-ones. They have two extra mounts, too."

"Ponies?" Arn brightened; she did like to ride. So far she seemed to consider this entire affair simply a pleasant jaunt, though I could not tell how much of her show of unconcern was meant to soothe my nerves.

Normally I was the one smoothing her sharp temper; she relied upon my wit as I relied upon her spear.

"Not ponies. Bigger. I do not know how they intend to feed such mounts in winter; they are but lightly equipped." Bjorn glanced at me. "I also do not know who will carry your chest, Solveig."

"They cannot expect me to come without a spare dress," I pointed out, practically enough, and winced as Astrid tugged at my hair. She was applying many red coral beads in with quick expert motions; I would not go uncrowned. Indeed I suspected Dun Rithell's entire stock of those lucky items was about to rest upon my braids. "How did Mother greet them?"

"With cup and bread." My brother's eyes were round. He pulled Astrid's skirt higher over his shoulders, like a child seeking comfort. The maneuver showed her knitted stockings—a pair I had made myself, whispering words of comfort and grace into each row. "She knows their ritual words. The youth said her phrasing is fine."

Well, my mother Gwendelint's people were traditionalists and she had been educated by a *seidhr* in her youth, so naturally she would at least offer welcome and farewell in the Old Tongue. Those with the power also teach the lesser though commonly available magics of writing and figuring, especially in houses where some strain of Elder, however fictional, is held as a matter of pride. My mother's bright gaze spoke of some such blood in our far past.

So does mine, though my eyes are winter sky to her deeper, richer summer.

"Just a few left." Astrid moved slightly, her knee digging into

Bjorn's back. "I will put every single coral we have upon your head, Sol. They will not lead *you* into a bog."

"It would be a waste of time for them to do so." I held very still against Astrid's pulling; she grows fierce near the end of hurried braids. "Unless their gods require it, in which case—"

"I may still challenge them." Arn, in her most well-beloved and comfortable hauberk with a few extra layers underneath, finished shrugging into her plain dun hooded overmantle, one slim callused hand questing for spear-haft and closing upon it without needing her gaze for direction. " 'Tis still an option, that is all I am saying."

"May all the gods save us from that." Ulfrica halted, bending swiftly to whisk a piece of straycloth from my fingers once I finished wiping. A hurried breakfast was congealing behind my breastbone; its traces were now gone from my lips. "Here, my lady. Your gloves; I shall have your mantle directly."

"Cannot leave that behind." Arn nodded, hopped on her boot-toes slightly to test the heft and fall of her armor; she settled upon her heels, satisfied. "And the undercloak, 'tis hanging right next to it."

"I *know*." With one last menacing movement toward a flinching Bjorn, her skirt fluttering, Ulfrica was gone. I had to hide a smile; I oft thought the sparks from rubbing against each other's temper could well denote some affection on her part. Bjorn seemed oblivious, only bearing her ill treatment with oxlike patience. If her father's hall were a little more advantageously placed Eril might have induced my brother to make some offer, but the son of Dun Rithell seemed only to see Ulfrica's sharp tongue and not the girl behind it.

Of course, they knew each other from childhood; a familiar chair is never seen until it is missed, as the saying goes. And though she was sharp with him, she was likewise with a few other young warriors.

I would not be here to watch what happened as spring came, or to weigh different marriage offers and give my support to one or another. The thought sobered me, and suddenly departure was a fearful certainty instead of merely a looming maybe. "I suppose I shall see what you packed as we travel." My neck ached, held at a precise angle so Astrid could finish her labors. "I mislike leaving my share of the sewing to you."

"I put a few pieces in, so you may have summat to work upon in the cold North." She turned slightly, still holding me as a hawk with its claws in prey. "Hand up a ribbon, Bjorn. No, not that one...not that one either. Yes, *finally*, thank you." Astrid made a soft *tch-tch*. "They will no doubt give you cloth there, though."

"Mh." I could sew just as easily at home, and some part of me still expected them to demand half the roof-gilt at the last moment instead.

So often we will not face what is before us until we are absolutely forced to. It was, I realized that fogbound morn, fast becoming one of my habits. Idra would have dispensed a sharp tug upon one of my braids and a steadying admonition, but my teacher was in Hel's country now, and probably glad of the rest after a lifetime spent in service.

That is another meaning to *seidhr*, and though there were others possessing the weirding in Dun Rithell I thought the community still might miss me. It seemed easier to think of their feelings than my own, especially when I embraced Astrid with an admonition to *be good, and do not weep.*

She disobeyed, promptly bursting into tears; afterward, in the hall outside the women's quarters Bjorn enclosed me in a bear's fierce silent hug. He said nothing, though his throat worked, and I knew he was sorry indeed.

"Comfort Astrid," I told him. "And, by Odynn and every other god, my brother, *keep your temper.*"

He nodded, disheveled and morning-rumpled, his jaw set as ever Father's was. So I left my siblings, with an eldest sister's nagging. I did not tell them I loved them.

I hope they knew, but how I wish I could be certain.

The hurry and bustle of travel-readiness turned to a breathless hush when I entered the greathall in my green undermantle, my overboots laced securely for long travel and my hair braided with every red coral bead Dun Rithell had laboriously bargained for in riverside fairs. I was nervous as I had not been since my fourth summer, when Idra told my mother I had the weirding and would survive the training were it begun soon.

Arn was stiff-straight at my shoulder as I paused upon the entry steps, her spear's blade—as long as her hand and forearm—glittering wickedly even in hornlight. My mother passed words with the Northerners, but I was too far away to hear.

At the moment, I was too busy keeping my fingers from knotting together. A *volva* must wear her bands proudly, a lord's daughter meet her fate with chin high and shoulders straight. I did not like the idea of facing the Northerners without the stairs granting me some additional measure of height, but at least their group separated smoothly when I approached, Arn prowling alongside.

A breath of smoke clung to their black-clad forms. Later I learned they had built the pyre for their fallen companion down by the riverbank, and stood vigil beside it as well. They did not suffer any southroner to bring fuel, nor to keen at the flameside; straight from the warm embers they came to my father's greathall.

I bent my head only to my mother, and when I looked up to her, tall and proud upon the second dais-step, the damp glitters upon her cheeks mocked us both. Gwendelint of Dun Rithell wore even her tears proudly, and silently dared any who would comment upon them to do so.

"Astrid tells me I am ready." I held Mother's gaze; she would not be shamed by her daughter before these men, or any other. "May I ask who among these gathered holds the pledge?" For a weregild is under some protection, from custom as well as gods, and woe to any who breaks it.

Or so the tales sing.

"My lord Eol." Mother gestured; I half-turned to see the Northerner with the jeweled hilt step forward. He made the same gesture some of his rune-marked friends had, his knuckles to left chest, his lips, and last of all his bent forehead. "He bears the authority of Aenarian Greycloak, the high ruler of the North, and was nearest in kin to one who rides West."

Riding West was an old-fashioned way to put it, but she could not very well say *My son murdered another's, and I am bearing this disaster as well as I may.*

"Your daughter and her companion are under my personal protection, my lady Gwendelint." Eol the Northerner's cloak was dark and the fur lining upon it glossy black, though I could not tell what beast it was from. And though he was unused to the southron tongue, he handled it well enough. Any insult to the weregild would be a slight to his honor, and Northerners, like my own folk, have ever been quick to answer such things. "There is a fate to this."

Mother regarded him almost balefully. "If there is, it had best end with my daughter returned. She is *seidhr*, my lord Eol, beloved of both your gods and ours." There was a challenge to my mother's tone, and her summersky gaze rested not upon the wolf-captain but the youth Aeredh.

"We may argue the names of the Vanyr and Aesyr for many a year and still reach no agreement." The Northern boy's clear tenor was pleasant enough. "The snow comes, fair lady."

"Oh, aye." Her eyes glittered; I had never heard my mother sound so bitter, especially to a guest so young. "And it falls more heavily upon us than upon your kind."

I did not wonder at her words, for the Northerners were held to be long-lived, a blessing from the vanished Elder.

"Does it?" Aeredh sounded only mildly interested, though courteous enough. "One would think the opposite."

I extended my hands, climbing the first stair of the dais; my mother clasped them. A susurration at the entryway was Astrid, peering in wide-eyed.

It would have been impolite for Bjorn to appear. We had already bid farewell, and I could still feel my brother's rough embrace.

Besides, he was never one to speak when an action would serve. A hot stone lodged in my throat.

A slight cough dislodged it, and my voice was a trifle huskier than usual. "I mixed more of the ague recipe, though it will not hold its virtue past a moonturn; Astrid knows where 'tis in the stillroom." I took a deep breath. My mother's fingers were cold; mine were not only because I was swathed in cloth and the great hearth had been prodded into wakefulness hours before. "Do not go forth thinking you are cured until snowmelt is well past, Mother. I would not have such fine work undone."

"I am supposed to chide *you*," she said, and the glimmering water in her blue, blue eyes hurt mine. Sometimes, when younger, I had wondered if my mother saw everything about her tinted with sky-dye.

Do not weep, Solveig. You have not for years, do not start now. "I shall think of you scolding me every night before I sleep. Will that do?"

"Only if Arn gives you a clout to make you listen." The last words caught upon a pained laugh, for my mother rarely ever had to raise voice or hand to me—not like Bjorn, who was endlessly, restlessly curious. So was I, but I learned to satisfy said curiosity discreetly, especially when my hapless brother could take the blame.

When thought of that way, 'twas only fair I was smoothing this wrinkle in the cloth now. "Do not give my small one ideas. You know how bloodthirsty she is." I squeezed gently. When had my mother's hands, so strong and sure, developed this faint tremor? Her fingers felt somewhat fragile in my palms, like birds charmed from a bracken or wide heather, trembling against the coaxing.

It is not right to wring the neck of a creature you lure thus; far better is the *seidhr* trick of letting the small thing fly free, returning to its business none the worse for wear.

"I will keep her safe, my lady." Arneior accompanied the declaration with a soft tap of her spear's blunt end upon the step, lending it gravity. "The Wingéd Ones are watching."

My mother accepted the oath with a tremulous smile and kissed my forehead, having to bend far indeed to reach me upon the lower step. "Perhaps you will return taller, daughter mine." Her smile cracked at the edges, so I stepped away as she straightened, smoothing my undermantle. Fine-woven green wool scratched comfortingly against my palms. "We shall have to make you a new cloak."

"Of a certainty Arn will hunt something in the North to line it with." I swallowed everything else I wished to say. "The sooner I go, the sooner I return. I shall dream of thee, Mother."

"You must. Or I do not know how I will bear it." She gestured again. "Go, my daughter."

There must be no wailing at a leave-taking such as this, so I nodded, turned, and made it almost to the archway before whirling and running back to the steps, pushing past the Northerners. I climbed the dais in a rush and threw my arms about my mother, squeezing as hard as I dared while Arn glided behind me, her face set and her gaze dissuading the foreign men from making any comment.

Or moving closer.

My arms did not wish to loosen, but I forced them to. I wiped at my cheeks, met my mother's gaze, and could find little else in my throat that had not already been said; thus it was Arneior and I left the greatest hall of Dun Rithell upon a morning of snowfog amid a deep hush, since nothing had thawed enough to drip.

Truth

I never returned.

Day Travel

*Through the bones of the world the Elder Roads run, and
those who step upon them must be wary.*
                    —Maelsana the Swift of Dorael

I had hardly ever ridden a horse so high. The cream-colored Northern mare was sweet-tempered and clearly knew her business was
to stay with her coevals; Arn's, however, had a mischievous glint to her
great sad eyes which promised trouble later. The dark-clad Northern
men closed about us; I did not see where my trunk was. Still, I had my
small, brightly embroidered *seidhr*-bag at my hip, the strap diagonal
across the chest of my undermantle. Arn had her own baggage, much
less than mine and easily added to her mount's tack. Thick winterfog
hid the road I had walked, run, ridden, or ambled along my entire
life, making it a stranger, and I was startled when the standing stones
at the east border of safe pasturage loomed wet and black around us.

It seemed far too soon to have reached them, but when clouds come
to earth they maze and dizzy even the most experienced travelers.

One of the riders muttered summat about ill luck in the Northern
tongue, and I suppressed another start. They spoke the old language
daily, it seemed; I decided to listen hard, adding to my store of it—
and to make no sign I understood, for we were two women among a
group of foreign men.

It is wise to keep every advantage one may need later, and in any

case I did not feel like speaking overmuch to warriors who counted
as kin a man my brother had killed.

I did keep my hood high, taking comfort in its warmth. I also whispered to the stones, wishing them a pleasant day as anyone who desires
to pass such things without malediction or ill luck is well advised to. The
fluttering in my bones—soft wings like my mother's trembling after a
seidhr draught eased her ague—intensified just short of pain in the center
of their cold, silent ring, and drained away as the horses plodded onward.

The one they called Eol rode to my left; the youth Aeredh might have
wished to take my right but Arn was there, and while her mare might
have a bit of spirit upon a clear day she was more than happy to let a
shieldmaid make the decisions in this baffling, almost salt-smelling cold.
Eol had wrapped his hilt, but I knew where the colorless gem was and
sometimes thought I discerned a stray spark from it as the fog thickened.

That weapon, I thought, *probably has a name.*

Had they not been grim Northerners, perhaps they would have tried
to make some manner of conversation. Instead, the dark-clad men rode
in what I recognized as a guard-pattern, having seen warriors take such
positions around my father more than once. Arn rode with her bright coppery head hooded and down, but I knew better than to think her unaware.

The fog brightened, new-risen sun warming its upper layers. Surely
it was not bad to feel a slight thrill of accomplishment—even if the
bonfire did not truly make the great light of the sky return, there was
still some satisfaction in performing the ritual to make absolutely
certain of the world's continuance.

And I had behaved as a lord's daughter and a *volva* during the
following disaster; none could say I had not. Though a tongue or
two might wag, saying a true *seidhr* would have foreseen and forestalled Bjorn's action or its consequence—but who can tell, as Idra oft
remarked, if we do not avert greater tragedies by the occurrence of
smaller ones? Perhaps, she would sometimes add, everything during
a life is the least of many evils.

Only the Allmother knows for certain.

Strangely, it was not my mother's farewell or my siblings' I
thought of, but my father. He would return to a hall in mourning,
and though he was Eril the Battle-Mad whose word and deed ruled

Dun Rithell and some distance up and down the river, my mother's grief would be difficult for even his broad shoulders to bear.

He probably would not miss his weirdling daughter overmuch, though, until Bjorn broke something else I was not available to mend. The thought gave me a shiver; the fur upon my hood was dewed with tiny water-jewels.

My motion was slight, but it attracted attention. Or perhaps they had been watching me with some curiosity, those Northern men taking me from my home.

"You must think us cruel," Eol said, in his heavily accented southron tongue. For a moment I was unsure whether he addressed me or his companions, but when I peered around the edge of my hood his dark gaze was fixed upon me.

Yes, weregild is cruel, but better than the alternative. The sagas say that before the last great war against the lord of the Black Land many a settlement was reduced to ashes and charred bones by vengeance raiding. The trading of child or warrior swiftly became an accepted practice after Wethik the Blue's innovation during the long-ago Great Alliance; faced with the Enemy's terror, ash, and despair, even the most warlike or least wise of mortals realized we could not well afford to strike each other down with abandon.

So I was called upon to make some small conversation after all. "I think you strange to be riding this far from your homes in winter, and so lightly equipped for it." I could have made another observation or two, but they would be sharp, and already I felt the constraint of a lone woman among those not of her kin.

If these men foundered during our journey, though, I was fairly certain Arn and I could make our way home. It would be a tale worth telling—she would hunt, I would use *seidhr* to smooth our way, and we would not lack for fire so long as we could find fuel.

"Need drove us. And I am not certain to what end." Eol regarded me somewhat curiously; of course, now that I was outside my father's hall, men could look all they liked. Arneior was a mighty defense, but she could not blind every passerby.

Though it would cheer her immensely to be capable of such a feat, I thought.

"The return of the Powers, and the final defeat of our foe." Aeredh's voice came light and merry through the fog; he was an indistinct shape upon Arn's other side, but I caught a sky-flash from that quarter, as of bright blue eyes. "A fated chance may still be a happy one, son of Tharos."

What foe? The Great Enemy in the north is gone. The sagas all agreed—the Black Land was spent after a great defeat, and its master vanished along with the Elder who fought him from the first rising of the Sun. The songs did not agree on precisely *how* he had been overcome, just that the great iron gates between the Two Fangs stood open and rusting while the land beyond slowly leached of his evil presence.

There had to be some new but purely mortal warlord in the North, perhaps one they were seeking allies against. And apparently this Eol was of Tharos—was that the name of his house or a mighty parent? I did not know enough of the North's holdings; what need, when they were so far away?

It was strange for them to journey to our relatively small world clinging to the riverbank. Despite my father's reputed battle-madness Northerners hold all who do not live in their harsh clime as perhaps not quite hard enough to wage true war. I had seen only one or two of Eol's black-clad kind at a distance during fairs or festivals; they did not come to my father's hall to give news or be greeted by my mother.

"Happy chance may yet strike. Though often just the opposite occurs, son of Aerith." Eol's horse drew nearer mine. "What say you, my lady?"

Was he expecting a *seidhr*'s pronouncement upon fates happy or otherwise? No doubt those of the far, cold, silent North had their own proverbs upon such things. Mayhap their home was so congenial to harsh tempers they did not wish to wend overmuch in our direction. Some said the North was but lightly populated and their numbers slow to increase; I could not imagine what manner of women they had, though Arneior would probably find them refreshing if their miens were as stark and traditional as these fellows'.

But that morn my new companions spoke of fate, and chance. An answer was required of me, so I chose the most diplomatic. "I say 'tis too soon to tell."

It amused more than one of their number; a mutter of laughter ran through the Northerners. The road lost its vestiges of ancient paving, becoming a rimed pair of parallel dirt tracks for cart-wheel or staggered riders, and I shivered again, wondering why we were not going south.

It was the furthest from home I'd ever been, unless one counted the other side of the river with Father. I visited the camps and small-farms at Tarnarya's feet more often with him as I grew older, gathering herbs and other things Idra thought I should know how to use. And listening, as those who were not quite under Lord Eril's command but close enough taught me the value of open ears; much of a *seidhr*'s duty is to discern what remains unsaid, and to keep the peace amid jostling holds, halls, and farms.

For a year-and-day Father would not be able to ask *Well, Solveig, what do you make of that?* At least he listened to my thoughts more than Bjorn's, which according to Idra showed some wisdom. But now he would not have me to uncover the truth of a matter or two, who would be troublesome or who wished to take what a riverlord might not grant.

Of course he would not send his son, his great blond copy, along with these men; of course he would not send Astrid since she did not have a shieldmaid. I could admit that morning I was the only possible choice, and I would even gain knowledge from the occasion. Such a thing pleases a *volva*, for knowing is power.

And yet I was not pleased.

Still…a traitorous bubble of excitement at a journey into wisdom none other in Dun Rithell could claim was very much in my heart. I rode sunk in silence and deep thought, disdaining to look at the white-wrapped world. What little I could see of the countryside looked very much like the slopes above our eastron standing stones, rocks lifting through winter-yellow grass, dark patches of thornleaf, or bright orange creeping everbranch. A distant inaudible creaking, muffled through the fog, was the breath of a forest surrounding us; perhaps we were upon a chain of heath meadows, though those who went through the eastron standing stones never mentioned such features in that direction.

There were some clear lines of the kind called "wyrmtrack" amid the trees a few days' journey north of Dun Rithell, though. We had not traveled that long, nor truly in that direction—but who could tell, in this weather?

Arn's horse pressed closer, and I felt her attention—not precisely worry, for she knows my silences almost as if she has *seidhr* of her own. There is oft no need for words between a shieldmaid and her charge.

I did shift uncomfortably in the saddle, though as unobtrusively as possible. Tomorrow would be a misery; adjusting to long hours a-horseback is unpleasant, but I would not give these men the satisfaction of seeing me flinch.

In any way.

"Sol." Arn leaned from her saddle; I took what she proffered automatically. She broke off a second piece of hard waybread for her own consumption, holding it in her teeth as she tugged her half-glove back on. "I think the fog is thinning."

I nibbled at the bread; Albeig had no doubt weighted Arn with a fair measure. Still, it would eventually run out, then we would have nothing that tasted of home. A few experimental sniffs, rolling the cold air over my tongue before taking a second bite, and I had my answer. "Mayhap, though it will thicken at dusk. We shall have snow soon, that is the larger worry."

"Fret not." The mist was indeed thinning, for I could see young Aeredh upon his mount much more clearly. No water clung to his dark hair, and his smile was bright. He seemed to enjoy riding for its own sake, or some other relief made his eyes spark so. "We can find our way through much worse than this, my lady."

I confined myself to a single nod. I knew the stories—they say the hunters of the North can track a direbeast through blizzard, or a bird upon the wing. Otherwise they would not survive between new winter and late far-northern spring, in that deep cold after the sun's renewal when screaming wind pours forth, piling ice upon snow and cutting through any wool no matter how well-woven, any hide no matter how thick. I busied myself with the waybread, and after a short while the track veered away. Aeredh took us to its side between two massive shelflike rocks, calling a halt.

There was no disagreement, though one or two of the Northerners glanced at each other with eyebrows raised. Perhaps they expected me to protest or faint, but I managed a creditable dismount into Arn's waiting hands. Her hauberk was slightly damp; tiny water-droplets festooned her ruddy hornbraids and dewed her freckled cheeks. "Walk a little." She drew me from the horse's side; I could still feel the riding motion in my limbs. "At least 'tis quiet here."

She was right. Father would be returned by now and home all a-bustle between the feasting and trade negotiations. I had often wished for a little peace while caught in new winter's beginning.

Wishes are dangerous things, Idra said, *especially when answered.* "How far have we come?" I did not stagger, though I did have to use my legs with care.

She shrugged; shieldmaids are not often troubled by such things as saddle sores. "Farther than we should have, unless the mist is playing tricks. I cannot even hear the stones."

"Nor can I." I halted, close enough to feel her heat. The Northerners made a loose ring about us, vanishing by pairs into the vapor and returning with eerily quiet steps. Even the horses were silent; the youth Aeredh went to each in turn, stroking their long faces and smiling as if they jested with him.

I watched to see if he performed any *seidhr*, but none was apparent. Perhaps he was simply a horse trainer.

"We should feel them all the way past the bend in the river. Instead, we're climbing, and have not…" Arn's hand tightened upon her spear as I finished chewing my noontide measure of bread; she had discerned the direction of my gaze. "*That one* is uncanny."

It was unlike her, for she knew I had been called the same more than once and the term irritated both of us. "Mayhap he has some weirding I may learn. Idra would be thrilled." Still, it was strange—for he carried a sword, and in the South those with *seidhr* may not use physical weaponry.

It is not proper. The virtue that makes a warrior is bled away by the contrasting power of *seidhr*, and one of my kind who uses aught but a healer's knife runs the risk of the weapon turning against them, not to mention losing the deep knowledge. In the sagas, it always happens at the most inopportune moment, and the cautions against even thinking of touching weaponry are many, deep, and insistent.

"Idra was mad," Arn muttered, and my laugh surprised me. My hand flew to my mouth to contain it, and her face eased, her dark eyes dancing. "So are you, sun-maid."

"Spear-girl, short but straight." I let one eyebrow arch, glad to be upon my own feet instead of a-horseback. "Shall I finish a few couplets? I begin to think I could."

She elbowed me, and I could not keep the merriment restrained. Still, the hush of the Northerners was not a thing to break lightly and I was under the constraint of a weregild's good behavior. So I sought mightily to trap my giggles, swallowing them as much as possible.

Two of the returned men conferred with Eol, and when they were finished giving some account or another he nodded, turning in our direction. Arn, attempting to keep her own chuckles muffled, dug under her dun hooded mantle. It was very likely Albeig had granted her a small skin of ale for the journey, too, and my spearmaid was not ever of the temper to let such a gift grow cold.

"My lady." Dark-eyed Eol halted at a respectable distance, and he held a small black glittering thing. "We shall stop as often as needed for your comfort. Try this."

I am not truly uncomfortable yet, but 'tis only a matter of time. I accepted the flask. It seemed made of smoky glass studded with small flickering red jewels, its cap attached to a thin, well-made silver chain. The liquid inside moved oddly, and filigree upon the glass sides reminded me of Kolle's lantern, said to be Elder-wrought. " 'Tis a beautiful thing," I said politely, attempting to restore it to his hand.

"Drink—a single mouthful should suffice. 'Tis *sitheviel*." He looked over my shoulder as young Aeredh approached, apparently to consult with Arn's mare and my own.

Of course it could not be true *sitheviel*, since the making of that wondrous drink was long gone with the Elder. What we of the South called by its name in those days varied from settlement to settlement, mothers swearing daughters to secrecy with recipes producing a drink of more or less medicinal value, more or less made of mead and a few herbs. At most I expected it to be some kind of distillation, clear and fiery-potent; I uncapped the glass flask and sniffed delicately, all my senses sharpening.

A faint, delicious drift of summer flowers brushed my nose. Arn, ever interested in anything given strength through fermentation, leaned over my shoulder; her blue woad-stripe was dry and cracking upon her cheek. "It smells good." Laughter still bubbled in her voice. "See if it will clear your head, weirdling."

I had my doubts any draught could ease the pain in my backside, but I brought the flask's mouth to mine. A single swallow—it burned, but not unpleasantly, and a golden glow filled my head as if I had downed one of Idra's many nasty-thick potions to strengthen *seidhr*-gifts or ward off illness. It hit behind my breastbone and spread; I all but staggered, the liquid sloshing. Arn steadied me, all levity gone and her hand tightening upon her spear. I coughed, loosely recapping the flask, and leaned into her.

If she was occupied with my support, she could not loose a sharp challenge at a man who might have wished to drug or poison her charge. " 'Tis strong," I managed, my throat coated with a sweetness I could not define. There was no ill in the drink, or I was no *volva*. "Will you have a swallow, Arn? I think you'll like it."

Eol looked as if he might protest, but at home Arn and I shared all. She took the flask, eyeing the Northern man balefully, and took a healthy draught. Her eyes closed, and though I could tell she was struggling to keep from coughing, nobody else could. Or so I hoped.

"Very strong indeed," she said huskily, capping the flask with a quick twist of her muscle-padded wrist. "My thanks, Northerner."

He accepted both his property and her thanks with a nod and moved away, the tiny glass thing vanishing. I caught sight of one black-clad man elbowing another; they found this amusing.

As weregild I could not be openly insulted, but any group—even a smaller family within a greatfarm's kinhold—has hundreds of ways to make a stranger feel unwelcome, or even merely bothersome. I rested my head upon Arn's shoulder, lightly enough not to drive iron rings or scale into my temple or her flesh. The Northern youth finished his visiting of every horse, perhaps listening to their ills or expressing his own, and I could not help but wonder who had trained him in horsebreaking.

Could this Aeredh light a bonfire, or hold one? Could he make the clouds thicken, draw darts of light from the glitter upon a river's back, or make a pebble twitch-dance? Certainly not, and neither could his fellows. They were warriors, and I was otherwise. All branches of *seidhr* were available to me, though I could touch metal only lightly; perhaps he was forge-wise? Frestis was a cloudshaper, and Idra could whisper to water in all its forms. The rest of Dun Rithell's weirdlings were not of their strength, though they had the cunning that lies within all *seidhr*, no matter the particular affinity.

Even among them I was different. Idra had been forced to teach me according to rede and lore, hoping the gods and spirits would provide what instruction she lacked. *You will know when you meet another*, she always said.

I hoped it was true, but if I am to speak with bare honesty, I ever felt some pride in lonely uniqueness.

In short order the rest halt was finished, and Arn did not have to help me mount. She did anyway, to avoid one of the men thinking he should perform the duty, and swung into her own saddle with no sign of stiffness. The *sitheviel* burned inside me, a steady flame, and strength spread from its glow.

Learning *that* recipe would be a worthy deed. I kept my eyes half-closed as the Northerners rode, attempting to follow each taste in the drink to its source, to discern the edges of whatever word or other act made for its potency. Aeredh began to sing in the Old Tongue, a soft naming of plants both healing and harmful I listened to while seeking the *sitheviel*'s secrets; the others passed infrequent, half-heard conversation while the sun rose to its highest and the fog drew away on every side. Arneior hummed part of the saga of Harald the Skald, a listing of the names of particular *valkyra* and the dead heroes they selected from a battlefield's fallen.

I held my peace. To be a *volva* is to listen, as Idra often said.

Great boulders brushed with damp rosy lichen squatting heavily on an orangish field, stubble-bracken and other slight grasses clinging to thin dirt—I did not recognize this place. After a short while there was no track anymore, even for cart-wheels, and it was a good thing I was so occupied with tasting the ghost of a foreign drink or I might even have felt some outright fear. Each step took us farther away from anything familiar, and as weregild I could no longer breathe or speak freely.

And it was only the first day.

At Any Age

*The Enemy hates the Elder, for they would not serve him.
Yet he reserves the deepest wells of hatred for the Secondborn, for it galls him bitterly that even such weak and perishable beings have defied him as well.*
—*The Saga of Redcloak*

The Northerners returned to grim silence as the sun fell earthward from nooning. At home Astrid would be at the looms or
her needle, singing amid women likewise employed. Bjorn would be
with other warriors, lending their strength to a neighbor's need for
something repaired, lifted, or thumped. My parents would be hearing legal cases in the greathall, one or two of Dun Rithell's other
seidhr attending to give weight to judgments or to find the hidden
truth of certain complicated matters.

Were we home, Arneior would be at her daily practice, spilling
other warriors of my father's hall onto hard-packed dirt with impatient flickers of her spearblade's flat or whirling through the complicated forms taught to girls the Wingéd Ones breathe upon. Most days
I would be watching her from the sidelines, well-wrapped against
winter, or in the stillroom concocting medicines. Today, however,
my duty should have been in the greathall, listening or lending my
own weight to certain judgments.

But Arn and I were with a group of quiet black-clad foreigners, wending east and northward, instead. This year the added respect and binding of a full *volva*'s presence would have stood behind Dun Rithell. It occurred to me—more than once as we rode—that when I returned from the North I would no longer be a familiar, known quantity. The travel would change me; even those of my home would regard me with deeper caution, perhaps even verging upon mistrust.

'Twas nothing new. There is more than one meaning in *"seidhr"*; loneliness makes its home in the word as well.

The Northerners halted just before twilight. A circle of great grey stones appeared amid thickening fog and slender firs oddly distorted by a low wind's almost-constant scraping. It had burned here a few years ago, if the winter-struck underbrush and youth of the trees was any indication.

The stones were not kin to those standing at the east edge of Dun Rithell's safe pasturage, nor were they the kind native to our riverside and Tarnarya's flanks. There was no accumulation of power—other than that of slow time—lingering in their hunched forms. Many a beast or creature had obviously decided such a grouping seemed fair protection for a short rest; we were no different.

The Northerners set about making camp as Arn steadied my dismounting, and after a day spent upon one of their tall pale steeds my legs would not quite do as they were told. My shieldmaid's mouth was set, whether a result of dislike or some stiffness in her own limbs I could not tell. "I need to fight someone," she muttered, and I could not hold back a weary laugh.

"My lady Solveig?" Aeredh approached, his sky-blue eyes dancing with a strange, merry gleam. Fog-droplets caught in his dark hair, and he moved with marked grace. Of course, he was used to days spent a-saddle. "I thought you might offer us some aid."

How did you travel without me, then? But I had to be mannerly all through new winter and spring, then summer and harvest-homeward-wending to boot. A weregild does as they are bid, unless the request be criminal. "In what form?"

"Come." He beckoned, not quite peremptorily, and Arneior bristled.

I knew she was a short breath or two from a sharp word, and that was an ill enough way to begin our first night with strangers. "If I may help, I will. Though I know not what a group of Northern war-riors needs from me."

Of course, I could not halt the latter slipping from my tongue. I may even have sounded bitter as my mother, and to a youth as well. He looked even younger than Bjorn, for all he carried himself with such dignity.

I was such a fool not to guess the truth.

"More than you might suspect." For the first time, Aeredh did not look amused; his eyes darkened and he watched my Arn very carefully indeed. "You are *alkuine*—elementalist, they call it now?" He made a slight movement, glancing at his companions as if he would ask another for the proper term, though he handled our tongue well enough.

None came to his rescue, though, all visible men being occupied with other duties. It was a relief to be ignored, even if I suspected 'twas half pretense.

Is that it? "I have *seidhr* enough to hold flame itself." I lifted my hands to prove it, but my gloves and the overmantle sleeves hid the marks. Still, the movement spoke for itself. "And you wish to test me." My tone was a restraint upon Arn's wrath. "Very well. What would you have, my lord Aeredh?"

"My skills lie in other directions." The youth's smile held an echo of sad memory. In fact, he looked a little like my father, when Eril could be induced to speak of some event he did not wish to revisit. "I thought perhaps you could light the fire."

I considered the request, glancing at Arn. Did they not carry firefelt, then, or flint to match their steel? One would think a group of such warriors would not overlook something so simple; they were making camp with every evidence of efficiency.

But why have a weregild and not require some little entertainment of it? Perhaps they were also grieving their absent companion, the one Bjorn had felled so ingloriously. His pyre was barely cold at the river-bank, and no doubt the tale would grow in the telling at Dun Rithell. My brother might even begin to preen at striking down a fellow with one blow unless Astrid and Mother punctured his pride with some regularity.

"Sol." Arn disdained to aim her words at the youth. "You are weary, and still not have recovered from the solstice. I have a flint."

Her offer was not quite an insult—every free person should carry such an article—but it could be taken as one.

I might have winced, were I not so bone-aching weary. "'Tis no matter, my shieldmaid. Better to see the sheep one has stolen earlier than later." It was not quite how the old saying went, but it brought a tight smile to her generous mouth, not to mention a tired curve to my own lips. "Where, my lord Aeredh?" *I will light it, but Arn will not fetch fuel.*

She was shieldmaid and I weregild, but neither of us were bonds-maid or thrall.

He led me to the lee of a large frowning stone capable of providing a measure of shelter and perhaps even reflecting some of a fire's heat; a ring of blackened stones set in the proper place showed more travelers than birds and beasts had alighted here. A stack of cut wood was settled in the lee of another rock—another sign this resting place was used by men, however infrequently—and someone had already arranged the tinder and kindling they wished me to light.

I sank down as gracefully as possible to consider the work, and frowned. The entire affair was arranged oddly, and it did not seem quite right. My hands itched, so I hummed softly while I set them free to do as they wished, realizing the strangeness of the stacking was a form of *seidhr.*

A test indeed; did he think himself a teacher, though he carried a blade? Or did they still doubt my ability? Irritation sharp-tasting as an unripe apple flooded my tongue, unease slid down my back on tiny prickling feet.

In short order my hands had redone the fire-setting properly; Arn was there to help me rise, or I might not have managed it without a groan. I backed up four steps, stripping my gloves free and shaking bark-bits from the right one.

Aeredh regarded me curiously. Perhaps he hadn't expected me to pass even so simple a trial as arranging a few sticks.

Earthbound clouds congealed as night dawned in the east; the damp cold nipped at my bare fingers. I shut out the aches of the day, the uncertainty of being far from home among strangers, the persistent thought that perhaps lighting the solstice bonfire, necessary an act as it was, had jolted the world from its usual course like a cart-wheel escaping a track and nothing would bring it back to the right course.

My breathing quieted. My heart was a muffled drum in my ears. My left hand leapt, fingers stiff, the pressure passing through my chest and down my arm demanding release.

The dilating flame was blue-white instead of orange. Perhaps they had doused the tinder with summat, for it burned with surprising heat—and once 'twas caught I did not have to guard the fire, which kept ribbons of blue at its heart. Aeredh knelt alongside, feeding the small blaze, and I shook both hands hard, for my fingers ached.

It had not nearly taken the effort I was accustomed to. The echoes of unspent force died but slowly, bouncing inside my body's walls like a brawl during a great feast. When my vision cleared the blaze was merry indeed, though still bluish and small; several of the Northerners drew close to its glow.

"*The only good luck we've had,*" one of them muttered in the Old Tongue, a broad-shouldered fellow who bore eyes like my mother's and Aeredh's—and my own.

"*Careful,*" another replied, and added summat I could not quite make out about enough slack in a fishing-net to let a large catch think it had won for a moment. I understood the gist, though; it sounded like a proverb.

I was glad to practice the Old Tongue, yet it still did not seem wise to let them know I could. They had heard Mother utter formulaic phrases of welcome and farewell, of course, but we were too far south for such language to be daily used.

Or so they might think. The instinct was clear and undeniable, and any *seidhr* trained by Idra the Farsighted would know better than to disregard it. I studied the fire, thinking furiously.

Arn and I were protected by her spear and by custom; if one were weakened the other might be too. Any additional defense was welcome indeed. So I listened intently, leaning upon my shieldmaid, who could no doubt tell my silence was not that of incomprehension or inattention.

"*There is no pursuit I can sense.*" Aeredh half-turned, still crouching easily, and regarded the two speakers. "*Strange, is it not? Almost as if...*"

"*Will no one say it?*" A dark-eyed one with a scar upon his jaw and another bisecting his eyebrow glanced in my direction, and just as quickly away. *"The big blond lout relieved us of a traitor; we should have thanked him with all we carry instead of taking recompense. This is not well done, Lord Aeredh, and our lord Eol knows it."*

Interesting indeed, though I was not certain of my translation of the word *traitor*. It could have meant *one who complains*, or *a cry from a high hill*. There were a few other terms I could not entirely decide—*recompense*, for one, or *lout*, since that last had turned into the southron word for *a good watchdog*. I tried not to stiffen, kept my face a mask as required often during training, negotiations, or adjudication. A *volva* must not be suspected of partiality, though of course her kin often share in the blessing of her position. And why not? A plow needs axes to protect it and axes need plows to produce unmolested, as the saying goes. Such is the price paid for survival, and most pay it gladly enough.

"Eol understands there is another power at work here, Efain." Aeredh's eyes glittered, that disconcerting light in his gaze brightening. His glance had more than the usual weight, and yet he carried a sword. And he had given a recipe containing *seidhr* for my mother's ague, not to mention built the fire in an unfamiliar manner. *"The West has not forsaken us."*

"So you say." Efain shrugged, and his gaze dropped.

I saw it then, and I almost gasped. For the Northern youth turned to the fire with a short, supple movement, pushing his dark hair back. The top of his ear's shell-curve was not a curve at all—it came to a high point, blushed faintly with the cold. I wondered blankly how no one at home had seen or realized what he was, but just as swiftly the old stories and sagas leapt through my head, and I knew why.

The Elder learned to disguise themselves when walking among our kind almost from the first, for long ago the Black Land was not merely a spent myth and all who lived in its lengthening shadow learned to mistrust every stranger—beast, bird, or otherwise.

The fire crackled, and the blue heart to the flames meant it had to be *aelflame*; I had never seen its like. He was doing a fine job of coaxing it to fullness.

Now that I had seen, it was impossible to miss. The restless grace, the seeming youth and strange restraint, a powerful recipe for a medicinal potion—it was a saga, a story, a myth come to impossible breathing life just before me.

One might expect one with *seidhr* to take such an event calmly. But so far from home, cold and unnerved, I had the urge to shout *fishguts* or something much stronger before fleeing into the darkness with Arn at my shoulder. Near Dun Rithell I could have escaped wherever I chose, but there was no palisade here, no outer wall, no greathall with corridors familiar as my own fingers, no green or Stone or well-worn paths to Idra's cottage or the closest farms. Even the sheep-grazing hills would have been welcome, and better than this.

I had to stay placed precisely where I was, all but shaking with... what? Was it fear?

The Northerners had to know, for they treated the youth with great honor. No wonder he bore a blade—the stories said Elder did not suffer many mortal prohibitions, which meant any *seidhr* he had would not go astray, nor warrior's virtue be drained by such an act.

"Sol?" Arn, softly, her breath brushing my cheek. Hopefully they thought me wrung dry by the effort of lighting their campfire. I shook my head; her short exhalation in reply said she knew I would speak upon it later, when we were as alone as could be managed. They had given us barely enough space to attend our bladders all day, and would no doubt hem us closely as we traveled farther north.

I cannot lie, I was then deeply glad that my father had sent me instead of Bjorn or Astrid, who had neither weirding nor shieldmaid for protection. Yet cold fear burrowed into my bones as well.

It is one thing to hear stories, sagas, tales. It is another to see a... I could not even call Aeredh's ear malformed, for it looked perfectly natural, even more so than a man of my own kind's. I stared at the fire instead, straining my hearing to its utmost.

But their conversation simply sputtered into commonplaces in the southron tongue, and few enough of those. Aeredh—oh, he was no youth—beckoned us closer to the fire, now blue at the base but fringed into cheerful yellow at the top. "*Aelflame*," he said, cheerfully, and I suppressed a start. "I am a traditionalist; I stack its house in the oldest way I know. Yours is much more direct."

It was twice he had complimented a piece of my *seidhr*, but now

I suspected it no true praise. My throat was dry, but I had to make some answer. "Your way must be old indeed, my lord."

"A habit may begin at any age." But he glanced sharply at Arn, who had gone still, her gaze roving the camp. "And old as I may be, I have never met a shieldmaid before." He slowed for the word as if it was unfamiliar. "You are sacred to the Wingéd Ones, then? The *valkyrja*?"

"Taken by them." Arn's chin rose. She did not bother to glance in his direction, her gaze circling the rest of the men as if she suspected them of ill intent. "And sworn. Where Solveig goes, I go."

"So it seems." He moved slightly, a graceful ripple like a granary cat waiting at a rathole, and settled a reasonably large chunk of wood upon the fire. The flames ran up its sides, veining eerily and refusing to be snuffed by such a large mouthful. "You will meet no insult among us, but much curiosity."

"I am glad to hear it." I cut off whatever reply Arn might have made, for I could tell by her expression it would not be conciliatory. "You must admit this is a...a strange situation. Even for Northerners."

"Even for..." Aeredh's pale eyes danced, and he threw back his dark head, laughing. The sound was pleasant enough, especially with the firelight taking on some of its accustomed warmth.

The merriment drew notice; we were eyed with some interest. But Eol had reappeared, and the two men with him carried a hunter's cargo—winter coneys, lean but still toothsome, already field-dressed. Arn finally shook her head, digging under her mantle; it was no use, for I was certain the aleskin was already dry.

"*I have not heard you laugh so in a long while, my friend.*" In the Old Tongue, the man with the gem-hilted sword sounded pleased and interested, instead of halting and grim. I could not catch sight of *his* ears, for the light was failing, but I did not think him like Aeredh.

"*The lady thinks this a strange situation, even for Northerners.*" The Elder—for I could not call him *boy* or *youth* now—chuckled again, shaking his head. "Your pardon, my lady Solveig; I have merely repeated your words. The North may seem dour, yet you will cheer it, methinks."

I could not begin to answer. An *Elder*, speaking to Eril's daughter and her shieldmaid. It was like a saga, except what happens later in those is generally uncomfortable or outright fatal, and I was not quite sure I would like a comedic tale better. The pursuit of knowledge was all very well, yet at that moment I was badly shaken. I wanted to be home, making certain traders respected Dun Rithell, restraining Bjorn's bullock-stamping, brewing cures or experiments in the stillroom, and roaming the fringes of the winter woods for certain components.

Not to mention being accosted by everyone within sight who had a grudge or wished a fortune told, and would seek to bargain for such an effort. *I will pay you,* volva; *tell me your price.*

Eol shrugged. *"Does she know us so well, then?"* He did not share his friend's amusement; some of his wolf-stamped men murmured to each other and no few laughed, though far more softly than Aer-edh. Still, their captain—for so he seemed to be, though no doubt the Elder was the true leader—halted, and gave a slight bow in my direction. "You need not fear, my lady *alkuine.* Our people were once one, and you will be held in high honor among us and our friends." He glanced at Aeredh, no doubt curious whether I had noticed what they traveled with.

Perhaps it would be best if he thought me unaware. Or stupid, though it irked me much to be considered so.

Never tell all you know, Idra always said. And though 'twas likely I would learn much that could benefit Dun Rithell in the North and any *volva* likes such a prospect, I did not enjoy their dark hints.

So I nodded and gave the most pleasing smile I could, though I have not Astrid's gift for such an expression, and held fast to Arn's arm. She did not relax, but then, neither did I.

So we passed our first evening in the company of Northern-ers. For all their quiet, they ate well; along with coney stew there was sweetish, unfamiliar dried fruit and waybread with a peculiar melting consistency, taken from what seemed like waxed cloth but was actually large, broad leaves from some plant or tree I had never encountered before.

I could not decide if I wished to see the living bearer of such foli-age, though I was somewhat certain I would before the year-and-day of weregild was over.

Notice Enough

Those the valkyra *take are mighty, and quick to anger. Swift do they strike and little use have they for men who are not dead heroes; to be a shieldmaid is to stand apart.*
—Harald the Skald

My mother's second-largest chest was placed near a pile of freshly chopped pine boughs snuggled against the now-dry rock shielding the fire and small dell; Arn and I would not feel the cold ground tonight. I did not try whispering to her once we had lain down, both almost fully dressed though her armor would be a mild discomfort. Her eyebrows raised, but she understood my significant glance and held her tongue.

A shieldmaid needs few words, as the saying goes. Besides, we had known each other all our lives. I was certain we would eventually find some time to speak unheard by the Northerners.

I woke only once that night, for which I suppose I may thank the weariness of travel. Arn's breathing was slow and deep against my hair, and her living warmth a great comfort under our pile of mantles and blankets.

Every other bedroll around the oddly burning campfire was empty. Aeredh the Elder crouched before the blaze, singing softly in the Old Tongue, his blue eyes bright as Elder lamps.

The song was a lament for the fabled long-lost home of his kind, long removed from the circles of the world, and he sang as if he had seen the place where gold-and-silver light mingles and the breeze of eternal spring carries warm sweetness. Each word held great grief, describing beauty long gone, and he paused often after certain lines, staring into the blue-hearted flames.

Amid his soft humming and half-breathed words, I listened hard for any sign of the other men. Nothing but the constant soft pressure of outside air and the fire's breath disturbed the night, and that was unsettling as well. I could still smell thick fog, which might explain it—but where *were* they?

A wolf's cry lifted in the distance. Aeredh tilted his head, his voice halting between one breath and the next. For the first time I saw an Elder's true age reflected in gaze and expression, and my breath did not catch only because I was still half asleep.

Another wolf answered from a different quarter, or so I thought. The vapor hanging in the air made it difficult to tell, and using hare-ears or any of a *seidhr*'s full attention would alert the Elder that I was not only conscious but watching this curious scene.

When the youth—I still could not help but think of him thus, even knowing what I did—returned to his lonely song, the cadence changed. A lullaby wandered between the shores of irregular wolf-music, and I fell into deep blackness interspersed with fragmentary, terribly vivid dreams.

I woke the next morning to the clash of combat.

Arneior's boots flickered light as snow-kisses, her spear whistling as its hungry leaf-blade carved predawn chill. I propped myself upon my elbow and yawned as Aeredh lunged, the flat of his hand blurring for the spear-haft. He had a longknife reversed along his other forearm, and looked as if he were giving a good account of himself.

But a shieldmaid is not to be caught with such tricks, if at all. She deflected his strike almost languidly, retreating a single step and popping the spear's blunt end to the side, smacking free his palm upon the haft with a small, contemptuous jerk when he attempted to turn his wrist and grab. Another small shake, a catlike leap, and she landed between me and the Elder, soft-light as falling leaves. Her spear-butt struck the ground twice, a familiar drumbeat of emphasis or approval, and she nodded. "Slow," she said, though not unkindly. "But you are capable enough, my lord Aeredh."

"Sparring before breakfast?" I was hard-pressed to restrain another yawn. My head ached from sleeping in travel-braids starred with red coral. "Your temper is ill improved by voyaging, small one."

"I might prove it even worse by turning you out of your blankets as your lady mother would, with a scolding." She did not glance at me, her dark, fiery gaze locked with the Elder's. Her face was freshly woad-striped, as if she expected more than one sparring-round today.

Aeredh bowed slightly, his smile young as the rest of him was more than likely not. "Indeed the *valkyrja* have blessed you, shieldmaid." He accented the word strangely, but of course his mouth probably remembered the Old Tongue in its purest form. "My lady *alkuine*, do not be alarmed; your protector and I were simply exercising."

"Oh, I've no alarm." I was, however, justifiably proud. " 'Twas too much noise for Arneior to be serious." I tasted morning in my mouth, and I found I had also stiffened from yesterday's exertions.

"Lazy one, so late abed." Arn's tone was sharp, but amusement lingered in her half-chanting. "Come, up. There is no ale, but we shall make do."

The Elder turned away, and once he did my shieldmaid finally relaxed, approaching and crouching next to our sap-smelling bed. It was not as cold as I'd feared, though I was loath to leave my shelter.

"He could give me some trouble," she continued in a low quick monotone, each word refusing to step far from her lips. Both shield-maid and *volva* have sharp hearing, and finally we had some lee to speak as the Northerners busied themselves with preparations to break camp. "Tell me I am not moon-foaming, Sol."

"If you are, I am too." Relief burst hot and sharp behind my breastbone, wedded to renewed pride. Of course she would notice aught amiss, and we would not have to speak much beyond signifi-cant glances. The eye may tell what the voice does not, as the proverb goes, and my small one was ever vigilant. "His ears."

"What? I mean the—" She halted, for one of our traveling companions approached with bowls for both of us and portions of their strange waybread.

It was the scarred fellow Efain, and his dark gaze was thoughtful. "A good fire," the Northerner said, allowed to hand me my breakfast when Arn gave a grudging nod. "Many thanks for its blessing, *alkuine*."

I longed to ask why they had fled during the night, did they consider it so blessed, but the same instinct keeping my knowledge of the Old Tongue private intervened. So I merely nodded, a *volva*'s politeness.

I would not give these men any cause to complain of their weregild's behavior.

"And you are swift as a minnow, spear-girl." He handed Arn the second bowl, a spark of amusement lingering in his dark gaze. "Does your weapon bear a name?"

"Soon." She accepted with a polite nod, and settled upon the stacked pine boughs at my feet with swift economical grace, turning her attention to food. He did not linger, and I found myself possessed of good appetite and also the means to satisfy it once he left.

But Arn and I could not speak until she moved closer with an aggrieved sigh, almost perching upon my feet. "Lazy," she repeated. "I should indeed scold you. How can a *volva* not notice?"

"I have noticed much, but apparently not enough." I forced myself to sit straight, my legs trapped in a complicated wrapping of underbreeches, skirts, mantle, blankets, and my stockings slipped almost to my ankles. "Tell me."

"Did you hear the wolves last night?" She applied herself to the business of nourishment, the waybread doing transport duty admirably.

"Some," I admitted, my lips cautiously shielded by the bread lest the Northerners had sharp ears as well. Aeredh and Eol were in deep conference on the other side of the fire, and their companions were eating in shifts, saddling horses, and generally attending to camp duties with little comment and much efficiency. "Perhaps you will have a chance to add to your mantle, though I will not do any sewing a-horseback." Spinning was another matter, but there was enough thread and to spare at the moment.

Indeed, the amount I had threatened to tangle me.

"And well you should not." Her gaze roved the camp, noting and weighing. I had rarely seen her this serious save when we were upon the far side of the river with Father. Arneior's tone dropped still further, and she muttered into her bowl. "I do not like this fog."

"Nor do I." It was not unheard of in winter, especially after the solstice and before the long hard freeze…yet, it *felt* wrong. "Teach me, Arn. What have you noticed?"

"Eyes too bright and teeth too sharp." She shook her head, her high-crested braids little the worse for wear after a night's rest. My scalp would not easily forgive its cargo of coral, though I had hardly noticed the discomfort last night amid fatigue. "Don't worry. I shall be watchful."

And so shall I. There was little time for more conversation, for we would be moving soon. I bent to my own work. The waybread was marvelously filling, though not quite as warming as yesterday's *sitheviel.* Was that draught mixed by Aeredh, too? Could I learn of its making, many in Dun Rithell would find it useful.

It was a cheerful prospect, even if we were caught in a tale. Daylight makes one doubt what the night has shown, as the proverb goes, and besides…

Well, I was curious. Any *volva* would be. Ours is the way of ambition, delving to find what can be unearthed much like the squat but doughty *thrayn* dverger who delight in ore and gem-shaping.

An actual Elder riding a horse, breathing, and speaking alongside us. What songs and *seidhr* did he remember? Would he teach me either? What great deeds had he witnessed, and how many of his people yet lingered in the North, mourning for their lost home?

How could I ask while not admitting I knew what he was?

I wished to be home in Dun Rithell, certainly. But I also longed to gather more of the Old Tongue, as well as whatever the not-youth could teach me if he would, and how I could manage the lessons. It somewhat salved the sting of longing for familiar places, and in my excitement I did not heed Arneior's words as I normally would have.

After all, wolves were everywhere, and she liked hunting them well enough.

Quite So Flimsy

The signs of the Enemy are many. Carrion he rules, and many misshapen things. Yet we must distinguish with care, for what is foul may seem fair enough at first, and the opposite is also true. Misjudging either is ill done, and brings more woe than even the Blessed can compass...
—Yevras the Bowman, *Collected Sayings of Aenarian Greycloak*

I t grew colder as we traveled that day, the mist clotting and cling-ing to our horses' legs. I did not like its greasy pallor, nor did I miss how the Northerners drew closer to Arn and myself in yet another guard-pattern. Aeredh rode slightly ahead, occasionally bending low over his mount's neck to study the ground. Despite that, he seemed to find our way with some sense other than sight, for more often than not he was tall in the saddle, his eyes half-lidded, singing under his breath.

I could hear neither tune nor words, though a shiver passed through me when I sought to sharpen my ears as Idra taught me. Whether 'twas *seidhr* or merely the cold I could not tell.

Besides, there seemed little enough "way" to find—what I could see of the terrain was strange winter-yellowed grass, grey boulders in tortured shapes as if by flood-carving along a dry river's lost course, and the occasional gaunt shapes of shrouded trees hunched against a wind that did not pierce or move the cold white muffling. My shield-maid and I exchanged many a dire glance that day, but held our peace. We did not even trade riddles, so eerie were our surroundings, and the Northerners did not speak beyond commonplaces. I could not add to my store of the Old Tongue if they would be so parsimonious.

How often had I wished for a halt to Dun Rithell's clatter and shouts, to the greathall's crowded roar upon a feast night? How often had I climbed into the forest or run along the riverbank with Arn matching stride for stride, seeking some corner of thoughtful silence? Here, the quiet was oppressive, my thoughts swallowed by clouds come to earth and the great even swells of the warming breath dispelling only physical chill.

At any stop a few low words were exchanged about the business of caring for the horses and—I realized after the last afternoon halt—for their weregild and her shieldmaid, since they seemed to consider us fragile indeed.

Did Arn discern that fact, she might well teach them otherwise. But she simply glowered at the fog as if it had challenged her to a flyting-match, and my unease grew.

In any case, it was during the final afternoon halt, the fog turning briefly gold as westering sun reached a low angle, that I finally made friends with my white mare by the simple expedient of softly patting her neck and intoning not quite a song, but a recital of the things I appreciated about her. It started with how her gait was much smoother than I had any right to expect, continued through her calm personality, and ended with a list of other pleasing features, like her high inquisitive ears, the sturdiness of her withers, and the fine fountain of her tail. I was justifiably proud of the couplet about her dark eyes and their sad wisdom lit only by gentle intelligence, and decided to call her Farsight.

It was a heavy name for a beast to bear, but she seemed equal to the task and consented to consider me a friend.

Arn shook her head, a line appearing between her coppery eyebrows. "I half expected you to start listing your flocks and fields," she said, but not very loudly.

"A horse seems a better marriage-contract than a man, certainly."

I was hard put not to laugh, and Arn's half-suppressed chuckle was a merry sound indeed.

Eol approached with some diffidence, and did not this time offer more of his flask. His cheeks bore the blush of cold, very like Arn's. "In some short while we shall halt at a steading." Fog-droplets clung to his dark hair, raising a stubborn curl. "It will be more comfortable. Afterward there will be snow, but we will not lack for nightly shelter."

I knew of no steadings, halls, free farms, or the like so near north of Dun Rithell, yet that meant little. While travelers go upriver with some regularity, they did not often strike away from the water's curve toward the faraway shadow of the Black Land's old, dead malice. Those who did might well never return—most likely from plain misadventure, or the call of the horizon. Better to stay upon the banks, and let our river-mother provide all necessaries.

Still, I was somewhat nettled at being considered so strengthless, and could perhaps discern why we were not wending southward instead. "We are not quite so flimsy as you seem to think, Arn and I."

"You are valuable, lady *alkuine*, and under our care. I gave my word to your mother Gwendelint and would not be forsworn." He nodded, sharply polite, in Arn's direction, and took himself away with no further word.

"Courteous enough," Arn observed. "But he flees speech with you as if he has heard you scold your brother."

I wondered how Bjorn was faring, and if he had committed another...I could not call it *indiscretion*, for that is a weak word for killing a man with a single blow, whether a stone had the final coup or not. Yet the Northerners seemed to bear our family little ill will, if any, and so far treated me well enough.

As if anyone would dare treat a *volva* otherwise, especially one with a sworn shieldmaid. And yet...*Traitor*, they said. Yet I was not certain of the word; better to simply listen and learn what I could.

I freed a small waterskin from Farsight's saddle, took a tepid mouthful. "I wonder how Astrid is faring." *And Mother.*

"I wonder if your mother has turned your father out of doors to sleep in the pig-hutches." Arn accepted the waterskin with only a token nose-wrinkle. The ale had not lasted. "He could have refused, and sent your brother."

"That would not satisfy tradition." It was not quite a defense of my father's choice, since I had silently bemoaned it more than once. Between us, though, only Arn would voice such a truth. "They are probably worried for us." If Father thought of me at all, which was unlikely except to feel some annoyance I was not there to keep my siblings from trouble or, in Astrid's case, tears. When I was small he was merry enough, but as I grew into my *seidhr* Eril held me in some caution, a constraint growing between us with each passing year. I did not doubt his pride in me, nor his protection—but perhaps he found it difficult to be affectionate with his uncanny eldest daughter.

For my part I preferred my mother, as some daughters do. The distance between the lord of Dun Rithell and his *seidhr* child had become mutual; we both added to its length like a spear with two masters.

"Oh, Lady Gwendelint worries, certainly. But he?" Arn shook her head, and took a short swallow as well—too little to slake a deep thirst. If it snowed we would not lack for water, but in the meantime it was best to be careful. "I know he is your sire, little weirdling. And yet."

A shieldmaid's tongue is sharp as it needs to be; the Wingéd Ones speak honesty enough and to spare. I might have made a light reply, were we still at home.

Of course, were we still at Dun Rithell, we would not be having this conversation. So I merely nodded, resealing the waterskin, and had to suppress a groan at the thought of more riding. My thighs trembled unhappily, and I suspected I had blisters in places Fryja rules.

Arneior stiffened; I stilled, my attention turning inward as *seidhr* prickled under my skin. The Northerners had gone silent, even Aeredh, whose hand blurred to hilt. Steel left sheath with a soft scraping, and the others followed suit. My shieldmaid stepped before me, pushing me against Farsight's warm bulk, her chin lifting and her right ear subtly presented.

Listening, through the fog.

I heard it too, a noisome burbling growl. Farsight laid her own ears far back, a ring of white appearing around each of her fine dark eyes.

"Up," Arn said softly, and I wasted no time clambering into the saddle. Without aid it was an inelegant scramble, but better than being merely afoot.

I gathered the reins in my right hand, leaning forward to flatten my left glove against Farsight's warm neck. *Seidhr* tingled fitfully in my fingers, but I have been calming the four-footed or feathered ever since I could walk.

It was one of the things Idra noticed, warning her of another *volva*. My mother, of course, had seen it too—she oft told the tale of how I used to charm the granary cats into playing with me, docile as dolls, and how even the ill-tempered black king of the goat herd would lie down when I approached, letting me clamber onto his back when I was but four winters old.

Arn was halfway to her own mount when dark shapes loomed through cling-greasy mist. One of the great pale horses let loose a rattling snort, and Eol lunged out of sight into the vaporous curtain. Aeredh followed noiselessly with graceful flickering speed, his swordblade gleaming blue. Scarred Efain and a tall Northerner with long dark hair bound in a leather-wrapped club were in their saddles with the same alacrity, both their mounts crowding Farsight and Arn's own horse almost before her boot could find the stirrup.

The growl turned into a chilling cacophony—more than one creature giving voice, something like barking but inexpressibly foul, yips, tearing noises, heavy snuffling. My heart thundered in my ears no less loudly. Farsight pawed, restless despite my fingers now twining in her mane.

My calm was tenuous; how could hers be otherwise even with *seidhr* between us? I glanced at Arn as she swung atop her mount; her hair darkened with damp and two spots of high color stood out upon her cheeks. Her spear's tip glittered; the noise from the fog reached a fresh crescendo.

A single beast burst from the wall of whitish cloudsmoke, a high-shouldered unhealthy hulk with spreading horns. Bright scarlet pinpricks flickered in its black pupils, its claws dug deep in winter-frozen earth, and it lowered its head to charge. Now the various sounds made sense—nothing with a nose so deformed could breathe or use voice with ease, and nothing so misshapen could walk, let alone run, without pain. A dart of similarly misborn agony speared my skull; I cried aloud and my knees clamped reflexively as Farsight backed away, tossing her head as if she too felt the thing's overwhelming *wrongness*.

"*Ai!*" Arn yelled, a shieldmaid's battle-cry. Had she not been a-horse she might have charged the creature despite its unwholesome appearance and the stink roiling from its steaming hide; as it was, her mare lost presence of mind and reared, shod hooves flailing.

The thing barreled in my direction. It really did look like a twisted, scabrous ram laden with ox-horns, but those claws were not of any creature that lived upon herb and its teeth were likewise altogether too sharp for a grazing beast, not to mention dripping with smoking black ichor besides. My weirding-hold upon Farsight was tenuous; the mare let out a high sharp fear-cry and would have reared as well had I not been locked with her in the way of *seidhr*, half myself and half a four-legged thing whose instinct and sense both screamed to flee.

Aeredh burst from the fog as well, lightfoot and eye-blazing, his blue-burning blade raised high. Efain—his mare trusting him far more than mine did a stranger—bolted forward, his sword a bright silver bar as the fog flushed, thinning under a last imperfect assault from the falling sun. Arn cursed, frustration ringing in her tone.

Farsight decided she had endured enough. *Seidhr* will quiet an animal before it is slaughtered, but I had no desire to make her suffer such an event and my hold consequently slipped a fraction. She wheeled, and bolted.

Clinging to the back of a maddened Northern horse, I plunged into darkening fog.

Night Falls

The Allmother's blessing rests upon the smallest of things—
a sparrow, a pebble turning underfoot, a single spark. Be
both mindful and merciful, for the sparrow may entice the
hawk to dash its brains upon the rock, a pebble under a hoof
may bring down the doughtiest rider, and a single spark
may, if breathed upon, grow until it consumes a forest.
—Idra the Farsighted of Dun Rithell

She did not throw me, at least, and for that I was grateful. A bone-rattling gallop thundered in my ears no less than my own panicked pulse, horsefear ringing through my bones. Wind-scoured boulders flashed by upon either side, crowding and rising in random bursts; Farsight's hooves sounded upon hard-frozen earth like bells. Dead yellow grass and rimed creeping-gorse flew in clods, and it was small consolation that at least the Northerners would be able to track our flight come daylight.

If, that was, they survived the attack. How many of those creatures were there? And Arn…

Of far more immediate concern was the mare turning a foot in an unseen hole, or launching herself from a hidden precipice—I could not see much of the terrain, but when one is stuck to the saddle of a plunging, maddened beast amid heavy cloudbreath all manner of strange fears become far more plausible and vivid. I had enough to do keeping myself from being flung to earth; I did not have breath or mind to mark which direction we were wending.

Sometime later, twilight swallowing the remains of a short winter day, the mare's terror was somewhat purged and she dropped to a bruising canter, then a jarring trot. Farsight finally halted upon a slope scattered with thinning cloud-fingers and large, secretively hunched grey boulders. Lichen clung to their backs and my head was not too mazed, so at least I knew where a *seidhr*-needle would point.

With north found, all else may be guessed at.

The mare hung her own head and shook. I clung to the reins and did likewise, my breath refusing to settle and my eyes watering. My mantle was askew, my skirts bunched, a stray tendril of dark hair fell in my face, and for the first time in a very long while, I had no idea what to do next.

At home there was always another task to accomplish, another petty or large crisis to manage, another trouble to soothe, another lesson to learn. Even traveling with strange Northerners and an Elder for a bare two days had its rhythm, but now the new dance was snatched from underfoot and I was left stumbling as if mead-sick.

I exhaled, hard, and patted Farsight's lathered neck with numb, gloved fingers. "I do not blame you." My voice shook, but I put all the calm certainty I could into the words. "Not in the slightest, my fair one. Easy now, let me think."

I received an ear-flicker for my pains; at least she was listening, and the connection between us firmed. The cold nipped at my cheeks and nose, for my hood had fallen and I dared not free a cramped hand from rein or soothing as I spoke gently to a beast made to endure too much.

"I may call a fire, but there is little fuel I can see. Nevertheless…" I hoped my tone and cadence would calm her further, for all she would not heed the meaning of the words. "I have never seen that manner of creature before. It stank of ill will."

Whatever it was, 'tis gone now, and night falls. You have only a horse and your mantle, now you must think of what to do.

I could not stay halt and trembling like a hunted rabbit or poor Farsight, who needed a walk to cool her, not to mention other care I could not provide at the moment. I slid from her back in a tangle of skirts and mantle, keeping the reins in case she startled—she would drag me, of course, but that could not be helped—and spent some time at her head, more soft speech and coaxing finally penetrating her exhaustion.

I also had my embroidered *seidhr*-bag at my hip. Dried herbs, a healer's knife from south-over-sea, a lodestone, and some other odds and ends...well, others had survived with less. When my pulse and lungs quieted I could use the warming breath, at least for a short while—like any burning, it requires sustenance. I was not hungry yet, but the duration of that mercy might not be long.

Darkness pressed close, ink pouring through night-thickening mist. It was not the weather I had smelled upon leaving Dun Rithell, and I had not heard of this landscape from the few travelers who passed through, wending south to the Barrowhills. This was not normal or canny, and even a *volva* may well feel a chill of apprehension when coming across weirding not of her own making.

Seidhr is by definition strange, for all we live and work within it.

"Come," I said finally, when I judged Farsight had regained enough of her breath and wits to be reasonable. "If you will lend me your nose, nervous one, we may yet find a fire tonight."

The waning moon would not rise for hours. Still, *there are many paths to seeing*, as Idra often remarked, *and the eyes provide only one*. Farsight consented to put her head over my shoulder and take a few circling steps to point us in the direction opposite our wild flight, her nostrils flaring, and I could tell from the way the damp skin upon her shoulders twitched that she was upon the cusp of understanding what I wished of her.

"That's right," I crooned, encouraging. "You know the way; your nose is finer than mine. We must merely retrace our route, and the smell is fresh now. Just a little walking, beautiful one."

If I could induce her to follow the scent of our passage, we had a chance of finding the site of the battle, and hence our companions.

I tried not to think about the misshapen things meeting us along the way. Could they smell us in return? What did such creatures eat, how did they live and reproduce? What were they called?

So many questions. Had this been a saga or traveler's tale I would be breathless with suspense. Curiosity was better than fear, yet I had a surfeit of both at the moment.

Arn would be beside herself. I could only hope her mount had not run, fear-maddened, in a separate direction. I could also hope the misshapen creatures—whatever they were—had all been slain, or taken themselves elsewhere.

The idea that the half-dozen Northerners might be slaughtered and my shieldmaid come to some harm I was not available to mend was bleak, and would not leave me.

Farsight was reluctant, but moving was better than standing in the cold. She plodded with her head at my shoulder, my numb hand grasping the reins and my own steps slow and faltering. When we drifted from the thread of scent spread upon the fog by our wild passage she would slow, not quite balking, and I would bring us back to the invisible line.

Sharing senses with an amicable beast is something many with a touch of *seidhr* may do, and I was glad indeed of such a simple trick that night.

The night crowded us as the fog did, but after a long while thinning vapor-strands streamed across more rocks I did not recognize. I looked up, halting as a faint patch of thinner cloud gleamed overhead. Fitful silver starlight struggled through. A weak breeze was rising—good and ill luck at once, for though bits of unshrouded sky could grant us some light Farsight might have difficulty with a scent blown hither and yon.

I tried to think of a wayfinding song, but I was so cold. My feet were insensate even inside felted overboots, and when I pulled my hood up the tenuous connection between horse and *volva* thinned, so I left it down. Every red coral bead braided into my hair was a chip of spreading ice, and I could perform barely enough of the warming breath to keep from deciding to rest against one of the grey, hunched, lichen-cloaked boulders.

If I halted now, I would slip into snowsleep and freeze to death. Farsight would do much better, having the wit to keep moving and perhaps graze, but she was unable to unsaddle herself and I could not inflict a slow, wandering cinchsore death upon her.

Though perhaps the Northerners would find her during daylight? I could not think upon that. Instead, I longed for Arn. We were so rarely apart; though my brother would marry out and Astrid bring a husband into Dun Rithell—possibly even before I could return home—my shieldmaid would never leave me.

The thought of Arneior's irritation at this turn of events braced me wonderfully. Which was a mercy from some passing divinity or spirit, I suspected, for the breeze intensified into a light wind and yet more starshine glimmered, the fog becoming patchy. Clear skies meant a hard freeze, one I tasted far back upon my palate. Farsight let out a low complaining sound, for she scented it too.

She wished for fodder, for a good rubdown, and for the company of others like her. "I understand," I whispered. "We came far, nervous one. I do not grudge it; you did well indeed. I should name you Fleetfoot instead."

A high, chilling howl rose in the distance, bouncing between boulders, distorted by the straggling mist. My breath caught and Farsight stopped, her head rising and her ears pricked. Another wolf-cry answered from a separate quarter, and the horse's trembling was mine again. Or perhaps I shared my own quivering fear with her, I could not tell.

"Do not worry," I told the poor horse. "If need be I will light a wolf on fire, and that should dissuade it."

I did not know if I could call a spark in such tinder, but I would certainly try. There was nothing about to build a campfire with. I could attempt thickening the fog to hide us from anything unfriendly, but such *seidhr* would mar and mask the scent-road leading us back to the others. Strengthening the breeze would do the same; calling rain would simply make snow and render us more miserable even if I had the concentration and will to do so at the moment.

Besides, Idra always said the weather was best left to itself. It knows its business better than the wisest *seidhr* can.

What was left to me, if fire, air, or water would not do? Earth? Perhaps I could call upon the boulders for some aid, or the hard-frozen ground, but I doubted it. There was no tree to ask for help; I carried a short curved healer's knife, the most allowed to one with *seidhr*, but even its metal was scant protection.

There was nothing to be done but keep walking, for the moment, and to strain my ears as well as Farsight's.

And pray, to any divinity who cared to listen.

Content with Simple

It is said the Enemy cursed those among the Secondborn who would not bend the knee, a slow creeping malediction making them more beast than man. Ever they fight the corruption, for like all his gifts it has its uses—which turn in the hand, and bring destruction upon the wielder.

—Tharos son of Ildar, lord of lost Naras

The howls grew closer. It became more difficult to coax Farsight along; she walked unwilling, her shoulders and hindquarters twitching. My feet turned to clumsy stone and I occupied myself almost exclusively with the warming breath, hoping I would not lose a tip—finger, toe, ear, nose—to the cold. My father's people called such wounds a toll paid to Lokji, while my mother's held them to be kisses from passing black-ice sprites. There is very little treatment for such things even with weirding, and the scars they leave are unattractive at best.

What manner of *volva* could not even keep the cold away? Yet another test, but with no Idra close by in case of failure, no pride shining from my mother's gaze should I succeed, none of Astrid's breathlessly whispered questions or Arn's broad, happy smile.

I would be content with simple survival.

The wind whispered over crowding boulders, ruffling rimed dead grass and bracken. More starshine fell, a pure cold light, the

Great River across the sky finally shaking free of high cloud. Farsight slowed still more, ears flicking nervously to match her anxious tail, each hoof-raise more tentative, though the scent-road was still there.

"Beautiful Fryja." I found myself half-chanting in the Old Tongue between bursts of warming breath. *"Summer-clad or iceborne, lady whom my mother loves, keep them away. Blind them, baffle their noses, keep them mazed."* *Seidhr* threaded through the words—not very much of it, for I needed to conserve my strength.

But it was enough to keep us from the wolves, if indeed they were wolves and not misshapen things like the sheep-creature. I had never heard tell of such things within a day or two's journey of Dun Rithell, and had they descended upon our flocks I could only imagine the hue and cry.

Farsight finally stopped amid a scattering of head-sized stones half lost in frost-withered grass, and could not be induced to step further. Too cold even to shiver, I tugged at the reins, prayer and *seidhr* jolted from my tongue. "Come, nervous one. We must keep moving."

But the white horse would not move. Her head rose, ears far forward, and her tail hung motionless. She was a statue in strengthening nightglow, tiny curls of steam rising from her flanks.

We were both losing far too much heat.

"Please," I whispered, as more howls rose into the night. It sounded suspiciously as if they ringed us save for a single slice of dead silence, fortunately straight ahead. "We may escape them, dear one, if we move. You must." I tugged at the reins again. *"Please."*

In the space of a few short days I had been reduced to pleading with a horse, unable to feel my extremities, while wolves or monsters closed in. It was not a fit end for a *volva*, and irritation fed by fear threatened to turn into full-blown anger.

I had never considered that I might hold my father's battle-madness. Yet that night, for the very first time, I think I came close.

Farsight consented to one more step, but only one, and halted again in the cold silver gloaming. My braids had slipped somewhat, and tendrils of dark hair brushed at my cheeks while I hauled upon the reins, too cold to attempt more *seidhr*. It was just as well, for the wind veered and I heard not wolfsong but what seemed to be voices.

Human voices.

Yet for all I knew it was the trickery of the cold, or mere wishful thinking. "Stubborn piece of..." I gave another harsh yank to the reins; Farsight did not even deign to notice. "I am trying to save you, stupid horse!"

It was laughable. When the beasts closed in, I would be hard-pressed to protect either of us.

"*Soooooolveeeeeiii...*" The wind, or something else, keened my name. I let out a despairing cry in return, for suddenly I thought it Arneior's voice, a shieldmaid's spirit riding through winter night in search of her charge.

I do not know how much later they found me, but it could not have been long. There were two glimmers high upon the slope of a hill to our left scattered with great hulking boulder-shapes, blue stars come to earth, and the wolves howled almost constantly as the lights approached. Despite all my entreaties, the mare still refused to move but instead let out a shattering neigh, and I heard similar equine replies.

Which did me little good, for in my frozen, fear-drenched state I thought them perhaps a cavalcade of the mounted dead come to judge before taking me among their number to Hel's country, and was almost petrified. Yet there were hoof-falls, and a string of curses in a familiar light alto.

I dropped Farsight's reins, staggering forward upon feet I could not feel. Everything below my knees was utterly numb.

Arneior fair leapt from the back of her mount and ran through flickering lamplight, throwing one arm around me while holding her spear well away. I buried my face in her mantled shoulder and breathed her in; she muttered relieved imprecations into my hair.

Aeredh was hard upon her heels, and 'twas he who beckoned Farsight. The beast obeyed *him*, of course, for the Elder have a way with every free creature, and besides the horses were busily greeting each other as well. The blue stars were Elder-wrought lanterns like Idra's prized solstice-light, burning clear and cold, held by Efain the scarred and another Northerner—Karas, with his hair in a leather-wrapped club, pale and with his hand to hilt as he scanned what could be seen of our surroundings.

I sagged against my shieldmaid, doing my best not to burst into tears unfitting for a full *volva* or even a mere adult with no weirding.

And the wolves? Well.

The wolves were silent.

Lady Question

Many are the great houses of the North, but there is a division in them. For some love the Elder, and fought against the Enemy. Others gave their allegiance to the Black Land, and on the Day of Ash they slew their brethren without mercy, even within greathall and family, yea indeed like ravening beasts...
— Aethrasil of Haradhrun, *A History of Töllmar*

Their camp was a fair distance away, and I heeded little save the warmth of *sitheviel*. Aeredh produced Eol's small black flask, encouraging me to take yet another swallow, and I rode double with Arn as Farsight, looking well pleased with herself indeed, was led by the Elder upon his own mount. I did not even see the camp clearly, save to note two great slab-rocks tilted against each other sheltering the fire, which had burned down to blue-tinged coals.

I did not ask how they had performed such a miraculous rescue. Arn joined our mantles and shared her warmth, and though the *sitheviel* burned in my middle and they plied me with much of their strange waybread I cared little for either, clinging to my shieldmaid. Eol and the others were absent, but I did not wonder at the fact.

I was simply too grateful for the luck of survival; great fits of shivering seized me over and over while I thought of the un-sheep creatures or the wolves finding this place.

At least the fire would keep the latter at bay. Or so I hoped, and fell into a deathly doze upon another pine-bough bed with Arn holding me close.

The next morn dawned bright, mostly clear...and shocking, for we were not merely two days' journey from Dun Rithell.

At that distance the terrain should still have been familiar enough; I should have been able to discern familiar landmarks. Instead, peering from the two boulder-slabs sheltering our camp, I saw what could not be. Somehow we were upon the side of a stranger's mountain, forested slopes stretching toward more great peaks and deep valleys almost sparkling with cold winter clarity. Upslope, bright snow mantled a knifelike summit I did not know the name of; we were upon a thin margin just above the trees.

Taking night-shelter in the forest might have been wiser. I could not say as much, though, for I was too busy gazing at sheer precipices and wondering how, by any and all gods, spirits, or *seidhr*, Farsight and I did not plummet to our deaths during our bruising, fog-choked gallop.

Morning also meant every Northerner had returned to the camp. Eol was deep in converse with Aeredh, their dark heads close together and the Elder occasionally tapping one finger into his opposite palm to accentuate a point. The rest set about their morning tasks as if it did not matter we were much, *much* farther away from Dun Rithell than we should be.

Of course Arn was awake far before her charge, and brought me a cup of warmed ale. "Drink every bit." She glowered mightily, her hornbraids redone, her woad-stripe refreshed, and her freckled cheeks cheerfully reddened with brisk weather. "You fair had my heart to stopping, Sol. What were you thinking?"

It would do no good to point out it was not my fault. My shield-maid's anger was quick and sharp, like her tongue; it also died almost as 'twas born, like lighting upon Tarnarya's hood. "There was not much thought involved, true." I accepted the cup, though hot ale is never my favorite drink. "What was that thing? Dare they name it?"

"At night? I should hope not. It died hard; the scarred one Efain had the honor." If that irked her, Arneior gave no sign; she folded into an easy crouch, her spear providing balance. "The rest were driven away or died as well. The youth merely said *they are twisted*. The one I saw was like a sheep, but a few such wool-bearers might well give even Mother Hel's shepherds pause." Her words became a whisper as I held my nose, attempting to down the ale. "I do not recognize these mountains. We are much farther from home than we should be."

Our gazes met, and held for a long moment.

I am more than willing, hers said.

Not yet, mine replied, *though I mislike the wait*. "So I see." Whether or not there was weirding in our passage, I was weregild and held to certain behavior—not bondsmaid or thrall but constrained to obedience with good grace, in whatever direction Eol of Naras chose to travel.

The rules governing such things are strict, for debtor and lord alike. He could neither rape nor starve me, nor force me to overly harsh labor. I could not refuse any reasonable request, nor deny any aid I was capable of, nor question his decisions. There are finer points argued in the South and entire hedges of restrictions upon both parties; I could not think the North much different. If anything, their expectations were perhaps more stringent, and it behooved me to keep both eyes and ears well open to discern any arcane points of etiquette.

I was, after all, Gwendelint's daughter.

Warm thick liquid hit my stomach, thought about revolt like a badly used thrall, and subsided. My position was not an enviable one, for all I had Arn to keep me from physical harm. I took a deep breath, held it, and swallowed the last half of the mug's contents, tasting a bitter medicinal herb or two at the bottom. "Gah. You should keep the ale for your own belly, Arn, and leave mine be."

"What manner of woman does not like ale?" She shook her head, and a flicker of a rueful smile submerged into watchfulness. "Your braids are coming loose. I hear they hunted more of those twisted things last night, in the dark."

I shuddered at the thought. The Northerners did not seem to spend much time in their bedrolls, but if such creatures were about in any number I was more than content to have it so. And yet, what

---

seidhr did they possess to stave off sleepless exhaustion? Such a thing would be worth knowing.

Perhaps it was an Elder trick. I would have to watch carefully—it is the height of bad manners to inquire too closely of another's weirding. Such things must be freely given, or learned by observation and native wit.

For all that, I felt the instinct to both keep my knowledge of the Old Tongue secret and seem oblivious of Aeredh's strangeness well warranted. Much of *volva* training is learning to listen to such small, still inner promptings. "Good fortune that you found me, then." So good, in fact, I was beset with fresh suspicion. "There is much weirding at work here, my Arn."

"*Now* this is revealed unto thee?" The old jest warmed her dark eyes for a brief moment; once more, she sobered almost instantly. "What should we do?" Her forehead wrinkled, and in that moment she looked very young.

Almost as young as Aeredh appeared. I could only hope my own unease was not so plainly visible. An uncertain *volva* is close to useless, as Idra oft remarked.

Once I settled upon a course of action, Arn would see it done. So it had been for many a year, and she was well content to have it thus. Whatever insecurity I felt had to remain unvoiced, and hopefully unseen.

"We wait, and watch." *Learn all we can, and I intend to learn much indeed.* I handed her the empty mug, grimacing again as swallowed ale fought for release. "Pay Dun Rithell's death-debt and return home intact. 'Tis all we can do."

She nodded briskly and rose in a fluid motion as a blue-eyed Northerner approached, the one with a brace of daggers at his belt. His nose was proud indeed; I thought his name was Gelad. He gave a half-bow and offered a wooden bowl laden with breakfast—more of their waybread, and yet more stew. They were hunters indeed, to find so much in winter. "My lady *alkuine*? Here." He handled our tongue well enough, and with a riverside lilt. "We have an easy journey today."

I am not here to take my ease, my lord. And I hoped the stew held no roast carved from that *thing* with its foul flanks and odd horns.

"We need not travel slowly on my account, my lord...Gelad? Have I your name aright?"

He nodded. "Indeed, and an honor to be named. I must offer our apologies, though our lord Eol will no doubt do so as well."

"None are necessary." Rumpled and aching as I was, in a nest of blankets and under Arneior's mantle as well as my own, I did not feel much like accepting pretty words. My disarranged hair tugged at my scalp when I turned my head, as if Astrid were braiding again. "My thanks for breakfast, my lord."

"And ours for your presence." The Northerner had a kind enough smile, though his bright gaze was watchful. No shadow of sleepless exhaustion lingered upon him. "We would not travel the Elder Roads save at great need; last night proved the risk."

"Elder Roads." I had never heard of such a thing; I wondered if the fog had been entirely natural or had merely masked some travel-weirding. It would be another skill worth learning, to go so swiftly—but if such roads held beasts like the sheep-horror, 'twas perhaps best to leave them alone. "Is that how we came so far?"

"It is." His smile was equal parts gratified and somewhat paternal; clearly the Northern men thought me simple for all my *seidhr*. Which pleased me well enough; being underestimated is an edge all its own. "There are things in the North which may surprise a southron lady, and—"

"Gelad." Eol cut him short, appearing over the fellow's shoulder with something close to a scowl. "Let the lady *alkuine* break night's-fast in peace."

I dropped my gaze to the bowl, and set to my work of consumption. But behind the disheveled picture I presented, my skull-meat was working furiously. Arn hovered over me, solemnly watchful as the leader of the wolf-stamped men crouched at a respectful distance, his hands hanging easily over his thighs and his wrapped swordhilt peering from his shoulder.

He had veiled the gem again, perhaps because its glitter might draw attention from a distance.

"I must offer apology to Gwendelint's daughter." At least he did not lack for formal address. A faint blush from the chill clung to his cheekbones; it was strange that the Northerners did not have beards. One would think them chilled by the lack. "Last night could have gone ill indeed."

"It went ill enough." I was too hungry to set aside my bowl; then again, when one is traveling, there is little need for overly fine manners. "Yet ended well, Eol of the North. Farsight and I would have found our way home."

It was not quite a lie, I told myself. Some chance, or even some *seidhr*, might have helped me survive until dawn, frostbitten but still breathing. There was no reason to contemplate any other outcome.

"Farsight? Oh, yes." He nodded, and his dark gaze was direct as Bjorn's, though shadowed by worry. "A fine name for a noble steed. I would assuage your worry, Lady Solveig. We will let no harm come to you."

It managed to nettle my pride, even after narrowly avoiding a plunging death upon a fear-maddened horse. "There stands my shieldmaid, and I am *volva*. I am not overly worried. I would know, though…" How far could I inquire? It might be best to test the limits of what this man would allow his weregild.

Eol of Naras stilled, and his dark eyes gleamed. He was much leaner than Bjorn, but his self-possessed quiet might well warn a fellow warrior not to taunt too freely. "What would you know?"

Several of his brethren cast sneaking glances upon us as they went about their work. Only Aeredh watched openly, a faint line between his eyebrows. Did Eol expect me to ask about the Elder who rode with us, now not bothering to hide his ear-tips? Or about that evocative phrase, *Elder Roads*? Did such tracks all run through cold fog, along mountaintops? How was the travel-weirding achieved?

"That sheep-thing, last night." I could not ask what I truly wished, but such is life—as Idra often reminded her student. There were other matters to inquire upon that could easily test his willingness. "I caught only a glimpse of it. What is its name?" Perhaps he would even label it in the Old Tongue, adding to my store of knowledge.

"Ah." Did he look surprised, or pained? It was difficult to tell; his reserve was near uncanny. "It is a twisted thing; in the Old Tongue we call it *grelmalk*. They are not common."

"That is a great comfort." I was somewhat gratified that he had given up a word I could use. *Grelmalk* was no term I had been taught; I would have to think upon it today, tasting its syllables to discover its secrets. There were other things a weregild could reasonably expect to inquire about as well, and he had opened the door a fraction to their urging. "How do such things breed? Do they come from the North? How often do they attack travelers?"

"We should name you *Lady Question*." Eol's expression changed again, a few fractions' worth of difference settling into faint bemusement, his dark hair full of blue glints in thin winter sunlight. "They come from the Gasping upon the borders of the Black Land, and are an affliction. You shall never see another so closely, for we will not use the cloaked ways again. We did not think…well, it matters little what we thought. I mean merely to reassure you."

I would know what he thought and more of these "cloaked ways," but he rose, nodded to Arn, and returned to Aeredh. His men busied themselves with breaking camp, and Arneior watched their movements with interest, her thumb moving slightly upon her spear-haft, an absentminded caress.

So he would answer a few things, but not most and certainly not all. Care and caution were called for here; my restraint would have to match his own.

I finished my breakfast in silence, and the food did not warm me.

Treesong, Welcome Cup

*Lokji invented winter, but it was the Allmother's eldest son
who filled it with terror. For the Enemy twists all things
he can, hating even the season of rest when the world is
quiet…*

—*The Proverbs of Graendel*

By midmorn we had descended well into the forest. Clouds
arrived from the north and east, and a thick tang of fresh snow
coated my throat. The trees, crowned by previous snowfalls, held a
profound hush as the air warmed—spring was a long time away, but
each day was now a few moments longer than the last.

Of course, in the North new winter warms only so it may produce another white veil.

I was well occupied in thinking upon and tasting the strange
word *grelmalk* while attempting to repair my braids and the red
coral beads when the first flakes floated down. Old snow had been
compacted by wind, its own weight, or slight thaws, swept into
almost-dingy drifts resting between thick trunks. Still, the way was
clear enough and the pale horses stepped more lightly than southron ones. Perhaps they had been bred for it; there were stories of
Elder mounts which could balance upon ice-crust, were it thick
enough.

I had become somewhat accustomed to the perpetual fierce silence

of the Northerners and even to Aeredh's soft, almost-swallowed singing as the horses plodded atop solid-packed snow starred with fallen
branches, depressions showing animal passage, and other detritus.
What made me cease my braiding and retying, swaying atop Farsight
with my fingers caught in my hair, was familiar *seidhr.*

The trees were singing, as they often do deep in hushed woods.
Even in the silence of falling snow—every hoof-fall muffled as our
route doubled and wound to avoid obstacles, taking advantage of
branch-cover or wind-sculpt pushing previous drifts aside—I heard
their murmurs.

Arneior rode with her hood back, her hair glowing in direction-
less grey light. A shieldmaid's hearing is sharp, but she did not glance
in my direction. No, what I heard was for a *volva's* ears alone.

It was not the creak of laden branches combed by wind or the
snap of ice-freighted twigs. The trees which bear new leaf every
spring muttered softly; those who wear their robes all winter were
a little louder. They whispered as humans or beasts do while their
dreamsouls—a third of what makes a living creature, some *seidhr*
say—wander night's country.

I was hard put to think *I* was not dreaming, my overlapping
selves disarranged by successive shocks and last night's fitful, shivering doze passing for sleep. For here we were, Eril's daughter and
her shieldmaid hemmed close by dark-clad Northerners, in a cortege
headed by an Elder after escaping twisted beasts hailing from near
the fabled wreck of the Dead Dust—called *the Gasping* in the Old
Tongue.

My braids were arranged as well as I could manage by evening;
the rest of me felt too rumpled for much confidence. The sun was a
mere handspan above the westron horizon, a strengthless smear amid
gathering darkness and heavy-falling snow as the woods drew away
and ribbons of smoke lifted from a steading. The greathall and its
outlying buildings turned their backs to the north wind, all crowding close. The central hall was quite fine, though not as large as Dun
Rithell, and the steadings' meadows were ringed with round, hip-
high grey rocks.

Most of the stones bore runes for health, warding, and protection

I knew well enough even if in somewhat ancient forms, but every so often they were shaped as squatting thick-bellied people with long earlobes, a few with ornately carved wooden pipes clasped to lichen-starred lips as if they longed for a twist of hemp or other herb-smoke to inhale. I almost laughed upon seeing them, for their expressions were comically surprised. Yet I sensed weirding drowsing within them, a different force than the tuneless hum of deep-carved, well-fed runes. The snow had been cleared in pathways, and hummocks in what had to be gardens during summer were domed hives, their inhabitants slumbering between tiny sips of honey produced against the long cold.

Had it not been winter I might have spoken to the bees, for they are powerful allies and enjoy a *volva*'s company. I touched the hard lump of my grandmother's torc near my collarbone, obscurely comforted.

Our coming had been noticed. Great shaggy dogs belled from the outbuildings and we were soon surrounded by a pack of brindle, tawny, and black with white socks and blazes. They looked no different than Dun Rithell's hounds, and the pale horses did not mind them; well-wrapped men with gazes both pale and dark clumped through the snow, hailing us in the Old Tongue. Steep-pitched roofs accumulating a fresh coating of white were a welcome sight, and I half-fell from Farsight's back into Arn's grasp.

Plunging into a hall's warmth at the end of a winter journey, even if travel has taken only a day or two, is what a red-hot blade might feel diving into oil. A welcome cup was pressed into my hand and I took a hurried gulp. It was mead with herbs; heat exploded in my middle, altogether rougher and somehow more comforting than *sitheviel*. Dogs nosed at my thighs, an excited babble rose around me, and Arneior all but drained the great gilded goblet figured with running deer, their antlers lifted proudly.

A tang of smoke, the close welcome fug of mortal bodies breathing and shedding heat, the smells of baking bread, rich roasting meat, and a sharp breath of mead—it was so like my home tears stung my eyes. My snow-caked mantle and overboots were whisked away, Arn's own dun greatcloak as well, but when they moved to take her spear she stepped before me, her upper lip lifting slightly and her shoulders square.

There was some discussion in the Old Tongue mixed with southron, while great waves of shivers passed over me. The body will oft save its protest until safety is reached; I was simply grateful to be out of the cold. If they tried to separate Arn from her weapon we might spend the night in byre or pig-wallow, and I would not mind overmuch except for the prospect of stepping outside again to get there.

Her charge was a weregild, yes. But none may separate a shield-maid from her spear.

Finally, thin strips of yellowed leather were brought, and one was tied around Arn's spear-haft. Eol's sword and the other Northerners' weapons received the same treatment, barring them from using a blade in anger. Such was the custom in certain parts of the North, the ancestor of our own pax-binding.

Hospitality requires different ceremonies in different places, but I did not care, for now that we had reached some warmth I was hard-put to quell the yawns which oft accompany the shuddering of deep physical relief.

That was how we arrived at the Eastronmost Steading, ruled by the Lady Hajithe—of whom I learned the next morning, for that eve I followed Arneior three steps into the hall's antechamber and swayed with weariness, whereupon we were whisked to a closet in the warm depths of the women's hall. I sank gratefully into a bed and knew no more.

Precious and Rare

Our pride is in loyalty, and in faithfulness our might.
—Asdrax the Tall, first lord of the House of Caelim

*T*he *Lady of the Eastronmost*—so they called tall dark-haired Hajithe of Caelim, her eyes blue as summersky and her mien as forbidding as my own mother's while judging inheritance or capital cases. Her infrequent laughter was merry as Astrid's, though, and she gave my shieldmaid high honor; the Wingéd Ones do not go North, it seemed. Even Arn's woad-stripe was the cause of some comment.

My own *volva*-markings and red-beaded braids fascinated the steading's children almost as much as Aeredh seemed to. Strangers did not often visit the Eastronmost during the winter.

The "Elder Roads" had brought us even farther than my shield-maid or I could have dreamed. We were well within the North proper, at least a moonturn and a half's worth of hard summer travel from Dun Rithell; I learned this from Arn the morn after we arrived, and my shieldmaid's gaze remained locked with mine for a few breaths after she granted me the news.

I could not say much in reply, for hard upon my waking there was a knock at the door of the closet given to our sleep-use, heralding a tray with breakfast and a tonic from the lady of the hall herself, full of herbs and honey but no *seidhr*.

I spent half that day abed, breathing deeply and listening to my body's many complaints while Arneior performed stretches in lieu of practice-sparring. The closet's door was propped wide open to let in heat—and perhaps to keep us from close counsel, for we could not help but be overheard by the stream of passersby. We excited much curiosity, and at regular intervals another thrall or freedwoman arrived with a tray of victuals, a wish for good health from the lady of the hall, a polite inquiry as to our needs, or some other reminder that we were guests.

Arneior did not complain, for they fed us well. Her appetite was that of any warrior's in winter, and excited no outright comment but many a pleased smile. They even had a proper sauna. Both shieldmaid and weregild availed ourselves of its cleansing, though I did not scrub myself with snow afterward as Arn loved to do and even there we were not alone, for a few other women had their turn in its warmth.

I bore no black-ice kisses, and was relieved to have escaped my first adventure in the North undamaged. I had much to think upon, but exceeding little time to do so.

The Eastronmost Steading was more properly a greathall and a swathe of associated smaller farms. Its name was ancient, and Lady Hajithe proud of her ancestors. She had once been married, though her husband had fallen to some ill chance not spoken of in the short time we rested there. Her children, son and daughter, were fostered farther northwest in some mighty kingdom, and Aeredh given tidings and small gifts to take thence.

It was the first intimation I had of our destination, though not nearly a definitive one. It did not matter much, as I was to go where Eol of Naras bid—and yet I wondered. Where had the bear-marked Northerners and Uldfang's men gone—farther south, on whatever errand, spoken of to the elders after the Althing, that had brought them all to Dun Rithell?

A weregild must be "stolen" from their hall, but this seemed a bit too extreme even for men of this quiet, grim stamp.

The lady of the Eastronmost seated me at her right hand during the evening meal; she was at pains to speak the southron tongue though her usage often waxed somewhat archaic. In her great carven chair, scenes of hunt and field deeply figured upon its back and its arms ending in thoughtful, frowning boar-heads, she sat straight-backed and used the antique horn implements common for eating in the North, unlike our more modern wooden ones. During dinner she asked of my mother, of the ways of the South, and, with an air of great but restrained curiosity, if the *volva*-markings pained me.

"All knowledge is paid for," I recited as Idra had years ago, just before the first line of ink was forced under my skin. "Arn gained many a bruise and scrape learning to wield her spear; I have these."

Those closest listened, though some of our traveling companions were pressed to translate our converse into the Old Tongue. I paid close attention to their speech during our short tarrying, though I did not stir from the hall itself. I would have liked to also examine the runestones and especially the statues, but the snow fell fast-thick and even Arn was content to stay inside.

Besides, each word I stored up now, each turn of phrase and meaning implied by context or expression, would likely serve us better than the stones.

"You are young," Lady Hajithe murmured that eve, gesturing for more mead to be brought to the lowers. Much attention was paid to the semicircular high table; every morsel Arn or I took was raptly watched. "And so is your shieldmaid."

"Three summers her elder," Arn replied, as she is wont to do. There was meat enough and ale to spare; the board met with her approval indeed. In the lamplight her woad-stripe gleamed richly. "They say *volva* are wiser, though I see it little."

"Someday I might find some wisdom," I agreed, selecting a bite of their sweetish bread. It was not the leaf-wrapped waybread; there was no mystery in its crumb. For all that, it was filling and quite welcome. Northern fare was not so different from our own. "And then what will you chide me for, Arneior?"

The lady of the Steading smiled, looking hard put indeed not to. "Are all shieldmaids so…" She wore fine dark-blue cloth and a torc of beaten silver; all things considered, I was glad of my own grandmother's bee-collar and red beads. I represented the finest of Dun Rithell here, and did not think they would find me wanting. "So forward?"

Did she think Arn forward now, she should see my shieldmaid in an altercation. "She was taken by the Black-Wingéd Ones, those who judge the dead upon battlefields and accompany the worthy to the halls prepared." It seemed strange the Northerners did not know as much; my words were taken around the table by the translating wolf-stamped men. Gelad's were the nearest to the proper meanings, I thought, though they all did serviceably enough—and taught me a few new terms besides. "Those the *valkyra* choose are granted much. Using such a gift to leave truth unspoken, or worse, would be a terrible thing."

"Yet there may be safety in silence, sometimes." Lady Hajithe's blue gaze darkened, her chin lifting. "Or even some profit." She gazed at the stairs by the great door, and the fire in its massive hearth crackled as if to underscore her words.

If I closed my eyes, I might even imagine myself at home. Even if the mead smelled different here and the accent of conversation was dissimilar too, being in the Old Tongue.

I sought to put our hostess at ease. "Our traveling companions certainly seem to think so. They pass barely half a dozen words in a day." It did not quite irk me—I was merely weregild, after all.

But even a thrall may remark upon the weather, as the saying goes.

"'Tis safest, traveling as we have." Aeredh, upon the Lady's other side, lifted his goblet of mead to her before each deep draught. His high regard was thought-provoking, indeed. "You will find us of better cheer henceforth, Lady Solveig."

And will your companions still vanish at night, as if my presence is not to be borne? My smile lacked nothing in politeness, much as if I were listening to a visiting warrior list his accomplishments in verse. "It would be hard not to, my lord Aeredh." I meant the sally to amuse, and at least the Elder laughed.

Lady Hajithe's smile faltered slightly, but Eol—upon Arn's other side—broke his usual quiet. "Lady Solveig has much to find us at fault for, yet has borne it with grace approaching yours, Lady of the Eastronmost. Her bravery puts us to shame." He paused, then continued in the Old Tongue. "*Hope cometh from the West, but also from other quarters.*"

"So my husband believed." The ruler of this hall—and much land within riding distance, I now knew—did not glance at him but instead gazed steadily upon Aeredh. "You rode south for aid, and return thus. Are we now seeking children to fight our battles?"

Her words raced through the hall, translated into the Old Tongue, and while a hush did not fall the hum of conversation and feast-riddling became somewhat quieter.

So. They were seeking some kind of alliance, perhaps against a troublesome Northern warlord. That would make some sense, but why not take me farther south to translate and perhaps press others to their cause with a *volva*'s skill and standing? Not only that, but they had not spoken of their fallen companion again—though that could be a prohibition upon naming the dead before they were safely in Hel's country—and I had to absorb more of the Old Tongue as they spoke it before I could be certain of that worrying word, whether it meant *traitor* or...something else.

I hurried to set my mead-goblet down in its proper place, very aware of my manners upon display. " 'Tis ill befitting of me to complain, Lady Hajithe Blue-Eye, and I beg your pardon if I have." I had clearly broken the merry mood, and so must repair it. Unfortunately, I had little idea of how, but it was no worse than lending my support to an unpopular verdict rendered by my mother, or even one of Eril's harsher pronouncements. "In truth I am well pleased; traveling north has been full of wonders so far, and I look forward to more."

"Wonders?" Her expression grew even more pained, were that possible. I did not like being so clumsy in conversation, and *children fighting battles* was thought-provoking indeed.

Why had they not taken Bjorn, if there was combat to be had? The entire group of Northerners had made some sort of appeal to the elders, my brother had said; could I assume the bear-marked ones and Uldfang's men were traveling farther south? I had not the time to discover the exact nature of their request before being dragged from home, and was called upon to make pleasant conversation with a Northern lady of great honor at the moment besides.

I would have to use poetry.

"Oh, aye." It took a bare moment to arrange a couplet, and I took a deep breath. Arneior settled back in her chair with her mead-cup, preparing to listen and respond. *"Far travel in fog and a sheep with wolf's teeth; I have not seen such a thing in all my few years."* The rhymes were not of my usual quality, but each syllable blent into the next with ease, and Arn's immediate draught from her goblet meant it was not bad at all. By the time she had swallowed, she had her reply ready.

"Less years than my own, and yet just as full; wolfsong we heard, and a fell beast slain." She flattened her hand to her breastbone, likely suppressing a resounding belch. Her rhymes were better, but she left the ending open.

I took it for the gift it was. *"Though into dim eve a horse took flight; met halfway on return by a belling pack."* It was short, each word containing an applicable double meaning, and I quite proud indeed.

Mystified silence met our contest. Even the translators had halted, though Eol buried a slight smile in his own cup. Why this should have pleased him I could not guess, but perhaps it was the pride of a man who has an exotic pet and makes it dance on festival days.

" 'Tis a game," Aeredh supplied helpfully, leaning against his chair-arm in our hostess's direction. The sharp tips of his ears poked through his hair; he made no attempt to hide what he was in this hall. Did they merely take the appearance of Elder for granted this far north? "They may spend whole evenings thus, speaking in verse. Sometimes a man's freedom is decided upon the couplets, or a woman's accepting a husband."

"I see." Lady Hajithe still looked puzzled, though she tipped her cup politely in my direction before taking a sip.

It was not quite the reaction I had hoped for, but Arn finished her drink, throat moving in long swallows, and tapped her empty goblet twice upon the table's rim. For all she is most martial, my shieldmaid concedes many a poetry battle to me. "I should know better than to play against you, Sol. A *volva* has a quick tongue."

"It follows a sharp mind, dear one." It was my turn to drain my own cup, which I did with good grace. Their mead was fiery, strong, and very clear, holding sunshine in its depths. "It is counted a politeness to our hosts to craft a few rhymes, Lady Hajithe. We pass many winter eves in such amusement, and in singing sagas old and new. Lord Aeredh has sung almost since we left Dun Rithell."

"His kind ever love music." The lady's berry-reddened mouth turned down at both corners. The hall quieted afresh, though the translators returned to their murmuring work.

" 'Tis said the Allmother sang the world into being and we merely follow suit, my lady." I could not decide if I was to pretend not to know what she meant. The Elder were indeed held to love all manner of song and instrument, and to have taught mortals their use. Mortals of Eol's kind were rumored to be great singers in their own right as well, though their sagas are rather dour, which was attributed to the weather or the memory of the Black Land's days of power. "What does the North do upon winter eves for amusement? It seems southron merriment is not to your liking, and we would be good guests."

"Ah, young one, you remind me of my Laleith; she ever finds most value in laughter." Lady Hajithe essayed a smile, and for a moment she looked much like my mother when a subject not fit for children's ears has been brought to their vicinity. "You are fine guests indeed; I am merely of stern temper. We play a similar game of a winter evening in the North, but in the Old Tongue."

"I am to spend a year and a day in the North, after all." I was tempted to bring forth a couplet in said language to please her. But a *volva* does not tell all she knows, Idra had repeated over and over, and the instinct to keep my cunning to myself remained clear and steadfast. Though I doubted myself in that moment, my conscience pinching slightly. "I should inquire how to best please my hosts."

"A year and a day?" Lady Hajithe looked to Aeredh, as if she had not quite heard me aright. The servers were busy bringing fresh platters and jugs from the kitchen, a familiar bustle. "Is it only expected to take so long, son of Aerith?"

It was Eol who answered, in the Old Tongue. *"This is a different matter, my lady, and one best not spoken upon."*

Arn glanced at me, then just as quickly reached for her newly filled goblet. I could tell her what was said later; now I was happy indeed I had held my tongue. There was something deeper than simple weregild afoot, and their unguarded speech might cast light enough upon it to grant my shieldmaid and me some advantage.

My unease sharpened; I sought to keep a pleasant, faintly mystified expression as if listening to neighbors argue over a wild, unmarked sheep.

"Are you the son of Aerith, to answer me so?" The lady's gaze sharpened, and a chill fingertip laden with dread traced down my back. *"There is no love between our houses, son of Tharos; I will have an answer from those I question in my own home."*

"By the vigilance of the house of Naras, too, are the Eastron Marches kept safe, my lady." Eol did not quite scowl, but his expression was not kind, and the chill down my back intensified. *"I do not seek to keep my lord Aeredh from answering, merely to save our precious guest from any discomfort."*

They spoke almost too swiftly for me to untangle meanings. My comprehension of the Old Tongue as they used it was improving at a marvelous rate, but I would have to think long and hard upon this to make certain I was not mishearing aught.

In any case, whatever reply the lady would have made was forestalled. *"Precious indeed, and rare."* Aeredh lifted his goblet again, honoring the ruler of this hall. *"We return northward without what we were sent for, but bearing hope nonetheless. More I cannot say at table, but would crave your pardon and ear in private."*

So I was not what they had been sent for, but a *volva* was a prize to be taken north instead? They had to have *seidhr* of their own, if Elder still walked their lands. I quelled a restless movement, listening so intently my ears all but tingled.

"Then you shall have it." Lady Hajithe inclined her head, crowned with braids longer and more complex than my own though no silver touched their strands, and her air was again so like Gwendelint of Dun Rithell's I was obscurely comforted. "Forgive us, young one. The wolves of Naras sit among us, and it moves me to caution. I should not speak in a language my guests lack."

Wolves of Naras, as if their sigil was famous in the North? Questions crowded my throat, and it irked me to keep my facility with the Old Tongue hidden now that she had spoken so fairly. "There is nothing to forgive," I answered, cautiously. "It is an ill guest indeed who brings discord, my lady. Perhaps I should retire."

"I would not have it so." She gestured as the servers finished their work with well-practiced coordination, and the next course could begin. "I miss my son and daughter, Lady Solveig of Dun Rithell, and you much remind me of the latter. There is a comfort in such memory, so stay if you will, and tell me more of the South."

What else could I do? I obliged, seeking to put her at her ease.

I do not think I managed it.

How Men Think

When they woke they were much amazed, for at their fire was one of the Elder, who sang to them in his own tongue. At first they thought him one of the Blessed and were afraid, but his song spoke to them of wonders and of kindness, and they listened with growing comfort. Thus it was Aerith met their chieftain Eofred, grandfather of Asdrax, and great was the love between them.

—*The Saga of Icevein*

W ell?" Arn whispered, snuggling next to me. We had been lucky indeed to reach this shelter before the new winter's deepsnow descended; the wind had risen too, though in the Eastronmost Steading's windowless depths I could barely hear its breath. "They gabble in weirding-speak like you and old Idra. I can make out a word or two, but only just."

"I can make out somewhat more, though they hardly speak enough to grant real understanding." The closet was warm, and paneled in some fragrant wood. I yawned, my mouth tingling from tooth-cleaning, and propped my head upon my bent arm. The luxury of being warm, clean, and alone with my shieldmaid—I did not know which to thank the gods for first. *Finally* we could be reasonably sure of privacy. "There is no love between the lady of this place and Lord Eol's family; she mentioned the wolves of Naras—I think that is his house, at least. They were sent south to find summat or gain allies against some foe, but did not manage it and perhaps consider me a replacement? Aeredh will be speaking to the great lady here in private; I begin to think there is some troublesome warlord in the North. But if so, why did they not take Bjorn?" Our whispers could not possibly be heard in the hall, and yet I was uneasy.

That is the wrong word. I was beginning to be afraid, yet I had no real hook to hang the fear upon.

"Perhaps they want my spear instead of his lumbering axe." Arn's laugh was not quite forced; a familiar line deepened between her coppery eyebrows. Her face was scrubbed free of woad for the moment. A faint yellowed ghost of its dye lingered, blessedly familiar, and for once she did not need me to warm her. "If they wished for a *volva* instead, though...what use could they have for you?"

"I will think upon it," I whispered. "And perhaps dream."

"You must dream of your mother, too." My shieldmaid moved restlessly. Her sleep-braids gleamed ruddy, and this close the fine lines of gold amid the brown of her irises were visible. "She will be worried."

"We have been gone hardly long enough to worry anyone, I suspect." Two days' worth of travel, and yet we had come so far—even for one familiar with *seidhr*, it was barely credible. Their Elder Roads were a mystery I longed to untangle, even if they were populated by fell creatures. "You have seen Aeredh's ears. He is *Elder*, Arn. We are lost in a tale, or a saga."

"His..." A strange look crossed Arn's face. "I thought him only like the others. And yet, if you say so...You are jesting?"

"I am not." My half-voiced hiss grew fierce; I was unused to disbelief from this quarter. "You said you noticed."

"I hardly think...well, Sol, the wolves." Her lips barely shaped the syllables. "Did you not see?"

"Upon their clothing, or singing at night?" Perplexed, I pressed my cheek upon my arm and studied her face.

She had gone pale, and her freckles glared. "*Them*, Sol. Their eyes are too bright and their teeth too sharp. I thought the boy merely too young to show any sign, but if you say he is Elder..."

"I do not…" I had thought her using some kenning to describe Aeredh's essential difference. But suddenly I understood otherwise, and despite the steading's shelter I shuddered as if lost upon the cliffside with Farsight again. "You mean they change their skins." Much more made sense, now—their empty bedrolls, and the wolf-calls that night driving me and the cream-colored mare back to safety. I wondered briefly upon the other sigils. Bear, and a torch-rune perhaps for no creature that walked under the daylit sky? "Fryja preserve us."

"We might do better to call upon Lokji, or upon Allmother herself." Uncharacteristically serious, Arn shuddered, and I slipped my free arm over her, hugging her close.

Nose to nose as if we were children again, I stared into her eyes, our breaths finally matching. Calm settled over me. There was no quandary we could not solve together, my shieldmaid and I. "An Elder, a group of wolves. And those things in the fog." I gave each word its own space, settling the problem in speech. Often, 'tis enough to bring clarity. "Why did they not take Bjorn? He would have noticed naught amiss, and probably thumped that sheep-thing upon the head to boot."

"Killed it in one blow, likely. We know him capable of it." Arn's dark gaze turned even more troubled, and a brief apology swam in it. "I thought, *We are only two days away from home, well enough.* But we are not, and we are at their mercy, Sol."

Well, of course. I was weregild, largely subject to Eol's command. And his kin, felled by my brother's hand and called *traitor.*

Perhaps I had translated the term aright after all.

"Or they are at ours." I did not like seeing her…afraid? Was that the word? I liked even less the way my voice sought to catch, as if on a stubborn nail in old wood. Fortunately, it was merely an internal sensation, not audible—or so I hoped. "A *volva* and a spearmaid are doughty enemies."

"The boy will give me some trouble." It was high praise from my shieldmaid. Then again, Elder had many a year to learn the use of weapons, and the light of the Allmother burned bright within them. They did not sicken as we did, even when grievously wounded—and though they may die by violence or anguish, naught else takes them over death's threshold. "As for the rest of them, well. Their kind is said to be strong, and quick."

"You have hunted wolves before," I pointed out, softly.

The truth did not bring a smile to my shieldmaid. "A wolf can be hunted because it thinks like a wolf, Sol. A beast which thinks like a man may not be so easy."

"But we know how men think, do we not? There is no mystery in them." Or precious little, I should have said. Neither Bjorn nor my father held any great riddle, nor did any warrior, freedman, bondsman, servant, or thrall of Dun Rithell.

Besides, *seidhr* oft uncovers what is hidden. I did not think myself a match for an Elder, naturally—but strength is not what may count most when it comes to weirding.

I was slightly nettled I had not guessed the truth of the Northerners before now—it was perhaps a sign I was not fit to wear the bands I had acquired so laboriously—but Arn saw what I did not. It was enough. The persistent unease retreated somewhat as I snuggled in fine linen and woolen blankets, and my shieldmaid's living warmth.

They did not know I could understand their Old Tongue. I was bound by the rules and obligation of paying a life-debt, but 'twas no different than being obliged by inheritance or other law. Every rule or custom may be turned if one has enough wit, just as a hare may wriggle through a thicket while the hunter is mired in thorny branches.

I was, after all, the eldest daughter of Dun Rithell. I had been negotiating since I could speak, and training in *seidhr* almost as long.

Whether we were caught in saga or song, at least we knew the rhyme or music now. And—oh, why deny it? I was intrigued. May the Allmother forgive me, I was also excited at the advent of new wonders, new mysteries, of things beyond the smaller world of my home.

What true *volva* could not be?

"I know that look." Arn's lips barely shaped the words. "There is weirding you wish to attempt. Something Idra would advise against, but you will do anyway."

"Would she truly advise against it?" I could not hold back a soft laugh; once or twice I had attempted what my teacher warned against, and though never leading to comfort it was also marvelously instructive. Now, though, I had no Idra to aid in undoing or mitigating an unexpected effect. "I am planning no *seidhr*, Arn, merely to keep my eyes wide open. To see what wonders can be seen for our year-and-day, before we return home with many a fine story to tell."

Arn's mouth thinned. I did not need further speech to sense her worry.

"They cannot keep us past then," I pointed out. "It is against law and custom both. And in a year we will have learned so much, Arn. We may leave after next winter solstice, whether they will or no."

She was still silent. We remained so, breathing together, until my eyelids grew heavy and we each turned to our halves of the bed, back-to-back in a small dark nest of warmth while outside a life-stealing storm drove white flakes before it.

I dreamt of Dun Rithell that night. The greathall was empty, though laid with a feast bearing a distinct resemblance to the Eastronmost's. My mother was in the carved high seat upon the dais, and when I descended the steps from the open doors she rose and smiled. I knew she had seen me in her own sleep, and was comforted.

But then the dream changed, and I trudged across a barren grey wasteland starred with dead trees and tangles of dark, thorn-thirsty bramble. In the distance a crimson glimmer crouched amid knifelike black mountains, and terror filled my night-wandering self as a single wolf's cry lifted in sere, corrupted air.

Fare-Thee-Wells

At the Dag Saekirrin—the Battle of Falling Ice—all was lost until Taeron Goldspear and his army arrived, from whence even the other Elder knew not, and fell upon the backs of the Enemy's assembled hosts like the avenging Blessed themselves. Great was the slaughter that eve, the Black Land's power seemed broken, and many were the fell things hunted to extinction in the days after. Yet three mornings past the victory, the assembled hosts of the Elder and Faithful woke to find Taeron and all his warriors had vanished once more…
—Daeron of Nithraen, On the Dag Saekirrin

The next day I added to my store of Old Tongue by listening to every scrap of women's conversation I could hear, made small repairs to Arn's clothing and my own, and used the sauna again. It was very much like being home, between the thump-clack of the looms and the singing of those at their own needles. There were constant offers of food and drink, which Arn availed herself of mightily, and many excited questions about the ways of the South. I learned a great deal by listening to the few who had a store of the southron language translating for those who did not, and my *volva*-marks were much admired.

That evening's feast was far less troubled, for I exerted myself in telling Lady Hajithe small stories of Dun Rithell and *volva* training before withdrawing as early as possible to the closet with Arn. The following morn bore no fresh snow, for the storm had taken itself elsewhere; I awoke to preparations for departure. Arn and I were excluded from any work save repacking my mother's second-largest trunk. None of the large white Northern horses were burdened with it during the day, though it arrived at our camp each night intact, and *that* was a piece of *seidhr* I deeply longed to learn.

Journeying with a trunk but without the need to haul it a-cart seemed a very useful bit of weirding indeed; I was much exercised in how to arrange witnessing the use of that particular skill but could find no graceful way of doing so. It did not help that Aeredh and the wolves of Naras were absent much of the daytime during our stay, returning only for the evening meal.

A chance remark by one of Lady Hajithe's warriors as he lingered in the door of the women's quarters, speaking to his sister, solved that last mystery. The Elder—whom the entire Steading held in reverence and the children crowded whenever he returned, forsaking even the novelty of my and Arn's presence—was in the forest, "speaking to the stones." It seemed he was strengthening invisible protections, rune-wrought or otherwise, with the wolf-stamped men accompanying him just as Dun Rithell's warriors flanked Frestis during the Midsummer boundary-walks, carrying the wicker baskets and keeping watch while he sang and made the sacrifices.

If there were more of those twisted, terrible sheep-things about, I could well see the need. And I pondered how we would travel in these conditions. There are ways to move through the landscape in any weather without *seidhr*, of course.

I merely wondered if an Elder and a collection of skin-changers would use the ones I knew.

We took our leave amid bright sparkling snow and thin golden sunlight. My mantle and overboots had been well cleaned; Arn was looking very pleased indeed, though sorry to leave their clear, fiery mead behind. Her spearblade glittered vengefully, the haft free of leather pax-knot, and she studied the dark-clad Northerners in turn while I cast my gaze over the assembled household. One of the children, a long-legged scamp of about nine summers, thrust his tongue out and squinted both eyes; I made the war-face in return, well acquainted with this game, and was rewarded with a cheeky giggle. His mother sighed, touching his peaked fur cap as if to ruffle dark hair, and I could not help but smile.

Lady Hajithe herself brought a great golden cup starred with clear fiery gems instead of the wooden welcome-goblet carved with antlered creatures, offering its contents first to Aeredh. *"Travel in safety,"* she said in the Old Tongue. *"If there is need, our House will answer. As ever."*

"As ever, and in return," the Elder replied solemnly, and drank deep.

I thought she would offer it to Eol next, but instead she paced to me, her great blue mantle bearing black fur at the hood and her indigo leather house-boots tooled with flowing designs. "You do your mother proud, young Solveig. I would call thee daughter also, and whatever aid this House of the Faithful may offer is yours for the asking."

Mighty promise or merely a traditional leave-taking, I could not tell. "You do me great honor, Lady Hajithe of the Eastronmost Steading. I shall do a daughter's duty, and dream of thee." The cup contained more mead, but this time the herbs in it were sweetish, and my tongue untangled them all. For health, for strength, for warmth—it was a good cup, and she offered it to Arn next.

"Fare thee well, shieldmaid. May your spear ever find its target."

"Farewell, Lady of the Eastronmost." My shieldmaid gave her the salute those taken by the Wingéd Ones pay to women they respect, a touch of left-hand fingertips to heart and forehead while her spear dipped slightly; then she drank. "May the Wingéd Ones protect thee."

Lady Hajithe offered to the wolf-stamped Northerners as well, but without comment. I ached to discern the cause of this among all my other questions, but we were soon a-saddle and leaving the Eastronmost upon a lane of much shallower snow between two of those curious full-bellied statues, passing through winter-blanketed meadow and broad fields into dark forest.

Singularly Incapable

For was not Erlitha the first sworn shieldmaid, given to the valkyrja from birth? Always do the Black-Wingéd Ones watch, and when a girl is born who bears their mark, many are the tests to prove her worthy. Strong is a shieldmaid's arm, quick is her temper, and sure her judgment; while she observes the spirits of Odynn himself bear witness through her eyes.

—*The Saga of Erlitha One-Eye*, attributed to Graendl

Aeredh led our group once more, and found a semiwinding way dipping between drifts. Occasionally a carven runestone rose to our right or left, and I thought it likely this was an ancient road of some fallen Northern kingdom. Our passage was easy even as we wended up tree-cloaked hills and into wide dales; we passed a few frozen streams, one with a trickle of moving clarity at its heart even in new winter. Eventually the ground firmed under its white carapace, but not in the manner of hard-frozen dirt.

There was stone lingering under the snow. Even if I could not sense it from the change in hoof-fall, the horses knew and their knowledge filtered into my own head. They stepped lightly indeed; I watched carefully, attempting to untangle the weirding that kept their hooves from sinking. Farsight was in fine mettle, tail flicking and her ears pricked no less than mine.

For the Northerners were no longer so silent.

Eol rode with Aeredh for some while, in deep conversation I could not quite hear even with *volva*-sharp ears. Soren with the heavy brows and the one named Karas with the leather-wrapped braid engaged in a lively war of riddles, using the Old Tongue.

I learned much by listening to their good-natured flyting, though Arn looked a bit sour at being left out. She did so love couplets, and any sort of combat appealed to her.

Blue-eyed Gelad rode to my left, gazing at the forest with a worried air between short glances in my direction. Scarred Efain rode a little apart, his head down, apparently sunk in profound thought. He and Elak—whose hair held ruddy highlights instead of the bluish sheen more common among his fellows—exchanged a few comments in the Old Tongue at intervals; they shared the hindmost duty and whoever was not behind our group rode slightly to Arn's right, trailing her as a guard yet not overly close.

They respected her temper, as any man should.

I was busy thinking about hoof-*seidhr* and trying to guess the answer to one of Soren's riddles—the latter purely for my own satisfaction—when Gelad cleared his throat and essayed some conversation. "We may be slightly merrier now, my lady Solveig, since we are not in the fog of the Hidden Ways. 'Tis a relief?" His voice rose uncertainly at the end, lingering in sparkling, pine-scented air.

"I am gladdened." Perhaps the fellow could be induced to shed some light upon a matter or two; I hurriedly marshaled my wits as Farsight's ears flicked again. "Do all Northerners learn the southron language, then?"

"It is the grandchild of the Old Tongue. Still, even in the North only the Faithful keep to the Elder's speech." Gelad cast another half-worried, half-gauging look at me, then toward the head of our small column. "Our lord Tharos requires it of all his people, as did his fathers before him. So does Lady Hajithe."

Tharos. Now I might ask in detail of the parentage and House of my captor, since one of his men had freely mentioned them. "So your leader is Lord Tharos's son?"

"Yes." He shifted uneasily in his saddle; his pale mount did not crowd Farsight but would have liked to. "Eldest, though not favored. It was his younger brother Arvil who…"

Who Bjorn smote, and killed. And was he some manner of traitor? All the same, I could only imagine how coldly polite I would be to a weregild were Bjorn or Astrid in a ship sent upon fire's back to the Allmother, or laid in forgiving earth. "I see." I settled my mantle's hood more firmly with one gloved hand, not quite glad to be a-horse again but heartened to finally be allowed some answers. "You must pardon me, my lord Gelad, if I ask something…improper. I do not mean to give offense."

My manners earned a blue sideways glance, and Gelad coughed slightly. "Of a certainty." A silver cloak-pin glittered upon his breast, simple work but well-made and of true metal besides, with a cold sheen. "We have been amazed by your quiet."

As if I have had any choice. "I am weregild; my reticence must befit my status. Though Arn can tell you I have never been chatter-some." I knew my shieldmaid was listening closely. For a moment, a swimming sense of unreality filled me—I was in a forest far from home, with an Elder and a collection of skin-changers. Would any at Dun Rithell believe this tale? I attempted to sort through every question I had, arranging them in order of most likely to be answered within the constraints of custom. "We are wending north and some little west, I see. Where shall we rest?"

"Tonight? In the forest, and for some days yet. We shall reach Nithraen soon enough though, should we make good time." Gelad shifted in his saddle again, as if I had asked something impolite despite my attempt at a safe subject. His mount snorted, a warm white plume upon frosty air. "'Tis an ancient place, and well-guarded. They are kin to our lord Aeredh there, and will welcome us warmly."

More Elder. I could not deny excitement at the thought. I was about to ask further, but Eol reined his mount and moved into Gelad's position, which meant the other man forged ahead to trail Aeredh. The maneuver was accomplished without a word and with the ease of long habit, much as Arneior and I might change places in a crowded hall if tempers became touchy and two warriors likely to trade blows.

Perhaps the captain did not wish to hear the voice of one whose kin had killed his? I did not know how strict his people were upon the subject of a weregild's behavior, either. My fingers tightened on the reins, though Farsight was relaxed enough, ambling along as if we rode upon summer sward instead of fresh snow that should have swallowed her to the hocks.

"I must apologize again," the leader of the wolf-stamped men said, without preamble. "We sought safety in speed and secrecy returning northward with such precious cargo, as well as a shortening of the journey. Aeredh judged the Elder Roads the lesser danger, and so did I."

"We are upon a very old road now, unless I miss my guess." I could not decide upon the proper tone, or address. How did one speak to this manner of man? Bjorn's blow must have been mighty indeed. In all the tales, those granted a second form possessed both extraordinary speed and strength, and were held well-nigh unkillable by usual means. "Is the danger lesser or greater here?"

"Both. Soon we will be in lands held by Aeredh's kin. They are skilled in hunting the servants of the Enemy, and yet those take many forms." His dark gaze rested upon the side of my hood. I could outright feel it; did all his kind possess some manner of *seidhr*? I did not know enough, for Idra had held tales of skin-changers to be largely poetic description despite some travelers—even one or two from the Barrowhills—swearing they had witnessed their truth. "You should not worry, though. We shall see you safe."

I do not even know where I am bound. I wished I could tell Idra these men were not merely poetry. Perhaps she was watching from the halls Hel reserves for those with *seidhr* after the physical body is shed; the thought was a comfort indeed. "We are bound to your father's house, then? Lord Tharos?"

It was not an unreasonable question, though if he took umbrage at being asked my alternatives seemed slim indeed.

"What? No." Did he sound shocked? It was difficult to tell; still, I thought a little astonishment colored his tone. "You mean you do not even know where we are..."

"I am weregild. 'Tis not my place to ask, merely to do as I am bid."

I recited it singsong, to show I knew what was expected of a lord's daughter. Perhaps he thought southron riverfolk savage, or untrained in proper behavior. "Besides, I had no time for gossip before leaving Dun Rithell, my lord Eol. I was busy with a *volva*'s duties during the Althing, too. It was my first time lighting the bonfire."

He was silent for a few breaths before granting me the honor of conversation again. "I had not thought you so young."

"I am old enough for every band I wear, my lord." Perhaps I was nettled; I had enough summers and practice to judge legal cases and to call fire from open air, after all. Astrid might be a child still, and Bjorn like most men a child all his life, but I was *volva*. I decided to hazard a bit more, since he seemed disposed to speak. "Whither are we bound then, and who is your enemy? Some new warlord in the North, raiding holds and steadings?" It was not a bad guess.

Certainly rumors of raids and unrest reached Dun Rithell, and the filthy blackrobes of the Falling Shelf past the barrow-country—always barking of their necromantic god—occasionally visited on their way upriver to visit other steadings. We did not cherish those particular visitors, and though we did all hospitality demanded my mother did not allow them to stay. It was not so much their god, though he sounded blasphemous enough to give any right-thinking person pause, but their physical filth and deplorable manners.

I wondered if these men had ever met one of their ilk.

"He is not *new*, my lady, though there is ever war enough and to spare in the North." Eol's laugh was short, sharp, and unamused. His mount arched his neck, and Farsight shook her head in reply, her mane tossing. "I wonder that your people have not heard, but at least we may be grateful our labors have made such a thing possible." He would have been hard-pressed to sound more bitter.

I pushed my hood slightly back with my right hand, glancing at Arn. Her eyebrows had raised, and she was a breath away from making a sharp observation or two. At my look she subsided, and I gathered myself for a parley beginning to feel more like a battle itself.

At least, so I thought then. I had not yet been upon a murderous field, hearing only the songs of such things; even my father had not been in battle since I was a babe still in swaddling. Not many dared his ire after the accounting he had given of himself against the last petty warlord to trouble our lands. Some few raids by desperate bandit-bands, certainly, but none of our neighbors cherished any hope of expansion while Eril the Battle-Mad and his followers could lay hand to axe.

"We hear nothing of the North in Dun Rithell." I hoped he would not take ignorance as an insult. The mornlight dimmed slightly, an edge of cloud touching the sun; I tasted yet more snow upon the frozen air, but not for some hours. I longed to ask why they had not taken Bjorn instead, for he would be far more suited to their company and furthermore oblivious to any weirding. "Truly we are occupied enough with our own affairs, and the Pale God's robed fanatics to the south. Last spring one came upriver and raved great blasphemy. He even offered violence to my teacher." I shuddered at the memory; not only had he attempted to attack Idra, but the robed man refused the healthful heat of the sauna and stank, always muttering about the corpse of his god tied to a dead tree—not like Fryja's husband Odynn or her son Tohr hanging from the great world-spindle in search of wisdom, but to expiate some horrific act.

Why worship anything so vile? It made no sense at all. The North's many saga-drenched mysteries, though baffling, could at least be *solved*. Or at least, so it seemed to me then.

"Pale God?" Eol's attention sharpened. "We have heard some fell rumors of that. Perhaps it is some gambit of the Enemy's."

"This enemy you speak of. You do not name him?" I shivered, though the cold was not nearly as intense as in the fog of their Elder Roads. Altogether I was more sanguine here, especially since there seemed little chance of another twisted sheep-creature happening along.

And so long as a man speaks, more may be gained than from his mere words. Tone, inflection, and expression all add to the tale—as well as what is *not* said. I was growing more hopeful I could at least reach some cold courtesy with Eol of Naras.

Not friendship, certainly. He did not seem the sort.

"Not anywhere his spies may hear." Eol grew yet graver, were that possible. He was not a cheersome fellow in the least; not even old Flokin was this dour. "Has the South forgotten everything? It was not so long ago the Black Land's iron gates were sieged; even less are the years between us and the Dag Saekirrin. Or at least, it is not so long as the Faithful count it, much less as the Elder do."

My pulse mounted in my throat, and threatened to fill my ears with rushing. "The Black Land's malice is spent," I said, as every deliciously frightening childhood tale had repeated at beginning, middle, and end. Farsight's tail flicked; she was now aware of my tension, and did not like it. "It was broken in the Battle of Falling Ice. Naught remains in that country but ruins, and the Elder are all gone into the West."

Yet even as I said it an Elder rode at the head of our cortege, his ear-tips poking through dark silken hair. He had not worn whatever *seidhr* kept his difference from striking an observer since Dun Rithell.

Or perhaps we simply had not seen it because we did not wish to, for who would credit such things while safe at home? Idra always said willful blindness is a deep darkness indeed; it hides much more than weirding could ever hope to.

"I am gladdened to hear as much," Eol answered, his tone oddly soft. Almost thoughtful, or more precisely, as if he had summat caught in his throat. "Someone should tell the *orukhar*, and the *trul* as well; it would make our lives much easier." Then he inhaled sharply, shifting in his saddle with a creak of leather. "Forgive my ill temper, my lady Solveig. It does comfort my heart to know there are places the Shadow does not touch."

I could stand it no longer, and pushed my hood fully back. Winter sunlight struck my braids, and my cheeks stung—perhaps with the cold, though I felt almost as if I had been slapped. Farsight's ears flicked again, as if she found this discussion interesting; Arn's were probably no less active.

It was all very well to tease one in my position—a weregild is not fully free, after all—yet it was not meet to do so in this particular fashion. "To speak of the Black Land thus is an ill jest, my lord Eol." Each word edged itself with brittle formality; it occurred to me I sounded like my mother. "I may be young, but I am not stupid. You wish to taunt your debtor, well and good. But 'tis a foul deed, and beneath one of a noble House."

I was not Astrid, to be frightened witless by dark stories. Oh, yes, there was an Elder, and skin-changers surrounding my shieldmaid and me, riding white horses who did not sink in snow. That much I could credit, especially seeing them with my own blessed eyes. But the Black Land? The *Enemy*, that shadowy thing, that first brother of Fryja and Vardhra, Odynn and Manhrweh, Nyssa and Mother Hel, Vollspa and Geledrail? The eldest son of the Allmother who committed acts so foul even *seidhr* does not speak of them, so awful even the robed fanatics of the Pale God are judged far, *far* less corrupt? The one who marred every peace, broke every treaty, the one even traitors and thieves would not swear by?

It was beyond belief, and no jesting matter.

"Noble?" Eol's laugh again held no merriment, and rang beneath snow-hung trees. The forest murmured, slim saplings shaking slightly and their progenitors loosing tiny spatters of bright white across our path. "Naras was ruined upon the Day of Dust, and its ruler the lord of nothing but beasts. I do not jest, my lady Question. Even my men might well think me singularly incapable of doing so." He regarded me steadily, his eyes, though dark, almost as bright as Aeredh's. "Your silence so far has been forbearance, well and good. But so has mine, and I will seek no pardon for what great evil had driven us to in order to combat its spread."

He touched his mount's sides with his heels. The white horse danced lightly over the snow; the son of Tharos did not take his place in the guard pattern but forged ahead of even the Elder. I glared after him, my jaw suspiciously loose.

"Solveig?" Arneior, tentative as she hardly ever was, urged her horse closer. "Did he say what I think he said?"

"He said much indeed, my Arn," I replied, numbly. My head began to ache, and the cold all through me was not merely that of a winter journey. "But I cannot believe…"

"If they jest at the expense of their weregild, it shows them poorly." A high flush stood on my shieldmaid's freckled cheeks. On her other side, Elak let his horse fall back, and though we rode amid the Northerners they now gave us as much space as possible. "It is an insult, Sol."

Was this some manner of gibe, or were they testing our behavior? They could no doubt hear every word we passed, though they might look studiously elsewhere.

"Yet not one we may take issue with." *At least, not at the moment.* I sought for an imitation of Idra's tone when she deemed certain behavior too foolish to even warrant a scolding. "Perhaps they must try the temper of every new travel companion with a tale or two fit to frighten children. It is no different than Flokin and his fellows every harvest-festival, making the littles scream."

Arn said no more, but her ire was plainly visible. She glared at each Northerner who approached, and they wisely did not seek converse. As the sun mounted and the forest breathed around us, my shieldmaid and I fell into telling riddles as we often do, working our way through the easiest ones first and falling silent when any of the men drew near or passed upon their white steeds, changing the guard-pattern.

But neither of us made a good showing, for our hearts were not in it. Each time I thought Eol's words could not possibly be true, I would catch sight of Aeredh, riding supple and graceful, the tips of his ears high-proud. And *seidhr* whispered inside me, just as if I were called to adjudicate a dispute between freeholds.

Truth has its own ring, and the Northern captain's words were brimful of its chiming.

Different Sparring

A quick eye and a quick hand,
A sharp glance and a covered heart,
A mystery in plain sight,
Such is the weirding way.
        —A Riverfolk counting-song

Aeredh led us a short distance from the ancient road as winter twilight swallowed snowy forest and iron-colored sky both, but there was yet more stone underfoot. A series of evenly spaced hummocks ringed what would, in summer, be a thicket-hidden dell—more runestones, but their thrum was not that of the Eastronmost's collection. Still, I heard the resonance in the space between my ear and jaw, whining like a marsh-mosquito in summer.

Seidhr lived in those stones, slowly weakening as the carvings were not fed. The snow was not so deep here, and in short order the Northerners had made camp upon a paved waystop. There was even a depression near the middle for a small fire, though somehow it was not blackened by heat and soot. Perhaps no blaze had been lit there for a very long time, since once powdery white was brushed free, the flat, cunningly joined rock underneath was cracked and worn in some places. For all that, it was shelter, and a screen of vegetation hid the road we had been following all day.

Perhaps I was acclimating to horse-motion. Still, I could barely bite back a groan as I landed with a jolt Arn could not quite cushion. She was pale, her woad-stripe glaring.

"What is this?" she murmured. For a moment we were left to our own devices, huddled between Farsight and her own mount. "They cannot expect you to sleep outside in this weather."

" 'Tis only the cold," I whispered back. "I am more worried about why we are still wending north. If they…"

But Gelad approached with a half-bow to lead our horses away, and the Northerners moved with swift purpose—clearing the snow, vanishing in pairs to fetch deadwood, building a fire they did not ask me to light, cutting green boughs to arrange as a tidy, interlocking pile in the most sheltered spot. This, I gathered, was to be Arn's and my sleeping-place, for my trunk had appeared in the short while it took us to dismount.

Perhaps they were hiding that bit of weirding from me. We were left with naught to do, but somehow one man or another was always well within earshot. Arn occupied herself with stretching, bending, and stamping the stiffness of horse-rhythm from her limbs, and if her spear twitched whenever one of them drew too close, at least the warning was respected.

Aeredh went from one horse to the next, and I watched carefully as he smoothed their faces, his lips moving slightly as if with dream-murmurs, or sounding out a rune's name. I saw no quiver of *seidhr* even when he drew his hands down each of their limbs in turn, but snow and ice fell away under his touch and the beasts did not flinch even when he crouched at their hind legs.

Arn gave me a sharp glance when I stepped away, but she knew the look I wore. I drifted closer to the Elder, hardly feeling the cold. For a few moments I became merely an eager eye and willing ear, straining to catch whatever skill I could.

He paused near Eol's proud-necked mount, glancing in my direction—I hurriedly looked away, ready for him to take offense.

" 'Tis nothing ill, my lady." The Elder spoke quietly, as if I were another creature to be soothed. Or perhaps his tone could be described as tentative; I could not decide. "Merely something natural, to aid and comfort the horses. I think your people call such things *seidhr* now?"

"I know how to calm a pony." *Little different than a sheep, though goats are slightly harder.* I could not ask directly, but I could certainly compliment. "I was admiring the care you take with their hocks."

"Would you like to learn?" A slight smile, a beckoning motion.

The Northerners paid no attention. I looked to Arn, whose coppery eyebrows rose. Of course I wanted to learn, what did this fellow think *volva* meant?

I brushed at my mantle-sleeve, working a small piece of solidified snow free. "What is the price?"

"Slight indeed, it takes nothing from me or the horse. Come, I shall show you."

I hesitated. Perhaps he did not understand, or he wished to show a pittance before asking payment for the bulk of the knowledge? Idra had warned me about such transactions more than once; curiosity may lead even a wisewoman to pay more than she should. Barter is not merely for ale and skins, as the saying goes. "I have little to trade for the knowledge, my lord."

"Trade for…" He cocked his dark head, momentary puzzlement wrinkling a smooth brow. It made him appear a little older—but only a little. "I would not take payment for the teaching, if that is what you ask. My people prefer to share what we can."

My people, he said? "Elder." I did not mean to make the word a challenge. But I ached from riding, we were far from home, and though I wished for these men to underestimate me I did not like the idea of being considered wholly stupid. "You do not mask what you are, here."

"There is no need when among friends," Aeredh agreed, cheerfully. Eol's horse lowered his head over the not-youth's shoulder, letting out a companionable sigh. "In the South, things are sometimes otherwise. Do you fear my kind?"

How was I meant to answer such a question? "Until a few days ago I would have said the Elder had all vanished, gone to the uttermost West." My chin lifted slightly, and Idra would have sighed at the motion, sensing some manner of mutiny almost before I knew my own mind. "So we are taught, and told as well that the Black Land's malice is spent, a myth to frighten children with."

Oh, a weregild must be decorous. But he had begun this conversation, and my brother had not felled *his* kin. I was still being polite, as such things went.

Barely, but enough.

Arn turned away, her back to me as she finished shaking her stiffness away. She had sparred with him once; now was my chance.

"There were some among us who thought the same a few mortal lifetimes ago." Aeredh's hand rose, stroking the horse's cheek much as my mother might an inquisitive hound's. "I am real enough, as you see. It…gladdens me, that there are places the Shadow does not touch."

Eol had uttered the same words, but not so wistfully. It was not quite an answer. Politeness forbade me from observing as much, so I held my tongue—and was soon glad of it, for Aeredh continued.

"We are on an errand of great secrecy, and speed is essential. Our former companions continue south to gather what allies they may, but our path is otherwise. The Hidden Ways were a risk, for any word uttered there may ring in an unfriendly ear indeed. Even here there are spies and other dangers, so we travel with much care between strongholds." He smiled, and it was strange to see such a being look…uncertain? "In any case, it ill becomes me to ask any price for the teaching of a precious guest. If you care to learn, daughter of Gwendelint, I shall show you what I may."

Was *precious guest* their term for weregild? I could find nothing unmannerly in his words, nor in his expression. An Elder, offering to teach me *seidhr*—it boggled the mind, and anything seeming so good must be examined from every angle to make certain there is no hidden hook within.

"I am a slow student." I had never sounded so tentative with Idra, but then again, my parents paid her well for tutelage, and 'tis an honor to teach another, as the proverbs say. "But a weregild must be useful. I would like to help the horses, my lord Aeredh, and I thank you for the offer."

With that, 'twas done, and there was no space nor lee for him to demand payment afterward. So it was I learned how to pass my hand down a creature's limb, pushing away ice and weariness, as well as a very subtle, simple *seidhr* for speaking to horses as the Elder do. Once I saw the method I wondered that it had never occurred to me before, and wished Idra was still alive so I could share it with her. Arn shook her head at my disbelieving grin, watching me stroke between Farsight's great brown eyes, half-closed with enjoyment, and Aeredh commented, very prettily, that I learned quickly.

For all that, I did not see how the Northerners produced the fodder, nor did they speak further of the Black Land. And they were never out of easy earshot, even when Arn and I retreated to the surprisingly deep pile of sap-fragrant boughs, the Northerners' bedrolls draped over it to provide cushion and insulation. Even with our mantles and under every horse-blanket it was still a cold bed, and I managed only a fitful doze, waking at intervals to use deep circular warming breaths.

Each time I did Arn was solidly asleep, a shieldmaid's hardiness far greater than mine; Aeredh was near the fire, feeding its bluish glitter and humming softly as an occasional howl lifted to the cold, overcast sky.

And the wolves of Naras were nowhere in sight.

⬧⬧⬧⬧⬧

There was no sparring-yard, but my shieldmaid was making do. Since she had already tested Aeredh, naturally she would turn to the others for some practice, and Efain had the honor the next morning.

Their feet sank in soft snow outside the bounds of the stone-floored wayrest, but there are ways to fight even while mired, and my Arneior knows them all. She slipped aside as Efain lunged, his sword glittering even in the dull grey of an overcast morn, and a great spray of snow rose as she skidded to a halt, fending him off with such speed her spear seemed to bend like a willow branch. It was an illusion, the eye not quick enough to track its quarry, but still marvelous to see.

My braids were only slightly loosened, but the warming breath was not helping as much as it could. I shivered even with my gloved hands wrapped about a heavy mug of warmed ale. It is the best thing upon a winter morn, and all our skins had been refilled by distillations of Lady Hajithe's making, with a distinctive tang to its afterbreath. Still, I had to hold my nose to drink the last half of the cup's cargo, and could not help but grimace.

"My lady?" Soren's heavy eyebrows raised; he hovered at a polite distance, leaning anxiously over his boot-toes. His handling of our language was heavily accented, to match his stocky frame. "Is it too warm, or not hot enough?"

I shook my head, exhaling sharply and lowering the mug as a fast light chiming echoed from the combatants. It was more like dance than a fight, though I had only ever seen feast-brawls and the occasional ill-tempered bout sparked by some insult or another between touchy warriors. Their blades barely touched before springing apart, and while Arneior wore only a look of fierce concentration, Efain's scars were flushed and he scowled in reply, though perhaps he was simply surprised at her skill.

" 'Tis very good." I enunciated clearly, wishing they would speak more in the Old Tongue. Still, with Aeredh willing to teach me Elder *seidhr*—however small—and Arneior learning how our captors liked to fight, we were doing quite well. "I have never been overfond of ale…Soren, is it?"

"Aye." He bobbed, not quite a bow but certainly more than a nod. He looked a little like Flokin's nephew Wulfgir, who blushed if anything female even breathed in his direction. "An honor to be named."

"Though I am not complaining," I hastened to add. "A weregild accepts what is given."

"Ah." He nodded, scratching behind his right ear with blunt fingers. The wolf-sigil stamped upon his shoulder snarled, teeth clearly visible, and I wondered I had not seen the similarity before. The men of Naras moved swiftly, with economical grace unlike Aeredh's, and after a few nights in the open each man's hair was somewhat tousled. "Is that what they say in the South? We do not often exchange hostages anymore."

Hostage was an old word, especially the way he pronounced it. I could hear the Old Tongue lingering behind its sibilant. "I thought the North kept to the old ways."

"The Faithful do." He shrugged while his gaze wandered past me, clearly distracted by the display. Efain was giving ground, fending off Arn's jabs with efficiency if not ease. "Is there summat else you prefer, Lady Solveig? We merely have travel-food, but we can hunt."

No doubt you can. The tart reply burned upon my tongue, but I could not give it freedom. "I am well enough, and thank you for your pains. Are we traveling far today?"

"As far as we can. Nithraen's close, but riding instead of running…" Another shrug, but he hunched his shoulders halfway as if fearing to speak too much—for his captain drew close, and Eol of Naras looked, as usual, coldly furious.

"Winter does not forgive incaution." Eol's southron was less accented, though still tinted heavily with the North. "The morning grows no younger, Soren. Saddle their horses."

I might have essayed some polite remark in return, but Arn's voice rose triumphantly, a curlew-cry barely muffled by the snow all round. There was a meaty sound, and Efain skidded backward, hunched halfway over as if he suffered the spine-curve. She had struck him soundly with her spear-butt, and he finished on one knee, glaring at her through a tangle of dark hair, his sword point-down and every line of him vibrating. His eyes glowed like hot coals, and a ripple passed through his skin.

"*Fool,*" Eol muttered in the Old Tongue. "*We have no time for play.*" Then his voice lifted, a harsh bark. "Efain!"

For a few moments they froze, shieldmaid and black-clad Northerner eyeing each other. Arn's ruddy head cocked, a flush of exertion on her cheeks, and her breath plumed silver in the morning chill. Her armor glittered, since she had laid her overmantle aside for this practice bout, and her spear did not quiver. Its readiness was perfectly leashed, and the featherbrush sensation of the Wingéd attention swirled about her.

Efain was perfectly still as well, but as a granary cat will freeze when it sees an oblivious mouse or a well-trained hound just before loosed to chase down prey. Another observer might well consider him a gifted warrior, one Odynn has blessed with the thoughtless grace of battle-madness or the quickfoot.

Like Aeredh, these men were now not masking what they were.

Eol tensed, and oddly, he took two swift steps—toward the impromptu sparring-ground, and one to the side, looming before me as if to block the sight. "Efain." It was not a cry, precisely, but the name carried a snap like a leather belt cracked against itself.

The scarred Northerner rose. The rippling was gone, and he was no more than an ordinary man now, albeit with a warrior's mien. "My thanks for the practice," he said, hoarsely. "You are quick indeed, shieldmaid."

Arn did not relax, but half her mouth tilted up into a smile. "Next time you will not hold back, then."

"Enough." Eol stalked to the edge of the wayrest, and I could not see his expression. Still, Efain shook snow from his shoulders and dropped his gaze. *Break camp, and stop playing about.* The command fled his tongue when he turned slightly in Arn's direction, though. "If you have had your fill, my lady shieldmaid, would it please you to attend your mistress? We must be swift today; I like not how the wind smells."

"Sol is not my mistress." Arn did not look away from her opponent until he left the invisible confines of the sparring-ground, then she turned her gaze upon the captain. "She is my *charge*, Northerner; a shieldmaid does not serve. Gwendelint's daughter is your weregild for year-and-a-day, but I am not."

"Then I crave your pardon, Arneior of Dun Rithell." Coldly polite, each word edged as ice upon the wind, our captor also gave a courteous half-bow. "My knowledge of southron ways is imperfect at best. The next time you wish to vent your anger, you may do so upon me instead of my men."

Oh, fishguts. " 'Tis not anger but friendly play," I said, hurriedly. "To be a shieldmaid's sparring-partner is a great honor among us, Lord Eol. Please forgive our trespass."

"Trespass?" He turned on his heel, and if I thought the sigil upon Soren's shoulder was a-snarl, the one upon Eol's looked for a moment as if it cried out in pain. The impression vanished in an instant; it became merely stamped leather and dye again, the elder son of Naras likewise merely a man with a proud nose, dark eyes, and a thin, drawn-tight mouth. "Hardly. We simply cannot risk a wound at the moment, my lady. It will cost us time, and we must reach Nithraen with all speed. We wait upon your readiness."

With that he brushed past me, and the camp was now a hive of activity for all it only contained a half-dozen men. I was left dangling an empty mug from numb fingers, wincing inwardly.

Arneior shrugged into her mantle and we made haste to comply. I could not blame her, for she had done nothing wrong.

Still, it boded ill.

Quick and Delicate

The lord of the Black Land cannot spark life; that is solely the Allmother's gift. Yet he may twist what he finds with little trouble, and seems to delight in misshapen things. Even his mightiest lieutenants bear some mark of foul seidhr, like Olvrang's obsidian tooth and Gortaum's hoof. This is why you must be careful, children, when you meet a stranger upon the heath or the road.
—The Saga of Tarit of Caelim

Deep soft snow-pregnant cloud closed a lid over the forest two days later; there were no more riddles among the Northerners but stony silence except for when travel made a word absolutely necessary. Arn and I traded a few couplets for form's sake when the silence grew oppressive.

At each halt I attended to the horses with Aeredh, and there was usually another small piece of *seidhr* granted while we worked. He was a kind teacher, never tweaking my braids or making a sharp spitting sound of annoyance as Idra did, but I longed to learn something larger and could not shake the sense that the Elder was testing me in some oblique fashion, or simply giving me child-baubles to play with.

I was never warm, even with all the heated ale they gave me and a scant daily mouthful of *sitheviel* from the black flask. At least the pain in my feet meant they were not frozen through. My head grew light and empty with lack of proper sleep, yet I clung to the saddle grimly, determined not to give the captain any reason to complain of his weregild's obedience.

Thankfully I had my Arn, and we gave each other many a troubled glance between our riddle-play. Most meant nothing more than *I am with you, at least*; nevertheless, they were still a comfort. I had difficulty imagining how Bjorn or Astrid might handle this turn of affairs. I could not even imagine Mother or Idra accepting proof of the Elder lingering in the North or of the Black Land's resurgence calmly, though Idra would not have been completely surprised at any dire prognostication. Whenever ill news came, she merely shrugged as if to say, *So the world is, why expect otherwise?*

My teacher found less joy in living the longer she endured it. Some are cheerful all their lives, but Idra's temper was otherwise. She might have seen what Aeredh was immediately, though, and perhaps stung me with a switch-strike when I overlooked it.

So much talent, and yet so lazy. Come now, daughter of Gwendelint. Look, and see more deeply.

We halted past nooning, and if the Northerners had guarded us before, they hemmed us closely as our own breathing now, giving each other bleak glances. I shivered as the wind rose, spatters of snow falling from gently moving branches, and Arneior stood at my shoulder while the business of the midday stop was attended to.

"Do you hear that?" she whispered.

I did indeed, though I did not know quite what it presaged. A jagged snarl rode the sharpening breeze, faint as the song of runestones and felt in a slightly different place. My eyes half-closed, my ears tingling through their numbness.

"It sounds…wrong," I whispered back, and deeper shiver slipped down my back. I patted the lump of my *seidhr*-bag, though I had not call to use anything in it yet.

I had not even time to look for winter herbs, or bark that might be useful.

Aeredh approached us as the Northerners tended the horses in the way those without Elder aid could. "You sense summat amiss," he said quietly, and the set of his shoulders told me he was far more worried about Arneior's reaction than mine.

"We are being followed." My shieldmaid did not utter it as a challenge; she stared at the forest, as if daring it to birth some danger. "Is it more of those sheep-monsters?"

"No." The Elder's cheeks bore no blush of cold and his hands were bare, lacking even the half-gloves the other Northerners wore. "Those cannot leave the Hidden Ways without great effort, and then they are easily dispatched. Especially by men of Eol's kind."

I wondered if he thought us unaware of those possessing two skins in the south. "That is a comfort, at least."

"Is it?" Aeredh looked in the same direction Arn did, and his look of listening was akin to hers as well. "There should not be such activity here, especially at this time. We have done ill, Lady Solveig, yet with the best of intent."

Arn had no sharp word, which was a wonder in and of itself. She merely leaned upon her spear. Her generous mouth was set with disdain, her dark eyes narrowed, and against her fair freckled face the blue woad-stripe stood out sharply.

She had not even drained the skin of mead gifted us at departure from Lady Hajithe's, a sure sign of unease. And she left the greater share of ale for me; I needed every drop, my body consuming its deeper stores to fuel the warming breath.

"Perhaps not so ill," I granted, not very grudgingly. After all, the sheep-things were dead, Arn and our captors had found me upon the mountainslope, I was learning *seidhr* and witnessing wonders. Besides, even if their leader disliked me for what Bjorn had done to his brother, I could not protest overmuch. Such is the fate of a weregild. "Though if 'tis war the North is facing, my brother would have been better for your purposes."

"Would he?" One shoulder lifted, dropped; the Elder was almost feline in that moment, wintersky eyes lambent in peculiar snowlight. "I ask you to pardon Eol. His temper is somewhat harsh, but he seeks not to offend. We rode south to find what aid we could in the houses of the South, for the fires of Agramar are renewed. Our journey has been marked with much misfortune; indeed, you represent our only luck, yet we were attacked upon the Hidden Road and nearly lost what we had found. And now this. We are balked at every turn, and grow passing desperate."

Indeed he was fair-spoken, and this was the most conversation I had been granted for two days. Yet my stomach was a knot at that word—*Agramar*. It was a term of ancient nightmares, and I did not like how the light about us dimmed when the Elder pronounced it. The ill shade was short-lived, certainly, but I did not even shiver.

I was too cold to twitch, and that was a bad sign.

These men had been closeted with the elders of Dun Rithell, making some manner of appeal. Was alliance, and a quota of warriors sent North, the sum of their pleading? But then, why would they ask for me instead of a youth gifted with battle-madness who could fell one of their kind with a single ham-fisted blow?

And now I thought I had not mistranslated that word, *traitor*. Some crucial piece of the design was missing, and thread I could have knotted into a pleasing tapestry pattern was all asnarl.

My numb hands, gloved and tucked safely inside mantle-sleeves, clutched at each other. "I am sorry your journey has been so ill-starred," I answered, cautiously. "My father's father, and his grandfathers as well, held it true that the Black Land is merely spent ruins. And in the South we think the Children of the Star either all departed or lingering only to leave in secret when it pleases them." I did not add that clearly his kind wished it that way, if they hid themselves with *seidhr*-seeming while traveling.

"Ill-starred? Hardly." Strangely, the Elder seemed pleased; his smile turned warm though absent, yet it soon faded. His cloak-pin gleamed, a silver wolf's head beautifully shaped with green-gem eyes, though it did not look of Elder make. "Yet it is true, my lady. We bought partial victory—or at least, a lesser defeat—over the Enemy at the Dag Saekirrin, and with the aid of those of your kind we call Faithful. After that even some among us thought the Black Land defeated, though the wise held we had achieved a mere breathing space."

"But…" I did not now think he would taunt a weregild; I was forced to consider him earnest. Why was he speaking upon this now?

"You asked the elders of Dun Rithell for warriors to ride north." I was careful not to let the end of the sentence lift as a question, though it was merely a guess.

And my patience was answered at last, for Aeredh spoke softly, in almost the same tone he used for conferences with Eol.

"We did, though they were not inclined to answer quickly, if at all. It is sad, for once your Dun Rithell was named Aen Haergar and many of your ancestors rode north to our banners long ago—including Hralimar the lord of that place." The Elder's gaze dropped to the ground, and the words turned quieter still. The sawing whine upon the wind grew no stronger, but it did not fade either. "None survived the Battle of Great Fires, and fair fields before the Cold Gate became the Gasping upon an eve of lamentation. The lands of Naras, among others, were lost in a single night of flame and hard battle."

Some have the trick of reciting sagas as if they had personally witnessed the deeds within. I could not decide if Aeredh was one of their number, or if his tone was that of memory itself. He was *Elder*; they do not age as we do. If no great grief or violence winnows them, they endure.

The Northerners were engaged in their own murmuring conference near the horses. I could not clearly discern the words, which may have been Aeredh's intent, and Arn did not know the Old Tongue. Something was decided and they broke apart, moving with purpose. Efain and Eol disappeared into the trees; Soren and Karas moved hurriedly about, finishing the last of the midday work. Gelad lingered near the horses, scanning the forest, and his left hand rested upon a daggerhilt.

My back prickled, though my voice was steady enough. "I know some little of that saga." I remembered tales of Hralimar, the son of Gwenlara from whom my own mother descended. After his fall and the loss of several warriors Dun Rithell had many a year of woe, though now we fared well enough. "Hralimar stood amid waves of the Enemy's thralls, and they broke upon him six times. Yet even he fell with many a wound at the seventh attack. There is a song." I had learned it to please Mother, and sang it in our hall one Midsummer.

Even Idra had judged that performance well done.

The Elder nodded gravely. "We sing some part of that battle as well, but not what happened after. It…" His throat worked for a moment, his gaze darkening. "It is a good thing, to know it is not forgotten."

Arn's shoulder touched mine, lightly. I leaned into that comfort.

"What…" I halted, for asking *what happened after* suddenly did not seem quite mannerly. I could not quite compass or absorb the rest of it—the Black Land renewed, the Enemy real instead of a myth to frighten misbehaving littles, the great twisted iron citadel of Agramar resounding with the screams of tortured prisoners…

I had to swallow hard, and row in another direction entirely. Fortunately, there was no shortage of questions, though I could not demand to know why on earth they had insisted upon *me* instead of Bjorn just yet. "I seem to do nothing but irritate my captor. What must I know to avoid giving offense, my lord Aeredh? My family owes Lord Eol a debt and I would have it fulfilled; 'twill be a long year-and-a-day indeed if I further insult him."

For not only had my brother slain his, but I had all but called him a liar to his face. Even one of my father's warriors might well take exception at that, and they had known me all my life. Besides, the man could hardly stand to speak to me, and each time he looked in my direction it was clear the sight pained him.

"Captor? My lady, you mistake him." Aeredh seemed somewhat shocked, even disregarding Arneior in that moment; his eyebrows rose and he shifted his weight uneasily, quelling the movement almost before it was born. "He carries a burden, and it makes him sparing with his words. Some hold the house of Naras as cursed, for the Shadow fell heavily upon their hall even before that battle."

Is that it? Relief burst upon me in a wave, almost better than a fire's heat. No wonder they wished to take a *volva* as weregild. "A curse, you say?" Perhaps that was the tale we were lost in, and I would be called upon to break some ancient malediction before returning home to forget such things as sheep-monsters, Elder wars, and Agramar.

I would not say the prospect of breaking ill-weirding delighted me, but it did not irk me either. Of such things is a *volva*'s fame made; it would be a proud deed, one even Idra might approve of. Not to mention accomplishing it could be held to cancel any weregild, and set me and my shieldmaid upon the road home.

"*I* do not say, my lady." Aeredh turned the question of ill *seidhr* aside very quickly indeed, but it is bad luck indeed to speak of such things and besides, we were now being pursued by something dire. "And that is not our purpose in bringing you hence. We have done you an ill turn, but we will reach Nithraen soon enough. And in any case Eol will take no insult from aught you choose to do."

"Even though..." If they did not wish me to break some kind of *seidhr*, what by Fryja *did* they want? Or was this an Elder test, to see if I had the skill to discern the form of the malison resting upon his friend? Was it a curse the Elder could not break, requiring a mortal to do so? Yet there was another consideration, and it leapt from my mouth despite all my caution. "If some ill has been done to me, why not return us to Dun Rithell and call the debt paid? Surely that is a little matter for one such as yourself. Or you may teach me the *seidhr* of your hidden roads; Arn and I will take ourselves home and trouble your friends no more."

Aeredh straightened, though paying little heed to Arn's concomitant tension. My shieldmaid's grip tightened upon her spear.

"No." His mien grew grave indeed, his mouth a thin line and his pale eyes alight. "We would rather lose ourselves than you, Lady Solveig. At Nithraen I may speak more freely, since the Enemy's ears do not reach inside that fastness. Until then I would ask you to simply accompany us with as much patience as you may."

The Northerners had finished their discussion. Efain the scarred drew close, his step almost as soft as the Elder's. "*It is indeed ill done,*" he muttered in the Old Tongue. "*The lady speaks fairly, Lord Aeredh. Surely you must see as much.*"

I longed to make a reply in their language. Instead I turned away from the Elder, leaning even harder into Arn's shoulder. "Easy, my shieldmaid." For I knew that look in her eye very well indeed.

"I like it not." Her brow was troubled, and she balanced lightly in her boots, her spear all but quivering with readiness. "They speak only of old nurse-tales when they deign to address us at all; even a weregild should not be treated so. And their weirding seems unhealthful. Perhaps we—"

"Aeredh!" The cry came from a few lengths outside our small group, and cloud-filtered sunlight grew sickly. It was Eol's voice, and I realized the horses had become restless, stamping in the snow. Farsight's ears laid back and she eyed me sidelong; a quiver of *seidhr* brushed inside my skull.

A four-footed cousin will remember you leading them out of danger and back to their fellows. Trust grows from such things, and besides, I had been upon her back for some while now.

Eol appeared between two trees, frozen white traces upon his shoulders as he moved with long swinging strides, breaking through soft, untrodden white with no more sound than falling flakes themselves. "A-saddle, and quickly," he barked.

Arneior lost no time pushing me toward Farsight. She all but tossed me into the saddle, and was upon her own stamping, snorting mount in a moment. The Northerners followed suit; Eol was the last, and had barely gathered his reins when a low, spike-edged howl rose from the east—the nasty scraping upon the wind was kin to that noise, I thought. It lingered somewhere between a brazen horn and an animal's cry.

It was also uncomfortably close. Mute during the disaster of the solstice, *seidhr* was now warning me. Unease turned to outright fear, crystal-clear and clarion-loud.

We set off at a bruising trot, our mounts stepping not quite as lightly as before. Each hoof-fall jolted in every joint I owned, and for some short while there was nothing but the muffled rhythm of our passage.

The calm did not last. "*Orukhar*," Soren finally said as he brought his prancing, snorting mount near, and cast me an indecipherable glance.

"And somewhat else, I think." Aeredh's steed matched Farsight's pace so closely they sounded a single beast. "How close, Eol?"

"Too close for comfort." The captain raised his right hand briefly; Gelad's horse moved nearer to Arneior's. Soren drew hard upon my left as Aeredh kneed his mount forward. Eol's breath came deep and fast, as if after running a hard league or three. He spoke rapidly in the Old Tongue. "*I can smell the filth. We have no choice but to stay upon the road, and yet—*"

"*We have not come this far to founder now.*" Soren's hand moved as if he longed to free his blade, but he looked to me and it fell back to his reins.

I found myself wondering, uselessly, about *Naras*. The name had never been mentioned in any saga I knew, but of course, that meant little. Sometimes when disaster looms the mind fills itself with inconsequentials to avoid looking directly into its eye.

" 'Tis ill-bred to mutter so in a foreign tongue." Arneior's chin was set, and her dark eyes flashed. Her hood had fallen free, her spear-blade glistered angrily, and to judge by her seat she was ready for all manner of mayhem. No doubt such exertion seemed more healthful to her than old legends, weirding, and half-voiced warnings. "What speaks in the woods?"

I listened intently, my head cocked. After a few moments I realized Aeredh's was held at the same angle, his ear-tips all but twitching. Farsight stepped nervously, lifting each shod hoof high, her nostrils wide as she caught a thread of evil-rotten scent.

It tingled in my own nose, and I suddenly wished I was not quite so entangled with her. Though the contact brought us both comfort, the stink was awful.

"*Orukhar*," Gelad answered, the word hissing-soft, laden with hatred. He pushed his cloak back, freeing his arms; it would be chill riding but he was now free to draw blade without hindrance. "They are foul, my lady Minnow, and strong. Your spear may acquire a name, should we meet them."

"Good." But my shieldmaid looked to me, both for guidance and any additional information I could gather.

My eyes half-closed as I concentrated. Even during a Northern winter, a forest is full of creeping life; small animals looking for food in the white wastes burrow when danger or storm approaches. Our morning ride had been surrounded by such tiny, stealthy motion, fading in stages as the overcast thickened at nooning and snow-scent turned dense as Albeig's summer sweetcake.

Now our surroundings were utterly silent, and the hush was not the velvety brush of falling white. No, it was a cold deep unsound, the wind's warning stoppered, raising the fine hairs all over my body. The pervading chill was not physical; another, more intense wave of shivering passed through me. Farsight shook her pale mane and blew an unhappy snort, which Arn's mount answered.

I had never felt this particular, nauseous anxiety before. *Seidhr* curdled in my bones, my head tipped back, and I searched for the source of the spreading stain. Each step jarred me in the saddle.

My hood had fallen; I looked to Arn. She nodded, and I needed say nothing. At least she was with me.

Our pace quickened, though the horses would begin to sink if we attempted more speed. There was simply too much snow.

"We cannot move fast enough, not like this." Elak was often the quietest of their number, a feat indeed, yet it was he who now spoke. "My lord Eol, shall I...?"

"Not yet," Eol replied in an undertone. "Not until we must."

I did not like the sound of that. I liked even less when another terrible, discordant cry lifted to the south; we were a few days' worth of travel away, but I found myself hoping whatever this was, it would not approach Lady Hajithe's steading.

They had many warriors, true, but I had not sensed a single *seidhr* among her folk.

Some manner of dark weirding prowled beneath the trees, yet could not quite grasp us. I suspected the runestones leading the road through bands of shallower snow helped, for as we approached each one the creeping dread lessened, and deepened as we left it behind. Still, the light was fading as the clouds thickened, and as the wind died scattered flakes began to fall. Steam lifted from heaving horse-flanks, each mount a small coracle upon rough water.

I became aware of Aeredh singing softly. There was *seidhr* in the words, the Old Tongue slipping free of solid meaning like a boat avoiding proper mooring upon a swift-rising river. The song lingered just outside comprehension, but you do not need to understand a chant to dance its rhythm.

It was like adding force to Idra's weirding. Such aid must be given free and lightly, akin to resting your fingertips atop a spear-maid's knuckles as she shepherds you between tables full of jostling feast-goers. Another thought occurred to me, tiptoeing catfoot-soft between worry, wondering, and mounting fear.

Snow is merely water, and air. The runestones, too—perhaps I could ask them? From one to the next, Sol, like hop-crossing a rocky stream.

Quick and delicate such work is, and would draw dangerously upon my inner reserves. My throat vibrated; I was hardly aware of my own singing, *seidhr* naming the stones upon the left, then the right. Between them a carpet of soft cold white was glad to aid me, did I merely ask with politesse.

So I did, conscious of Arn's familiar closeness. She was a sword of hot, disciplined brilliance at my side; Aeredh, leading our group, was much brighter, a warmer blue than the Elder lanterns' gleam. The rest of the Northerners shifted oddly to my inward sight, but I had no time to examine them.

It took all my concentration to clear the road.

I could not coerce the snow away, of course. I could only *ask*, and that faintly. Sometimes I wished I had been born with a deep affinity to one of the great branches of *seidhr*'s tree, for such narrow chan-neling provides power much as a stone-girt stream will acquire speed and strength, pushing all detritus before it.

But I was elementalist. I could only whisper to the deep forces—water, wind, stone, metal, fire, good fruitful earth—though all of them were available to my urging.

Sometimes small persuasion is all one needs.

Arn hummed tunelessly, attempting to follow the thread of my quick-chant. Our mounts shifted from snow-walk to trot, and their hooves sometimes chimed upon leaves littered over stone. I *felt* the road under us, freed of its snowy cover and quivering like a plucked string.

My throat burned, my eyes prickled. Fierce stinging cold swal-lowed my fingertips, my toes. Farsight's hoof-rhythm altered again, gathering speed, and her fear was a sharp ragged blade against my concentration.

She scented something terrible, and very close. Only the Elder's will and the presence of her fellows restrained her; she understood very well there was safety in a herd, however small, and had not yet been terrified into another wild flight.

I became aware of the Northerners exchanging terse half-whispers, and the slight scraping of steel drawn from sheath. The foulness was ever closer, dragging at my will, spreading like liquid ordure in clear water.

"If need be, I will hold them. Protect the girl." Eol, in the Old Tongue, harsh finality snapping at the end of every syllable.

Aeredh's voice changed, took on new urgency. My own diverged, soft and clear, persuading the snow to flow from beneath hooves, the infrequent runestones on either side adding help—but not nearly enough. I could not keep the weirding alive for much longer.

I did not have to. They boiled from the forest. Farsight and two other horses shrieked with fear, Arn cursed, and there was the clash of steel upon steel, married to a slavering, disorienting howl that is the battle cry of *orukhar*.

Edge of Foolhardy

You always remember your first, whether it be battle or love.
—Riverlands proverb

They are large, the thick-hide servants of the Enemy; their armor is blackened and their fangs sharp. Their bleached eyes are oft alight with a sickening, corrupt gleam when there is some chance of murder or torment, and rarely are they seen otherwise. Some say the lord of the Black Land took several Elder in the dawning of the world, and later the Secondborn when they appeared, blinking and barely capable of fire in the primeval woods. Those so kidnapped were held in thralldom, and slowly, surely *changed* into ashen foulness by merely existing under his rule.

Others say the eldest son of the Allmother committed a mockery of her greatest *seidhr*, fashioning forms from materials at hand and breathing a travesty of life into them, creating abhorrent puppets unable to do other than work his will. Yet the *orukhar* and many other spies of the Enemy sing, however discordantly, and that is the mark of a creature that may be free if it wishes—by flight, fight, or battering against cage bars until the release of death is won.

Still others say the truth lies somewhere between, that he took what people he could of the twin strains Elder and younger, twisting them at once and wholly in an act of unholy *seidhr*, letting them thereafter multiply in the usual way. For some of them appear as youths, and some parts of their rough language speak of mates or family left in the Black Land's distant reaches as surety for their cringing return to its master.

What is absolutely known is that they hate the Elder, and to a lesser extent the Allmother's younger children; they fear bright sunlight, but can withstand it for short periods at great need. They are swift, hardy, and deadly, and very often their broadswords bear a sharpened, triangular metal flag at the tip, meant for ripping great gashes in the bodies of foe or victim. Sometimes, when one of those straight, awful blades cleaves the air, a particular deadly sound is heard.

The Elder call it *kwiseirh*, a crushing whistle.

Arn's horse pressed upon my right, her knee almost upon mine, for the Northerners drew close around us. A lone rider may be surrounded and pulled from his perch, and they sought to do so to Soren. His mount did not rear, but responded to the pressure of his knees and weight by lashing out with hindfeet. Shod hooves sank deep into unhealthful flesh the color of a smoke-tainted snowdrift, and dark ichor spattered.

Their band was small, eight to ten warriors, but I only knew the count much later. In the snow-choked light I thought them far more, and clinging to a trembling Farsight took all my strength. A long ribbon of cleared pathway trailed behind us, an ancient stone road brushed free of old drifts but showing a skin of needles, leaves, and moss vanishing under a scrim of fresh white flakes. Near every rune-stone the clear patches spread, giving the impression of a serpent's undulation along our wake.

That much I glimpsed before a deeper darkness rose behind the attackers. It was on foot as they were, but much taller and leaner than their hulking; its shadowed head bore a spike-crowned iron helm. Reddish glimmers deep in the gloom sharpened, and a gout of whirling snow pushed through rents in its great sable mantle, turning into a billowing stain.

A cold deeper than winter spread from it, and a sense of twisting, deepening *wrongness*. My head, tender from holding *seidhr* for so long, crunched with pain. I thought something had hit me—a flung stone, perhaps, much larger than the pebbles Idra used to toss at me near her woodpile, reserving her true aim and force for when I could reliably dodge or deflect their path by will alone.

Like many weirding-games, it was practice for battle. But I had never imagined anything like this.

Aeredh's voice rose in a shout. Farsight quivered underneath me, and another white horse reared, a black-clad Northerner sliding from its back.

I caught only scattered flashes of the fight. Aeredh driving forward a-horse, his sword running with cold blue radiance—he fought with blade and *seidhr* both, clearly suffering no loss of strength. The black-cloaked *thing* parrying with a dull-gleaming blade, and the impact shivered through me, crown to soles. Eol and Efain both were dismounted, the Northern captain cleaving the head from an ash-pale shape, letting loose a high spraying jet of dark blood. Efain's shape blurring like black clay in warm water, and the shrill protests of maddened horses ringing under moaning trees—it seemed to take forever, yet I remember only small bits, reflected in shards of polished ice. Arn leaning in the saddle as her spear flickered, driving deep into an attacker's throat and tearing free. Shieldmaids are trained to fight upon horseback if they must, but she did not charge, keeping her white mare near Farsight.

Aeredh's voice took on a deep, belling sonorousness. It was a battlesong, and had I any wit at that point I would have been listening to learn its cadence and content. I could have added more of my own *seidhr* to his than the trickle I managed, for though a *volva* may not touch or use weapons of honest combat, we are more than permitted to aid warriors in our own way.

But I was useless, mazed and blind, frozen and clinging to Farsight's reins.

There was a final burst of noise, a deep foul howling, a choked gurgle from the last dying *orukhar*, and the spike-helmed thing retreated with its last defiant scream piercing my head as well as all my joints. I cried out too, shrinking and shaking so badly I almost slid from the saddle.

"*Solveig!*" Arn's voice, very far away. I clung to consciousness, despite the world turning to midnight around me. My body loosened; I swayed drunkenly.

A vise closed about my upper arm. Arn shook me—not overly rough, but still a sharp movement. She repeated my name, but I could barely hear her. The quiet of falling snow had crawled into my head, perhaps a reflex against the dark-cloaked *thing*'s terrible, piercing scream.

Gelad, Karas, and Elak went from body to body with quick efficient movements, gathering what knowledge they could along with items fit for later use. Aeredh's horse stepped delicately onto a patch of cleared road; the Elder's eyes blazed while the sickening unphysical darkness fled, pure snowlight returning in a flood. His sword hissed itself clean as it swung, *seidhr* smoking along the blade; sharp metal returned to its home in a single fluid movement. A very disheveled Eol stood aside, his own blood-streaked broadsword held low but ready. The Northerner glared at the woods as if to challenge the foul thing to return. He waited until the Elder had joined us; only then did he clean his blade upon a fallen foe and sheathe its shine. Efain stroked his horse's head, speaking to the trembling mare in the Old Tongue.

Soren, hard by my left, scanned the forest from horseback-height. His mount turned, obeying the pressure of his knees, and he kept hand to hilt.

"Solveig." Arn's tone assumed its proper volume and dimensions. I stared at my shieldmaid, and for a dizzying moment did not recognize her. I barely even knew I was upon a horse, let alone where we were or the names of my companions, and my own name seemed too great a riddle to even pretend thought upon at the moment.

"Arneior?" I sounded like Astrid after a night-terror; she had them often before reaching her blood years. Once she gained full womanhood they abated; I was glad of it, though I did not grudge their soothing. Sometimes even our mother could not calm her, and I had to sing her back to sleep with *seidhr*. "Oh. Yes."

"Here." Arn let go of me, but only to attempt freeing the meadskin from her belt. "Here. Take some, and don't argue. You have *that look*."

I shook my head, waving the proffered drink aside. She was

about to curse, but I was not precisely arguing. I merely had to lean over, clinging to the pommel with both hands, and retch. My middle twisted upon itself; I could only produce a thin thread of colorless bile. Their strange Northern waybread I had taken at the beginning of our nooning halt did not burn when it escaped like some other foods do.

But all the same, I did not like losing it.

A breathless, strengthless moan left me at the end. Though I was cold, sweat dewed my forehead, and I hoped I had not fouled my mantle.

"First battle?" Soren still scanned the forest, tense and ready. The Northerner even wore a slight, fey smile; his dark eyes were live coals. "Aye, I remember the feeling. You did well, my lady *alkuine*."

I was not so sure. It took all my failing will to straighten as Aeredh kneed his mount closer.

"Very well indeed." Aeredh granted the compliment in a hushed tone. There was a light in his white horse's gaze that almost matched his, as well; his kind are held capable of infusing even mute beasts with courage. "Steady, young one; all is well."

"That was not one of the Seven." Eol backed onto the road, turned sharply, and strode for his horse. "Was it?"

"Oh, no." How was it possible for a man to look so young and old at once? Aeredh was the same youth who had visited in Dun Rithell, but his expression was akin to one my father sometimes wore while speaking quietly to warriors who had witnessed the deadly battle of Nath-Imil, the year before he wedded Mother.

A mildly successful warlord—one too victorious to be called "petty," and Idra once said she suspected he had some weirding despite his use of paired blades—had met his end upon Eril the Battle-Mad's axe, but Father did not listen to the songs sung of the event, nor did he speak upon it to his children. The silence said more than any saga could; did a guest begin to intone familiar verse about that long-ago deed, Father left the high table and would not return. Even Flokin did not boast of that victory, for it had been a terrible one. The fighting had been without quarter or ransom.

What came after was worse yet.

The warlord had died upon Eril's axe, yes, but a third of his warriors had been sent to slay the women and children huddling in Imil Steading. Such a thing is simply not done, and every last survivor of that accursed man's horde had been hunted down.

Found, but not killed. A brand was laid to their faces instead, and their right hands mutilated before they were driven into the wilderness with whips. Such signs speak plainly to any in the south, even past the Barrowhills, and those so marked would find neither food nor shelter in any hall, farm, or even thrall-hut.

A great gripping pang seized me, scalp to toes. I longed for home, and even Flokin's greybeard dourness. The wish to see Ulfrica shook me, and I wondered for a moment why I should suddenly miss her, and not Astrid or my mother.

The homesick heart fastens upon strange things.

"Merely a lich," the Elder continued, and urged his horse almost close enough to touch mine as Soren's moved aside. Aeredh studied me closely, traces of that cold blue radiance cloaking him.

I was seeing too much. I inhaled sharply, and almost heard Idra's snort. *Do not wander half out of yourself, girl. What you do, do at once, and wholly.*

"*Merely*, he says." Leather creaked as Soren's horse stamped; the Northerner did not roll his eyes only by an effort of will, it seemed. "I like this not. Too small a band, yet with a lich holding the leash?"

"Peace, my lady. The battle is over." Aeredh leaned from his saddle, brushing two fingers against my mantle-clad shoulder. The brief touch sent a bolt of heat through me, strength shared through *seidhr*. I was too dazed to wonder if he would teach me the trick, for Idra had known how to perform only a slow seeping exchange of vitality. "Are all southron women so brave?"

What bravery? I could not produce the words. Was he mocking me? *There is nowhere to flee, even if I could drag Arn away.* I blinked several times, the world flickering. The thing's cry still lingered in my memory, spreading its oozing black frost.

"Solveig." Arn crowded closer. "Look at me."

It took a great effort to turn my head. She thrust the meadskin at me again; I took it more out of exhaustion than obedience. I knew from long experience she would badger me until I did what she considered healthful.

My stubbornness is deep, but hers approaches the truly legendary.

I would rather not have even smelled the mead, for my stomach did not wish to seat itself properly. But I took a fiery mouthful and our surroundings roared back into life around me. The black thing's voice fled entirely, and the shivers gripping me eased all at once.

Lady Hajithe might have no *seidhr*, but there is a weirding in any act of creation, no matter how small. How much more, then, in distilling? I shelved the thought for later examination.

Had I the lee to do so, it would mean we had survived.

The skin sloshed as I handed it back. "I am well enough." My throat was raw, words husky like the morning an illness takes hold. "I...I cannot clear the road again, though." In fact, I doubted I could use any *seidhr* at all, at the moment. "I am sorry."

For a long moment they were silent, and Arn's gaze kindled afresh. The stripe upon her face glowed; she had pleased the Wingéd Ones mightily this day. "Of course you cannot," she said, loudly. "They should not expect it of you, either."

"Of course not," Aeredh hurried to agree. "'Twas a mighty enough feat as it is, and then to render aid against a lich? Not many of your kind are capable of such things, even among the Faithful. The wonder is you are still conscious enough to speak."

"I can ride." *Do not ask me to sing, though. Or to dance.* I forced my shoulders back, my chin to rise. My arms ached, and my legs were full of strange fluttering. But Farsight was steady underneath me, and if I watched her ears and nothing else, I would not embarrass myself. "How much farther?"

"We have only to reach the Ford. The waystones grow stronger with each step." The Elder twisted to look at Eol as the Northerner mounted, his cream-colored steed sidling uneasily, but too well-trained to protest more. "Some few leagues, easy riding."

"Unless the lich returns with the rest of the war-band. They cannot be far, and 'tis well past noon." Eol's boots were crusted with snow, and he looked as if he had been rolled in it. Blood, bright crimson but drying, striped his roughened cheek—they did not grow beards, but now the black-clad Northerners all bore some evidence of stubble. His dark hair was wildly tousled, and he shook his head irritably. Everyone bore some sign of hard activity; even Arn's horn-braids were mussed. "Soren, take the *alkuine*'s reins. Shieldmaid, keep close watch, and should she swoon call out so we may halt. Efain, take the rearguard; should you sense them…"

Scarred, solemn Efain nodded, dropping back. Elak followed suit. Arn did not bother to protest; the command was what she would have done anyway, and Eol of the house of Naras was after all their captain. In a few short moments we were moving away from a ring of shattered *orukhar* corpses twisted amid bloodstained snow. Oddly, the stains seeping from their dead were not bright scarlet.

The attackers' blood looked old, and dark. I could not even shudder at the wrongness. The fearsome thought that the terrible thing— *lich*, the Elder called it—could return made my heart pound so hard my vision turned dark at the edges. Tales and songs mentioned such things in bloodcurdling detail that did not even remotely begin to describe the true horror.

And Aeredh had met it in battle; he had, burning with that strange inner radiance, driven it away.

"Brave indeed, my lady Solveig." The Elder touched my shoulder again. There was no burning jolt this time, but he nodded. "You are upon the edge of foolhardy. Should the dark thing return, do not attempt to aid me again."

I do not think I did too badly. But of course, what I thought of my own performance did not matter. I managed a nod, and turned my gaze to Farsight's ears. Even the familiar sting of disappointment from the teaching after a failed test did not bother me overmuch.

Besides, if the lich returned, I could not follow his advice. Strictly speaking, I had not attempted to aid him. I had simply been thrash-mad with fear, like a bolting horse, and striking out with every weapon I had.

There was, I knew, no bravery in that.

Across the Ford

O sing of Nithraen, the many caves,
Of the mirrored water before its gate...
O, sing of Aerith's kingdom, for it is gone,
And never shall its like be seen again.
                    —*Lament of the Uncrowned*

The Ford of Nithlas was indeed close, but the hours to reach it were a miserable eternity. More snow whirled down, branches overhead unable to stifle the flood, and the wind returned. At first, the breeze was almost playful, but it quickly lost interest in restraint. The horses trudged wearily, and even Aeredh's singing grew fainter, with short gaps between some phrases. Once he coughed, and Eol silently urged his tired horse forward, offering the glassy black flask without word. The Elder took a swallow of *sitheviel*, nodded his thanks, and returned to his song.

Seidhr had hold of me, the veil of the physical world drawn aside as cold, hunger, and fear mounted in my limbs. I could almost-see how words and cadence infused strength into faltering legs, warming the beasts we rode. But I also saw strange things in the whirling flakes. Some fantastical shapes were fair enough, merely curious, but others smoked with ill intent. The latter fled before strange subtle forms bearing the faintest hint of chill blue light, and I heard voices without the help of my ears. Even though Arn pressed the meadskin upon me twice more I was only half awake when the snow thinned, drawing back in a curtain as hooves rang unmuffled on small splashing stones.

At that time the Nith had never frozen save once, and the tale of that winter—told to me long afterward—is terrible indeed.

The ford is always crossed in stages, for there the Nith runs shallow over many gravel-beds before it gathers two tributaries, Shaerith the Cold and Eleth-mir the always musical. With their aid it becomes much mightier than our river at home, turning southward with a vengeance to come, after long wandering, to the sea. On the far side of the Ford's broad shoals forested hills rose, their foliage oddly tinted, and the air was not nearly so frozen. Falling snow vanished, though the sun's light still filtered through endless heavy cloud.

I was glad to be out of the whirling ice-feathers, not to mention those strange *seidhr*-shapes. The stone road broke through a thinning white carpet, breaching to leap like a fish. Beyond a short rise, the forest bore more paleness upon its shoulders and hood, but not below the canopy. Crisp cleanness shone between pillar-trunks, as if we were high upon a mountainside again, the air thin and crystalline.

Our horses lifted their heads, snowmelt dropping from hocks, withers, and tails. The Northerners exchanged relieved glances, but Arn urged her mount closer to mine. She was deadly pale, her freckles glaring like the blue stripe on the left side of her face, and her knuckles were bloodless as she gripped her spear, apparently not trusting the saddle's bucket to hold it.

If her nape was crawling like mine, if the fine hairs all over her were rising, if she was suddenly sweating under her mantle—while still chilly, it was appreciably warmer than upon the other side of the river—I did not blame her. I felt the weirding as well, though I was too exhausted to do more than wonder.

There is a word for an animal made so placid by fear or tiredness it simply ambles, head down, toward the burden-release of the knife, and now I know its depths.

Hills rose in great pleats, the trees so old and large not much undergrowth gathered between them. They had to be evergreens since they bore their finery even in new winter, but their leaves were deciduous-shaped and tinged with gold at the edges. Great greygreen boles lightly touched with lacework lichen made hallways in every direction, and in summer the sward would be verdant.

It was beautiful, and the tree-leaves familiar, since I had seen them wrapped around the Northerners' strange melting waybread. But the unnatural blunting of winter's chill and the loveliness of the groves were both…disturbing.

There is no other word for the feeling, though I racked my porridge-impersonating skull-meat to think of one.

We rode for some while upon the newly freed road, its surface innocent of fallen leaf or branch, moss or stray pebble. Aeredh's song dropped into a hum, echoing the inaudible ringing from the rune-stones at now-regular intervals. Passing from one stone-singing tone to the next produced a strange thrill along my back and upper arms; Farsight's ears were pricked so far they almost seemed ready to slip free and go galloping themselves.

Arneior pulled her mount to a sharp halt; it took a moment for me to convince Farsight to stop though Soren had her reins. It also hurt, vaguely, to use the savagely overstretched willpower-muscle inside my aching head and chest, but if my shieldmaid would go no further, I would follow suit.

Besides, the idea of sliding from the horse's back, taking a few staggering steps into the woods, and sinking down upon the banks of yellowed grass with only the thinnest thread of green at each blade's center was incredibly appealing.

"Hold," Soren said, pleasantly enough. "Does the lady require—"

"We are being followed, again." Arn turned as far as she could in her saddle, looking behind us, her spear almost quivering. "And there are voices. Sol?"

"I hear them." My whisper was a singsong; I clutched at the pommel and tried to focus through the swimming before me. Even Farsight's neck was undulating. "I do not think they mean us ill."

"But do they mean us well?" Arn shook her coppery head, leather-wrapped braids vigorously brushing her shoulders. "They may show themselves, or I shall not allow my Solveig another step. There is weirding here, and I *do not like it.*"

It was Eol who answered. "We are in the lands of our lord Aeredh's kin." His cloak dripped and his hair was wildly unhappy at the battle we had just suffered; the rest of him probably felt the same. "Nothing here will harm you or Gwendelint's daughter, lady shieldmaid. We are very close to shelter."

Arn gazed at me, but I could say nothing. I felt the watchers as well, their interest sharp but not unwholesome. Still, if my shieldmaid was cautious, I would not move.

I trusted my Arn. The rest of them? Perhaps, to a degree.

And perhaps not.

So there I remained, with Arn at my side and the Northerners passing whispered arguments, until there was a slight sound within the trees. Riders on slim-legged white horses like our own appeared, melding from the spaces between greygreen trunks, their cloaks woven in greengold-grey and their hoods pulled high. For all that, their gazes were bright in the shadows underneath, and skilled hands held bows when they did not rest upon fluidly shaped hilts chased with gems or stark with plain loveliness.

Thus it was we were introduced to the folk of Nithraen. I heard little of what was said, but we set off again, Arn's mouth pulled tight and her mare matching Farsight stride for stride. The hills rose but the road was laid to be very gentle to both foot and hoof, and by the time we passed over the Great Causeway above the lapping mirror of Nith-an-Gaelas—a naturally, partially dammed branch of the river itself—I was all but insensible. I did not see the Gate carved with runes of strength, bound with flowing hammered metal and seamless once closed. I did not see the shadows part under the great hill, nor did I hear the silvery trumpets echoing deep in the halls where the Elder lived, sang, and wrought their wonders.

It was enough that we eventually stopped, I plummeted from the saddle into Arn's waiting arms, and we were taken to a place of resting.

PART TWO

NITHRAEN

Morn in Nithraen

*Before Faevril was born, his queenly mother Mieris went
to the northernmost shore of Valhalle, to the cave where the
Three Kind Sisters weave. Much was her joy upon hearing
that her firstborn would be a flame bright enough to light
the world, but deep also was her unease, for that was not
all the Njorn said...*

—The Annals of Valraëne

To wake upon a bedstead carved from grey stone is strange
enough, even when its mattress is soft as a cloud and the linens smell of summer freshness. To see the bed's curtains hanging
from a loop of more carved stone overhead, the ring depending from
a rough mass of almost-triangular rock, is even stranger. There was
a small stand next to the bed, a pillared dish growing from its surface like a twisted tree-trunk and bearing a single, heatless, glowing
golden globe. The light it shed was clear and forgiving, brightening
when I yawned and scrubbed at my poor head. My braids were in a
sorry state, coral beads digging unmercifully amid the tangle, and as
I sat up, pushing unfamiliar, finespun blankets aside, I also dislodged
Arn's arm from my middle.

She muttered a curse, turned over, and returned to the deep shadowy land of sleep with little ado. Her spear was propped within easy
reach of the carven bed; I realized, staring in wonder, that the entire

room had been hollowed from grey stone. A columned opening along one wall let in a dappled glow of shifting leafshadow, accompanied by the sound of voices lifted in song and laughter.

There was a stone table too, but the chairs were—thankfully— made of wood, and in the usual fashion besides, though highly carved. A stone wardrobe with varnished, likewise sculpted wooden doors stood sentinel in one corner, and before it was my mother's trunk, still securely fastened. My *seidhr*-bag, with Astrid's beautiful stitchery making runes of health and protection upon its sides and flap, was tangled in the bed's blankets near my shieldmaid's knee. Arn's mantle and mine hung upon wooden holders set nearby, dry and clean, looking very companionable indeed. The walls were alive with stonework of climbing vines and leaves, a screen-trellis with stone flowers shielding a small sitting room. I peered through the holes, running a tentative fingertip along hard petals.

It was a representation of no plant I knew, but the rock remembered tiny whispers of *seidhr*-shaping. If I listened deeply enough, I could perhaps untangle the words used to make stone behave so.

The artisans of this place were skilled indeed, for even small hairs along the flower stems had been rendered. The rooms were wide and airy, holding a faint indefinable floral fragrance and the faintest breath of stone-smell, as of a mountain's slope upon a sunny summer day. On the other side of the sitting room—it held low wooden couches upholstered with velvet, clearly this was a hall much greater than Dun Rithell or the Eastronmost—was a door I felt no need to examine just yet, being too busy freeing my braids.

My scalp tingled with relief, and the prickling slid down my back. I found the colonnade along the bedroom's wall looked over a tree-lined street, quiet and deserted; the voices came from elsewhere, rising and falling in lapping waves. The trees drove their roots into, over, and past stone containers that had held them as saplings, their branches stretched upward under a shimmering radiance from a great golden thing hanging far above.

It was not the sun, and my fingers froze in my hair. I retreated once more, working coral beads free and whispering a small *seidhr* against enchantment and ill will with each one. I did not think such caution precisely necessary, but the disturbing feeling under my breastbone would not go away.

Another archway led to a small grotto with water sliding down a stone cliff-face subtly shaped into spiraling designs; it was close and half as warm as a sauna, tiny vines and moss festooning its walls. The light was an indirect golden glow, from whence I could not tell. There was a smaller stone column, too, somehow feeding bubbling cold water into a basin. An entire family could have lived in these rooms and had plenty of space to share with bondsman, thrall, servant, and free retainers alike.

The wardrobe's shelves and cubbies were empty, and sweetly redolent of resinous wood. I decided against trying to heft the trunk into its embrace, for there was no telling if this was our final destination or how long we would stay.

Finally, clean and warm—and is that not a joy after any voyage, no matter how short?—I took my carved-horn comb to the balcony over the street, setting to work upon my damp hair. The voices had not stopped, merely shifted like river-chuckles running over a stony bed. I studied the bright golden ball hanging high above, realizing it was akin to a great gem. The stars scattered about it were other jewels set in the roof of a vast cavern, but if they were constellations I could not tell, being none I had ever seen.

Under hill, under stone they live; Where singing echoes deep and bold. An ancient saga, telling of the waking of the dverger in the first ordering of the world; I shivered at its unbidden appearance in my head. My second-best dress, of very dark heartsblood wool, was more than fine enough for visiting other halls.

Was it enough for an Elder city? It did not *smell* underground here; there was no cave-reek. On the far side of the river from Dun Rithell there was a noisome cavern Idra swore had once held an evil hulking stonehide thing finally killed by a distant ancestor of Gwenlara my own mother's progenitrix; there was no breath of anything so foul here.

The pillared balcony had a pretty carven balustrade; I studied the trees and smoothly cobbled street below. Had they found these caverns and enlarged them, or did an Elder lord look upon a hill ages ago and decide to carve within it? Or perhaps others had made these halls? There were stories of the *thrayn* dverger, short squat people whose hands know the secret of every earthly crafting and who lived in halls of stone; they were held to have departed the world when the Elder did after the Black Land's fall, but by burrowing inward instead of taking ship to the far, glorious West.

But apparently the Black Land was risen again. And now I wondered what else lurked in the far reaches of the North, how much would I see before returning to Dun Rithell. I could not think beyond seeing Mother again, and Astrid and Bjorn. Even Father's bluff, uneasy greeting would be a relief and a joy.

While the cold North might hold wonders like this place it also held things like sheep-monsters in hidden ways, and *orukhar*. Not to mention the lich we had so narrowly escaped, and that was a terrible memory. I shuddered, drawing the comb through my hair, and sensed more than saw movement below. I peered over the balustrade, narrowing my eyes. A blurring shape slipped through liquid tree-shade, moving between patches of deeper shadow.

My fingers cramped upon the comb. I sucked in a soft breath, and he must have heard me, for Eol paused and looked up, peering between heavy-laden branches. He had put aside his blackened armor, but his new garb was sober-dark as ever, leggings and a long tunic of some soft material I learned later was Elder-woven. His eyes gleamed, his face patched and seamed with moving shadows, and the gem upon his swordhilt, now unwrapped, glittered savagely.

"*And there, in her tower, the daughter of a king; Looks upon me, and her gaze is as a knife.*" He murmured in the Old Tongue, some manner of song or riddle, for the accents were pleasingly arranged. Then he shifted to the southron speech, raising his voice as if he thought my ears were stoppered instead of sharp as a *volva*'s. "Be untroubled, Gwendelint's daughter. You are safe in Nithraen, where Caelgor and Curiaen now rule."

That means nothing to me, son of Tharos. But excitement rose behind my heartbeat, largely dispelling unease. "This is an Elder place, then?" I had to lean over the balustrade, my damp, unbound hair swinging, and pitch my own words loudly enough for dull hearing.

Although his ears were perhaps as sharp as Arn's, considering what lived in his skin.

"Of a certainty." He stepped out of lacework shadow, his eyes bright and whatever golden thing burned overhead wringing a hard dart of light from the gem in his swordhilt. "The great city of Nithraen, in a thousand caves beneath the hills of Nithlas-en-Ar. Do you ask him, Aeredh will tell you stories of its building. May I come up, Gwendelint's daughter, or will you come down?"

Arn was still asleep, and I loath to wake her. "Am I called, then?" For a weregild must attend where they are bid, and we were not traveling at the moment.

"Only if it pleases you." Was it chagrin, crossing his face? I could not quite tell. "Aeredh is hard upon my heels; we thought to be your doorguards. There is much curiosity about an *alkuine*."

So I am to be an amusement. I was not quite hard-pressed to find a polite reply, but it was close. "I have much curiosity about the Elder, so we are well-matched."

"I begin to think you fearless." He did not move; a breeze ruffled branches and sent dappled light cascading over him. How vast was this cavern, if the air moved so? "Grant us leave to linger at your door, Gwendelint's daughter, and emerge when it pleases thee."

So you can speak with some politeness, when you choose to. I heard stirring behind me—so Arn was awake, after all. "It will not be long," I promised, and retreated, working at my hair.

My shieldmaid yawned, regarding me from the carven bed. "What is that?"

"We're in an Elder city, small one, and my captor wishes to show me like a prize sheep." The last tangle yielded fully under the comb's teeth, and now I had only rebraiding to accomplish before I was decent again. "What have you seen of this place? How large is it? The cavern seems deep indeed, yet it does not reek, and—"

"Only you would find this a pleasant turn of events." She rubbed at her face, yawning afresh, and my own throat ached to answer with a corresponding sigh. "Where is breakfast? And, by the gods, I could do with some ale."

"As ever." I carried my *seidhr*-bag to the table; I could tell it had not been disturbed save to place it in the bed, which was heartening. I lowered myself cautiously in one of the chairs and found it far more comfortable than it looked. "I saw Lord Eol below, but he did not seem to be carrying a meal."

"No surprise there. The man seems to resent even bread." She pushed back the covers and flowed from the bed with her usual grace, bending to touch her toes, stretching her hands to the ceiling, and embarking upon the regular, stylized movements a shieldmaid performs to press sleep from stiffened muscles. "And this is not one cavern but several, each deeper than the last. I do not like it, though the air is sweet enough."

"There is *seidhr* here." My hands knew their work; my braids began to take shape. Red coral, solid and healthful, warmed my fingers as I braided, snugged, and looped; the ribbons were Astrid's and well treasured, but she had slipped them into my luggage anyway. "I shall learn much, and so shall you."

"Mh." She wrinkled her nose and disappeared into the water-room.

A Promise So Often

For Lithielle did not wish to be taken, and struggled; as they rode past Bjornwulf leapt to her aid, dragging Curiaen from the saddle. The lady fell too, light as a leaf, and Bjornwulf might have killed an Elder prince in that moment, for great was his wrath at any who would lay hand upon his love…
—*The Hunting of Lithielle*, attributed
to Daerith the Elder

There is no night in Nithraen, merely a period of dimming and shadows at the dawn and dusk of the world outside. Each cavern had its light-orb, sun-golden or moon-silver; the more shadowed passages and streets had graceful, bluish Elder-wrought lanterns burning endlessly at precise intervals. Some caverns blent into each other at their edges, and the mingling of orb-light was beautiful indeed.

Homes, workshops, halls for dining or dancing or music or weighty discussion, storage for various items—all were carved from the stony hills, and in the streets there were no broken cobbles or cracked ancient paving, only round granite river-eggs whole and complete. The trees grew as if upon sunny hillsides, and if leaves dropped free of their arms there was always fresh green to replace them. Gardens there were, with fruit-bush and healthful herb, not to mention flowers grown simply for the joy of their foliage or flowering.

Fountains played, sweet water speaking in garden and plaza, and the singing in Nithraen followed that music.

I must have gaped like a farmchild brought to a greathall for the first time, or a youth seeing his first love at a riverside fair. Between Aeredh—in no armor but a long coat of black Elder-woven velvet and trews to match, like Eol—and my shieldmaid I did not have to worry overmuch about placing my feet, though Arn caught my arm once or twice as I fair tripped over the satin-smooth cobbles in my eagerness to absorb some new vista. The air itself hummed with messages I could not quite hear, brushing like butterflies above a meadow.

Idra had been fond of those bright-winged creatures, often letting them rest upon her greying hair while she tended her small garden. The memory was piercing, and my first unease in Nithraen was that, beautiful as it was before the breaking, there was no birdsong threading through the lifted voices.

But I did not think upon such a lack then, for there were Elder everywhere.

They are tall, the first-awakened of the Allmother; though most are dark-haired their eyes shine with fierce light and are often blue as my mother's. They did not quite stare, though a few in bright flowing armor standing guard at some post or another glanced at Aeredh more than once, not bothering to gaze upon my own strangeness. Most Elder look youthful indeed, though for some grief or great wisdom may grant them a gravity approaching an aged warrior's. For all that, they are quick to merriment, and the sound of their enjoyment is often silver as the night's largest light. They do prize the sun, for it keeps evil at bay—but their hearts are given to the stars, for they woke in starlight and marveled much later when the Moon first sailed across the sky.

The women among the Elder examined me boldly, most with their hair unbound or held back with simple silver fillets. Yet some wore braids as complex as mine, though none with red coral. For all that, their gazes were not unkind, and the men did not linger-look overlong.

Perhaps they found Eol's glare daunting; I know Arn cast more than one sharp glance at any whose scrutiny verged upon the importunate. Most of Nithraen's citizens, however, were more interested in Aeredh, who appeared not to notice. He did not meet their gazes, and almost it seemed our small group was amid the wilderness's vast loneliness instead of a collection of stone houses. I did not see the other Northerners; no doubt they were glad to be resting in such surroundings.

But we were bound for the palace at the heart of the many caves, the very center of Nithraen. Street after street of houses, other buildings, wide gardens, and so many people—at times my breath stopped in my throat, and a strange uneasiness turned my fingers cold, rushing down my back, attempting to raise the fine hairs all over me.

Aeredh pointed out small details—*my father planted that tree, there is where casks of new springwine are kept, archers practice amid those trees in certain seasons, we shall soon pass a fountain that sings like one across the sea.* He kept a steady pace, and though I might have preferred breakfast, there was wonder enough in seeing that I did not mind very much. Three great caverns melded into one as we walked, and the path under us became a road thrice as broad as the one before my father's hall.

Had all paved ways once looked like this? The way the blocks were laid reminded me of the trade-road running past Dun Rithell, but this one looked fresh-new, not a crack or discoloration to be seen.

Then we turned again. A wide avenue of white stone with multi-colored gems laid in a branching pattern at certain junctures hummed with force, rather like the runestones. Both Arn and I avoided placing our feet upon the glitters, though Aeredh trod firmly. "No need to worry," he said. "They are meant for dancing upon."

"It feels wrong," Arn muttered, and I could not disagree.

At that moment there was a belling, and I halted. From a cross street some distance ahead a pack of giant wire-haired hounds, grey as mist and graceful as deer, crowded a high-prancing white horse. The hunter was dark-haired, in greenglitter armor, and turned toward the shining spires of a palace boiling with silvergold light—for this great three-lobed cavern had *two* light-orbs, silver and gold, the only one we had seen so far possessing both types at its apex—without casting a glance in our direction.

"Curiaen," Eol said, quietly. "The fifth son of Faevril, my lady *alkuine*, and returned from hunting the Enemy's servants upon the borders of Nithraen. His brother should be...ah, there."

A second hunter, his hair bright gold as Astrid's, was the true center of the pack. The horn at his hip glittered fiercely, and he looked over his shoulder. Though his eyes were dark his glance was like a dart; Aeredh again appeared not to notice, though I all but heard the missile whistle. It did not strike, or if it did, the impact was silent.

"Caelgor," Aeredh said, mildly, as if I had inquired. "Faevril's third, and a mighty hunter indeed. Though he has lost his best hound."

"*None would gainsay you.*" The Old Tongue burst from Eol; Arn tilted her head slightly at my side, listening hard to tone and hue though she could understand neither word nor accent. "*I wish you would simply—*"

"*My father's people chose.*" Aeredh shook his dark head, and his faint smile held no amusement. "*I have also chosen, my friend.* Forgive us," he continued, in the southron tongue. "We should not speak so before you, Lady Solveig. We are bound for the palace, and will have a draught there to ease whatever hunger you and your shield-maid have. Afterward the rulers of Nithraen will question you, though not overly harshly. You need fear nothing."

I fear little with Arn next to me. Though that was not quite true— my anxiety at this place's strangeness could be diminished but not wholly elided, and the memory of the lich sent a fresh shiver down my back. Regardless, Eol wished for me to attend, so I must.

I could not help it; the question bolted free. "Do you think they found it? The thing with the iron helm?"

" 'Tis likely, and if so it will carry no tales to its master. We may be grateful for that much." Aeredh's smile turned passing bitter, though, and he did not look thankful at all.

"*Usurpers,*" Eol muttered.

I did not like the turn conversation had taken, and had to appear oblivious or merely curious while I examined the buildings, the glittering streets, the trees of several different kinds. A large, spike-limbed evergreen of a type I had never seen before thrust skyward as if it longed to reach the roof, and though its trunk was massive there would be many a long year before its crown could reach close to its goal.

Certainly longer than a man's life, or even two.

"*Soft, my friend.*" Aeredh did not sigh, but he looked very much like my mother when she wished to do so. I found myself wondering if he had any children, though he looked far too young. "*I have left the matter behind; so should you.*"

"Sol?" Arn, very quietly; did I wish to let these lords know I understood their ancient speech? Or perhaps she was asking something else. I did not like being unable to discern or anticipate my shieldmaid, but we were both disarranged by travel.

Not to mention our surroundings. This place was so vast, and so many Elder were breathing within it. I wondered they had not run out of air, and *that* was an uncomfortable thought indeed.

"I am hungry too," I murmured, as if she had meant to inquire about that. "At least there is a chance of breakfast, small one. Though I am uncertain if the Elder have ale."

" 'Tis the time for winterwine." Aeredh's good humor returned, the sun freeing itself from a cloud. "You may find it a worthy substitute, shieldmaid."

The breeze touching my braids was sweet indeed, but I was unsure if I could truly like this place. I took to studying where my slippers landed instead of the buildings or gardens; the ground was so easy I did not need buskin or boot. My bee-torc rested comfortingly against my collarbones, but I did not think its work would impress those who had hollowed out this lovely, uncanny place.

No one likes to feel insignificant. My delight in seeing the new and strange soured some little as the palace drew nearer, lifted voices and the sound of stringed instruments as well as pipes echoing from its wide-open doors. Hound and hunter were gone from view; so were the crowds of Elder folk, yet the music remained. Another chill touched my skin under heartsblood wool, and I looked to Arn.

She felt it as well. My shieldmaid's dark eyes were wide, her freckles bright against paleness. For all that, the light suited her, burnishing every edge and glittering upon ring- or scale-mail. She had reapplied her woad-stripe, and it glowed reassuringly.

Of course the orbglimmer was likely picking out my own imper-
fections, but *she* was beautiful. So I have ever thought of others,
especially other women. Astrid would glow like the pearls carried
upriver here, and I found myself not quite wishing they had asked
for her as weregild instead.

Not quite. And yet.

"We are being followed," Arn declared, flatly. "Though your
people stay well back, still they come."

"Yes." Aeredh glanced at me, as if I had been the one to speak.
"There has never been an *alkuine* in Nithraen. Do not let it trouble
you, my lady shieldmaid. They mean no harm."

"No elementalists?" I could barely believe it. The Elder are mighty
in *seidhr*; it never occurred to me that with all their inner sight and
invisible strength they would lack even the rarest flowerings of the
Allmother's gift. Then again, Aeredh's share did not bar him from
carrying a weapon—was he counted weak among them?

It was a strange thought.

"You are the first of your kind to set foot here, my lady Solveig."
Aeredh's smile was beneficent, and his pace did not alter, drawing me
onward. "The Elder have only ever had one *alkuine*, and some hope
we may never be afflicted by another. Yet you are blameless in that
matter, and a remedy besides. Do not fear, I shall not let any ill come
to you."

It struck me, then, that the Northerners would not utter such a
promise so often were there no danger of it needing fulfillment. And
from Arn's expression, she had realized as much too, though well
before her charge.

I watched my slippers—not so fine as any Elder raiment, certainly—
avoiding gems in white stone, and redoubled my efforts not to lay
even a toe upon one gleaming jewel.

It seemed safest that way.

Sons of Faevril

Then did the king lay his circlet upon the throne, and declared that any his people would follow could wear it with his blessing. None moved, and the City of Caves was silent as he took his leave, walking beside Bjornwulf as two friends upon a summer day.
　　　　　—Baelor of Quaencis, *Saga of the Uncrowned*

Broad white steps swept us through vast high-arched doors and into the palace of Nithraen; the many-pillared halls were magnificent indeed. As we crossed the threshold, silver chalices were brought by Elder in livery blazed with embroidered representation of two shining trees, their boughs interlaced.

Some say we learned of the welcome cup from the Elder, but others say each of the Allmother's children hews to the ancient laws of hospitality in their own way. All agree it is best to do as your hosts require in the moment of arrival. A good guest is polite, as a good host shares both food and fireside.

Arn drank deep of hers; I took a token sip followed by a startled, much deeper mouthful as heat slid through me. It was close to *sitheviel* but far more substantial, with a taste slipping through many different forms. First, it was Albeig's special crisp-crust harvest bread, the very thing I had been longing for though I knew it not until that moment. A second swallow was honey from hives Kolle's family tended; there were fields of aromatic purple laventeli their bumble-winged gatherers loved to sup from, and it ever gave a fragrant tinge to their mead.

The third taste puzzled me, for it was roast mutton, and filled me the way only meat could. I lowered the silver chalice, disturbed and attempting to separate each ingredient in the draught from its fellows.

Yet I could not.

"It tastes of memories, my lady Question." Eol watched my expression, and his smile was somewhat pained though his tone kind enough, for once. He did not drink, but of course he must have upon arrival, not being half-dead of exhaustion. "I remember my own unease, the first time I drank."

At least you do not hide it. There was no poison I could find in the liquid, and I handed the heavy, gem-crusted silver item back to its bearer with what grace I could muster. "Many thanks," I advanced, tentatively, and the Elder cupbearer—he looked no older than Aeredh, but that was no indication—gave me a startled, blue-eyed glance.

"It is my duty," he replied, in a heavily accented approximation of the southron tongue. He looked to Aeredh, as if his fellow Elder would take issue with the words, and then cast his gaze down and hurried away.

I could only watch him vanish into a nearby hallway. "Did I offend by—"

"No." Eol's eyebrows drew together, very nearly wearing a scowl again. In this light, the sharp vitality burning in him—different than that of the Elder, but bright nonetheless—was more evident than ever, and his hair glinted blue-black. "Another used to rule here, my lady Question. More I cannot say."

Many were the halls of Nithraen's great palace. Our own great timber warrens were trifling in comparison, but I would have given much for a friendly hailing from a table of my father's warriors, or ale drawn from Dun Rithell's casks though I ever prefer mead. I missed Ulfrica's smile, Albeig's anxiety, Ulveig's fierce swearing, Astrid's worrying, and even Bjorn's great graceless self presenting me with a problem to solve.

At least Arn was with me. A vast central hall swallowed us, its pillars tree-carved so finely I expected to hear the subtle brush of moving leaves. Aeredh glanced at me twice, perhaps measuring the effect of such grandeur upon one of my kind, or attempting to encourage.

Or for another reason entirely.

Curiaen and Caelgor were now the rulers of Nithraen, and they often came from their hunt to the great ruling hall. When we emerged from a stone forest the light was cool gold, the stone underfoot cushioned by soft carpets woven to resemble close-cropped grass, and the rain-colored hounds milled excitedly, too well-bred to bay at our approach. They ringed us as we walked, but more in the manner of curious sheep than hunt-bred chasers.

It was strange, for they did not smell of dog but only, faintly, of fresh air and musk.

Some few Elder scattered about the bright, incongruous sward. A group had gathered about a harpist, whose playing grew softly plaintive when we appeared. Guards in bright greengold armor attended at intervals, while two slim Elder maids in matching pale dresses halted dancing and withdrew, bright blue gazes startled as young deer. Movement whispered behind us, and in the center of the woven meadow was a small rise with a round bench carved of living grey stone polished to smoothness, its cushions brighter than the "grass" and well arranged. A greater circle of white paving surrounded it, and the two hunters, bright-haired and dark, stood at its edge, conferring with each other while making every effort to appear unaware of our approach.

Yet tension sang in the air around the brothers, and the fair one, his shining hair a little deeper gold than Astrid's, very carefully did not turn his back. Both bore great curving Elder bows, their quivers half-empty from the hunt; sword and knife rode their belts. The folk of Nithraen were proud indeed, holding their lands against any incursion, yet they bore arms more to show the skill of their crafting than for brawling. I did not know as much then, though, and was glad of Arn's spear close by.

We halted some small distance from the hunters, and Aeredh stilled. Arn examined everything about us with wide-eyed interest, her right hand easy upon spear-haft. Eol moved to stand to her left, but slightly behind; his eyelids dropped halfway and the gem in his swordhilt gave a single bright dart.

A tall female hound approached me gravely, fringed tail held high. She examined my skirt with some attention, and presented her head for a pat. I bent to smooth soft fur, peering into her dark, intelligent eyes. Farsight had the same air of good nature, and I have ever liked dogs.

"*Beware, brother,*" the dark-haired hunter said in the Old Tongue. He was the taller, and his smile was thin. "*You may lose another hound.*"

Perhaps he did not think a *volva*'s ears sharp enough to hear, or a shieldmaid's. Eol stiffened; I sensed more than saw the slight movement.

Aeredh said nothing. He appeared deeply interested in the carving of the roof, highly figured and rising on dome-ribs to brilliant golden orb-light.

"And what is thy name?" I murmured to the dog. "Fair and sleek you are, and swift as the winds, I judge."

I meant no ill, of course. Complimenting a hunting pack is simply good manners, especially when there is some small unpleasantness or hesitation to smooth over in a hall's conversation. It was my duty as *volva*, and as the eldest daughter of Dun Rithell, to save guest or host from embarrassment; now I was called upon to use that skill as a weregild.

Why else had Eol brought me here?

The blond hunter tilted his head slightly, and his gaze came to rest upon me. An Elder can show their displeasure with such a look, and it is heavy indeed. "*Well, perhaps the haughty-brought-low must find his dogs where he can.*"

It sounded like an insult, but their accent was archaic and though I was used to the Northerners, they had hardly spoken enough for me to discern nuance. Yet a tone, a swift glance, a gesture—or even the tiniest shift in breathing—can express contempt, and the Elder have much time to learn such display if they wish.

The hound nosed at me again, not quite demanding but certainly hopeful. Canines always sense *seidhr*, and rare indeed is the *volva* or seer they—or cats—do not like. If the power curdles through viciousness or great evil, though, they cringe, and their obedience becomes reluctant just as that of the two-legged, though even the most helpless among Secondborn turn on our tormentors long before a dog would ever think to.

The most polite thing, of course, was to give a couplet in praise of our hosts' possessions. It might even stave off unpleasantness, and would certainly fulfill my responsibilities as weregild. Arn, though she did not have the Old Tongue, could very well tell a sneer from a smile, and our gazes met.

Shall I take offense? hers asked.

Not just yet, mine answered.

I do not know from whence the poetry came. I know only that it left me in a voice not quite my own, deeper and more resonant than my ribcage could ever produce. For all that, it was achingly sweet, and it spoke the southron language as I smoothed the dog's head again, marveling at the texture of her coat. "**Well-robed you are, by noon or night; A shining jewel among many prized.**" Each syllable in southron was neatly balanced, a play upon a highborn lady's great furred mantle lurking in the first half, the second holding the rhythm of running our bards call dogside, for the lolloping sideways motion of an excited puppy. It rhymed both at midline and end, and I could only think a passing divinity—or one whose veiled gaze had been upon me since the journey's start—had poured it into my mouth with Elder winterwine.

The cavern reverberated as if I had screamed a river-rowing obscenity, or a drunken warrior's challenge. The dark hunter's chin lifted and his gaze kindled; he stepped forward, though the fair one's arm rose across his chest, a restraint matched by the blond's narrowed eyes.

Arn tapped her spear's blunt end twice, both to honor whatever invisible beneficence had granted the words and to show her approval. And apparently the passing god or spirit found that pleasing as well, for the sound was also granted uncharacteristic weight, as of blade meeting blade.

"Did you bring another speaking dog to mock us, son of Aerith? Quite rude." The dark hunter looked a hairsbreadth from drawing steel; a bone hilt chased with silver hung at his hip, and the sword was greatly curved in a manner I had never seen before.

Aeredh stepped forward, but only because Arn had as well, her spear a diagonal line and her gaze fastened unerringly upon dark-haired Curiaen. Her hornbraids glowed, and in that moment my small one looked tall as an Elder herself, and fierce as a Black-Wingéd *valkyra*.

"Please, my lady shieldmaid." Aeredh raised his hands slightly, and though his tone was courteous enough, its edge of command was unmistakable. "Be at ease. Guests were once welcome in these halls, and I cannot think the hospitality of Nithraen so far changed."

I straightened. It was Caelgor the blond who spoke; his south-ron was accented strangely, the Old Tongue attempting to draw its descendant back from a precipice. "My brother is simply surprised," he said, and though he appeared languid, his arm all but vibrated with strength holding the dark one at bay. "You thought to return with an army or two, as I recall."

The hound at my feet flowed away, her tail still held high. I suppose she must have seen a great many wonders since birth, living among the Elder as she did; I was nothing in comparison.

And keenly aware of the fact.

"We rode south for allies, aye." Aeredh no longer looked so young. Here among his fellow Elder some force was unveiled in him; it was not the terrible blue flame that had driven away the lich but a vivid depth speaking of age. And yet he was the same youth, only a shade less tall than Bjorn, who always had a hint of amusement about his mouth as if the entire world of the Allmother's making was secretly delightful and he had the key to understand its kenning. "But we returned with far more, sons of Faevril. This is Solveig, daughter of Gwendelint of Gwenlara's line, and she is *alkuine*."

The Elder had gathered between the stone trees, a crowd far too solemn-quiet for its size, and a murmur took Aeredh's words racing for the door. The dark hunter relaxed, and the blond one's arm dropped.

Much is given to the Allmother's first awakened, and they may see deeply into another's heart. It is a manner of *seidhr*, but not of the type which comes unbidden even to warriors. There are forms of pressure, or even actual combat, both Elder and *seidhr* of my kind may engage upon with will alone.

Curiaen's dark gaze met mine. I *felt* the strike, as if he had somehow pushed past my shieldmaid and laid hands upon me. It was not the lich's foulness but a sharp intrusion; not abhorrent, but still vibrating with arrogant strength. Idra had told me such things were possible, of course, but neither she nor I had the power to accomplish them without some aid, divine or otherwise.

The Elder lord had such force, and to spare. The marks upon my wrists flamed. Idra had taught me much, and though my response was weak—a kitten's paw, attempting to fend off a bullock—it was wholly unexpected.

Even a tiny claw can sting.

Not Hospitality

Seven were they, the sons of Faevril, and all took the oath
that led him to doom. If even one had turned aside, perhaps
the rest might not have happened—but great was the wrath
of their father, and its burning filled them too.
                                    —*Song of the Breaking*

Dark Curiaen made a short, incredulous sound, but his surprise was a mere lightning-flash. As soon as it showed 'twas gone, and he relaxed with feline swiftness, not to mention disdain. Of course I could do no real damage to one such as he; my *seidhr* was not enough to challenge, merely to sting.

And yet I may have pricked his pride. Every man, even Elder, has a measure of self-regard, and it curdles swifter than any milk.

Caelgor turned, and his attention settled wholly upon me as well. At least he did not try to pry with *seidhr*, though my marks ached afresh. I was painfully conscious of my few years against theirs, for these might be Elder who fought during Hralimar's life, when the Black Land was alive as well.

Our captor said that time had come again, and Aeredh agreed. We were lost in a saga or plain myth, I and my Arn; and now I did not think it very likely to be a comic tale.

"*Now I see,*" Caelgor said, softly, in the Old Tongue. "*You know where the Freed Jewel is hidden, and think to claim it yourself.*"

I listened for all I was worth; their word for *jewel* carried much significance and a suffix to denote an item of great worth or import as well. I glanced at Arn, who visibly did not like the Elder's tone. The faint brushing of the Wingéd Ones' attention intensified—perhaps 'twas one of them who had given me the couplet. My shieldmaid's ring-and-scale glittered as her spearblade did.

They used no yellow thread or leather cord for pax in Nithraen.

"I have no desire to possess anything, save perhaps a sword to strike *him* down with." Aeredh wore a faint, icy smile, and the change from his usual self was startling. Tall and black-clad, the youth was gone and in his place was a forbidding statue, every line of his face grown sharp-carved. "This pair of Secondborn girls have traveled with more bravery than I have seen many a Child of the Star display in battle against Agramar, son of Faevril. And yes, if Taeron will lend his aid we may yet reclaim all that was stolen from you. Then perhaps the Blessed will admit us to pardon, and those of us who wish to may return home." He paused, whether for breath or because he sought to control his wrath, and the caesura was sharp as an Elder blade.

Reclaiming something stolen? Had that been their errand in the South, and asking for aid against the Black Land merely a pretense? But if that was so, why would they bring Arn and me hence?

None of this made sense. The frustration of sewing with tangled thread filled me, and at Dun Rithell I would have been off to walk along the river or perform some other activity so I could think without interruption.

"Will you take up your father's crown, then?" Curiaen's accent in our southron tongue was like a mountain-dweller's, and I thought it likely he had lived among those of my kind to speak it thus. "And lead your people forth to assail the Cold Gate?"

No few of the crowd around us—for the Elder drew closer, listening intently—gasped, or made a restless movement, almost instantly controlled.

I did not, though a chill slithered down my back. Any passing mention of Agramar was bad enough, but speaking of the vast iron gates between the two stone fangs guarding the entrance to that citadel was ill luck of the very worst kind. Any lingering disbelief I carried was put to rest; these folk would not speak so if the Black Land were indeed spent.

"Will you stain the halls of Nithraen with another kinslaying, do I take a step toward the throne?" Aeredh's eyes blazed, and even though I knew him somewhat, the urge to back away and perhaps quietly leave the hall was all but overwhelming. "Or perhaps you think to place me and my companions in a dungeon my own father carved?"

I do not think the desire to flee was cowardice on my part, for the two sons of Faevril might have shared the feeling. They exchanged a meaningful glance, much as I would with Astrid or Arn. Much may pass between kin in that manner, and swiftly, too.

These Elder lords held Aeredh in some caution, which was thought-provoking as well. We had stepped into matters much larger than mere weregild, and little did I like the event.

"Perhaps we should ask you where Taeron has hidden our property." Caelgor sounded merely thoughtful, but his gaze locked with Aeredh's, and though neither of the Elder drew a blade the impact all but shivered air.

"He came when most needed—as you well remember." Aeredh had never used such disdain during our travels, and I was glad of it, for it is profoundly uncomfortable to hear contempt so deep even if it is not aimed at oneself. "And now he wishes to live in peace, without traitors baying at his door."

My hand curled over Arn's shoulder. She heeded the pressure of my fingers—though I could tell by the vibrating readiness under my palm that she did not wish to—and remained silent.

This was not our matter. Indeed I was hard-pressed to discern precisely what, under the Allmother's sky, they were discussing. Yet there was that word again—*traitor*, though in southron instead of the Old Tongue.

"*The Goldspear cannot hide forever.*" Now Curiaen was cold, and while he addressed Aeredh in their Elder language his gaze shifted to Eol. "*In any case, work might be found here for a kinsman's Second-born witch, repairing some old toys and trinkets. An odd pet, but then, the son of Aerith has a weakness for beasts.*"

I had ever heard the Elder hospitable, and these were obviously weighty affairs a weregild could not comment upon. Still, it irked me, especially knowing that Eol and his men had the gift of changing skins. It is a heavy *seidhr*, but I could well imagine the comfort a hall or steading might feel in sharing such strength during a battle, a raid, or even simple misfortune. To impugn that defense seemed ill manners at best.

And to call a man a dog is not hospitality, even if you love your hunting pack. To call a *volva* a witch—or more precisely, a word which means something like *chanting beldam*, carrying overtones of ill-wishing and hatred too weak to wound—is not mannerly either. It is beneath a great lord, though it may be indulged in by a petty one.

"My lord Aeredh." Eol's tone approached lightness for once, as if he were only half-interested in the conversation. "Your people watch."

The assembly did not mutter or shift as a mortal crowd might. They were deathly silent, and why was I witnessing this?

Put that way, the answer was simple. Eol and Aeredh had some deeper use for an elementalist, even a mortal one. These other Elder lords seemed violently opposed to the notion; something of theirs had been stolen. The word *traitor* had been used in my language as well as the Old Tongue. There were liches and *orukhar* here, as well as terrible sheep-monsters. The Black Land was no mere child's tale but a living, looming terror, a ghost story suddenly given new breath and force with the advent of dusk.

And I? I was far from home, with only Arn as protection despite any promise a Northern captor might utter.

Whatever measure of excitement or anticipation I had at the prospect of learning deeper *seidhr* in the North or history only the Elder could teach was well and truly vanished at that moment.

I do not mind admitting the feeling did not return for a long, long while.

"Let any among the people Aerith once ruled witness this; I welcome the scrutiny." Aeredh's right hand flickered, indicating me. "An *alkuine* has come to us, sent by chance—or the Blessed, I know not which. You took up your swords and followed your father, sons of Faevril, well enough; I am serving the memory of mine. He lent his aid to a mighty undertaking, and in it a Secondborn achieved for love more than the Children of the Star have by wrath since the darkening of the West. I do not wish for your Freed Jewel, even were it gifted me by the Allmother herself. Do not accuse me of your faults, Curiaen the Subtle, and I will not accuse you of mine." The last held all the quality of a proverb, and I could hear why—in the Old Tongue, the phrase would bear a crackling lash of consonants.

"How very noble." Caelgor's smile was thin ice over a deep well. He still did not reach for a weapon, though one of his elegant fingertips twitched. Orb-light glowed in his golden hair, and though he was fair as Astrid my sister's is by far the greater beauty, for it was ever unmarred by cruelty. "Let us hear from your Secondborn witch, then. What wonder does she hope to accomplish?"

My fingers tensed as Arn's shoulder turned to stone under them. "Do not," I murmured. "If Lord Aeredh forbears, my shieldmaid, so shall we."

"She speaks," Caelgor said. "Your lord Aeredh, Secondborn? Has he taken a kingdom among your kind, then?"

At the moment I did not compass what an insult that was, but the rising ire in the crowd—invisible and silent, to be sure, yet still palpable—was warning in and of itself.

Captured to pay off a life-debt or not, I was still a lord's daughter, born free and *volva* besides. Being addressed in such terms, I *had* to speak.

"I am weregild to my lord Eol of the House of Naras for a year and a day, Elder, and Lord Aeredh has treated us fairly." I pitched the words as if rendering Dun Rithell's judgment to a possibly restive pair of combatants, and the whisper of a passing divinity still lingered in my throat, for the words rang bright with truth. Even the most forbearing, that tone said, could point out that a host was not behaving in mannerly fashion. "Even in our halls, far less grand than yours, we know how to repay a kindness."

"Son of Aerith." An Elder stepped from the crowd. It was the harpist, tall and spare in dark-green velvet; his stringed instrument hung loosely from one hand as if he did not feel its weight. He spoke in southron, whether to be courteous or to indirectly answer my likewise oblique challenge. "Have you returned to lead us? Your father's crown rests there, and though we have followed others we remain your people."

Ah. So that is a missing piece. Much about Eol's deference was now clear; the Elder I thought a mere youth was a king in exile, and Curiaen and Caelgor, sharing another speaking look, well knew their rule rested upon a thin board indeed.

Aeredh continued in the southron tongue, and the vivid power in him had not waned either. "Not so long ago you spoke differently, Daerith. I brought the son of Tharos and the lady *alkuine* here because we had little choice, being pursued by the Enemy's thralls. We should be setting our swords solely against *him* and not each other, as we so often have—to our grief, as the sons of Faevril should know well enough." He paused for a brief moment, but none dared speak in that interval. "When the lady and her companion have rested enough, we shall continue upon our journey."

"Perhaps we shall escort you hence." Caelgor's fingers now toyed with the jeweled horn at his belt, though no doubt he wished to employ his grasp otherwise. Sometimes my father touched his beard-pin while mastering his wrath, and this looked much the same. "For the safety of the *alkuine* child, if such she indeed is. Secondborn are…fragile."

"One took you and your brother both from the saddle not too long ago." Eol's silence apparently had its limits too. If he suffered a curse and wished me to remove it, perhaps he chafed at this time-consuming display? But that did not explain this talk of jewels, or of treachery. "And thus freed a woman held against her will."

Curiaen's hand fully clasped a hilt now, and the dark hunter was only restrained from drawing steel by his brother's arm once more.

"Where is your brother, son of Naras?" Caelgor, I thought, was by far the greater danger, for he not only leashed his sibling's ire but turned a searching look upon Eol, much as I might at once restrain Bjorn and question one of my father's warriors. "The girl speaks of weregild; thy father Tharos should be told."

"Were he here I would have already attended to that duty, my lord Caelgor. I thank you for the reminder." Icily polite, the Northerner otherwise held his stillness, but it was not like an ordinary man's. It had a peculiar animal quality; I saw what Arn must have, in that moment—eyes too bright, teeth too sharp for all they lingered in a human mouth. A ripple passed under Eol's skin, just as it had Efain's during sparring, and perhaps I should not have found the sight comforting.

Yet I did. For all their difference, those who possess a second skin are still of my kind. Amid all this strangeness, even that slight kinship was a blessing.

Whatever I expected next, it was not Aeredh turning to me, his shoulder pointedly excluding the hunters upon the rise. A twinkle upon the bench they stood before—it occurred to me they did not dare to set themselves in that seat, confining themselves to behaving as regents instead of true rulers—was an Elder-wrought circle of gold so pale it appeared silvery, set with a single great gem clear-bright as the one upon Eol's swordhilt. Its gleaming eye watched this event, silent as my mother while listening to opposing arguments.

The crown of Nithraen. Later I learned it had not been worn since Aeredh's father left his palace for the very last time upon a mighty undertaking, one which had cost his life. His son had never touched it since, and perhaps gem and circlet lie there still, buried under wrack or sunk in deep darkness.

"My lady Solveig." No trace of chill formality or anger marred Aeredh's tone; he obviously meant to be encouraging. "You have been brought to Nithraen's palace and given the welcome cup. You are a cherished guest, and we shall leave when you are fully recovered from the perils of our journey so far. A mighty deed you performed, clearing the road of snow and furthermore aiding in battle against one of the Enemy's undead servants; all who live here owe you honor. I should hope they realize as much." He offered his arm as well as a smile. The light in his wintersky gaze was akin to my mother's, and a curious comfort as well.

"I thank you, Aeredh son of Aerith." My knees were none too steady. Still, I squeezed Arn's shoulder before releasing; we had been cast into a battle not our own, and I liked not the implications—*traitor, jewel, undead* were all heavy, nasty words. I also did not wish to set her spear against either of the Elder hunters. "Your city is beautiful, but I do not think we shall linger overlong."

The gathered citizens of Nithraen parted before our departure, and the sons of Faevril—I did not yet know the name, more fool I— said no more as we left the hall.

The Tale Bleaker

O where is the horn, and where is the harp,
And where is the cup ever-flowing?
Gone into darkness, gone into stillness,
Left where there is no morning…
　　—Harkel of Dun Ysaer, *Aerith's Song*

Pained silence enfolded our quartet; Aeredh did not point out any more Elder wonders and I had no further desire to gawk. Sometimes in dreams I walk those broad shining avenues again, and hear the singing of fountains which mimic those from the West.

When I wake, I oft wish I had looked more closely, in order to remember.

At the time I had more than enough to occupy me from toes to crown and all the way through my hair, as the saying goes, and though Aeredh kept a steady pace it was not nearly quick enough for the questions building inside me.

Questions…and anger. I breathed deep, seeking to dispel the latter. Emotion is fine fuel for *seidhr*'s fires, but it oft distorts a *volva*'s inner vision.

I needed calm, and clarity.

When we reached the graceful white stone building Arn and I had awakened in, my shieldmaid tapped her spear-butt once upon the lowest step leading to its archway—in Nithraen, most entrances were unbarred, needing neither wood nor iron doors to halt theft or attack.

Warlike the Elder may be if needful, but they like the peace of growing things best. Or most of their number do.

"Sol?" The word held a wealth of warning. She had not heard half of what I did in the palace, but she had heard, quite plainly, enough.

Arneior's task is to win those of our battles *seidhr* cannot; mine is to choose those carefully. "Yes." I removed my hand from Aeredh's arm and climbed two steps, placing myself firmly upon my shield-maid's other side. Even to myself I sounded somewhat stunned. "I am only Eol of Naras's weregild, my lords, and have done as I am bid. We may travel as quickly as you demand, but you might wish to grant me some answers before the event." I thought it reasonable, all things concerned.

And—I will not lie—I needed the scant height the steps would afford. I was lost among giants, and though full *volva* I did not feel my cunning nearly enough to match even Arn's strength.

"I have half a mind not to let you stir a step further without some truths uttered, indeed," Arn muttered darkly, and I did not argue, nor did I chide her.

Even a life-debt has limits.

"Perhaps inside?" Eol did not glance over his black-clad shoulder, yet I thought he perhaps wished to. " 'Tis not a conversation for house-steps."

"The fault is mine." Aeredh bowed slightly, that strange vivid power not quite drained but somehow lessened, a cloud over the sun's face. Still, I doubted I could ever see him as a simple youth again, after even a single unveiling. "I told you I would explain as much as I may in Nithraen, and I will. But yes, inside is better."

"*I accepted the weregild, my friend; mine should be the burden of their anger.*" Eol's Old Tongue was not sharp, but soft and reflective; the Northerner shrugged when his Elder friend looked to him. "It is as you wish, my lady Solveig. Shall we?"

I entered the stone house again with Arn behind and my heart heavy within me. I have attended many a council before and since, but this one still causes me a chill to think upon. I took one of the two chairs from the stone table, turned it toward the room and sat, folding my hands together and wearing my best inquiring look in conscious imitation of my mother's posture when a difficult, unpleasant case was brought.

Arn did not wish to seat herself, standing instead at my shoulder—all the better to express her displeasure with some speed and thoroughness, should it become necessary. Aeredh leaned against the wall near the doorway, his ear-tips poking through a silken mat of dark hair; the sound of water from the inner rooms was not nearly soothing enough.

Eol stood before me like a penitent, and he began explanation with a phrase worthy of any saga. "The Children of the Star—for they remember a time before even the Moon, my lady—have only ever had one *alkuine* among their number. His name was Faevril, the heir of a high king, and he was mighty indeed." The son of Tharos clasped his hands behind his back, disdaining a seat; in any case, there were only two. The second sat somewhat forlorn, pressed against the table like a colt near its dam.

"*I should tell this part,*" the Elder said, but Eol shook his head. He observed some distance from us, almost as if he feared my temper—or, more likely, the reach of Arn's spear, since she gazed harshly upon him, fresh distrust evident even in the stiffness of her shoulders.

"*You would wish to sing it, and I doubt they have the patience.*" The Northerner coughed slightly. "Forgive us, my lady. We are used to converse in the Old Tongue."

"So I have noticed." Ink forced under the skin of my wrists and forearms tingled, and the runes between the bands might have moved. It could have been a warning; still, it was wasted. Never could I have imagined what I was about to hear.

I have since gained much more than the bare map of events Eol gave. Each retelling or fresh detail makes the tale bleaker.

Of Faevril's works he spoke, many wonders of *seidhr* wrought by an Elder *alkuine*'s hands in the uttermost West. Of how the Enemy, granted grace and lee to repair damage he had previously wreaked, betrayed that ruth with the murder of Faevril's father and the theft of many great works, as well as a crime so dark the Elder do not speak of it, dimming the light of their home well before Moon or Sun arose. Of Faevril's sons and the vengeance they swore with their wrathful father did Eol speak, and Arn grew paler and paler.

So, I suspect, did I. For of that terrifying oath came another crime, committed not by the Allmother's first son but the Elder themselves, setting blades upon their own kin.

Of the Elder passage to our shores Eol spoke in only the barest terms, the pursuit of the retreating Enemy ending in Faevril's death. Barred from their home by the shedding of kin-blood, the Elder settled to siege the gates of Agramar, for though the lord of the Black Land is of the Allmother's greatest begetting they had no choice but to set themselves against him—not only to save their own lives, but as a bulwark between his malice and the southron lands, where my people were barely beginning to stir, having only just discovered fire—that great gift of Tyr the Ever-Burning, who of all the Vanyr or Aesyr loves the Secondborn most.

Eol passed over many of the wars which followed. The campaigns had not been wholly in vain, for one of Faevril's mighty treasures had been wrested at great cost from the Enemy and taken to a secret place, both to keep it from their foe and to rob Faevril's oath of a chance to beget more bloodshed. And so it remained, even while the most recent battle broke the forces of the Enemy and brought a measure of surcease. For many mortal lives the iron gates had stood ajar, though no rust appeared on them and nothing moved in the Black Land's ashen, misshapen wilderness.

And yet...some time ago, the watchers in the North had discerned stealthy rumors, padding footsteps, thickening shadows. One dusk the Cold Gate stood open; by the following dawn it was closed and the sky beyond underlit with hellish, fiery gleams.

It was that sudden. The Black Land was awake, the Enemy's servants suddenly active once more.

"*I should tell the rest,*" Aeredh said, but not very loudly. Eol cleared his throat—the tale was long in the telling, but he did not reach for his dull-black flask or the slim jug full of clear cool water upon the table. Two gemmed cups accompanied the pitcher, beautiful as all Elder make, but their glitters merely taunted.

I doubted I could swallow anything, though my throat was very dry.

"*Peace, my friend. Let their anger fall upon me.*" The Northerner held my gaze, steadily. "The Enemy's servants and spies have thickened. We rode south to ask the Secondborn kingdoms for aid against Agramar's malice, but the great houses are broken. Few wish to risk the journey north, with previous battles so bloody and return so uncertain. Then we came across your home, my lady Solveig, and in the riverside market we heard tales of Dun Rithell's eldest daughter, able to bring flame from the air as only an *alkuine* may. We had already decided to speak further with your father, since he had argued for war against the darkness, yet when we saw him again it went somewhat ill. Gelad remarked that your sister was perhaps the *alkuine* herself, for she is Elder-fair indeed, and my younger brother Arvil…"

"He laughed?" That much I could guess, from Bjorn's account. My fingers were cold, knotted against each other. And to think I had been ready to leave my home with good grace, to gain adventure and knowledge while paying a debt.

Now I was being gifted knowledge indeed, and for once the gaining did not please me.

"And somewhat more, my lady." Eol's mouth turned down, his eyes glittered, and he had paled. He made no mention of traitors or treachery—even now, there were hidden matters. "I would not repeat his words; your brother answered them well enough."

So he did insult her. It did not help, but it might have eased my brother's mind somewhat. It must have pained the Northerner to tell this part, and yet I did not feel much grief over his suffering at that moment. I was too busy with the implications of the tale. "So you saw a chance to bring an elementalist northward?" My lips were numb, and I sounded as if I had been struck breathless. "I see."

I did *not* see. What did all this have to do with me, even though I was like their long-ago Elder craftsman? A simple accident—being born *volva*—should not have led to this.

"Not quite." Aeredh made a restless movement. "I suspect our errand was betrayed at the outset, my lady Solveig. We had much trouble traveling south, and no sooner did we find a welcome answer to our call than it was stifled. Yet since leaving Dun Rithell with you, the…incidents…of the Enemy's devising vanished. Of course there was the *grelmalkin*, but those are drawn to the Elder Roads. *Oruk* war-bands are now oft upon Nithraen's borders, too; I expected some trouble once we passed into Lady Hajithe's lands. We were—*are*—hard-pressed for time, and this was the closest safety. At least here we do not have to fear the Enemy's thralls, merely Faevril's cursèd oath."

"Your father somehow aided in the retrieval of this…treasure, the victory." It was not so bad a guess. Now I had more pieces of the puzzle, yet I could sense I still lacked a crucial few. A jewel, a victory, a bloodstained oath. "Faevril's thing. And lost his kingdom for it."

"After a fashion." To see an Elder blanch at a terrible memory almost makes one's own limbs flinch. "My father Aerith did what he must, my lady *alkuine*, and so will I. He…cherished the Second-born, ever since he found them camped singing upon a riverbank so long ago. There is much in your kind to admire, and your bravery not the least."

I was glad I had the chair, not to mention the bracing of Elder winter-wine burning in my middle. Arn's hand descended upon my shoulder. She did not squeeze harshly, giving me pain as an anchor; instead, the tension in her fingers said she was just as astounded as her charge.

I marshaled what wits I had; it was not so difficult to see the next link in logic's chain. "You wish me to use this…this treasure, this thing left by Faevril, in your war against the Enemy."

"We have a hope, my lady. Not a wish." Aeredh said no more. His gaze met mine. Unfortunately, though I knew the Old Tongue and the southron language both, I could not decipher what was to be read in its depths.

I turned in the chair and stared up at Arn; she looked back at me. Her grip changed slightly upon her spear, but not upon my shoulder. She was not ready to attack, not yet.

"Lady Hajithe," my shieldmaid said, flatly, before her tone shifted. " '*Is it expected to take only so long, son of Aerith?*' " My shieldmaid produced a creditable impression of the Lady of the Eas-tronmost Steading.

Of course, Arneior oft arrived in one leap upon a far pinnacle while I was occupied with watching valleys and wondering what they contained. "You did not truly wish weregild." My lips were all but numb. "You merely wished to prize me from my home, since I am like him. Your Faevril." Was I merely the first elementalist they had found? Idra and Frestis concurred that my type of *seidhr* was rare indeed, so that was not entirely out of the question.

And yet…

Eol did not bother with denials either. "Our need is too great and the opportunity too sudden to do otherwise. That is why we would take no other."

Now Efain's objections made sense, as well as Lady Hajithe's expression—though she had made no mention of treachery, she no doubt found it strange to go south for armies and return with a pair of women, even if one of them was a shieldmaid.

If his traveling companions had already suspected Eol's brother of being a traitor, though, a life-debt did not apply. It was ill done indeed to take a weregild in such circumstances.

"Do not blame Eol." Aeredh had grown grave indeed, and spoke with some speed and force, almost as if facing Curiaen and Caelgor again. "Mine was the deciding voice, my lady Solveig. I counted the… the event unfortunate, yet one which could be turned to greater use. And…forgive me, Eol, but I suspected. Your brother has ever had a cruelty in him. It is as well he was not gifted with your strength."

"*Curse*, my friend. Not strength, and my father would be the first to remind you of it." Eol's grimness deepened, if that were possible. Indeed he stood as one expecting execution in a judgment-ring, with jeering warriors looking on. "My brother might well have been how the Enemy's spies followed us. Which means I have done you ill, Lady Solveig. I set our course, and told your father we would take no weregild but you. Here in the North you have an opportunity to strike a blow or two at the Enemy, and keep Dun Rithell unconscious of the dark which looms. I ask no pardon, for what we have done—and will do—protects your household as well as our own."

"You have no intention of letting us return home." Arn arrived at the realization after I, but to her went the dubious honor of voicing it.

I was, for once, too mazed to speak. They spoke of a curse as well; just how much *seidhr* was I expected to perform for these men?

"None." Eol's answer was immediate, and likewise sharp. "And though you might wish to test your spear against our unwillingness, my lady shieldmaid, I would counsel you not to."

"I heed not the counsel of false men." Arn still gazed steadily at me, and I could only guess at what she saw in my eyes, for I was surprised by the swift flash of pain in hers. "Sol?"

Now is not the time for open battle, Arneior. The words curdled in my throat. I would have suspected some manner of *seidhr* to stopper my tongue, but it was not so, even in that Elder city where invisible force filled the very air and sang between fountains' waterdrops. I could only shake my head, my braids heavy with red coral beads, resting against my scalp.

Despite the power of such ornaments, the Northerners had led us into a bog after all.

Offering Apology

Though orukhar *are foul they are also hardy, and may march great distances with untiring swiftness. Many times have they appeared where all is considered safe, and their greatest strikes are against the unsuspecting. They delight in battle, and it is well they are so fond of it, for did they not fall upon each other when left to their own devices they might trouble us all the more...*
— Tharos of Naras, *History of the Northern Houses*

At dusk or dawn the orbs of Nithraen dimmed and a hush fell over the city. The songs of the Elder turn slow and thoughtful, lullabies or laments, and sometimes halt altogether in soft restful silence. Upon the balcony of a beautiful room turned into a trap I paced, occasionally glancing into the street below.

I could not see the Northerners, but I could very well feel their watchfulness that eve—or I thought it likely to be evening, though time under the hills was strange and I had no way of aligning myself with the sky. Slipping away from men with wolf-keen senses was a daunting prospect even with my shieldmaid's spear to meet any direct challenge. Traversing the unknown streets of an Elder city and gaining the outside was another, and after that, the snows of deep winter and more things like *orukhar*, the twisted carnivorous sheep-creature, and liches?

Even a *volva* might be net-caught in such a collection of quandaries.

There was enough space inside for Arneior to practice her own form of nervous pacing, following her spear's bright whistling as she parries and attacks invisible opponents. As practice, it clears the mind wonderfully, and its sweat wrings anger away so one may think clearly.

I was not so lucky, too scattered to engage in our usual game of dodge-dancing. So it was the balcony for me, back and forth as a sacrifice in a wicker cage or a fish trapped in a drying puddle. I could not tell if anger was what I felt; the mix inside me was eye-watering volatile as strong mead. The excitement of a journey promising much knowledge was stained with rage at my own blindness, the anxiety of possessing too little *seidhr* to avoid the snare, and nauseating homesickness.

I could at least be glad the Northerners had not taken Bjorn or Astrid; my siblings were safely at home with my mother. If things like the *grelmalk* or the lich wended their way southward, though…

Every time I thought of those creatures near Dun Rithell, I shuddered. My father was mighty, and gifted with the battle-madness, but against a lich even that gods-granted fury might fail. Especially if I were not there to sing strength into the warriors' arms, or meet the thing with whatever *seidhr* I could. Desperation might strengthen us in that battle, but the Northerners spoke as if liches were almost common in their lands.

And that was a chilling prospect indeed, for a single one had reduced me to quivering terror. What else—or worse—might Arn and I face if we escaped our captors, or as we were dragged northward to the hiding place of some strange Elder weapon?

Still bleaker realizations crowded me. What might eventually make its way not just to our riverside but beyond if the Black Land was indeed resurgent and the Elder lacking will, numbers, or weapons to meet its terrible master? For Eol had a compelling argument, and all the sagas say the Enemy is never satisfied with what he holds, always seeking fresh lands to conquer.

I could barely imagine the carnage, did *orukhar* overrun my home. To think of Astrid broken upon their blades, or my brother pierced by many wounds and collapsing in battlefield mire…no.

No. I refused to think further upon that path, but the mind, like an inquisitive goat, goes where it senses its master does not wish it to.

Silvery shadows moved, tree branches ruffle-rustled, and I halted, my skirts swaying and my fingertips resting against a bee-end of my torc, once considered the very height of fine craft before I witnessed Elder work. On the street below was a flash of dark blue, a glitter of pale gems, and Caelgor the Fair moved with a purposeful step.

He did not look up, but strode for the door to our refuge. No Northerner appeared to gainsay him, so I left the balcony, my sudden purposefulness attracting Arn's attention.

"What now?" she snarled, and my own expression could not have been pleasing either.

"The blond one comes. Caelgor." I cast a longing glance at my *seidhr*-bag upon the bed, discarded the idea of ducking through its strap. Instead I tugged at my sleeves, made certain my skirts were in order, and was glad my hair was suitably adorned. A *volva* does not wear a warrior's armor, but a woman has her own sheathing. It is the mail of skirt and accoutrement, jewelry and hair-twisting.

Unless that woman is a shieldmaid, of course. Arneior's ring-and-scale was full of Elder light, and her spear whirled in a complicated pattern before its blunt end came to rest with a sharp tap against stone floor. "If he insults you—"

"Then I shall respond as seems best." I did not wish to let her swear an oath, and wished even less for a pair of sharp Elder ears to hear one. "This is not Dun Rithell, Arn."

My shieldmaid gave a short plosive sound of irritation, but by the time our visitor had climbed the gently winding stone stairs she was at my shoulder, her spear a vertical bar and the flush of exertion fading in her cheeks, pale and blue-striped alike.

I stood behind the chair I had listened to Eol's explanation in, my hands tense upon its carven back and my chin raised.

A mannerly knock upon the side of the stone hall-arch heralded the Elder. "One seeks entrance," Caelgor said, in the southron tongue.

At least he was courteous. "Then enter, and be welcome." *Though I like not your advent.*

No armor, no weapons, merely a blue tunic and easy-fitting

trousers, boots of Elder make and a silver fillet holding back his fair hair, Caelgor the Hunter—so they named him, since it was ever his joy to ride with hounds even if there were nothing to be flushed or taken—stepped over the threshold and bowed with every evidence of respect. The horn alone was still at his belt, a restrained jewel-glittering curve shining with Elder skill. His ears were just as pointed as Aeredh's, and the shape of his chin much like his brother's. Both had long narrow noses, too, but Caelgor's gaze was far more meditative, and his restraint of Curiaen the Subtle—for so the Elder named that younger scion, regarding him skilled in the making of ornament and weapon—spoke of patience and forethought.

A rash man, even among the Elder, may be tempted to mistake. It is those who *wait* one must be most cautious of.

"Many thanks, child of Hralimar's house." He straightened, and his gaze passed over the room in a swift arc. At the time I thought he disliked to see Secondborn in a place more suited to Elder grace. Later, I would see the same look upon men taking in terrain where a battle must be joined. "I would begin by offering apology. My brother does not like the son of Aerith overmuch and the house of Naras even less; I am not fond of either. Yet you are a guest here, and should not have been treated so."

You called me a Secondborn witch, my lord. "We have been brought hence by chance and do not know your land or customs, my lord Caelgor of the Elder." Watching my mother use a few fair words to restore peace in a hall stuffed brimful of angry, prideful warriors was good training for this. "Whatever lies between you and our companions I do not share, and neither does my shieldmaid."

Arn tapped her spear's blunt end once to agree, and the sound was sharp in the dim hush.

"Well spoken." He did not move past the door. "I knew Hralimar some little; he was doughty for a Secondborn, and did what he had sworn to. I think we might find each other of use, my lady—Solveig, is it?"

"Solveig, daughter of Gwendelint," Arn answered. "*Volva* of Dun Rithell."

To prove it, I lifted my hands. My sleeves fell back, and the bands upon my wrists, runes between their roof and floor, were clearly visible. "And with me stands the shieldmaid Arneior of Dun Rithell, taken by the Black-Wingéd Ones."

"Interesting indeed. I am Caelgor, third of the seven sons of Faevril." Another bow, his handling of the southron language improving almost between each word. *"May the stars shine upon the hour of our meeting."*

"May the Allmother have it so." The proper reply in the Old Tongue slipped free before I could halt its passage, as I replaced my hands upon the chair's back.

"Ah." His smile turned gracious, and perhaps even charming. "So they do remember somewhat in the South. May I enter, and speak?"

I can hardly bar your passage, though Arn might like to try. "This is your home, my lord."

"Is it? They call my brothers and me the Great Dispossessed, for our father gave up any claim to kingship before the Sun rose. But that is no tale for tender ears." He glided into the room, careful as a forest creature stepping from tree-shelter into meadow. "So, this is your… shieldmaid?" He all but tasted the word, pronouncing it with care. "I wonder how such a creature came to be, for the mark of the Blessed is upon her in a way I have not seen among our kind, or even the *majaiar*. And you are said to be *alkuine*. A strange pair."

Were there truly no shieldmaids in the North? "If it pleases Arneior, she will tell you of her kind," I said, steadily enough. "I am *volva*. I have performed the silent tasks; I am also elementalist. It may be what you and Lord Aeredh call *alkuine*." I did not think it wise, before this particular Elder, to claim a title belonging to his dead father.

"He would not bring you here, were he not certain indeed." Caelgor's smile could be counted a handsome sight, had I not witnessed his treatment of Eol and Aeredh. My feelings upon our traveling companions were far from kind at the moment, and yet their welcome in the palace hall irked me. "Which leads me to wonder what proof he has; I am told you performed a trick or two fleeing one of the Enemy's war-bands."

Arn all but vibrated with irritation behind me. My mother and

Idra agreed a man who insults a woman once will try the trick again, unless met vigorously indeed upon the first offense. This was no worse than a petty warlord or a man from a neighboring greathall expressing polite disbelief in order to strengthen his position during trade, peace, or marriage negotiations. I held my tongue, for he had not uttered a question.

Perhaps it was childish of me. The Elder live long indeed, and to one such as he I was no better than a swaddled babe—less, even, for their kind are said to be born knowing much. Yet silence is a weapon in and of itself, and I had few enough to gainsay whatever Northerners or Elder wished to do.

Even Arn's spear might not deter either; 'twas my responsibility to keep us both in whatever safety could be found. So I fixed an Elder many times my paltry mortal years with a steady look, and hoped my patience would outlast his.

Remove All Doubt

Great was Faevril's wrath, and too rash his pursuit. When they found him upon the smoking heath many of the Enemy's fell creatures lay dead by his hand, but his armor and flesh were both rent and he died within sight of the Fangs. Some say his body disappeared into ash, consumed by the flame of his spirit, but his sons do not speak of his passing. And they were the only witnesses.

—Gaemirwen of Dorael

The silence was not quite heavy, but it was marked. Finally, Caelgor nodded, as Idra might when I had passed some small test. His hands flickered, a gleam appearing between them, and I did not miss the breath of *seidhr* as he produced the article from some hidden place. "Will you do me an honor?"

"If I may," I replied, cautiously. "I am a guest here, and bound to honor all I can."

The blond Elder halted a fair distance from us, perhaps because Arneior took a single step to the right, assuring herself of combat-space. It was warning enough, and if I know my small one, she was glaring at him with no respect for age, wisdom, or power.

So far as she was concerned he was, though Elder, only a man. And those creatures are not held in any great esteem by the Black-Wingéd Ones who comb every battlefield for brave souls, leaving the cowards to Hel's lowest holdings.

"My father made this." Caelgor presented the gleam for my inspection. A bright silvery orb, its surface scored with strange supple lines, rested in his palm. "'Tis a treasure brought over the sea before the first rising of the Sun, though but a small one. I wondered if you might open it for me."

"What does it hold?" So this *was* a trial, and one he arrived alone to administer. I kept my hands where they were, resting upon the chair's back; the carving was not quite sharp enough to bite yet. The orb glinted, a faint shimmer moving through those deep fluid lines. They shifted lazily, as if it rotated of its own will.

"Nothing harmful." He tilted his palm slightly, gazing at the thing; its gleam underlit his face and glowed in his pupils. "Should you open it, my lady Secondborn, my brother and I offer you—and your shieldmaid—our protection and escort."

"We already have escort," Arn murmured, as if for my ear alone.

"There are dangers you cannot imagine in the North, maiden-of-steel." The play upon southron words must have delighted Caelgor, for he smiled again, still gazing at the silver orb, tilting it this way and that. "I will not dissemble; should you deny our aid we will simply follow as hunters. Aeredh means to take you to a hidden place wherein rests summat else our father wrought. We swore an oath to reclaim what was stolen, you see, and it will not let us do otherwise."

They spoke of a jewel, a treasure, and of a weapon. It could not be a mere sword or axe, and in any case I could not touch either, nor spear, nor bow. Each fresh answer merely unveiled more riddles, crowding upon me like starving fleas in an abandoned stable.

"I have heard some little of your father's saga." I was glad to be upon my feet, and even happier to have the chair as a shield. Still, the thing in his hands was…tempting. An Elder *seidhr*, older than the Sun's rising?

What might it teach me? And what might this "weapon" truly be, especially since "jewel" could be a term I did not know the proper meaning of? Even to gaze upon such a thing would be a powerful feat for a *volva*. Worthy of a song, at least.

"It is not a pleasant tale. Yet…" Caelgor's tone softened. What was he remembering, this ancient being who looked a little younger than Bjorn? "Were I granted the chance I would, I think, perform my part again."

A curious thought struck me. If this small Elder thing did not open, would Eol and Aeredh—despite my lighting of their campfire, and what little *seidhr* aid I had rendered since—know me elementalist but not this *alkuine*, and send us back to Dun Rithell? It would be deeply, ironically amusing if this entire affair proved simply an error of translation from the Old Tongue to the southron.

I could return home somewhat wiser, though not much older. "If I do this thing," I said, slowly, "you will be as allies to Arneior and me? And if I am unable to, and our companions know I am not what they seek—will you and your brother give us safe passage and escort to our home in the South?"

"My lady." Caelgor straightened, and the light in his eyes was fierce. "Do you open this *taivvanpallo*, Curiaen and I will accompany you to your destination and guard you against all peril. We will even offer what apology we might to Aerith's son, though he may not accept it. And should you be unable to alter this toy, swift passage homeward is a small matter easily accomplished." He paused. "Even if the son of Aerith and his tame wolves wish to gainsay us."

"Sol." Arneior turned her head slightly, though she kept the Elder well within view. "You are weregild."

So I was, offered in good faith though stolen with a lie. What was proper behavior in this particular situation? I could only hope my shieldmaid did not find me lacking in propriety.

"And yet." I was loath to lay the entire tale before this lord, polite though he might be at the moment. These two of Faevril's sons were arrogant as any petty warlord my father had defeated or my mother outfoxed; I liked neither the Subtle nor the Hunter. But more protection, and a chance to return home, was high inducement to at least hazard a single toss of the bone-dice. "Better we should know now if I am truly what they wish, is it not?"

"They all witnessed you..." She halted, her hornbraids glistening ruddy. One was slightly disarranged from her practice, and a trace of sweat showed upon her woad-striped cheek.

"What did they witness, my lady shieldmaid? I am most curious." Caelgor turned his attention to Arn, though he still held the orb as an offering.

I did not think it wise for Arn to answer; fortunately, she did not deign to. My knuckles were not white as I held the chair's back, yet the carved wood pressed harder into my fingertips. "Is it some insult you wish redress for, or some mischief you wish to do Lord Aeredh? I would not be used in either fashion, my lord."

Nithraen's hush surrounded us. The entire city seemed breathless, waiting; at any moment I expected the singing to start afresh.

"Nor would I stoop to such." At least Caelgor met my gaze directly, and either honesty or its seeming lingered in the blue depths of his. "I make my offer plainly, my lady. Do you leave Nithraen with Aeredh and his fellows you will become a means of finding what was stolen from us, and we shall ride in pursuit. How much better to remove all doubt now, and gain our protection? Should you be unable to perform this one small thing, I cannot think it likely they will take you to the Hidden City."

Hidden City. It was the first breath of our true destination I had heard, and it came from *this* quarter—if I could believe it. "I know not where we are bound," I admitted.

His expression did not alter, though a glint of satisfaction lit his summersky eyes—like my mother's and my own, and yet unlike. "Do you not think that strange?"

Oh, he was the more dangerous of Faevril's sons in Nithraen indeed, for all his brother had attempted *seidhr* upon me. I weighed my response carefully before setting it free. "A weregild does as they are bid, my lord."

"And so you are thrall to the house of Naras forever now?" His eyebrows rose the barest fraction. "Forgive me, I am unfamiliar with the fine points of this particular Secondborn custom."

"I was to be weregild for a year and a day." 'Tis is not thralldom or bond, and even an Elder unfamiliar with southron ways should know as much. I did not feel the urge to teach him the difference, though. "Then the debt is fulfilled."

"Ah." A studied nod, as if he thought deeply upon my words. His back was to the open doorway, yet he betrayed neither impatience nor unease. I wondered where our Northern wolf-guards were, and if they knew of his visit. How much time did I have before one or two appeared? "Did they not tell you any who find the Hidden City do not leave it, save by death or the leave of Taeron its king?"

Please, continue speaking. I will sift the truth from your words later. I held my peace. Arn shifted, her armor making a soft sound.

"And again I ask your pardon, my lady," the golden-haired Elder continued, "but should you be able to use a stolen Jewel against the Enemy, do you think *his* defeat will be compassed within a single mortal year, and do you think they will let you return to your home before it is?"

Lady Hajithe had also asked much the same; it might please her to hear an Elder lord making the same point. Yes, Caelgor was more dangerous by far, though many held Curiaen's temper in more dread. I could only wonder what Faevril's other sons were like, and what their sire had been.

And now I knew something else. This "weapon" was indeed the jewel, and there seemed to be more than one of its make. Though that could have been another Elder riddle; there were plenty of them in this place.

"No," I said. "I do not think so at all, Caelgor the Fair." And though he was fair indeed, in many senses of the word, still I thought my Astrid fairer.

Arn perhaps knew my decision before I did. "Is it dangerous?" Her chin thrust forward, indicating the orb.

"Of course not." The Elder looked mildly baffled, his eyebrows rising and his mouth softening. "Merely a small wonder, an amusement, but one an *alkuine* must unlock. Do you think me likely to harm a woman by guile, maiden-of-the-Wingéd?"

"I am not of them," she returned, almost hotly. "I was *taken* by them, my lord Elder."

"My apologies." He rolled the orb from palm to palm, a slow easy movement he must have performed many a time while watching light play upon its surface. "I did seek to keep a woman against her will once, but not with violence. And for my part I regret it; *that* I would change, if I could. You see I give you the honor of honesty, my lady Solveig, even when it does not flatter my pride. I suspect even now Aeredh hurries hither, since one of the wolves watching your door must have gone to tell him I visit."

And what is he likely to do when he arrives? I could not look away from the silver gleam. Even just to touch something so old, so stainless… "Arneior?"

My shieldmaid looked to me. She did not like his offer; then again, nor did I—and yet. Arn nodded, a fractional movement.

"Very well." It took most of my courage to let go of the chair and skirt it, seating myself with as much grace as I could muster. Compared to an Elder's ease, I felt gawky indeed. "Will this thing injure a Secondborn with no *seidhr*, my lord Caelgor?"

"Of course not." Again he seemed perplexed. " 'Tis merely a toy."

"Then Arn will take it from you and place it in my hands. I will do what I may, and it is her duty during such matters to keep all who might seek to touch me at bay." *And to kill them, should they persist.* It seemed unwise to add that codicil; I contented myself with understatement. "I would not like there to be any… misunderstanding."

"I see." Caelgor grew somber, but he offered the orb afresh, extending his arm. "I have no objection, my lady Solveig; I can only thank you for your willingness."

Arn's spear dipped slightly; the Elder did not flinch at the motion. Instead, he cocked his golden head a fraction and watched her approach, then dropped the small silver sphere into her free hand.

With that accomplished, she backed away, catlike-ready at every moment, and as the glow strengthened in the window, Nithraen's dusk or dawn receding and orb-light intensifying, she deposited the Elder thing in my own cupped, waiting palms without needing to look.

A Riddle in Light

You must know your own strength before attempting to surpass it, child.

—Idra the Farsighted of Dun Rithell

Heavy and strangely warm, that smaller orb was also silken-smooth, its texture more like heavy cloth than metal. An unheard hum filled my palms, reverberating like the whisper of the black standing stones to the east of Dun Rithell or the sensation upon waking from a dream sent by the gods. It was also akin to the prickling-skin rush of a blade mighty enough to be named leaving the sheath upon a moonless night.

Though those with *seidhr* are barred from wielding physical weapons, we still know very well their secret songs.

Arn's boots settled, and her spear slanted slightly forward, ready to strike. "Do as you must, my weirdling. None shall touch you." It was the duty she performed least often, but perhaps the most important. Interfering with a *volva*'s body while one or more of her selves are elsewhere—or while she works a great *seidhr*—is dangerous for all involved.

"My thanks, small one." I cradled the orb as Caelgor had, then stroked its carving with my thumb. The lines moved and yet were motionless at the same time, an eerie dichotomy. *How beautiful, and how strange.*

There was a rushing sound in the hallway, and a shadow filled the door. "You." Eol did not sound pleased to find the Elder hunter here. "What are you—"

"Be at peace, son of Tharos. I merely brought a gift to the lady." Caelgor could have sounded a little less amused, but clearly did not care to.

I ignored their voices. The Elder toy was fascinating indeed. The etching was but a single line for all its twists and doublings, it tricked both eye and hand into sensing motion—or did it? The shifting was nothing I'd seen before, yet held a familiarity nonetheless.

"*A riddle.*" The Old Tongue escaped me, dreamy and slow. It is, after all, the language of *seidhr.* "*I see.*" For I did, and my fingers played upon the surface, following its whispers.

"Do not." Arn's tone was level as her spear, and chill as the snows outside. "If you seek to touch her, wolfling, I shall strike to kill."

Then I heard no more, for the *taivvanpallo* was indeed one of Faevril's works, and it swallowed me whole.

⬙⬙⬙⬙⬙

Yes, it was a riddle, as Idra had often posed while teaching Gwendelint's daughter the road of *seidhr.* A *volva* is not made, nor is she born; instead she must be both born *and* made. Uncontrolled talent is worse than no ability at all, or so my iron-spined, iron-haired teacher oft repeated.

Look more deeply, child. Look again, and do better.

Some riddles are for drinking, others are for war. Some are for travel, some are for dinner, and others are for marriage. But there are riddles only those with *seidhr* may answer—indeed, every branch of the great tree holds mysteries only those with its affinity may approach. And among those, lying hidden where even those of water or air may not discover them, are the ones only elementalists know.

The *taivvanpallo*, mute since it had last left the hands of an Elder *alkuine* both unsurpassed in crafting and near-unrivaled in war, was of the latter type.

It took time, of course. Arn later said she was half afraid I had stopped breathing while I sat with my fingertips dancing upon the silver surface, my eyes blank and my lips moving slightly as the Old Tongue ran beneath my heartbeat.

For all that, she was not overly worried. In childhood and during early training 'twas my shieldmaid who made certain I did not fall into a brook and drown when one of my selves departed to gather information, or wander from a cliff's edge when a sudden flood of insight pushed at my feet. She had seen the strangeness, and it bothered her little. It was she who listened to and remembered my halting recitation of what I had prophecy-dreamt, she who watched over my physical self as Idra taught me to breathe deep of drugging fumes and go riding the winds east, south, and as far to the west as the high cliffs broken by cold deep spear-shaped harbors, the Great Sea beyond containing its own *seidhr*.

Yet I never rode north. At the time I had not wondered at the prohibition, merely accepting it as law. For I loved Idra and trusted her much as I might my own mother's mother, though that lady had been sent to the god-halls upon a burning boat well before my birth.

The bands at my wrists and forearms sang with piercing-sweet pain, as if the ink were forced under the skin all at once instead of agonizing pin-by-pinprick. I was only dimly aware of my physical self, for I followed the *taivvanpallo*'s carving through each element in turn.

Metal I tasted, and rich black earth. Fire and smoke filled my veins, ice and limpid wave running underneath their brightness. A cold fresh wind and a hot forge-breath mixed with an indefinable lift, as under the feathered wings of a hawk before diving. A tree's trunk groaned as a breeze caressed its high crown, sunshine touched my fluttering eyelids, and the peculiar smell which rises from hill and valley late in the darkest of autumn nights filled my nose.

Behind the elements both large and small lingered the invisible spark, the ineffable they flow from. The great tree of *seidhr* holds endless branch, bole, and leaf, yet the sap rising through its heart is another secret still.

It is that an elementalist touches, or so it has always seemed to me.

My hands moved of their own accord, fingertips brushing or pressing in particular patterns, and cloth-soft silver flowed underneath without a mountain-heart's heat to make it pliable. The red coral in my braids sang piping-sweet chorus, not a stone but a collection of infinitely tiny skeletons somehow pressed into hard durability; the wool of my dress was made of the sad gazes of sheep and the grazing they did upon sunny hillsides as well as the thump-whirr of spinning and the clack of a loom, the stab of bright needles and the chatter of sewing women. The felt of my slippers, the thread of their embroidery, the precious beaten ore of my torc and the dreams of the smith who crafted it—oh, all, *all* of it I felt as the *taivvanpallo* opened like a flower.

The "toy" showed me glimpses of hills so green they hurt to gaze upon, a conical forge glowing hot, and a tall Elder man, his dark hair with a single streak of pure sunshine along one side, his hands sure and deft as he tossed molten metal from one palm to the other. He whispered a *seidhr* that burst against the white stone walls of a workroom cluttered with fascinating implements, drenched in silvergold light the hanging globes of Nithraen could not rival. He spoke in the Old Tongue; my own mouth followed the shape of his words, the accent ancient and unbearably pure.

"Thus I make you, and thus you shall be."

It was no longer a sphere. Instead, a silver flower bloomed in my hands, its cupped petals holding captive a single point of brilliance. Shadows, knife-sharp and ink-black, painted the walls—for not only did my shieldmaid stand straight and slim, barring all from approaching as her spearblade hung in readiness, but Caelgor the golden-haired son of Faevril stood in that room of Nithraen-that-was, as well as Eol son of Tharos and Aeredh son of Aerith. One of Eol's fellow Northerners was at the door as well, and his shadow had star-bright eyes and shaggy edges.

A *taivvanpallo*, after all, will show the truth even in what its light does not touch. But I did not know it then.

It was open for a few heartbeats, no more. The petals whispered as they closed, and I heard every word of impossibly ancient *seidhr*. I could not fully remember nor replicate what he said. But I knew the voice was of the man who had created this thing, and that he had taken joy in its making.

A further pang, hidden but incontrovertible, was the deeper satisfaction in knowing none but an *alkuine* could open the toy, loosing its beauty into the world. Only an aching glimpse would be granted those who did not share an elementalist's gift, and the knowledge pleased him mightily.

For he knew well, did Faevril the Dispossessed, that he was unique among his kind.

Arn afterward said it took a long while indeed for the thing to open, while Caelgor and Eol exchanged sharp words and Aeredh arrived, alerted by an almost-breathless Efain. The scarred Northerner had been set to watch the house door, and had seen the blond hunter's approach. All told an hour, maybe more, passed while I sat bolt upright in the chair with my hands working at the orb's surface, and she was quite content to let the men wrangle as long as they did not attempt to approach me.

And then it glowed, Arn said, dismissing the wonder as only a shieldmaid can.

For me it was no longer than a few breaths before the flowering of the sphere, and when the light receded and I was left holding a smooth silver globe, the carving on its surface had changed. Oh, it still looked the same to those without *seidhr*, I suppose.

But to my eyes the marks made a word, though not in the runes Idra and my mother had taught me.

And that word was, simply, *Light*.

Half Done, Worse than Not

Once the Enemy did not cover himself in darkness. There was no need, for he was the Allmother's eldest, most glorious son. But no heart may be satisfied once envy has filled it, and no soul untwisted once lies have taken deep root in the tongue. Now his malice is blacker than cave-night, and of all things he fears the cleansing of light. Even stealing the Jewels did not sate his greed, and he takes no joy in their beauty.

Because it burns.

—Anonymous, from the Paehallen Manuscript

O rb-glow had returned. Nithraen was once again full of song threading through paved or cobbled lanes, blending in every corner. I cradled the *taivvanpallo* in my lap, staring at stainless, secretive curves; Caelgor the Hunter took his leave of me as if there were no others in the room. *Keep it*, he said in the southron tongue, *as a gift from one you have done a great service, albeit unknowing. When you leave Nithraen, my lady* alkuine, *my brother and I ride with you.*

Then, with a courteous nod in Arneior's direction, he was gone. He passed Efain at the door, and the scarred Northerner's gaze upon him was unkind, to say the least.

Not that the Elder deigned to notice.

"Well," Aeredh said heavily, his hands clasped behind his back. "Faevril's Oath continues to cause grief."

"I thought you were to guard our lady *alkuine*." Eol faced Arneior as if challenged, but my shieldmaid's spear was steady and her shoulders relaxed. "Yet you let that—"

"He caused no harm to us." Arn would not brook scolding, especially by this Northerner. "Indeed he was more honest with my Solveig than you cared to be, wolfling."

"Was he?" Eol's ire mounted, and leapt in my direction besides. "Whatever he told you was only in service to finding what Bjornwulf and Lithielle won at great cost. He and his brother will slay any who seek to keep the Freed Jewel from them, even their kin—*that* is their oath, and they swore it upon the Allmother and Unmaking itself. They will hunt us when we leave here, and the rest of Faevril's living sons will come riding upon their trail."

I stared at the *taivvanpallo*, breathing deeply. Its *seidhr* settled within me, a sweet-edged burning I did not know how to quench; I felt as an almost-consumed candle must, eaten even as it flares.

Arn's shrug was a marvel of loose fluidity, though her spear-point did not move. "Perhaps they will treat us with more honor than you have."

"*Soft, my friend.*" Aeredh laid a hand upon Eol's shoulder as the Northerner took a single step forward. "Look to your lady, shieldmaid. It is no small thing to master even one of Faevril's minor works, and she is pale."

Pale? No, I felt as if I had Mother's ague, but the shivering was turned inward, sharptooth mice nibbling at my bones.

"Then withdraw," Arn snapped. "I will not have liars near my weirdling. Sol?"

Water. I thought of the great broad-backed river at the foot of Tarnarya oozing through mud at the reed-banks, or the soft sliding sound clear liquid makes upon stones. Snow-fed in spring, our mother-stream was clear and cold even in summer, though she rarely froze even in deepest winter. She teemed with fat silver fish, and even the sucking black clay in certain places along her shore could be used for pottery or dye, not to mention wattle and daub. A giving dam indeed, our river, and though I was far north among strangers I could still summon the scent of her wide rippleshimmer back, familiar as my own breath.

"*Hurry,*" Aeredh said in the Old Tongue, from very far away. "*Bring me the flask, there are cups aplenty.*"

Cold liquid memory met the burning of the *taivvanpallo*; I expected steam to burst from the two opposing forces, leaking from my skin and clouding the room like herb-water cast over hot-glowing stones in a sauna. My heart was a blacksmith's fastest hammer in my throat and wrists, and my scalp was damp. Saltprickle moisture collected under my arms, behind my knees, and I shuddered hard enough that the chair shifted under me.

When the seizure ended, I sagged, blinking at the bright smear of the world. Arn's face swam into view, blue woad-stripe down one side cracking though it had been recently reapplied, and she did not touch me. Nor had she allowed anyone else to, for which I was most grateful. Still, my dress was all but sopping, and the soft almost-constant singing of Nithraen's Elder citizens scraped against my ears. I had sweated through fine heartsblood wool; I could have eaten a whole chunk of salt and asked for more, like a great antlered winter-deer.

"Here." Aeredh was at Arn's shoulder, and he offered one of the jeweled goblets from the table. The liquid within shimmered restively. "We must have her drink, shieldmaid."

I am well enough, I wanted to say, but my voice would not do its duty.

"We cannot touch her." My shieldmaid straightened, and I suspect she did not attempt to strike him only because her current anxiety outweighed the matter of his proximity. "Not even a fingertip, Elder. Step away."

"What is it?" Eol hovered as well, but farther away. Efain drifted close to his captain, his scars pale and the rest of him following suit. A shaggy blurring hung over the Secondborn men; the Northerners were black blots, and for the first time I wondered why they wore such cloth.

Our riverfolk love color, the brighter the better. Not only does it show one's wealth, but it is cheersome to look upon, and lifts the spirits when the long dark nights of winter settle over the world.

My hand twitched. It took a great, drowsing effort to lift my fingers from the silver orb, still in my lap. Then to make my entire arm move, my fingers stretched pleadingly toward Arn, was another deep, terrible striving.

Her hand met mine with a shock like two angry warriors upon Dun Rithell's training-yard. Her skin was dry and warm, my own flesh terribly cold despite the burning. More than that, the *seidhr*-sense of another thinking, breathing life swamped me. A clear disciplined heat-haze hung upon her, and a great rushing of soft feathers passed through us both.

It helped, though not nearly enough. I exhaled harshly, my lung-cargo chopped into segments by a wave of trembling. "Arn," I whispered. "Arneior."

"My weirdling." But her smile was a shadow of itself, and though her gaze was not nearly so piercing as my mother's when she suspected wrongdoing, it was still a blow against my own. "The Elder has a drink he says may help. Will you take it?"

It could hardly hurt. I could not even nod; all my will was focused on clasping her hand. She did not let go, but she did suffer Aeredh to lean close and put the goblet to my lips.

Whatever the cup contained was warm, strangely spicy, and drowned the embers buried in my chest. It did little for the weakness, but my consciousness did not gutter like a candle in a cold draft again either. My joints ached, like Idra's when the weather changed.

At least none of the drink ran down my chin. Aeredh let the liquid retreat when he sensed I needed a breath, and offered it afresh when my gaze turned questioningly to his. "*Yitherin*," he said, quietly. "A restorative; there is nothing harmful in it. I will teach you the recipe, if you wish to learn."

So now you wish to give me more Elder seidhr. *How kind.* The thought was uncharitable, but I was in no condition to give it voice.

With his patience and my willingness helping at either end, I drained the goblet to the dregs. He retreated, I shuddered once more, and Arneior still clasped my hand, her coppery eyebrows drawn together and her full mouth drawn tight.

"I have not fallen in the river yet." My tongue was unwieldy and my throat dry despite the Elder drink, but my shieldmaid granted another ghost of a smile to the old joke.

"Not for lack of trying, weirdling." She squeezed my fingers before drawing away, casting a dark look in Aeredh's direction. " 'Twas beautiful, Sol. Idra would be proud."

Would she? For all I loved and respected my wise teacher, I had what she did not—not only as eldest daughter of my mother's hall but as a *volva*. Power I held, and she made no secret it was more than hers; all of Dun Rithell took pride in it no matter how uncanny its bearer.

And so did I, ever since I began upon the path of training. My arrogance might be small compared to an Elder's, yet it was mine, and all I had.

Caelgor called the thing in my lap a toy. Such *seidhr*, counted weak among them, could burn me from the inside out.

And once more an Elder drink bolstered me. It returned some manner of strength to my limbs, but I was not at all certain I could stand. Still, my arms worked now, so I cupped the silver sphere and lifted it. "My lord Aeredh." The words hurt, scraping their way free. "Here."

"My lady?" The Elder stilled, the empty cup dangling from his fingers. Its gems glittered sharply, spearing my tender eyes; the world was a bright agony at the moment, and yet curiously darkened by the absence of the orb's inner shining.

"Take it." I could barely shape the words; it was an effort not to speak in the Old Tongue after the silver thing's deep, undeniable whisper.

"Only you may open this item, my lady Solveig." And of course, because he was Elder he now looked handsome indeed, his head tilted slightly and his blue eyes kindled. His gaze was far kinder than Caelgor's, but still burned like the silver thing resting against my trembling fingers. "I lack the—"

Must I beg? "Please."

Arn solved the problem in characteristic fashion, snatching the thing with her free hand and pushing it toward the Elder's chest. "It is an ill deed to refuse a *volva*'s gift," she hissed. "Have you no manners at all?"

He did take the sphere, perhaps sensing she would throw it if he demurred. "*Is this some southron custom?*" Perhaps he was startled, for he looked to Eol, who shrugged.

"*None I know of.*" The Northern captain studied me for a long moment and turned to Efain, who still lingered in the doorway, though his ribs no longer heaved. It put Eol's back to Arneior, and I could not decide whether he considered her little threat or could not bear to look upon me, useless as I was. "*Well done, my friend.*"

"Babbling away in weirdling-speech." Arneior addressed a point over Aeredh's head, and her hand tightened upon her spear. "It seems a lying tongue, to suit them."

You forget I speak it as well, Arn. Or perhaps she did not, but I was too weary to care. "Let them say what they will." My voice was a bare husk of itself, and my hands were empty in my lap. Even my sleeves were damp. "As long as they leave us in peace; I'm weary."

I could not help it. A tired child will whine, and that is what I felt like.

"*'Tis worth more than my father's entire treasury, save perhaps the necklace given to Lithielle.*" Aeredh's hand tightened upon the glass goblet, yet he cradled the *taivvanpallo* in the other gently. "I shall hold this for you, my lady *alkuine*. And we shall withdraw so you may rest."

The urge to howl *fishguts, just take the shitstained thing away* was sudden, overpowering. I denied it, shutting my eyes again. I could not bear to look at its alien gleaming now. At least they left with no more speech, southron or otherwise, and Arn let out a soft but exceedingly obscene term no other warrior of Dun Rithell would have dared utter in my presence.

"Finally." She descended upon me to set all right, much as Astrid or Albeig would have. "You're soaked. Come, to the water-room." Her fingers bit my arm as I swayed. She meant no harm; the movement simply surprised her. "What is it? Shall I call them back?"

"Gods, no," I whispered. "The water-room. Yes. I..." How could I explain this? "Arn, that thing..."

"Beautiful," she said, matter-of-factly. "But you will have to train so it does not do this to you. Just like a weighted practice-axe."

If only it were so simple. "Elder *seidhr*, Arn." I found my legs would support me, but only just. "And yet it..." I could not even explain.

So far from home, and at the mercy of these men who had no intention of letting us return—and I had just been shown, in the most visceral way possible, that I was infant-weak even compared to their toys. I was no longer Dun Rithell's pride, the first full *volva* in generations and elementalist to boot. Caelgor and his brother might have sent us south with a blessing and escort, had I not managed to crack the fishgutting silver egg.

It had nearly killed me.

Half done is worse than not done at all, Idra often said, and like all such lessons, it did not sink below the skin into full knowing until I had failed.

Dread News

Before the door a shadow appeared
The guards quick-slain, the Mere
Fouled by a scaled length. A rush,
A slithering, a rasp-choked cry,
And then Nithraen knew. The bridge had
Betrayed them, as the Crownless warned...
—Daerith the Younger, *The Rape of Nithraen*

Our remaining time in that Elder city was short, though we did not know it. I did not even dream that last bright night we spent in the bedstead's stone embrace; I could have blamed my exhaustion or the taste-shifting winterwine, brought in graceful silver pitchers by a somber Soren and all-but-scowling Efain, who clearly considered us troublesome.

At least they refrained from sharp words with my shieldmaid, merely left us to our meal. Soren gave me a long look, as if judging whether or not to speak—then caught Arneior's eye, and hurriedly retreated.

When I awakened, I could not tell if it was morn or eve. A deep hush pervaded the street, though the strange Elder orb-light did not alter. Even the breeze stilled; no whisper of moving branch or thread of song reached us. No visitor braved our doorstep, and the remaining winterwine tasted of sweetened oatcakes my mother made to celebrate her children's naming-days.

I wished to weep, but the tears would not come. I was dry as summer-dust upon the trade-road outside my father's hall.

That morning—or so we thought it was, the constant orb-light was disorienting indeed—we were both somewhat out of sorts. The silence was vast, as if we were the only living things remaining in the cavern; Arneior's practice in the middle of the largest room given to our use made far more noise than the rest of the entire warren.

My second-best dress of heartsblood wool was already *seidhr*-clean and dry, packed in my trunk, and I paced before the archway to the balcony in my grey traveling-gown, almost wringing my hands. My shieldmaid could swing her spear to rid herself of an ill mood, but I could not run along the riverbank or venture into copse or pasture seeking the same relief.

I could only fret while treading, and wrestle with the knot of my own anger, bafflement, homesickness—I could not name all the emotions, and that is dangerous for a *volva*. Weirding sometimes leaps to follow a strong feeling, even if its holder would refrain.

"*Shuh*," she huffed, finishing, the weapon held level and almost quivering with battle-hunger. "They cannot expect us to stay trammeled much longer."

"We are penned goats, Arn." Even if no bar had been placed upon our wandering, I was sure we would not be allowed to go in any direction without an escort. Normally I would have longed to see the sights of an Elder city, stuffing myself with the strangeness, learning all I might. Now, each loveliness it held was merely a cat-tongue rasp across my nerves. I had not thought my mother's daughter so small and envious, but it would have been worse had I attempted to lie to myself. "Do you think we should leap the fence?"

"This is unlike you." She whirled, light upon the forefoot, and her spear-butt stamped the stone floor with a sharp crackle of irritation. "You will tell me what ails you sooner or later, Sol."

Maybe. "'Tis too quiet." I found my fingers threaded together and clasped bloodless-tight. "I like not how the air feels."

"Your mantle is ready, and so is mine. It would be a shame to lose the trunk, but we may both carry a saddlebag." Arneior's freckles glowed, her cheeks bearing a bright pink tinge of exertion, and she regarded me narrowly. "I say we attempt to find an exit. There cannot be only one."

"And then what?" I did not point out that wandering an Elder city in search of some egress might be frowned upon by our hosts, for she would blithely assume I could keep us from much notice. Even if that were within my power, what would happen afterward? "League upon league of deep winter and more of those sheep-things, not to mention *orukhar*?" I could not even bring myself to mention the iron-helmed lich.

She dismissed my objections with an eye-roll very like Ulfrica's when confronted with one of Bjorn's clumsy sallies. "Oh, you may find those fog-bound roads the boy did, Sol, and have us home in a trice."

"I am not so certain." A shudder walked down my back. I wondered if perhaps I *should* tell her the source of my brooding, though it irked me to admit any shortcoming at all. Who, Secondborn or Elder, feels easy with such an admission? It is harder than the most impossible *seidhr*. "Arn..."

"Just spit it forth, weirdling." She glared at me, though she did not thump the floor again. "Idra would pull your braids, Sol, but I have half a mind to make you dance until you cease fretting. We may do something about what ails thee."

There was always a cure for my Arn, and it usually involved spear-play. Dodging and weaving as she jabbed at me was an old game, and cheerful enough even when there was some ill feeling the dance was meant to purge. "There are some things you cannot kill with stabbing, small one."

"Of course, and that is what I have you for." But she cocked her head, her red-tawny braids dangling over her shoulders; she had not wrapped them yet today. "I mislike this quiet as well."

"Perhaps it is some Elder observance." My shoulders ached; the tension was well-nigh unbearable. And the lack of dreaming in what sleep I had gathered made me wary indeed. "This part of their city seems but lightly inhabited."

"Or abandoned." She stalked to my side, peering out onto the balcony. Though bright with orb-light there was no singing to be heard, neither of fountain nor of Elder throat. "Something troubles you, and has ever since that hunter brought you the silver apple. Out with it."

To be so thoroughly predictable is only a comfort until there is an event one wishes to chew privately. "There is much to be troubled over."

"I thought you giddy at the prospect of more weirding." So easily did she say it, my shieldmaid; she knew me almost better than my own mother. She adjusted her grip upon the spear, her fingers fanning out to stretch before closing again one by one. "Is it the weregild troubling you, then? I have been thinking, and praying. The Wingéd Ones are silent, but…"

"It makes little difference whether they absolve us of oathbreaking at the moment." Though being granted some sign, *any* sign in that direction from a divinity would have been welcome—even one of Lokji's pranks, and he is a fellow no sane person, *seidhr* or otherwise, wishes to gain the attention of. "There is still the snow, and those *things*."

"But will the dark things be interested in us when there are other…" She halted, her head cocked. "Hist."

I heard it too. Hurrying feet in boots, light and quick. The sound rang oddly in empty stone lanes, and though I did not have the strength for Elder *seidhr*, I had at least enough of my own to dread the news such a step brought. "Something is very amiss. It is as well we are packed; quickly, let us be ready."

Arn hurried for our mantles and her braid-wrappings while I made certain our trunk was well-closed. Consequently, when Efain and Soren appeared, bearing signs of great haste and their own black traveling-mantles, we were unsurprised. Sword-bearing, both also carried their bows, and their quivers were half-empty as Curiaen and Caelgor's after a long hunt.

"My lady *alkuine*." Efain's scars were flushed afresh, and he took in our readiness with a single glance. "We must go. They have broken the great door, and—"

Arn's blunt spear-end struck the floor, cutting across his words. "*Who* has broken *what*?"

"*I told you.*" Soren put his hand to his side and exhaled, as if to quell a muscle-cramp. The Old Tongue was harsh in his mouth, and high color stood in his thick cheeks. *"They both might be of some use in the battle."*

"And be killed or worse, not to mention prove to the Enemy what he might only suspect?" Efain shook his head and shifted to rapid southron speech, sharply accented with his mothertongue. "The Great Doors of Nithraen have been breached, my lady Minnow, and the battle-rages. Our lord Eol charged us with your escape. 'Tis a relief to find you so ready."

That was when we learned there had been battle before dawn upon the causeway leading to Nithraen's outer gates—great stone slabs, silver-chased and cunningly balanced over the Nith's mirror-like mere. Arn had seen them upon our arrival but hardly studied their construction, occupied as she was with the burden of her half-conscious charge. Later, we knew the war-band we had met upon Nithraen's borders was merely a tiny scouting party, spray before the wave; a strong force of *orukhar* and other noisome things had issued southward from deep, new-made clefts in the ice-cliffs of the Marukhennor, those perennially frozen peaks raised by the Enemy to guard the eastron plains of the Black Land before turning north toward the Cold Gate.

It was the first army to do so in many mortal lifetimes.

Such was the cause of Nithraen's sudden silence. Those who could fight were called to the many layers of defense, for Aerith the Delver had thought long and wrought hard to provide his folk with safety in caves the dverger told him of, long ago while the Sun was new. There had been little warning of the disaster though the folk of Nithraen held the hills above their deep homes with bow, sword, and spear no matter the season; some even lived among the trees in summer, free of a stone roof.

It may not have mattered. Warning is not the same as enough strength to fend off vast hosts of terrible creatures bent upon destruction.

My heart leapt into my throat. I could have wished for a true measure of my father's battle-madness, for at that moment it seemed far better than my own cowardice.

Arn's expression was merely thoughtful though her knuckles were white as she gripped her spear, and in her dun mantle and fresh woad-stripe she was the very picture of a shieldmaid ready for the work she prefers above all else. "How long, before…"

"They may yet drive the foul things forth at great cost." Efain shifted slightly, exchanging yet another telling glance with Soren. Had they expected to roust us from leisure? Perhaps that was fair, for I clearly had not *seidhr* enough to suspect their purpose in Dun Rithell. "Regardless, we have brought danger here."

"And while Curiaen and Caelgor are occupied, your lords may whisk their prize away." My chin rose, and I drew my gloves on with sharp tugs. "Very well."

Efain stiffened, but it was Soren who answered. "No matter what you think of our captain, the Black Land is far worse. Will you consent to accompany us?"

I could have remarked that my consent meant little, but a massive noise boomed through Nithraen, bouncing from wall to stone paving, from the houses to the great dome-ceilings. The orb-lights shuddered, trees quaked, and shadows danced. A bolt of pain lanced from my braids to the soles of my overboots; my strangled cry was lost in blaring, echoing cacophony.

Arn's hand fastened upon my arm, and she hissed an imprecation at the Northerners to dissuade them from seeking to bolster me as well. Efain whirled, preceding us from the room; as soon as we burst from the house another massive impact boomed through Nithraen. At first I thought rain or hail was pattering around us.

Then I remembered just where we were, under the hills of Nithlasen-Ar, and realized the small stinging drops were falling pebbles. The dome far overhead shuddered, creaking. Arn yanked harder upon my arm, and we ran in perfect accord, following a Northerner's black-clad back.

Death of Nithraen

The first of the great wyrms was wingless, and it is said the thing left Agramar against the Enemy's command, eager for plunder. For they are ever greedy, those things bred in foulness and fed upon giant carrion in the darkness under the Ash Citadel; they will swallow all they may, even as the meal chokes them.

—Eohyna the Riddlemaker,
On Wyrms and Their Habits

Just as there are sagas about its glory, there are laments of the Breaking of Nithraen. No few tell of how the battle veered across the causeway and many a great deed was performed by the two sons of Faevril, or by the Crownless—for so they called Aeredh, whether in mockery or strict truth—and his Secondborn friends. It was not the great iron-tooth ram the Enemy's servants christened *Krog* which broke the doors but something else entirely—a long sinuous shadow running with wet, wriggling flame, its snout dripping vile orange-yellow heat and its eyes deep glassy crimson, a creature grown immense by rancid feasting in the Black Land. Its teeth were chips of glassy stone, and its hide was thick.

It heaved itself against the great doors of Nithraen thrice, and it was a wondrous mercy none of the cavern roofs broke during that battering. But the thing—afterward named *Ugurthal*, the Glutton—was a burrower and delver itself, and perhaps knew precisely how much force to exert in order to gain its new home.

Ugurthal's unholy presence was such that terror smote even the brave under his lidless red gaze, and if it did not the great belching heat of his breath would. He heaved through the wreckage of Nithraen's well-wrought, deep-carven gate on a tide of clinging slime-flame, and the inner defenses fell one by one upon a morn of lamentation and fear.

Some sagas tell of after the battle was done, the wyrm drove even *orukhar* and lich, whip-wielding *trul,* and other foul beasts of the Enemy's army from the defiled caverns before settling in spaces rendered dank and lightless. He was not drawn forth until some time later, but I do not ever sing that particular tale.

Through shuddering streets under fading orb-light we ran, Efain keeping just in sight before us. I do not know how long we stumble-staggered between the peppering of tiny rocks falling from great heights, stinging as they landed. At some point Gelad and Karas appeared from palls of rising dust, both with blazing eyes and unsheathed, ichor-spattered blades. That left only Elak, Eol their captain, Aeredh—and Soren, who I discovered was not behind us after all. I tried to halt, digging my heels into stone with bruising force, but Arn merely hauled me along, perhaps thinking me struck with fear or *seidhr.*

Rumbling, crashing, overlapping echoes and screams, the ground itself trembling like a living thing with a twitching hide—just a short while ago, we had been trapped in a great silence, and now all was chaos.

Seidhr was lost to me, and in any case I could not hold up hill or mountain from underneath. But I could pray, and I did, crying aloud to Tyr who loves the Secondborn, to Ullwë-Aol the Smith who shaped the very bones of the world, to Fryja the beautiful whom my mother loved most. I prayed to Velundh the vengeful and to the Allmother herself, the Old Tongue falling from my lips of its own accord, unheard in the noise. Falling pebbles showered us, dust rose in choking veils, and a huge jagged chunk of grey rock calved from the roof as if from the ice-floes the seashore folk speak of in whispers, breaking from white ice-walls to splash into grey, wind-whipped waves.

I sensed more than saw the stone's descent, my entire body turned cold, and I yanked against Arn's grasp, terror granting my smaller frame a measure of strength and bringing us both to a skidding halt. The crash sent sprays of jagged spears and sharp chips in every direction; its bulk broke a graceful stone house and landed in what had been a garden. A great spreading tree gave a forlorn creaking cry as it was crushed. A smaller rock—I say *smaller*, though it was twice my height and wide as the stable doors at Dun Rithell—slammed onto white stone where Arn and I would have been, had I not stopped us. As it was, it barely missed Efain too, but I do not think he noticed.

The boulder tumbled upon its way, smashing against the house opposite. Arneior let out a hawk-cry, her lips skinned back, and we bolted forward afresh, running side by side as if we were upon the riverbank in girlhood again, my single braid bouncing and a shorter, weighted practice spear clasped in my shieldmaid's not-yet-adult hand.

Karas had sheathed his sword, and grasped my free arm. Between him and Arn I was carried along almost bodily, and thank the gods Efain knew where we were bound, for I was half-mad with fear. I caught sight of ash-pale skin and a fanged mouth opened wide in murderous mockery—*orukhar* were in Nithraen, though not many this deep in the caverns.

They had not yet time to plunder, being occupied with murder and other business.

Gelad's black-clad form flickered between dust-veils, billowing like ink dropped into swift water before stretching into a man's shape again, and the foul thing died upon his blade with a howl lost in the vast noise of breakage and ruin. Efain spun aside into a shivering house carved of a single block of gleaming white stone, and I might have attempted to balk again like a frightened horse if my feet were anywhere near the ground.

A hall with trembling, carven pillars on either side swallowed us; Efain darted aside, and I was hauled after him like so much laundry. We plunged through a narrow aperture and it was not so bad for the first few steps, for some light filtered through as well, but then the stairs began.

When Gelad wrenched the cunningly designed stone door closed behind him, a vast darkness swallowed us whole. And I was a sorry excuse for a *volva* once more, for I was still screaming prayers to any god, Aesyr or Vanyr, who might listen.

⬛️⨯⨯⨯⨯⬛️

It is said Aerith, the king of a mighty people who followed Faevril to the mortal shores not for gain but because they loved their kin and wished to right a great wrong, had the aid of the *thrayn* dverger in building Nithraen. I can well believe it, for there were secret ways from the city's deeps. Dverger have a fondness for such things; a cave without a second—or third, or more—exit is, when all is said and done, merely a hole.

In other words, a trap, no matter how cunningly wrought or beautifully lit.

The darkness of that passage was not like a moonless night. It was not even that of a cellar with a thick door. Perhaps it was the consciousness of what was happening overhead as we huddled on broad, spiraling stone stairs, or the cold blue gleam of the Elder-wrought lantern one of the Northerners produced, light holding us in a fragile sphere. Outside that thin scintillating glow, the blackness was a living thing, a cold empty smothering, an *absence* like the Unmaking.

Only the Allmother knows the secret of holding that endless, devouring nothingness at bay.

My throat was raw with screaming, but so was Arn's. We were all coated with fine floury dust, the Northerners almost as grey as *orukhar*. Their eyes blazed just as fiercely, too, and Efain set off down the stairs.

"Soren," I managed, husky from screaming and dust. "He was not behind us. We have to—"

"Don't worry for him." Gelad's sword whispered back into its sheath. "Filthy *orukhar*." His lip lifted in a snarl, and the wolf in him was visible for a bare moment, turning inside a man's skin as a hound will settle in a corner to sleep.

"Are you hurt?" Karas, his dark hair a wild, dust-stiffened mess, let go of my mantle-clad arm. "Or you, my lady Minnow?"

"I am well enough." Arn's teeth showed, a brief grimace. Her chest heaved, deep breaths wringing gleams from her ring-and-scale. "My thanks, Northerner. Sol?"

I was numb from head to toe; had I any injury, I suspected it wouldn't show for some hours yet. "Soren," I repeated. "He was not behind us. We should wait, or—"

"No waiting," Efain said, grimly. With Eol gone, the burden of decision apparently rested with him. "Karas, take end-guard. We must move."

"If there are fallen, we shall sing their names when we reach some safety." Arn's expression was as grim as I'd ever seen. She examined me, brushing at my mantle with one hand, tugging sharply at my right sleeve, peering into my eyes. "Well, my weirdling?"

I swallowed a suspicious weight in my throat. I had never in my life wished to be other than a *volva*, the eldest daughter of Dun Rithell, but at the moment I longed to be a shieldmaid instead. At least Arn was always *certain*.

If I had been chosen by the Wingéd Ones, though, I would not have been taught by Idra or taken from my home. "You've a cut," I managed. The woad-stripe upon her face was cracked and drying, and a dark thread ran through it—blood, from a shallow slice over her eyebrow. "Hold still."

It was a moment's worth to draw the pain out with shaking finger-tips, to convince the flesh to reknit. I did not even have to imagine a starglow to eat the discomfort.

Though Efain shifted, clearly wishing to be gone, he said nothing. I took my fingers away and flicked them, dashing the tiny bit of pain and damage to the floor. Stone still groaned madly outside the door, a muffled thunder. The closeness, and the dark, clawed at my aching throat.

Arn's eyes reopened, wondering as Bjorn's when I performed this duty. "Hardly worth troubling over." It was her way of thanking me, and a slight, pained smile bunched my cheeks.

"'Tis all I can do." I could not keep the bitterness from my tone, but I set her mantle to rights as well with a few swift tugs, and shortly after our small group set off down the stairs.

I did not ask if the Northerners were wounded, since they all seemed hale enough.

The sunwise-turning stairs did not last nearly so long as I thought they might, and at their end was a passage with rough sides but a smooth, even floor, traces of sand gritting underneath the Northerners' and Arn's footwear. My own felted overboots were in reasonable repair, though they were made for snow-travel, not combat or walking over sharp broken stone. Filthy with dust and sand, they dragged at my feet, and deep cold fear mounted in me despite the light of the Elder lamp.

The corridor seemed untouched by the rivening overhead, but I still did not like the sensation of earthweight pressing upon us. Efain led, Arn paced slightly ahead of me, Gelad and Karas behind; a new silence unlike Nithraen's hush wrapped us in black velvet.

My hands were damp inside green, fur-trimmed gloves. Anything could be hiding in the ink-pall beyond our small, faint sphere; the cessation of noise was not comforting. I did not even want to blink for fear of losing the light.

"You could have told us there was battle," my shieldmaid said, when we had walked some distance.

"There was not time." Efain did not turn, and though he did not whisper the vast silence nibbled at the edges of each word. "And my lord Eol would not wish to risk either of you near such a thing."

I found I could speak. "Or he thought we might try to find some hidden egress from the city, did we know our captors distracted." It was perhaps unwise to observe as much, especially with my voice broken from screaming prayers.

Efain's shoulders stiffened, but it was Gelad who replied. "He thought you might seek to help, and be injured or worse. Aeredh agreed, and sent us to take you to safety. We would rather lose ourselves than you, my lady *alkuine*."

Of course, I was a means to an end for them—or so they thought. I could not tell whether it would be better or worse to inform them Faevril's "toy" had almost burned me to emptiness, like a wicker cage upon a solstice fire.

It had occurred to me, as I woke that quiet, dreadful morn, that I was near useless to any of their possible designs. Which meant Arn and I could possibly go home—I could think of nothing else at that moment, and my eyes welled up not merely from the dust.

"Aeredh foresaw an attack, just not where. And Nithraen was supposed to hold." Karas spoke softly from his place as rearguard. The Old Tongue halted between his lips, sorrow-laden. *"Next the Enemy will take Dorael. If he can."*

They still thought us unable to understand their language; it was a slim advantage, and one I was glad my fruitless screaming amid the earlier noise had not broken. Arn cast an eloquent look over her shoulder. I held my peace. The rabbit-trembling still shook my bones, but at least I was not sweating with fear anymore.

Now I was chilled, though the tunnel was neither warm nor cold. I do not know how long we walked, as the passage sloped gently upward. Perhaps we had all been crushed by falling rock or slain by *orukhar*, and were now wandering in one of Hel's lands while that great goddess decided what to do with us.

The more I tried not to think such things, the more plausible they seemed. Sometimes the invisible selves are knocked free by mischance, after all, and though *volva*, I was just as mortal as any Secondborn. I was busy holding what little remained of my courage close-trapped and biting my lower lip to halt yet more useless prayers; I could not even perform a simple test to see if I was still in my body or…otherwise.

Would my companions be whisked into a vast ruddy-lit hall with warriors laughing and Wingéd shieldmaids, their service done, trading riddles as the mead flowed? Would I find myself upon a grey hillside with white flax-flowers, denied the reward of those who had died bravely in battle? Since I had been contemplating abandoning the weregild, would I drown in the cold lake of oathbreakers, numb and struggling to breathe for an eternity as my choked cries rent an uncaring, smoke-lensed sky?

Perhaps my cowardice would leave me, quite simply, alone. In the dark.

Forever.

The journey, however, came to a far more mundane end. Efain slowed, and the Elder lantern swung slightly on its thin, very fine chain. The rock face on either side smoothed, the hallway narrowing before reaching a blank terminus. "Gelad?"

"No pursuit," the other Northerner said. "Yet." He and Karas slipped past, hands to hilts. Arn motioned me slightly back; the wall of blank stone before us was sheer and polished almost to a gleam. Thin lines of moonlight ran against its surface, sparked by the Elder lantern's glow. It looked a mere drawing of a door, and the fear clawed at my chest again.

"Perhaps I should look past it," I heard myself whisper. "To... to see if it is safe?" The thought of sending one of my selves to the other side of the barrier was almost as terrifying as being trapped in this hole while an entire city shivered overhead. We could not hear Nithraen's death-agony, which was perhaps the only mercy the day offered to that beautiful place.

A short silence ensued, almost embarrassed, while the men glanced at each other. "No need," Efain said, finally. "Though I thank you for the offer, my lady. You are indeed brave."

Liar. I was merely cringing-grateful they had not accepted. Arn glanced behind me, though there was little enough to see, then turned to the silvered drawing and settled herself, the wicked leaf-shape of her spear's very tip glittering coldly.

She did not ask where the door led. Perhaps, like me, she was not certain it would open.

Neither Foolish nor Hardy

We won upon the stony beaches of Nar Aemil, and when the Sun rose we drove the Enemy into his iron pen. We won the Dag Nariae-li, after which our tears were like rain. Dag Jinar, Dag Gaesion, a score of other battles leading to the Liar's Truce, all victories. We kept the Long Vigil after Dag Skalda-en-kar, and met every egress from Agramar with swift vigilance. We won on the Day of Ash, and though it was cruel, we won the Battle of Falling Ice as well. So many victories, bought with so much sorrow—and yet, having carried every battle, we have somehow lost the war. The Enemy is beyond us.
—Unfinished Saga, attributed to the Crownless

A steep wooded hillside, a frozen stream at its foot under snowy starlight—it sounds simple enough. Also upon the hill was a hidden cleft snugged among tumbled boulders and the strange yellow grass of winter in Nithraen, thin threads of green lingering at the heart of every blade. The trees, their giant golden leaves holding fast instead of dry-fallen, rustled uneasily as Efain stood at the end of a short corridor between moss-grown rocks, a pool of deep shadow behind holding his companions as well as Arn and me.

The door was closed at our backs, invisible once it had sealed. We no longer needed the Elder lamp, and I finally saw the trick of extinguishing one by watching carefully as Efain did so. Kolle had always jealously guarded that small bit of weirding; the Northerner was not nearly so cautious.

After that was done the scarred Northerner tested the cold breeze, his eyes closed while I strained to hear past snowbound quiet and a trickle of running water—music indeed after the tunnel's complete, unnatural silence. Tiny hard flakes whispered past the leaf-roof; whatever vast *seidhr* held snow and the worst of the cold at bay in the land above Nithraen was weakening, if not yet broken.

Even with *volva*-sharp ears, I could barely hear a distant pounding, like thunder so far in the distance it seems imaginary. Enough starglow filtered into our almost-cave to show Arn's expression—she heard nothing, and shook her head slightly at my inquiring look.

I could say I was overjoyed to be out of devouring darkness, not to mention breathing free air, but such words could not ever express the sheer depth of my relief. My knees were not quite steady, so I leaned against the round back of a moss-coated, massive granite egg, my gloved hands already numb with cold but unwilling to peel themselves from its support.

Thank you for not crushing me. The thought, somewhat incoherent, nevertheless met a sleepy stirring inside the boulder. It had stood here for a long while and not crushed anyone, but was glad enough to be spoken to.

I was still *seidhr* enough for that, at least.

"Nothing," Efain finally muttered. "My lady Minnow, should we meet a war party, we will hold them while you take your lady *alkuine* west into the Wild. If you follow the setting sun and cross the Lithak, then aim for the outstretched arm of the mountain looking like a hooded man, you may well reach the edges of Dorael, and—"

"Perhaps." Arn did not think much of these instructions. "Or I may take my Solveig south and east, returning us to Dun Rithell."

"You are neither foolish nor hardy enough for such a journey." Efain beckoned us forth with a swift, irritated motion. A faint puff of stonedust shook free of his black mantle, and though his scars had flushed the rest of him was deadly pale. "Come."

There was no path from the hidden door; we simply filed down the hill and turned what had to be west at the stream-edge. The water's margin held growing feathers of slush—not frozen yet, but only a matter of time.

My overboots were glad of the change in terrain. I pulled my gloved hands into mantle-sleeves, feeling very rumpled indeed. The deep circular warming breaths would not seat themselves properly in my lungs; I could have blamed the fine floury dust. Arn paced just behind me; now Gelad had rearguard, and the Northerners moved very quietly indeed.

The silence of a wood upon a winter night is rarely complete. Even if no animals are about night-hunting there is always the wind, and the trees' slow breathsong. That night there was also the hiss of small ice pellets falling, and when the breeze shifted a faint, distorted howling rode its spiked back. I pulled my hood up, after making certain Arn had arranged hers as well.

Weather cleared, the threat of snow retreating slightly as we crept along; the ice falling now was shaken from branches instead of sky. The cold intensified, a deepcrack freeze approaching—so named for its habit of making trees in a forest's far cold reaches explode as if struck by lightning. It is the weather Lokji rules, that mischievous, contrary, high-horned son of the Allmother. A good sign, since he often worked against her eldest child's plans.

He does not like mischief not of his own making, nor cruelty to the innocent.

Or perhaps it was a bad omen instead, since he had often aided the Enemy's party, thinking himself fighting for freedom, during that unfilial divinity's first rebellion before there was a world or anything living to inhabit it. Or so the sagas say. No god is so great they are without a mistake or two, even the Allmother by whose grace we are made—for what else are suffering and malevolence but errors, even if their eventual end is far greater than we may compass?

Soon I was fully occupied with the deep, circular breathing to stoke my body's inner furnace. Broad leaves began to fall, each one coated with clear, heavy ice; the night was full of tiny groans, the snapping of foliage from branches, and occasionally a greater wave of sound as the wind pushed another cargo of freezing over the lands of Nithraen.

Efain halted at intervals, his tousled bare head upflung; shieldmaids love the cold, but the two-skinned Northerners did not seem to even feel it. The distant pounding and weird howling from a violated Elder city vanished after a long time of steady movement. Glancing at the sky was disorienting, for the stars here were different than Dun Rithell's.

The Elder Roads had brought us far indeed, and I could not find a friendly light in the heavens.

We followed the stream's wandering for some time until its curve bent far to our right, intent upon its own business. Winter had been denied too tight a grasp upon this land, but in the end, the frost always wins. The groaning and creaking around us intensified, and when ice-freighted leaves hit the ground no few shattered with small, forlorn tinkles.

At least I was now certain we were not dead and trapped in one of Hel's many halls or countries. The comfort was short-lived indeed, though I was still utterly grateful to be out from under so much rock and earth. I had never been uneasy at close spaces like Ilveig our kitchen-queen—who disliked even a cellar with its door carefully propped open, turning pale and accomplishing any task in the depths quickly—but after that night I never bore them comfortably again.

Efain halted once more, and after listening intently, turned to face the rest of us. We huddled at the foot of yet another hill, sheltered from the wind but not for long. I realized dawn was tiptoeing, grey and hushed, between the forest's wooden pillars.

It had not been morn in Nithraen after all, but dusk. Now the night and the city itself were both broken—though I was still somewhat confused, and hoped the foul invasion could be dispelled. The Elder were mighty warriors, were they not?

Yet the stonedust upon us was so thick, and the damage to those vast caverns likely immense even if not fatal.

"The border's close," Gelad said quietly. "We can reach it by nightfall, even on two feet."

"If our lady *alkuine*'s strength holds." Karas did not look at me, and his next words put paid to any small hope of Nithraen's continuance. "They will be about the wrack and ruin of the city for some while, and will drive the captured northward."

My ears tingled upon hearing that, and my restless yearning seized upon possible escape. "Let us go." My whisper was as fierce as Efain's. "You can escape to this Dorael, and while the *orukhar* are busy Arn and I will slip by."

I was weregild, yes; but the one holding my pledge was not here. Between those two conditions I had some room to maneuver, and even to negotiate. I could even use the charge of a dead man's treachery to free Arn and me from this madness.

"We cannot." Gelad was still pale, though bright spots of high color stood on both his stubbled cheeks. He had managed to shake much of the dust from his hair, and his left hand rested upon a dagger-hilt. "You are a long journey from your home even during summer travel, my lady. Please, let us arrange this, and—"

"Do you not hear me? I am useless to you, and to your lords. I cannot do the thing you want, and you have a chance to right a great wrong by freeing us." At least I was still *volva* enough that my hiss forestalled any interruption, and though Efain opened his mouth I silenced him by glaring, knowing my eyes were bright with *seidhr*. "It was ill done to take a weregild by lies, but you may set the matter right, and in turn, the gods will smooth your own journey."

I did not quite apply the pressure of my will to the words, as a *seidhr* often does when facing a wrongdoer who may easily become violent. Besides, such a weight can wear off with distance and time, and I did not wish pursuit.

Not by Northerners who could change their skins.

"*It was ill done indeed,*" Karas said. "*But they will not last a day without us.*"

"*Try explaining that to stubborn women.*" Efain sighed, and when he spoke in southron, the words bore sharp accent. "My lady, did you have even a slim chance of reaching your home alive, I might agree. But if they have taken Nithraen the South Gap is blocked unless you can use the Elder Roads, and the Enemy watches those so close to the Black Land. 'Tis why bringing you north upon them, even at the very fringe, was such a risk, but we knew there would be an attack soon. We simply did not know whether *he* would first take Dorael, now that Aenarian is—"

"This is no time for a history lesson." Gelad had turned his attention to scanning our surroundings just as Arn was. She was leaving persuasion to me, but I thought it very likely she would attempt to free us from our companions in her own way should I fail, and soon. "The sun rises; every moment we linger means the greater chance of discovery by roving filth."

"Let us go." I focused upon Efain, for I knew his conscience spoke in my favor. "You knew it was not right. More than that, I cannot use your Elder weapon, *seidhr* though it may be. Taking us any farther north is a waste, and a violation of hospitality. The gods themselves will be angered."

"*As if the Blessed care for aught we mortals do,*" Gelad scoffed. "*Will we have to drag them? We must go; I like not the way the wind smells.*"

"We can make our way south." It was difficult not to shift to the Old Tongue, and curse them in the deeper language of *seidhr* for good measure. "I am *volva*, Arn is shieldmaid, and the gods will protect us. You can travel for whatever safety you may find among the Elder or your own kind without our weight. Nothing of the Enemy's will care for us, we shall simply slip by—"

"Please." A muscle flicked in Efain's cheek, twitching the scar upon his jaw. He swallowed hard, the stone lodged in every man's throat bobbing, and continued in a harsh whisper. "Please, my lady *alkuine*. Do not force us to anything we might all regret."

"That," Arn said softly, her gaze settling at a point just above his shaggy black-haired head, "sounds like a threat."

"I would ask you to trust us, though we have given you little reason to." Efain did not move, though he was tense as any warrior who suspects the strike will fall soon. "The Enemy's spies do not care for gods or the Blessed. They will find you; they will slay a shieldmaid and take an *alkuine* by swift passage to meet their master. Neither of you will survive long in the North without aid, and you are fools to spurn ours."

"I would rather face those spies than endure further travel with liars." I did not bother to whisper now, and the words rang like a shout among the chimes of falling ice-leaves. "You are given a chance to right a wrong, Efain of the North. I suggest you take it."

Arn moved, her spear dropping into guard, and I was ready, backing away to provide what *seidhr*-aid I could.

Swearing Alliance

During Aenarian's illness his wife led their people; even as darkness pressed against the borders did she sit in judgment and rule upon the green hill of Paerunn-il. Sadness was etched upon her loveliness, but though her silent grief made every song a lament and dimmed the light beneath the trees she made no move to leave their land, for she knew there was one more guest to welcome.

—Daeglan Silverthroat the Elder,
The History of Dorael

It is said the Black-Wingéd Ones themselves train shieldmaids; it is close to the truth. It was Idra who noticed Arneior's grace and unflinching; test after test was conducted to disprove a child's selection, for the path is harsh and those not truly called will die in horrible fashion upon it.

Yet each time Arn passed the trial, often with a cheeky grin and a toss of her ruddy head. *That wasn't so hard; the feather-ladies help me.*

After the final ordeal—the Hunt of Marrow, performed naked and weaponless in deep winter—proved her worth beyond doubt Arneior sparred with the warriors, and any who thought a girl-child easy prey was roundly disabused of the notion. The Wingéd whispered in Arn's ear, pulling her limbs into the proper places, and sometimes it was chilling to see her young face blank except for shining trust while she swung a shortened spear or pair of weighted, child-size axes.

That day she was light as a feather herself, her boots whispering as we retreated from the three Northerners. Dawnlight was strengthening, no longer merely grey but shading into gold at its hem. The stars were fading, and it would be a bright winter morn soon enough.

None of the men put hand to swordhilt just yet; I had no idea how long such luck would hold. We had no saddlebags, no trunk, nothing even approaching winter gear except our mantles and my *seidhr*-bag. Yet I could call fire to any tinder and keep it alive, at least, and Arn had her spear. I knew very well returning home was not likely at this point, and Arn likely concurred.

Yet we would go no farther north as weregild. As prisoners, perhaps, without a polite fiction to smooth our captors' paths and allowed or even encouraged to attempt escape as often as seemed possible—or as allies, able to exert some small effect over our own fates.

Better than none. My patience might have been thought weakness, but now it paid handsomely, as such things often do.

"This serves nothing." Efain kept his tone low and reasonable, and though his two companions stepped aside as necessary for three men with a single foe, still none drew. "I am sorry for my part in it, my lady *alkuine*, but I cannot return you to your home nor let you wander unprotected."

I have Arn, thank you. "Then you will either take us prisoner or become our allies." I did not speak overloud now, but I did not whisper. "I suggest the latter."

Arn retreated another step, ready to dance. With her spear level and her gaze clear and direct, she was every inch the shieldmaid. Some few bits of melting ice clung to the dust upon her ruddy hair. We were a sorry-looking lot indeed, and I did not like to argue with *orukhar* and possibly more of those lich-things about.

But I would not have a better chance to alter our captivity, and Arneior visibly agreed. At least I had the comfort of knowing she judged my behavior well within the bounds of propriety. I was not shaming Dun Rithell with breaking a compact; the Northerners had marred it at birth.

"*What is it she wants now?*" Gelad's eyes, blue as my own, narrowed as he glanced to Eol's lieutenant.

"*Clever girl.*" Efain shook his head slightly, forestalling his companions' further argument. "My lady, we are honored to have you as an ally. Let us leave this place."

"Not quite." Arn's braids swung gently, caressed by cold wind, but her spear was solid and level. "Swear to it, Northerner. And you two as well."

"*There is no time for this.*" Karas's fingertips brushed a swordhilt, and if he drew to strike we would not leave here without spilling Northern blood.

Arn's stance changed. Just a fraction, just enough. A great brushing calm spread from her in overlapping waves, a sign the Wingéd were watching closely. I hoped they found this acceptable. Since *we* had done nothing wrong, and were facing men besides, it seemed likely they would lend at least a fraction of their aid.

I hoped it would be enough; the question of just what helpful *seidhr* I could perform now loomed before me.

"*It makes no difference.*" Efain studied me closely, as if Arn were not between us—and as if I had done something very interesting indeed, like a saga-hero's horse deciding to speak at a critical juncture, or a stone moaning a riddle in the night. The slight sounds of ice-leaves falling changed; thin freezing mist crept between the trees as the sun rose. "*We may promise them whatever they wish.*"

I drew back into the shadow of my mantle's hood, hoping my face was a mask. "Decide quickly."

"Then may the Blessed witness we are glad to have you as an ally, Solveig of Dun Rithell." Efain managed to say it as if he were giving a promise of great import. "And for their part, Gelad and Karas will swear the same."

"Oh, aye." Karas all but spat. Strands of hair had freed themselves from the leather club he usually bound it in, and the skin-ripple I had seen on others of his kind passed through him once, a warning flicker. "Now may we leave, my lady? If *orukhar* find us—"

"I will not be further shamed." Gelad's sword left its sheath; Arn did not move, though the feather-brushing intensified. The

Northerner took two steps toward her, drove the point into frozen turf, then sank to one knee despite the ice creep-clinging to the grasses. There were no threads of green at their hearts now; any tender new growth had faded with the night. "This is how we swear such things in the North, my lady Solveig; I am Gelad son of Aerenil, and I pledge myself to our alliance." His blade gleamed, and Efain muttered a term in the Old Tongue I had never heard used as an obscenity before. "It is little enough, in light of your bravery."

"Eol will not like this," Karas muttered, but he performed the same movement, kneeling with his bared blade a gleaming upright bar. "So do I, Karas son of Nareal, pledge myself."

Efain did not give his father's name, but he performed the maneuver as well, then it was done. I was no longer weregild, but an ally. Such a position has much more freedom than one paying off a life-debt, and if Eol of Naras were dead in the ruin of the Elder city…

I did not like thinking upon that possibility; I had enough to worry over at the moment. If the Northern captain by some miracle appeared again, I could use an oath sworn by three of his men as leverage.

And if they treated me as a prisoner afterward, it relieved me and my shieldmaid of any polite behavior, unquestioning obedience, or of the duty to aid our captors. I did not think even my mother, well known for her skill in negotiation, could have done better.

Arn did not lift her spear until they had all resheathed, and we set off again through the rapidly rising mist gilded with dawn. My shieldmaid's shoulder brushed mine before we followed the Northerners, though, and it was heartening to feel her approval of the gambit.

"We could still make our way home," she said, not very loudly.

"Soon enough." My gloved hands were fists, my fingers numb. I was glad of a bloodless victory; no doubt much crimson had been shed the night before, and my stomach flipped uneasily. We were weregild no longer and I had one other piece of useful information gained from the moment: Karas considered their captain still alive. I did not wonder why that realization caused a great burst of warm relief in my middle. "We are not helpless now."

She did not sniff that we had never been truly helpless, which told me she considered my solution to our predicament canny enough, though perhaps not completely elegant. "Next time, let me stab someone."

If I thought it likely to get us home, I would. I edged closer to Gelad, walking as softly as possible. "My lord?"

The Northerner kept moving, his boots landing soundless as Arn's own. "What now?" His whisper was fierce again and his mien severe, but neither were enough to dissuade me.

I had a further purpose for this man, especially if his captain was angered at my new status. It was no different than breaking steading-lords away from a warlord grown too large, or uniting a pair of fractious warriors in common cause to make them cease yapping at each other.

"I wish to thank you," I murmured. "For your honesty."

He made no reply.

Individual, Complete

To fight the orukhar, *a sword; to fight a* trul, *the spear; to fight a lich, an Elder's touch. But to fight one of the Seven, you can only die well.*

—Northern proverb

Fog thickened as the sun rose. Yellowing grass, falling ice, mist that distorted every tree into an enemy's shadow—there are songs of the beauty of lost Nithraen in spring, and of the glory of colors in autumn when the great trees painted their leaves but did not lose them, the song of its fountains in coolness during summer-shimmer heat-haze.

We saw only its demise. Even then, as ice-freighted debris struck the ground like a child's playful slap during a game of touchwell, there was a sad majesty to the forest, helped by its eerie lack of undergrowth.

Even I heard them before we saw aught, of course—creaking movements, broad boots crushing fragile ice, growls and shouts in a tongue bearing no resemblance to the Old or the southron its great-grandchild. They made no attempt to be silent; Efain gestured our small group toward a tumble of moss-grown boulders, dripping with mistbreath and edged with frozen fragments. I accomplished hiding with very little in the way of noise, though my heart threatened to thump through my ribs and my breath tore at my throat as if I were running instead of creeping in felted overboots.

The Northerners arranged themselves before Arn and me, and I did not need their grim looks at each other to understand the situation, for the voices in the fog were many.

I flattened my gloved hand against stone. Arneior's freckles glowed and her woad glared, for the rest of her had turned pale. A shieldmaid does not necessarily quail before an uneven fight, but the sounds were a river dividing around us—a tramp of marching feet, clatter of metal gear and bits moving in rhythm, some manner of chant which approximated music but was perhaps intended to keep them shuffling in unison.

Hide us. I did not have strength enough to manage an Elder toy, but there was a great deal of mist—water hanging in air, and easy enough to thicken if I asked politely. *Please. Just a little, and a little more.*

My lips moved slightly, my *seidhr* not quite painful but certainly stronger than usual. No doubt fear added to its potency. Thickening vapor-streaks slipped from my overboots' toes, tiny curls rising. The strands wove together, a tapestry of smoke, and the mist swirled into heavy clots.

The Northerners did not seem to notice at the beginning, though Arn relaxed slightly and Efain glanced in my direction, probably thinking I was about to faint or make some sound.

My eyelids fluttered, turning winterlight to a candle's flickering. The *seidhr* intensified yet more; this time there were no strange half-seen figures in the fog, no lich-shapes or ghostly outlines running with cold blue radiance. Nothing but my own will, subtly adding embroidery to a woven screen.

Soft and gentle such sewing must be, and the necessity of silence made it more difficult yet. Still, my throat swelled, words running just under my motionless tongue, and I held to my task as the sun mounted. Left to itself the mist might have cleared in patches, but around our tiny shelter it turned to churned milk just upon the edge of butter.

Efain gripped Karas's arm, for the son of Nareal's jaw worked and his hand was knotted about his swordhilt. Gelad gazed at the mist as Arn did, yet without her relaxation.

Her faith in me was a bright comfort, much less distracting than the Northerners' tension.

I shuddered, my mantle's hem brushing mossy stone. *Please*, I pleaded, over and over. *Keep us from their notice.*

The stamp-shuffling of *orukhar* moving past lasted a long, long while. Their chanting worked against my *seidhr*, sawing at the strands; it took a great deal of concentration to repair the fraying. Mounting cold ate at me, though I sweated with effort under my mantle.

It was not the devouring fire of the *taivvanpallo*, but I could not even feel grateful for such a mercy.

By the time the sound of marching diminished I trembled like a rabbit in a snare, driving my fingers hard against the green-clad skin of a boulder almost twice my height. My knees threatened to give, tipping me against Arn's shoulder; the sense of warm breathing life she contained helped somewhat, though yet more mist-strands slipped from my mental grasp as it blasted through my raw, open inner selves.

She flinched, knowing the contact would distract me. It could even be fatal were I engaged in some different feat of *seidhr*. As it was, her movement thrust me back upon the stone's support, and my shivering exhale made the fog billow uneasily.

I sagged, icy-feverish, red coral beads digging into my scalp and my skirts quivering. I even laid my cheek against cold, gritty rock, my hood shutting out all daylight. It was still not as dark as the passage under Nithraen.

A faint scrape assaulted my ears, tender from *seidhr* despite the well-furred hood. I cowered as if struck, and there was a sound like an axe sinking into good dry cordwood. It faded into drywhistle croaking, like a grass-jumping insect rubbing its legs together.

It took all my strength to shove my hood back with cold-clumsy fingers, and turn.

Arn's spear was buried deep in the belly of a rather large *orukhar*. The deathshine upon its rolling dark eyes gleamed, and he might have cried our presence aloud as he died—save for Efain's sword-tip in his throat, blocking the way. The *orukhar*'s ashen fingers spasmed, his sword dropping free; Gelad lunged to catch its hilt, keeping it from clattering, and the huge fur-wearing thing's left hand flickered for its belt.

It had not quite the strength to drag a long, wicked dagger free, though it tried mightily. Its gaze was fixed upon me, and when the strange sheen upon its eyes faded I felt its life leave, a candle carried down a dark hall before winking out under a cold breath.

Its armor was iron, and cruelly spiked at shoulder and elbow; Arn's boots slipped as she fought to keep sudden limpweight from crashing earthward. Gelad surged upright, Karas sprang forward, and they eased the corpse to the ground as Efain drew his swordpoint free. A gout of blackish blood spilled down the thing's front.

The *orukhar*'s skin looked perfectly natural despite its greyish, sickly paleness. *As natural as Aeredh's ears*, I thought, and a swimming weakness nearly leveled me. He was strongly built, his cheeks turning to wattles along the jaw, and there were marks of either laughter or grimacing upon either side of his wide mouth with its strong pearly teeth. His hands looked like my father's despite their unhealthy pallor, callused and broad. One of his boots had a broken heel; a metal cap on the other showed what had torn loose.

Hel, take him gently. The prayer caught me by surprise; I almost spoke it aloud, for it is only right to speed a fallen foe along thus. *Wingéd Ones, judge him surely. Allmother, may he rest with thee; may Odynn and Manhrweh welcome him.*

Hel has many halls and countries; one of them might accept even the Enemy's servants. If they are indeed twist-descended from the Elder, they might go to that place the Children of the Star never speak of to mortals, where rest from life's labors is gained before they issue forth again, memory and spirit intact, at a time of their gods' choosing.

I did not know. And it troubled me as I gazed upon the body amid filigreed leaves and yellowed, dying grass.

The Northerners attended to searching the corpse with silent efficiency; he had little enough—a waterskin, another skin containing foully alcoholic liquid, and hard waybread with a faint oily coating. His cloak was too rent to be of much use, and I was useless as well, for I had not hidden us well enough and furthermore could barely stand, let alone stagger unaided, for some while.

It was not the first time I had seen death, even of a violent sort. But I was...astonished, I suppose. The dead *orukhar* in the lich's party had not seemed so individual, so complete.

I could not help but wonder, did we look the same to them?

Tasks and Remembrance

Far from home we die
Wife and child left behind
We may scream, but do not whisper
For our ashen Lord hears all.
— Gurukhun the Subtle, *Marching Song*

We did not linger there, for which I was grateful despite my weariness. Even Arn did not want the *orukhar*'s small skin full of acrid drink. *Smells like griping*, she said, and put her arm about my waist until I could walk without help.

We wended westward and only slightly north, as quickly as Arn could drag me. It would have been a sparkling, cheerful new-winter day except for the mist and the knowledge of what had occurred before dawn. When he deemed it safe enough, Efain finally told us of the battle in an undertone.

He spoke of those who raised the alarm, and of the battle upon the causeway—Aeredh had been among the first to arrive, and Eol, roused from slumber, was at his friend's side amid waves of *orukhar*. The wolves of Naras fought with the Elder; Curiaen and Caelgor joined battle as well. There had seemed some hope, the great doors closed fast at terrible cost, almost upon Eol of Naras's very heels... but then the ram appeared, and when Krog seemed unable to finish its work the great wyrm arrived.

Lost in the North amid Elder and liches, neither Arn nor I thought his tale embellished to any degree, even the actions of his clearly beloved captain.

We were not hungry yet; yesterday's winterwine still filled us. Still, I kept a sharp eye for anything herb, berry, or bark to serve as food later. They had bows; we could hunt, and would not lack for fire. Still, it worried me, and so did the infrequent, unnatural sounds in the thinning fog.

Near the nooning only faint patches of vapor hung between the trees, and there were many stealthy noises usual in a winter forest on a bright day—birds and foraging creatures shaken from lethargy by the light, attempting to find prey or grazing despite the sudden flow of time and cold into their land. The ice-coated leaves were not falling so frequently, and we worked along a hillside in single file. At the bottom was a much easier path an enemy would find just as acceptable, so we went quiet as mice along the harder way, hoping the columns of trees would hide us. Tangles of bracken appeared wherever the *seidhr* prohibiting undergrowth had weakened, a thin glistening layer of freezing turning thorns into diamond arrowheads and vine-branches into glass rope.

And we found other bodies.

Three small groups of dead *orukhar* lay in tangled heaps, stiffening as the cold covered them with its cloak. The Northerners searched the corpses, finding nothing of use; the marks upon them were of Elder blades and queerly blackened, for those scorch the flesh of the Enemy's servants when they burn blue during battle. One carcass had a broken arrow lodged in his throat; it could not be wrenched free, but the fletching was of Elder craft as well.

The dead seemed, to our companions, stragglers or warriors on patrol duty. Efain said it was unlikely the army that had broken Nithraen would take this route; they would either return straight northward to whatever newly created pass through the Marukhennor's ice-pinnacles they had used before or strike more southerly after leaving shattered silver-and-stone gates. If they did the latter, they would soon find the broad, ancient west-running road to a different kingdom's borders—Dorael, a name conjuring old sagas even Idra had only half believed.

Just after the sun began its daily descent we found a larger band
of ash-pale dead, and the battle here, though small by comparison
to the city's breaking, had been fierce indeed. Some of the *orukhar*'s
wounds bore no black-crisp burning; the Northerners' relief was palpable. At least one or two of their comrades had survived and were
still fighting, but there were worrisome signs as well—drying blood
upon an ice-sheathed tree-trunk, where a wounded man had leaned
to rest. I did not yet know how Elder bled, but the marks were not
orukhar ichor either. Torn strips of black Northern cloth showed an
attempt at bandaging had been made, scraps left behind as unsuit-
able. All the arrows, even the heavy spine-fletched ones of the Enemy's make, were gone.

Which meant the survivors had bows as well, a happy chance
unless they mistook us for the Enemy's servants. Not that there
seemed much hope of finding anyone but more *orukhar* in this quiet,
freezing forest.

Karas took the lead now, his proud knifelike nose all but twitching, and we set off at a quicker pace. My legs were heavy, and the
cold intensified as undergrowth thickened. Whatever *seidhr* kept the
woods of Nithraen unstained had no clear border in this direction,
simply fade-fringing into more natural effects. I could see no sign of
passage; nor could Arn, but the Northerners became fractionally less
dour.

Gelad caught my elbow as ice-freighted thorns threatened to tear
my mantle; the slope was unforgiving and it took a careful step to
cut across instead of slipping downward. "Do you need rest?" The
words were barely a murmur, ready to be lost amid the stealthy bustle of a winter forest on a bright day.

"I am well enough, merely clumsy," I whispered in return, grimly
determined not to slow them or Arn further. "Who do you think
it is?"

"Elder." He caught himself, glancing down at me. "You are so
quiet, my lady, we forget you do not know our ways. At least a dozen
Elder, maybe more. One or two of our kind, though that is difficult
to tell—the Firstborn with them are covering their passage much as
Aeredh did for us."

Was that what his singing was meant to do? It would be a good *seidhr* to learn, if I could manage to arrange the lessons. I nodded, and his hand fell away once he was sure of my footing. "Do you think…" My throat was very dry; I muffled a cough before I could speak again. "Do you think Soren survived? He was behind us."

He glanced again at me as if startled; his eyes were blue as my mother's but not so deep. "He has his task, as we have ours. Don't worry for him."

"Ah." I nodded, seeking to appear brave—or at least, unsurprised. At least he seemed disposed to speak, so there had to be little danger of being heard at the moment. "What was his task?"

"Don't know." One shoulder lifted and dropped as he moved, feline instead of wolflike, and though the sigil upon it opened wolf-jaws wide in song, the rest of the emblem had a watchful cast. "Our sole concern is you—and your shieldmaid, naturally. Efain to lead us free of the city, and Karas to find the path. He has a gift for it, you see."

For the wolves of Naras to call one of their own a great path-finder was thought-provoking indeed. "And what is your task, son of Aerenil?"

"Merely to lend my sword, my lady. Or to die in your stead, should it be necessary." He studied me sidelong, placing his boots without looking and making no noise at all. The dust in his hair had turned to clay, slicked down with mist-moisture. "You remember my father's name."

"Of course." How did one respond when a Northerner said *to die in your stead*? Arn did not speak so, for all her duty is to guard. She knew very well it was my task to keep her from Hel's lands, or to go with her if we met a foe too large for our combined might to vanquish.

An event which seemed more and more likely indeed the farther we traveled. I had never thought of our compact in such stark terms at home.

Gelad was silent for a long moment. "It was only said once."

Once is enough, when Idra the Farsighted has taught you. "A *volva* remembers what should be remembered." Besides, the eldest daughter of a hall keeps such information ready. Many of our duties involve the soothing of tempers, and honoring a man by remembering his lineage is a small, disproportionately useful courtesy.

Efain, drifting behind us in rearguard, gave a slight disapproving exhalation. Silence returned to our group. We walked through the icy woods, alert as deer who sense the wolves—or wolves themselves, wary of a hunter's snares.

When disaster struck, it was quick. Arn halted, her chin rising and dun hood falling free. Her hair, still grimed with Nithraen's choking stone-powder, nevertheless glowed fiercely, and the blue of her woad, with a thin line of dried blood slashing over it, was likewise vivid; a stray gleam was wrung from mail through a small rent in her mantle I would have to repair if we ever reached safety.

I froze. Gelad reached for his sword and drew a dagger in his other hand as well; behind us, Efain's blade whispered free of the sheath.

Karas turned to grant me a meaningful glare, pointing at a nearby tree with one half-gloved hand. The other was upon his swordhilt, and when the *orukhar* boiled from a scattering of boulders downhill, evidently surprised during a rest, I darted for shelter as I was bidden.

Battle, Persuasion

I have wrenched the secrets of seidhr *from the roots of the Tree, and thus I decree: Those who use what I have discovered may not touch blade, nor bow, nor spear, nor any other weapon save a healer's knife. It is an affront to the gods.*
—Anonymous, *The First Saga*;
said to be sung by Odynn himself

My first pitched battle was a jumble of disconnected images amid whirling snow, the terror of the lich staining every moment. The second stands clear and sharp in memory, not least because it was so *loud*.

Clash-slither of metal against metal, Arn's sharp cry as her spear's point plunged through armor and burrowed deep before ripping free, the war-shrieks of the *orukhar* and sharp oaths from the Northerners—the sudden clamor was overwhelming. My back slammed against a tree-trunk wider than I am tall, and for a few moments I could do nothing but stare.

Gelad, ducking away from a wild swing, stepping in with broadsword held almost level and lunging with nearly Elder grace, tearing open an *orukhar*'s belly when he moved away to the next clash, stabbing with the glittering dagger in his free hand. Efain engaged with two swift-slashing opponents, a stray shaft of sunshine glaring over his shoulder to strike their straight, flag-tipped swords. Karas giving ground, feinting, and nearly lopping the head from a squat, muscular *orukhar* whose war-bellow was disconcertingly deep.

And Arneior? My shieldmaid danced, her spear glittering and her armor whisper-silent. She had already downed one opponent and spun in, finishing one of Efain's; with that done she whirled again, spear burying itself in a throat, breaking free with a whistling rush. A black ichor-spatter flung from its passage hung in the air for a bare moment, horrible in its beauty, and fell.

It was a battle, I was *volva*. I had to do something, but what?

None of the sagas or songs speak of crippling fear upon a bloody field. Now I know why—it is of the *seidhr* nobody wishes to attract by mentioning or even thinking upon for too long. Warriors are trained to keep moving, for freezing in terror means being felled almost at leisure; *volvas* are not taught that particular skill. I knew the battle-chants, of course, to lend strength to arm and blade, to fill companions with the gift of fighting rage, to proof skin and armor against stray breaking, and more. I had learned them painstakingly, under Idra's watchful glare.

At that moment I could not remember a single note, nor a solitary syllable.

Arn retreated, slashing; there was a clot of the ashen creatures gathering and her practice-cry was now a full-fledged war yell. The difference was unmistakable, for all I had never heard her produce such a sound before.

My gloved hands leapt up at the sound, fingers spread, and I whistled. The high-drilling noise shaped what *seidhr* I could reach, and one of the *orukhar* pressing my Arn flinched, sunlight striking its eyes just enough to alter battle-rhythm. Her spear leapt to take advantage of the motion almost of its own will, and she stamped at the end of the blow.

It wasn't much—tiny light-darts, a child's game on a river's dappling broad back. *Think a little smaller, Solveig,* my teacher said more than once when I bemoaned my own ineptitude, my inability to accomplish some worthy feat. *You see? Great things need not be large.*

It is a terrible thing to find, after being the pride of Dun Rithell, that the wider world esteems one small indeed. Yet there was no time for self-pity of any stripe. Sunlight, for however long we had it, was an ally if I could just be persuasive enough.

The inked bands on my wrists twinged, *seidhr* flaming. A large shadow detached from the tumble of boulders our opponents had been resting in, ice crunching under its gnarled, hooflike feet. A thundercrack leapt across the clearing; my head snapped aside, my cheek stinging.

Faint iron-taste filled my mouth, my teeth piercing my own flesh. I stared at the thing, near-dazed with horror.

One greenish-pale, heavily muscled shoulder much higher than the other, its broad face set with terrible blank fury—the monstrosity was taller than the Northerners and impossibly broad. Steam curled from its shaggy sides; either it was furred like a bear or it wore the pelt of some terrible misshapen animal, I could not tell which.

It had been twisted by some monstrous *seidhr*, I realized. A hazy shadow wrapped about the creature, leaping and fringing like flame; it looked like a lopsided clay figurine made by an enthusiastic but terribly untrained potter. Something crouched inside its body, and though the invisible inhabitant burned it did not consume.

The monster stomped uphill with ponderous almost-grace, far too quick for such a bulky, limping thing. And it *hurt*, though not with the lich's cold piercing. This was a battering; for a moment I thought our new opponent the thing which had wrecked the gates of Nithraen, and was slightly puzzled at its small size.

Another whistle shrilled between my lips, my upflung hands shaking as the thing's invisible will buffeted me across empty space.

No, not empty, for Arn was there, and the monster was no longer too small to batter down a city gate but far too large compared to my shieldmaid's slender glitter. Sunshine burst in dapples across Arn's back, and where the light fell past her and struck the burning thing, actual smoke arose. Thin weals appeared upon its pelt, bubbling with blisters.

The *trul*—for that is what Northerners name the smaller form of these fearsome things—actually staggered, its deep-cloven hooves stamping frozen earth. Ice shattered, and I could think of nothing save blinding it and hoping that someone, *anyone* else would some-how make it go away.

Arn's spear flickered, stinging the monster's larger hand. A coil of what looked like tar-smeared rope swayed in that hairy three-fingered fist, and the knowledge of what the weapon was arrived with another sickening swell of fear.

The *trul* bore a whip.

It flinched again, and I tried to think of something else to do. The sun might drop behind the hillcrest at any moment, and this creature was not ordinary. Even its stink was a violation. Its *seidhr* battered at me once more, driving my shoulders against the tree with a jolt. My cheek stung afresh; I had never been struck so, not even in childhood.

Arn flicker-stabbed it once more, a deep gash opening on the back of that huge fist. Of course she had realized that if it unlimbered the massive whip it could easily hold a sword or two at bay, and there were still so many *orukhar* left.

The whistle died in my throat, replaced by a rising shout I had never heard from my own chest or any other's. It was like Arn's war-cry—a day of firsts, for both of us—but more piercing, for it was loaded with invisible force given weight by my frantic horror.

It struck the monster squarely, but had little effect except to madden.

The thing howled in reply and surged forward, whip uncoiling in a fat sinuous tarry ripple thudding upon cringing ice-grass. Next it would draw back, arm becoming a tight-wound spring soon unleashed to terrible effect. Worse than the strike would be the *seidhr* wedded to the weapon, and I was wretchedly certain I would feel it first.

Arn did not hesitate, driving forward to stab once again, and I was so occupied I did not hear the others until they were upon us.

Allies So Few

Three things make an alkuine: *fire from air, water from stone … and light from darkness.*
—Faeron One-hand, *My Father's Words*

A gleam at the corner of the gaze, a flash of chill blue radiance, blades bright burning blue and their boots whisper-quick, the Elder crashed into the *orukhar* party's flank. A great bow hummed and its arrows whistled, quivering after they struck in the *seidhr*-monster's side. Two indistinct blurs—like shaggy ink splashed upon a wall—attacked the burning thing, and in their wake a black-clad figure swung grimly, the gem in his swordhilt blazing like a star.

The monster screamed again, though in pain instead of rage. My own battle-cry died, and my legs nearly failed me as well. I slumped against the tree, amid daggers of silver ice falling from quaking branches.

I did not know *truls* were among the weaker of the Enemy's *seidhr*-servants, especially against the wolves of Naras or bears of Tavaan. Nor did I know how such creatures were hunted or dispatched, but I learned that day. The thing's sickly shagfur hide smoked with fresh weals raised by darts of flung sunlight as well as the touch of Elder steel; there was a deep reek of foul roasting.

More Elder followed, most dark-haired and many blue-eyed, two with spears a little longer than Arn's. That pair moved with swift grace, holding the *seidhr*-thing almost immobile while Eol clove its head free, a maneuver looking quite practiced indeed. A jet of burning black bubbled from its thick stump-neck. The battle veered so swiftly it was finished before I quite understood what had happened, a great gout of *seidhr* draining away inside me and deathly chill taking its place. The small clearing, glittering with freeze and gilded with mistbreath, had been tranquilly beautiful just a short while before.

Now it was a death-carpet. Ash-pale bodies lay sprawled and slack; a horribly wounded *orukhar* was given a mercy-blow while it made a thin sound of great pain.

Silence fell, the crackling quiet of a battle's end.

Efain let out a disbelieving laugh; Arn spun upon her forefoot, gazing uphill at me. I dropped my hands, the inked bands on my wrists alive with pain. My knees were soft as festival bread's dense, thick crumb.

The two black smears were Elak the quiet and Soren, both with dust-stiffened hair turning them into old men with young faces. Elak moved immediately to Eol's side; the Northern captain's head bore a glaring-white bandage, his clothes were torn, and his scale-and-ring appeared not so much battered as chewed. His hair was singed as well as dusty, and so was Aeredh's—the Elder conferred quietly with another carrying a great longbow, who I recognized as the harpist from Nithraen's palace.

None of them paid any further attention to the dead *seidhr*-monster, to the ice underfoot, or to me. I could not remember the harpist's name despite having heard it once, and oddly, at that moment my inability to do so bothered me most of all.

Arn strode uphill, arriving before me flush-cheeked, her woad glaring and her armor winking brightly. "Not like killing wolves," she said softly. Her throat worked once, a convulsive swallowing.

"I thought us both dead, and the men too." The truth spilled from me in a rush, and I tasted yet more iron blood in my spitless mouth. My face throbbed. "That…that thing…"

"I do not like the North." My shieldmaid's arm slipped over my shoulders. Her forehead touched mine, both of us sweating. It would leave a trace of blue woad upon my skin; I shut my eyes and breathed her in. The Wingéd Ones had been watching, and the immense feathery weight of their approval filled us both.

It did not help me very much, but she had recovered her usual color and much of her strength when footsteps approached, deliberately loud against ice-freighted hush. Arn whirled as if expecting more *orukhar*.

Aeredh halted well outside the range of her spear, his sword sheathed and his singed, dust-laden hair a wild mass.

"Thank the Blessed," he said, quietly. "Are you hurt? Either of you?"

I took stock of Arn. A single splash of rancid *orukhar* blood touched the hem of her torn mantle; that was all. "None of them even touched my small one. A fine dance indeed." The words shook, my weakness on full display.

"Easy enough to spit a blind pig," she returned, but one corner of her generous mouth drew up. "Well done, my weirdling. And you?"

"That thing...well, it is dead now. And you, my lord Elder?" At least I could still use brittle formality, though my voice shook. Much as I sought not to, I sounded like Astrid after a nightmare—young, and somewhat unsteady. "Yours is a timely arrival indeed; I must see to the wounded." Now that the battle was over, a *volva*'s work began. I was glad of the tree's bulk behind me, and its dozing *seidhr* sharing a trickle of strength as well.

"I crave your pardon, my lady *alkuine*." Aeredh's slight grimace held equal parts chagrin and weariness, despite his unlined face. "Nithraen's gates have held firm against the Enemy before; we thought there was no need to trouble you with the news of an attack. Eol feared you would wish to join the battle, and that we cannot have. You—"

"We found a battle nonetheless." I forced myself away from the tree, an unfamiliar heat quelling the shaking in my limbs. It was, I realized, anger—and it bolstered me wonderfully. "This is a second deceit, son of Aerith. How many more lie in store?"

Yes, it was somewhat unfair for me to behave so, but now we knew Eol was alive and I had been granted the chance to make our new status not only known but irrevocable. The sooner the better, and the more lee Arneior and I would have to exert some small control over matters.

At that moment it seemed the most important consideration in the world, outweighing even my own stupid, trembling nausea.

The black-clad Northerners were busy greeting their captain, who leaned upon Elak's shoulder, haggard under his bandaging. Of them all, he looked the most grievously hurt—in fact, the only one bearing much evidence of injury at all, for though the Elder were dust-covered and their eyes bright with battle-wrath none of them seemed to have suffered any great damage.

Most importantly, my shieldmaid and I had survived. I did not know whether to thank Aesyr, Vanyr, the Wingéd, or a lesser spirit passing by pure chance. I touched Arn's shoulder. "Come," I continued. "There is healing to be done."

She half-turned, effectively halting whatever answer the Elder would make. "Should you not rest a moment, weirdling? Your cheek is swelling; it will bruise."

"It is nothing." The betraying quaver in my voice irritated me as well. "Though I could use a skin of mead and some of Albeig's roast fowl, certainly." I was deeply, almost angrily grateful the *seidhr*-monster had not been able to put more force behind its invisible blows, or my neck might well have snapped.

We were allies to the Northerners, and that comes with responsibilities. I had to do something, especially since I had proven so singularly incapable at every point even before I held the fishgutting *taivvanpallo*. I tugged at my mantle-sleeves, touched one of my bead-freighted braids, and set off with what I hoped was a determined stride. Ice threatened to slide underfoot, and Arn had to catch my elbow halfway across the clearing. She righted me with a quick yank, her fingers sinking into mantle-sleeve and flesh underneath.

I did not demur, though later a bruise rose upon my arm. The bodies stank of brassy death and ordure; I was somewhat glad there was nothing in my middle but Elder winterwine. Had my stomach contained that longed-for roast fowl, or even bread, I might have lost it upon seeing intestines spilling loose in wet grey tangles, or drawing nearer the bulk of the dead *trul*.

As the servants of the Enemy rot they breathe more than the usual stink of decomposition, and swiftly, too. Sometimes a deeper contagion rises from their decay—*foul as the Black Land's breath*, the saying goes, and *plague rises with it.*

The Northerners quieted as I approached, except for Efain murmuring to Eol—perhaps granting him the unwelcome news of our changed status, or simply making a report as a warrior charged with a completed task must. Elder moved among the bodies, stripping what might be useful; the harpist Daerith—it was a deep relief to find I could now remember his name—was busy salvaging what arrows he could, even the sharp-fletched *orukhar* shafts.

"Well?" It was not precisely diplomatic to address the heir of Naras and his wolves as I would Bjorn and his fellow warriors after an ale-soaked pigpen brawl, but I was afraid if I sought a softer tone the words might break upon an unwilling sob. "Who needs attending? The daylight wanes."

It was an afternoon of surprises; the black-clad men exchanged guilty glances, for all the world like errant boys taken to task by Idra or Corag. Arn's shoulder brushed mine, much closer than she usually stood.

She could perhaps tell my legs were none too steady.

"My lady Question." Eol's gaze was fever-bright, and he was pale as I felt. His armor indeed bore rents looking uncomfortably like toothmarks, blackened metal strangely deformed in places as if melted by some caustic forge-breath. "I am relieved to—"

"How badly are you hurt?" The inked marks upon my wrists twinged dully, and so did the rest of me. Half my face felt tight-swollen, and I blinked furiously, for my left eye was swelling too. It was no worse than feeling Bjorn's pain after a clout from our father, or so I told myself.

"Who struck you?" the Northern captain demanded in turn.

"The thing is dead now, it matters little. 'Tis a *volva*'s duty to provide healing after a battle." *Since apparently I can do nothing worth mentioning during one.* I could not unclench my fists or make my voice behave with its usual smoothness; each word held a shiver. "The Elder seem well enough, but you are not."

He might have made some answer, but a shadow passed over the battlefield, along with a ripple through every remaining living thing. I shuddered, swaying; Arn's shoulder bumped mine, hard.

"*Hurry.*" An Elder I did not know, his long dark hair held back with a silver fillet, held up a gauntleted hand, and the Old Tongue was a barbed comfort. "*They are scouring the forest. The Enemy is not content with Nithraen's fall.*"

"*Redhill is just within reach, even with Secondborn to carry.*" The harpist had just finished collecting arrows, and straightened, casting a curious glance in my direction. "*My king, we must away.*"

Even though riding was uncomfortable, I would have given much to pull myself into Farsight's saddle and let a beast take the burden of moving us to safety. It occurred to me the horses, if trapped in an Elder stable, had probably suffered summat dreadful during the breaking of the city. Strangely, the thought pained me far more than the twisted, stinking bodies crowding upon every side. Aeredh approached with an Elder's soundless step; he halted and gazed at Eol for a long moment, a speaking look.

"*Daerith is right,*" the Northern captain said, finally. They had returned to the Old Tongue, and seemed likely to attempt disposing of Arn and me to suit themselves once more. "*But she looks near to foundering.*"

"*Then we will carry her.*" Aeredh's shoulders were stiff, accepting a burden—I had seen both my parents tense in that manner more than once, when some unpleasant decision must be made for the good of Dun Rithell. "*We have come this far, my friend. The Blessed will not fail us now.*"

"Again, you mutter in your foreign tongue." Arn leaned fully against me now, and I suspect we both drew no little comfort from the contact. "If this is how you treat your allies, I can see why you have so few."

"Let them speak as they please." My tongue was clumsy-thick; the sun dipped fully below the hillcrest, continuing through its afternoon walk with no thought of any mortals trapped below the sky. The last dregs of Nithraen's ancient warmth fled. So far as I know, it has never returned to that place. "It matters little; the sun is falling."

Even then I pretended not to understand the Old Tongue. The misdirection had become a habit, and one I was grateful for. The *orukhar* were foul and the Enemy a nightmare, but I did not wholly trust these men either, and we were alone among them. Eol regarded me, the fevered glitter of his gaze bespeaking some pain, but he made no move to accept a *volva*'s care.

I found I did not wish to press it upon him, if he would treat me with such disdain.

"We go, now." Aeredh's tone shifted; this was the voice of command, for all he spoke in the southron language. "We must reach Redhill, even should we travel after dusk."

"*And what of Faevril's sons?*" another Elder asked. "*They are drawing pursuit away; will we leave them to run as hares, alone before one of the Seven?*"

So the blond hunter and his easily angered sibling were occupied elsewhere, well and good. Perhaps I could use the information later in some fashion, but at that moment all I felt was weary stomach-rolling disgust.

"Very well." I hoped my aching face was a mask once more, and turned away from Eol. My overboot crushed a shard of ice, and the breaking was as of a tiny bone snapped in half. "I am gladdened to see you survived, Soren. As for the son of Tharos, he may spurn my aid if he likes; the rest of you may keep your secrets and chatter in your Old Tongue too. But let us do it while walking, for soon the woods grow dark."

Arn moved with me as I set off, and I aimed us for the upper edge of the death-ground. We had been moving westward all day; though my legs were leaden and both my face and wrists pained, walking was better than waiting for men to finish their nattering. It was a torment to work across the hillslope instead of down.

"*I do not worry for Caelgor and Curiaen,*" Aeredh said. "Give the women some *sitheviel* and what other aid we have, and let us move swiftly as we may."

Not by Foe

*Mortal time may be held in abeyance, but not forever.
Only in the West does the blossom not fade, the fruit not
rot, the tree not wither.*

—Elder proverb

The first traces of snow quickly became long clutching vein-streaks reaching for the shattered city, and mounted to drifts shortly afterward. At last my overboots no longer crunched in thin tinkling ice; steadily intensifying cold swallowed us as the sun descended.

When the drifts reached knee-high, the group halted. I thought they wished to give us more *sitheviel*, though the scant swallow I had taken earlier—the last in Eol's black-glass flask—still burned inside me. Instead, each Secondborn was given to an Elder companion, who grasped their arm. By some seamless *seidhr* our steps were lightened, and we walked *atop* the snow's white crust, as if we had left our heavier bodies behind and went forward with only our subtler selves. Even Arn, once she understood what they wished, consented to give her left elbow to Daerith the harpist, his bow riding his back and her spear riding hers.

Only infrequently and at great need does a shieldmaid carry her weapon thus.

Daerith also sometimes touched my shoulder, for Arn suffered him to walk between us since he carried no blade save a short curved healer's knife, and no other weapon save his bow. A burst of *seidhr* from that brief contact warmed me each time, and even soothed some of the swelling upon my face.

Aeredh tucked my hand in the crook of his right arm as if we were about to ring-dance around a summerpole, and the first few steps upon unbroken snow, my boots weightless against its smooth clean sweep, were almost a joy. We forged onward, some of the Elder singing softly, their voice barely disturbing the sough of wind among treetops. Bare branches appeared, and evergreens weighed by white blankets under a thin gleaming ice-skin.

I stared at my feet moving as if unconnected with the rest of me, the tang of *sitheviel* mixing with blood in my mouth. The cut inside my cheek stung if I tried to speak, so I did not bother. I could not even concentrate enough to untangle what weirding they used to walk thus.

A stream too swift to freeze still bore ice at its fringes, a single slender stone bridge over its silvery back. On the far side a bloody sunset dyed snowy forest, and I gathered we were no longer in Nithraen's lands. I expected us to make some manner of camp, but the Elder continued walking so the Northerners, Arneior, and I were obliged to as well. A short purple dusk gave way to clear new-winter night, the kind that kills if one has no shelter or fire.

Yet the Elder are hardy, and one or two were always singing. The music, laced with *seidhr*, was part lament for Nithraen and part quiet exhortation to keep lungs and limbs from freezing solid; I sensed, almost *saw*, how it drew strength from earth, stone, and tree, feeding trickles into the Children of the Star and their more fragile companions.

Shivers gripped me. Aeredh freed his arm from my hand only to slide it over my shoulders and draw me close, his warmth somehow spreading to drive back the killing cold. Arneior made no objection; she was too occupied with the warming breath, a shieldmaid's strength pitted against deep winter. The harpist no doubt helped her, but I was too weary to worry.

I merely endured.

Starlight filtered through snow-laden or bare boughs. Soft bluish radiance strengthened around the Elder, not so much actual light as a form of clarity. Eol was braced between the two spear-wielders, breathing shallowly and staggering oft. I did my best not to trip, and after a cold eternity the waning moon shed more faint glow from a bright, cloudless sky.

At some point I thought longingly of Dun Rithell, and lifted out of myself.

※

Under a vault spread with diamond-chip stars, the greathall stood silent. All were abed—all save one, for a single candle burned in the stillroom, where a golden-haired girl stood before a wooden table cluttered with familiar implements.

Astrid, her face buried in her hands and her shoulders shaking, wept. Even in the dead of night she muffled the sound. The candle flickered under a breath from nowhere, but she did not notice, too sunk in her grief.

The warriors were at muttering, soft-breathing rest; the women's quarters deathly quiet. Up stairs and down a short hall, in his closet a short distance from our parents', Bjorn curled upon his side, a great strong body sleeping curiously childlike, damp traces upon his bearded cheeks as if he sorrowed while dreaming. A few rooms away my mother lay in her husband's arms, both deeply unconscious, but my father's brow furrowed as his eyes flickered under their lids.

My mother's lips twitched. She, too, was dreaming of something. Her outflung hand, resting upon a fold of woolen counterpane her daughters had embroidered a few winters ago, stretched pleadingly.

I am well enough, whatever self I had sent home whispered, anxious to ease her. *Be at peace.*

In the stillroom, the candle flickered again. I sought to brush against Astrid, to comfort her. But the vision was fading like sun-bleached cloth, and I burst from the roof of Dun Rithell as a white-wingéd bird, circling once before arrowing northward.

Above, the great river of stars echoed with faint sweet voices. Yet a dark grasp was upon me, drew me steadily, swifter and swifter, my heart thundering with each wingbeat.

Long I flew, under a waning moon turned leering-yellow as bad cheese. Forest, river, mountain, infrequent steading—they wheeled below my tucked-tight claws, barely glimpsed before vanishing. Snow gleamed, and knifelike peaks rose in sawtooth progression. Starlight faded, soft silver voices suffocated behind a thickness neither cloud nor mist.

Sickening heaviness clotted about me, a terrible pressure squeezing both breath and pulse. The subtle bodies do not need such things, but they are anchored in the physical, and 'tis air and blood which fuel every living thing. Even the subtle selves may be injured, if their bearer believes the strike does some damage.

Or if the attacker is strong enough, and skilled enough, in seidhr.

I struggled, but it did no good. I was drawn inexorably northward, and in the far distance a low crimson glow rose, swelling like a boil as I approached. Great black towers rent the sky, their angular battlements sharp as needles, and endless, terrifying screams rose from deep vents in riven stone. A sickening fog drowned all healthful light, leaving only a pale fungal glow in secret caves; leaping ruddy fires gave no cheer, for they were unwholesome and feasted upon flesh as well as other noisome fuel. Orukhar *and worse thronged the vast citadel's ramparts and battlements; underneath their anthill seething I sensed passages, hallways, and mines carved deep in tortured earth.*

Something else lived in those depths. The rubescent smear woke, glittering balefully, and above it lingered two pale gleams almost suffocated by a hatred so massive, so twisted, even glimpsing it threatened to strike me from the sky—

▨▧▧▧▧▨

"Solveig." A hand upon my throat, massaging. "Drink, my weirdling. There."

The liquid was cold, yet burned at the same time. I coughed, choked, and blinked blearily at Arn's face, seen through a haze. I could not feel my hands or feet, and was forced to keep swallowing or drown in whatever she was pouring through my unresisting mouth.

Yet I made no demur, rammed back into my physical self and glad of the event. It takes much effort to fly forth in such fashion but hardly any to return; the ship of any invisible self longs to moor itself to the body once more.

The drink did not taste of Elder vintage, but rough mortal alcohol without the body of ale or the healthful tang of mead. When she took the container away, my eyes welled with hot saltwater. "Ugh," I managed, feebly. "Have we halted?"

"Only for a few moments." Her eyelashes were white, and frost lingered upon her hair as well as her shoulders. Despite that, she looked relieved, though her woad-stripe cracked, flakes falling free. "Asleep on your feet like a horse. We have only the liquor from the pale things left; the Elder did summat to render it less harmful. Come, take a step or two."

"The worst is past." Aeredh's arm was still over my shoulders. I barely felt his warmth; the entire world was ice. "Dawn comes, and we are almost to Redhill."

It meant nothing to me. "T-towers," I managed. Arn's attention sharpened. "Made of iron, and inside it a red thing. It knows, Arneior." *Seidhr* gripped me; the unbidden vision had to be spoken, lest its memory slip away. "No. Not it." My hand flew up, gripped a fold of her mantle's front. "*He.* He knows I am here. North, amid the ash."

"*What does she say?*" Daerith the harpist swam into view over my shieldmaid's shoulder. My head tipped back, and it was a relief to see a few stars glimmering cleanly between snow-laden branches.

Even if unfamiliar, they were still real, and whole, and good.

The forest was grey—Aeredh was correct, dawn approached. The entire world was hushed as if immured in the Unmaking, that great void broken by Allmother's first song. She is at once ever-singing and music itself, but even the greatest *seidhr* has a beginning, vast ongoing notes which brought the world into being and kindled secret fires in the depths where nothing had existed before.

The wise say that music has always been, and will always be.

"*It is as we feared.*" Aeredh's breath touched my ear, hot as a brand. The Elder's fingertips scorched my cold forehead. I had rarely been this close to man not of my kin before, and was too frozen to feel anything at the event. He made a swift motion, and I thought for a moment I was flying again—but no, he had simply bent to place my arm over his shoulders, and his own left arm slipped about my waist, holding me indecently close. "Come, as quickly as we may. How fares Eol?"

"Well enough, Efain says, though only half-conscious." Arneior thrust the stopper into the skin-mouth, and eyed the Elder balefully. "Neither of them will last much longer in this weather. We must find shelter."

"And so we shall." Aeredh set off again, carrying most of my weight despite my twitching attempts to help.

I wished I could walk unaided, for even a few steps. To be still in deepfreeze winter is to court death; the blood stops moving and lethargy grips the entire body.

I had to make them listen. "He knows." I forced the words through a burning throat, through numb lips. "He knows I am here, *he knows.*"

Aeredh froze, his stillness that of a hunting creature sensing it has been seen. So did every Elder, and a blade rang from its sheath— Efain's, I thought, for he was the one who spoke.

"*I can smell you, idiot,*" the Northerner said in the Old Tongue. "*Come out.*"

The next voice was a surprise—a man's, deep and resonant, and very amused. "*And I heard your approach since before moonrise. What brings a king and his wolves to Redhill, my lords?*"

We had been found, and—for once during that terrible journey— not by a foe.

PART THREE

REDHILL TO
THE WILD

Laden with Discoveries

He was not born curst, but the Enemy hated his family above all other Secondborn. And over and over, the young lord paid the price.
　　—Reikat Halfhand, *The Third Saga of Hajithe's Son*

Karat Vaerkil—literally, "the blood-colored hill"—protected a large swathe of Dorael's southeastron border in those days; a column of solid rock rose, stony and mostly sheer, to a great height. Whoever held its windswept tower could see far in every direction, and wherever one trod in those lands, its stony crown was easily visible. It was honeycombed with smooth-carved passages, and hidden ways radiated veinlike from it as well, for the hill had been delved by those most cunning.

A clutch of spiny, ice-freighted bushes protected a scattered tumble of boulders; deep in the pile's heart was a crack wide enough for a man to slip through. Inside, the dimness was uncomfortably akin to the passageway out of quaking, riven Nithraen, and it was warmer though my breath still turned into a thin cloud. Bands of different rock in the tunnel's walls glowed enough to give faint illumination more than enough for Elder eyes, yet I shuddered at the return of darkness.

I was not even embarrassed at being carried between Aeredh and another Elder whose name I did not know. Even my shieldmaid accepted Daerith's aid in the final stretch, leaning upon his arm, her silence of the peculiar type meaning she kept herself from foul language only by a supreme effort of will.

Less than an hour after we were hailed by a voice from a thornbrake, firelight painted the walls of a half-timbered, half-stone room, and we were made welcome with deep brown ale and dense, sweet waybread of a type Arn and I had not tasted before. There was also Elder winterwine from a great cask, and the lord of the hill himself brought a wooden cup to Aeredh.

The garrison here was Northerners, clad in black cloth and oddments. A few were people of Lady Hajithe's hall, though most hailed from other quarters, and the man who held Redhill—for in spring to autumn the rocky prominence was covered in a plant which dyed it ruddy, especially at sunset—was accorded all the honor of a steading-lord. But 'twas not he nor any other Secondborn who had wrought its tunnels.

Our mantles and undermantles were taken, Arn and I wrapped in rough woolen blankets and placed near the fire, and every hospitality possible pressed upon us. I sat and shivered in great waves, my body accepting the warmth only fitfully, and Eol, his rent armor stripped free, was laid upon a hurriedly cleared table. He was more wounded than he had appeared; I had failed in a *volva*'s duty once more, for I should have tended him despite his reluctance.

Yet now I saw a fresh wonder, for a small figure bustled about the table, sometimes standing upon blocks placed just so, giving access to its height. He looked almost childlike, but his proportions were fully adult and he had a dark, well-braided beard only lightly touched by grey. Even Flokin my father's oldest warrior might envy said beard, for it reached his knees.

"*Quite interesting*," the small man said in crisply accented Old Tongue, peeling aside a piece of rent black shirt and peering beneath; his gaze was odd, for his eyes held flecks of gold like sparkling river-mud from an ore-rich hill. "*I have not seen these burns before.*"

I realized what he must be. "A *thrayn* dverger?" I said blankly though chattering teeth, and the fire spark-crackled in reply.

"Indeed." The man who had greeted us was tall and somber, his dark hair indifferently cut and his clothing rough black. His armor was blackened as well, ring-and-scale very much like Arn's except in its heaviness. For all that, the sword upon his back was of Elder make and his boots, though worn, of high quality. His entire air was of tight restraint; his nose was proud, and his features echoed Lady Hajithe's.

Indeed they should, for he was her son Tarit.

In his dark eyes and tight mouth lurked something very familiar as well, a cousin to Bjorn's temper or my father's battle-madness. In spite of his size—he was tall as Aeredh—and the brace of daggers at his hips as well as the shortbow strapped for easy use, not to mention his mail and the lightness of his step, I felt a curious comfort.

This was a manner of fellow I knew quite well how to handle.

"This is Mehem son of Dísara of the line of Ivaldi," the hill's lord continued in thickly accented southron, indicating the dverger, who snorted and bent to his work, spreading some manner of paste from a shallow wooden bowl onto Eol's burns. "Redhill is his home, and we but guests. I am Tarit son of Taliurin, and any friend of Aeredh's or Eol's is most welcome wherever I lodge." His gaze lingered upon my bruised face, but he did not ask how I had suffered the wound.

"Guests." Mehem poked somewhat ungently at Eol's side, and the Northern captain, only half-conscious, did not even twitch. The dverger's handling of my language was very precise as well, each syllable clear and sharp. "Is that what it is called?"

Arn stretched her legs as far as they would go, drinking deep from a wooden goblet. Her eyes were half-lidded; I had rarely seen her so weary. My own exhaustion had passed the point of rest; I could barely believe we had gained any shelter at all. Aeredh poured another measure of winterwine from the tapped cask and drank deeply, his ear-tips all but twitching. The harpist and other Elder attended to their own business after our journey, and while most of the Northerners followed suit Efain and Soren hovered near their captain instead, watching the dverger work with narrow-eyed, intense interest. Eol breathed shallowly, submitting to the small man's ministrations as he would not to mine.

"We can leave you and this place to the Enemy's mercy, Mehem my friend, if this is indeed your wish." Tarit did not shrug, but he also did not glance at the dverger. "I am surprised to see you here, my lord Aeredh. How fared you in the South?"

Aeredh broke his steady consumption of winterwine, drawing a deep breath instead. His blue gaze held renewed fire, and his shoulders relaxed. "*We did not find what we sought, but something far more precious.*" He indicated Arn and me with a brief, economical motion. "Lady Solveig and her shieldmaid Arneior are in our care; we visited your mother not so long ago. She sent tidings and gifts with us, but sadly the latter lie now in Nithraen's ruin."

"Ruin? That is heavy tidings indeed. I would ask—" Tarit glanced at a carved stone doorway; motion within it was one of his men, peering at the new arrivals. "Kaedris. What news?"

"*Orukhar* and lich." The man, bearded and broad-shouldered, lingered in the doorway. Despite his rough cloth he was too well-bred to express curiosity at our presence, though it shone in his gaze and he glanced often in my and Arn's direction. "Some other foul things, too, no doubt tracking our new guests. Shall we harry the filth, or simply watch?"

"How many?" The lord of Redhill was abrupt, true—but he was also fey in battle, and no few of the Enemy's servants had met their end at his blade or bow.

He was like his father in that respect, and consequently had earned the hatred not only of the thralls but of their master too.

"Two war-bands, a score each." The bearded man's gaze flickered toward me again, cut away to settle upon his commander. His hand rested easily upon a sword that had to be of Elder make; the plain metal hilt's curve was too lovely to be aught else. "A larger group just at the edge, aiming south for the Cleft. As far as we can tell Dorael's Cloak still holds, but…"

The lord of Redhill had heard enough, and his tone was now very like Lady Hajithe's. "Make certain all our men are accounted for, then close every entrance. Some misfortune has befallen Nithraen, and until I know its tale I will not risk any of our number. Have Gerell and Flokis strengthen the watch, and ready a safe room for our gentler visitors."

"Women here." Kaedris did not quite grumble, but his disapproval was plain. Still, he no longer stared at me and my shieldmaid. "It will make trouble."

"Better here than in the Enemy's clutches, my friend." Tarit half-turned, staring into the fire. His dark eyebrows drew together, and his fingertips lingered upon a knifehilt, tapping thoughtfully. Though his hands were dirty and mud daubed his clothes, he possessed all his mother's nobility. "Have Mehem's sons returned?"

"At the far northern entrance just past dawn. Right glad we were to see them, and they come once they have stowed their burdens."

"That's something, at least," the dverger grumbled, and dropped the bone implement into a bowl with a faint clatter. "Fear not, this one shall live. He merely needs rest; the burns are not envenomed."

"Blessed be praised." Efain sagged with relief, leaning against the table. All of us were draggled with dust and wet with snowmelt, not to mention splashed with battle-grime—a sorry lot indeed, though the Elder shone through the dirt as if they could step out of it at a moment's notice, leaving all smears and stains to collapse upon the rush-strewn floor. "Our thanks for your care, my lord Mehem."

The dverger merely grunted. I was too exhausted to wince at the reminder of my failed duty. It took a concerted effort to lift my own cup, and though I am not overfond of ale, at that moment it was sweeter than any Elder drink. I had thought I would never be warm again, but a trickle of strength returned as the fire shared itself with the entire room. I did not even wonder how they had such a luxury without smoke rising to warn enemies of their location; later, I learned it was a trick of many dverger dwellings.

Their forges burn clean, and they consider flame an honored cousin instead of a mere helpmeet.

Kaedris disappeared to carry out his lord's instructions. Tarit approached Aeredh, and they fell into murmured conference. Aeredh clasped the tall man's shoulder, and it looked as if he were delivering even heavier tidings than Nithraen's fall, for that was the only time I saw Tarit son of Hajithe pale and almost stagger.

The songs say he loved one lost in that cataclysm, an Elder maid—but I do not know. He never spoke upon it afterward to me, or indeed to any other I heard from.

Arn's gaze met mine, and her relief at the fire, not to mention a chair to settle in, was palpable. Flakes fell from her woad-stripe, and her eyes bore dark rings underneath. Her boots were filthy, and mine scarcely better.

"My lady *alkuine*?" Soren left his captain and approached, bowing when I looked to him; I almost flinched, thinking him about to take me to task for not aiding his lord despite Eol's refusal. "Efain tells me you worried for my safety. My thanks for the compliment; I am well enough, as you see."

"I am glad of it." What does one say to a man one had thought dead? "Your captain, is he…"

"He has survived worse; my lord is too sharp a morsel for even a fire-wyrm to chew, and the dverger are skilled in treating many things." Soren scratched at his stubbled cheek, his fingertips rasping; for all they sometimes bore beard-shadow late in the day the wolves of Naras did not let it linger overlong. "We also hear you hid our companions from pursuit and dueled a *trul*. It seems Eol was right to fear you would risk yourself in the battle, and perhaps rob us of hope."

"I did little enough." To be complimented for it was awkward in the extreme. The shivers sank inward, quivering in my bones, and I was so grateful for the fire I could barely contain the feeling. At last my teeth had halted their clattering. I could not bear to think upon what a sorry sight I presented at the moment; tiny curls of steam rose from my sodden skirts and my hand trembled, though there was no ale remaining to slop inside the cup. Arn's ring-and-scale would need cleaning soon, and a layer of *seidhr* applied to keep rust at bay. "In any case, we are allies now."

"Gelad mentioned you accepted their oaths. I wonder…" He glanced at Arn, as if gauging her temper; my shieldmaid simply took another healthy swallow of ale, looking very much as if she considered hefting a cask and drinking straight from it a distinct possibility. "Had we told you of our need, would you have agreed to come of your own will?"

I longed to shame him, to say *perhaps I would*. But I was weary unto death, and in any case Arn was listening; she would hear a lie. And I could not give these men any advantage, either. "I do not know." It seemed a poor answer, even if honest. "My father might have forbidden it, despite any weregild."

"Your father was near to breaking pax upon us when Eol insisted." Soren was pale, but evidently determined to have his say. "And now you see what Aeredh feared. Nithraen is gone, and we are as hunted beasts. Dorael will feel the full brunt of the Enemy's wrath soon, and though the lady of that place is mighty and Aenarian Greycloak, even in grief, is most fell when there is need, they cannot hold against *him* forever. The South will not come to our aid, for all they are next to suffer the Enemy's grasp once we are dealt with. You are the hope not just of our lands but of your own."

I merely longed to crawl into a bed—failing that, a pile of straw, or even a corner of a disused room—and close my eyes. "Little hope indeed," I muttered, and sagged against the chair's back.

"Eril threatened to break pax?" Arn clearly saw I wished no more discussion of what I would, might, or should have done. She bit at a hunk of waybread and chewed with great relish, her spear propped within easy reach. Despite the weariness graven on her own face, her eyes were bright and every line of her expressed readiness.

"Oh, aye." Soren shifted as if his booted feet pained him; they were probably swelling now with the sudden return of warm blood. "He said, *I prize my eldest daughter, I would not send her North with wolves.* And while I have the chance, my lady Minnow, I shall tell you that your spear is mighty indeed. Not many face the Enemy's whip-bearers with your courage. I will name any weapon you carry *Trul-killer,* and all who hear of your deeds from me shall be impressed."

"My thanks for the compliment, friend." Her sudden grin was shadowed with exhaustion, but genuine enough. The Northerner retreated, leaving us sole owners of the fireside.

I stared at the flames. Split wood, stacked neatly upon one side of the stone hearth, was ready to be fed into the maw; the image of deep furnaces under iron towers struck me again, as a dream sometimes will after one wakes.

"Strange." My own voice, soft and wondering, surprised me. "I would have thought him glad to send me." After all, Bjorn was his son, the precious copy of his maleness, and Astrid—well, who could not adore her?

But I have ever been uncanny, and difficult; Eril, no matter how doughty upon the battlefield, held weirding in proper caution as a warrior should. For all that, he sometimes expressed a measure of rough pride at having sired the first full *volva* in generations, and no festival or feast passed without him pressing gifts and signal attention upon Idra for her care and training of me. Of course losing such aid was an inconvenience, especially with trade negotiations and legal cases swarming at the year's turn, but of his three children I was the easiest to send far afield.

When I was young, I thought him near Odynn, or Tohr the thunderer, or even Manhrweh the Great Judge—large, powerful, and booming with authority, possessing no frailties or even gentle feelings. What need had he of them, with my mother nearby?

Now, I wondered. Perhaps every child finds their parents a foreign country as the years accumulate.

"So would I," Arn agreed. "This journey is laden with discoveries."

"Few of them pleasant." My eyelids had grown passing heavy. I sagged in the chair, its wooden back biting my shoulderblades. "But now your spear bears a name. Congratulations."

"Not yet." She finished the waybread and let the aleskin dangle from her left hand, mere fingerwidths from the smooth stone floor. These seats were well-made, but slightly too small. "I did not kill the foul thing, after all."

"Nevertheless." *I did nothing but delay it for a few moments.* Between us, my shieldmaid had the higher honor, and I hoped she knew as much. "You accomplished more than I could."

"I shall show you to a quiet room; he needs only sleep." Mehem the dverger had finished his ministering and stepped briskly away from the table, brushing his small capable hands together. "'Tis best for him, now. A hillwyrm, you say? One large enough to batter city gates?"

"The Enemy has devised some way to breed them for size." Efain motioned to Elak and Karas. "Come, let us make him more comfortable. Soren, Gelad, look to the ladies. We are safe here."

"For how long?" Soren murmured.

"As long as the ruling line of Kharak-Ûn endures in this hill, it will not fall." Mehem fixed Soren with a baleful glare. His eyes were even stranger, now that I had chance to examine him more closely— the specks of gold caught in his irises moved in slow streams, and his pupils were not round but goatlike. "And I have no intention of giving up my home just yet, even should the Enemy of our great maker Ullwë pound upon the doors."

I heard the tale of Redhill's eventual fall sung much later, in a saga of Tarit the Ill-Fated. But that morn I was merely glad for the fire, and stared into its comforting glow until Mehem and Soren led Arn and me to deeper chambers—a small alcove and a water-room—where a narrow pallet upon a rude wooden frame accepted both shieldmaid and *volva* for rest we sorely needed.

The True Difference

It is said that the Great Smith Aol created the dverger in secret, and thus courted the Allmother's anger. Indeed they reverence him as their Maker, and give the rest of the Blessed cursory—though traditional—honor. There is an argument that the Allmother put the desire to make them into the Smith's heart, and so was not truly angered but merely playful. Upon these matters the Delvers are silent.
—Stachil of Dun Kaenis, *On the Thrayn Hill-Delvers*

We were awakening in stranger and stranger circumstances, Arn and I, first in an Elder city and now inside a dverger-hill upon a thin mattress stuffed with fragrant ruddy herbs, a water-room close by. The latter was of different make than the Elder one in Nithraen and there was no sauna, but we could clean ourselves, and the enclosed privy was a distinct relief. Veins of glowing rock threading through the walls provided low illumination, not nearly as bright as Nithraen's orbs; and most blessed of all, it was warm enough to be comfortable without sweating.

Not only that, but when I woke my mother's second-largest trunk was set in a corner of our room, and the saddlebags draped over it were familiar, being my shieldmaid's private luggage. How either had arrived, brought somehow out of the ruin of an Elder city, neither of us could tell.

Arn poked lightly at the trunk with her spear as I propped myself on my elbows, blinking. "Weirding," she muttered, her horn-braids disarranged by sleep and her sleeveless linen undershirt slipping from one muscled shoulder. "Sol?"

"I think it unlikely to attack, unless 'twas badly packed." I ached all over as if I had my mother's ague, and the bruised half of my face was stiff.

A short while later, I sat on the side of the neatly made bed in my green winter dress, fragrant of packing-resin and bearing Astrid's rune-tangle embroidery at neck and cuffs, rebraiding my damp hair while Arn, in fresh linen and quilted padding, worked her way into her second-best hauberk. I could have wished Astrid was there to help with both Arn's armoring and twisting my hair into submission, but I had to content myself with each red coral bead being a reminder of home. The door to the hall, slightly ajar, quivered under a mannerly knock, and at my bidding to enter opened silently to reveal Eol, his scorched mane neatly trimmed and the rest of him haggard, but his dark gaze clear and his black cloth reasonably clean. The gem upon his swordhilt winked at us, unwrapped and catching a stray gleam from the wall-illumination.

"My lady *alkuine*." He even bowed—somewhat stiffly, true—and though I did not like a man not my kin seeing me in the act of braiding, there was no help for it. "And my lady shieldmaid."

Arn muttered what might have passed for a polite greeting, yanking at the hem of her hauberk to situate it correctly, and my fingers were oddly clumsy. A chunk of red coral almost skittered free, but I held it grimly to its task, and the ribbon too.

"You seem recovered indeed." It did gladden me, though even to myself I sounded merely, coldly polite. "I am sorry I did not attend to your wounds, my lord. It is a *volva*'s duty, and I failed in it." *As well as everything else.*

It stung all the more deeply because I had not seen or avoided the trap in Dun Rithell. Was being ignorant of the danger lurking in the North better? The question occurred to me over and over, while my hands were busily attending to other matters.

Even the dream of ash-choked iron towers and that low, awful reddish glow did not occupy me so much.

"Ah. Well." Eol's black eyebrows drew together, his mouth turned down at either corner, and he stood very straight indeed, though something in the set of his shoulders said it pained him. His hands, kept at his sides, were tense as well. "The house of Naras is hardy, my lady; I did not wish you to waste your strength upon my small hurts. We were more concerned for your injuries, and none can tell me who struck you."

I glanced at Arn, who settled upon the trunk to deal with her boots. She wished to be fully armored for the day, and I could not blame her. I could not touch a bee-end of my torc, and while occupied with twisting my hair I was at a distinct disadvantage in this conversation. "The whip-monster—it had *seidhr*. I could do no more than scorch and slow it, and it marked me in return." I finished the recalcitrant braid, secured it, and set to work at the next. The stock of beads, ribbons, and bent pins in my lap shrank correspondingly.

"It is a mighty thing to even delay a *trul*. The Elder are saying that if the women of the South are this brave, the Enemy will find them a difficult foe indeed." Eol paused, closely regarding my work; perhaps Northern women let any man watch them thus. It is one thing to speak half-glimpsed from a window with your hair unbound, it is quite another to let a strange man see your ribbon-weaving performed—or so it suddenly seemed to me that day. "There are some matters we must speak upon, Lady Solveig."

Could you not wait until I have at least had breakfast? "Then speak, son of Tharos." I might have added I could hardly avoid hearing him, that as weregild or ally I was still obliged to listen in any case, and a few other sharp observations besides, but I was not at home and could not give the sharp edge of my tongue so freely.

I was beginning to suspect I would never see Dun Rithell again. Sometimes I flinch to think of how long it took me to realize as much.

"We are safe enough here for some short while," he began. "The petty-*khazal* Mehem and his sons know these passages, but 'tis easy for others to become lost. You will need a guide, do you venture into the halls."

Khazal. I stored the word for later tasting; if it was the Old Tongue, I had not heard it before. "Very well." I did not add that I could simply touch a wall, or the floor, and more than likely garner enough information to wend my way to an exit if need be.

Just like untangling a snarl of thread, or of yarn. The fact that I was lost in a larger mess of half-sensed ropes did not bear mentioning either.

Eol paused as if expecting me to say more. The silence was not quite excruciating, but the fire snapped as if it had an opinion, and when it had finished he continued. "Tarit leads the Secondborn here; he is Lady Hajithe's son and was fostered in Dorael for some time. Some of his men are not of the Faithful, but *he* can be trusted." Another pause, as if he expected some reaction, but I gave none, merely gazed steadily upon him until he coughed slightly again and continued. "You will be well-guarded here, yet eventually we must leave. Should the worst happen, my lady *alkuine*, I must ask you to let us fight without worry. You cannot risk yourself." His gaze settled upon Arn, perhaps seeking to enlist her agreement; she busied herself with her boots. "I would bring you safely to our journey's end, and I beg you to understand as much."

"I understand you will not tell me where such end rests." It also nettled me that he would dare to *beg*, as if he did not hold the upper hand—at least, until I could manage to wrest the advantage away, as I had with his men. At least three of them had sworn allyship, and that is a weighty oath. "But perhaps you should. I am no longer your weregild, son of Tharos. You would do well to treat an ally with less secrecy."

He could have sought to challenge my assertion, to demand the life-debt's payment despite any treachery his brother had committed. Then it would become a case of legal argument, but he had a half-dozen warriors set against one lone spear and a *volva*—and possibly Aeredh's help as well, to corral a pair of intractable women. I did not think the lord of Redhill would intervene on our behalf unless I could put the matter to him with both urgency and unimpeachable logic.

I waited, my heart attempting to lodge in my throat, for Eol of Naras's next words.

"So you know." Did he wince? If he did 'twas no more than a

flicker, there and gone like lightning. "I deserve your anger, and you may vent it as you wish. But you must not risk yourself, Lady Solveig. On this point the Elder and the house of Naras are in complete agreement."

I could not let my relief show. His acknowledgment meant my status was no longer mere weregild, and welcome was the change.

"Neither you nor your Elder friends need worry," Arneior said, tartly. She did not reach for her spear, but straightened and gave him a baleful glare. Her hauberk gleamed; metal loves the light of a dverger home, and takes on a richer glow under it. "Sol has me."

"Even so." Eol granted her a short, stiff nod. "We would not like to lose you either, my lady shieldmaid."

"Arn and I look after each other, my lord." Having achieved at least one goal, I did not think it wise to let Arn's temper mount even further; she had achieved no breakfast yet either, and consequently was in no forgiving mood. "I ask for your honesty, which is little enough to grant a woman you have wronged. Where is this Hidden City you mean to take us to, and shall you begin treating me as an ally deserves or must I expect more lies and obfuscation? I can hardly distinguish between you and the Black Land's lord at this point, for he is said to be false as well."

I did not expect my words to have such a marked effect. Eol paled, his mouth turned to a thin line, and his gaze kindled with anger. Arn was on her feet in an instant, though but newly shod and without her woad, her spear making a soft sound as its end touched the floor, braced in case she needed to move swiftly.

At least I had enough *seidhr* to see the wolf in the Northern captain, peering through dark eyes, its muzzle lifted and a growl just on the edge of loosening from a black-furred chest.

"I hope you never learn the true difference between me and *him*, my lady." Brittle formality edged every word, and his right hand twitched as if longing for a hilt. "I regret I am not at leave to discuss the end of our journey, even did I know its exactness. A heavy charge is laid upon all who know even of its existence, and despite what you may think I would not be forsworn." He visibly swallowed other words, perhaps not so restrained, and gave a final short, stiff bow. "I shall send someone to bring you to breakfast, so you are not forced to endure my presence."

With that, the heir of Naras turned upon his heel and vanished through the door.

I finished my braids in silence while Arn studied where he had stood, her brow furrowed. The silence between us was familiar, and comforting.

Finally, she turned to me, the ghost of woad lingering yellow upon her cheek and forehead. "Well done." No sarcasm sharpened her tone; so long as my behavior gained a shieldmaid's approval, I could be certain of its propriety.

She was my *seidhr*-needle, my small one, for all her usual solution to any problem was a quick application of her spear. Mine was to wait until I knew more, and between the two of us, the eager and the dilatory, we managed well enough.

"I am no longer weregild, or at least not completely. Perhaps he will grow weary of my badgering and send us home." My braids were done, ribboned, and pinned. I stood, my fists at my lower back, and stretched as my mother often did. My skirts made a low soft sound, and I was glad of their weight. "Though what good that will do, I cannot tell."

"I have been imagining those pale things coming south." She returned to the chest, finished her own buckling, strapping, and tying, and rose with swift grace to bounce upon her toes thrice, making certain her armor was settled. "Or one of those whip-monsters. No wonder they wish some aid, Sol. I would too, faced with those...*things*."

It cheered me, albeit only faintly, that we were in accord upon that point. "I do not know how much aid we will be." My legs were not as steady as I liked. Yet I rose, shaking my head to test the seating of my braids, and the dim glow from rock-veins made my eyes hot and grainy. "That toy of Caelgor's nearly killed me, Arn. This *seidhr*-weapon they wish me to use may finish the job."

"Ah. So that is the burr in your skirts." She tapped her spear-butt once, indicating readiness for the day's battles, and regarded me. "Idra did not train you for nothing, my weirdling. If you simply practice—"

"It is not like that, Arn." I settled my sleeves and brushed at my skirts, heartily grateful for the appearance of our baggage. Being reduced to a single dress was not nearly as awful as the appearance of *orukhar*, but so often we brood upon a smaller fear to forget larger ones. "I wish it were."

"Don't worry." Her smile held only the barest trace of anxiety. "The Wingéd are with us. That has to count for something."

"Indeed." I sought a better subject, and luckily one was handy. "I should have asked him how they dragged our trunk here. That would be *seidhr* worth knowing."

"Now there is my weirdling; she sounds much more like herself." Duly comforted, she glided to the door, peering into the hall. "Do you think you can untangle these passages? I like not being trapped."

I rubbed my palms together briskly enough to warm them. "Mayhap I shall touch them, and see."

Yet a few moments later Mehem arrived to guide us toward breakfast, accompanied by Gelad. I did not have time to test myself against dverger work that day, or any other during our stay.

It was probably for the best.

Atop the Listening Hill

Long live the lord of Redhill
A thorn in the Enemy's side!
Long lived the lord of Redhill
Until at the Leap he died…
—Hillel Brightblade, *The Second*
Saga of Hajithe's Son

I did not quite like our sojourn at Redhill, though it was far more comfortable than traveling in the freeze.

For one thing, we were kept far below the hill's surface, and it was neither so light nor so airy as Nithraen. The hill had been hewn for smaller creatures, and most passages were somewhat cramped. Arn had the worst of it, with her spear to manage as well as her greater height; I was, for once, glad to be less tall.

For another, we were daily hemmed by the men of Naras, though all the Elder, those of Tarit's warriors unwounded or not engaged upon the guard of the hill, and most of Eol's companions left before dawn and returned after dusk. They not only kept watch upon each league the hill guarded, but also emerged at carefully chosen points to harry whatever foul thing or servant of the Enemy could be found. There had been an increase in such things of late, and Nithraen's fall left a large gap in the Elder siege of the Black Land.

Yet there were always at least two of Eol's wolves left behind, and neither Arn nor I could stir a step without their attendance save with the Elder, or Tarit himself. It rankled my shieldmaid, for any of her kind dislikes close watch, and it drove me to near peevishness. I was used to wandering Dun Rithell as the mood took me, river-bank to woods, the green to the Standing Stones, with only Arn for company. Often physical movement will bring an answer to some quandary of *seidhr*—or any lesser sort. Yet in Nithraen we stayed in a single house, and at Redhill a cramped warren enclosed us with little glimpse of sunlight or hint of fresh air.

I might not have minded so much, for there were fires in the deeper rooms, and the cold outside did not break. The return of the men after dark each day brought melting ice dripping from boots and mantles, grim looks, and tales of sharp close combat with *orukhar*.

Not to mention other fell creatures.

Tarit had a great horned helm—Aeredh told us it was dverger-work—and its leering was deeply unsettling. The mask struck terror into foul and fell alike; it had belonged to his father, Lady Hajithe's long-gone husband. It was there I also learned the tale of Taliurin, beloved of the Elder and vanished, thought dead at the hands of the Seven.

Lady Hajithe's gravity was the result of much sorrow. Though her daughter was safe in Dorael and her son presumed there as well she refused that shelter, holding to the belief that somehow her husband would one day return to the Eastronmost. Besides, the stead-ings around that hall looked to her for guidance and rule; like her son, she was not one to shirk any duty, no matter how small.

In any case, it was the son of Hajithe who took Arn and me to the summit of Karat Vaerkil sometime after we arrived.

The top was overgrown with *vaer*, the reddish herb granting the hill its name, but none was evident amid the snow-smothered scrub tortured by constant wind when not under a depth of fluted, air-carved white. Still, there was a hexagonal stone floor large enough for a smallhouse's foundations, flags fitted together without mortar, and I saw the distinctive look of dverger work there. In the precise middle was a stone shape—a throne, with a high back, a wide broad seat, and arms ending in frowning faces akin to the visor of Tarit's horned helm. No snow touched either floor or chair, though I could detect no *seidhr* lingering in either.

The sky had cleared, a bright pale piercing blue, and though the bruise on my cheek had faded somewhat it still throbbed when the cold stroked my face. I used no healing for the wound, for I had not attended Eol's hurts either. My mantle fluttered under a knife-sharp wind; I had repaired some small damage to it and to Arn's, glad to have time for such a task.

Very little is as soothing as sewing, especially while one is kept trammeled by weather.

My shieldmaid stood with her eyes closed, basking in thin golden sunshine. The frigid breeze brought a blush to her cheeks, made her freckles glow, gilded her woad-stripe, and burned in her hair.

Eol's cohort clearly judged Tarit unlikely to offer me any insult, unlike his men. There was some manner of reserve between the two groups, though both were glad enough of an Elder presence. Today the lord of Redhill was at home instead of striking at his enemies, and I fair leapt at the offered chance to see the crown of his domicile.

Besides, it gave us lee to speak without other ears lingering close by, and I was curious what he would make of it.

"You met my mother," he said, after a short while of grave attention to the wind's formless song. "How was she?"

"Gracious and kind." I tucked gloved hands into my mantle-sleeves, and could not help but smile. "She reminded me of my own mother, though sad. There is steel in her." I paused, and perhaps he expected more. "I can see her in your face, too."

"Can you?" If he was pleased at the notion, he did not show it. Then again, the son of Hajithe did not often betray any emotion other than mild disdain, or fury at the Enemy's many servants and deceits. He even seemed to scorn the cold, not bothering to shiver though his black mantle, in the manner of Northern wear, was thin. "It has been long indeed since I saw her; I thank you for the news."

"She did me much honor." I suspected that had the lady of the Eastronmost known me brought North with a lie she would have done all in her power to gainsay Aeredh and Eol's purpose. Little good it would have achieved, indeed. "I would aid her all I can, and her son as well."

"A fine promise, though there is nothing I would ask of you, my lady Solveig." His tone robbed the words of any sting; it was a mere statement of fact, nothing more. "You must chafe at being so closely held, but 'tis for the best. We do not see many women here, and my men are…well, we were bandits together once, and I suppose we still are."

"Is that so?" I knew of bandits, of course, though only by report since none truly troubled Dun Rithell while my father was present to dissuade them. Only outlying steadings and smallfarms were ever touched by their depredations, and then only until a war-party was dispatched. "You do not seem desperate men, or honorless."

"That is a comfort, my lady." Now he wore the very slightest of smiles, and his dark gaze gleamed. Like the Elder and the men of Naras, he grew no beard; the raffishness of stubble suited him, and he oft let its growth linger for a few days while hunting his foes. "The Enemy deforms even those who fight him with the best of intent."

I thought Eol would agree with the statement, but I did not think it quite wise to remark as much. The two Northerners seemed to hold each other in polite caution, nothing more. "In the South they think the Black Land spent. I gather it is not so here."

"No, my lady." The son of Hajithe regarded me steadily, and had Eol answered me thus, perhaps I might have come to belief more easily. It was not easy to discredit anything the lord of Redhill cared to say; as the sagas point out, though he oft chose not to speak. Much pride had he, and it was visible even in his silences. "The Enemy is alive, the gates of Agramar have closed, and new flame burns in the depths of that cursèd place."

"The Enemy…" I shuddered, for the wind grew even more piercing. It was perhaps ill luck to mention such a creature even in the southron tongue. "Is he truly the Allmother's first son?"

"You should ask the Elder; they know more than I." Tarit paused, glancing at Arn. His stubbled cheeks blushed with the wind's force, and even here in some safety he rested a hand upon the hilt of a plain, well-crafted dagger. "There is some disagreement, Lady Solveig. Daerith and the other Elder say you should be taken to Dorael, where Aenarian

Greycloak and his queen will offer you refuge. Aeredh and Eol will not say whither they mean to wend, but 'tis clear they have some other destination in mind. I thought to ask where it pleases you to go."

It would please me to return to Dun Rithell, my lord. And yet… the idea of a lich or vast army of *orukhar* descending upon my home filled me with dread twice as cold as the wind tugging at my mantle's furred hood. I was to wield an Elder *seidhr*-weapon, I knew I lacked the strength—and the men who had taken me from my home were not bothering to ask an ally her wishes, but arguing with other men over my fate.

I did not know what to do, and could not tell how to aim my cunning or craft to find an answer.

Arn did not tap her spear-butt against the stone, but her arm tensed as if she wished to. Her eyes were closed and she still drank in all the sunlight she could, but no doubt she weighed every word.

I had been excited at this journey, especially by the thought of learning new *seidhr*. Perhaps Lokji had been listening to my inner counsel and decided to grant me what I longed for, accompanied by the twist he gives every gift.

Lady Hajithe's son deserved my honesty; I could give at least some measure of it with good grace. "I think Aeredh means to take me to a place they call the Hidden City. An Elder named Taeron is king there, and will not suffer me to leave once I arrive, or so Caelgor the Fair told me."

"Caelgor?" Tarit's lip curled slightly, and he made a restless movement. His use of the southron tongue improved much with practice, though each word remained achingly formal. "A mighty lord, but I have never liked him overmuch. Still, the Elder care not for my like or dislike. They are above such things."

Perhaps. "Yet I should think every man or woman free to dislike whom we will, my lord."

"Well spoken." Tarit eyed me closely, and his gaze was piercing. There was very little difference between iris and pupil, granting his glance almost *seidhr*-weight. No breath of the wise art hung upon him, but he saw much—and in him ran a streak of wholly mortal strength, all the more unforgiving for its presence in a perishable host. "Taeron Goldspear. I have heard the name."

I waited. I was warm enough, well-swathed in wool, with venison stew as well as waybread filling my stomach. The men of Redhill were hunters not just of the Enemy's thralls, and it was a relief to eat again instead of merely quaffing Elder draughts. Arn was pleased with Redhill's ale, and even I liked it well enough. One of Mehem's sons—Jeherem, the younger—held the title of brewmaster; his stills and casks were well-kept. The dverger ferment without bitterness, holding life has enough of that quality, so their drinks often bear a certain sweetness, probably from the great starch-roots they jealously guard the secret of. For they do not brew with grain or honey, and those roots also give their bread its distinctive, dense tenderness.

Finally, Tarit reached some decision. His shoulders stiffened, and he turned fully in my direction. "My father sojourned in Taeron's city while he was young, and all he ever said of that king was fair indeed. Should you visit there I cannot think it will do you any harm, and since he let my father and Aeredh leave his halls I also cannot think he will gainsay one so fair as yourself. Yet Taliurin my father met his fate expecting some aid, and none arrived. We are as butterflies or nightjars to the Elder; we dash ourselves against their rocks, and they do not feel the breaking."

Arn returned to my side, either having her fill of sun or wishing to join our parley. Her shoulder touched mine, and she regarded Tarit with sober seriousness and the honor of her complete attention.

"I at first thought Eol mistaken or jesting when he told me of the Black Land." My gloved hands knotted against each other; somehow, in the mad scramble of leaving Nithraen, I had not mislaid such small articles. "I thought it but an old tale to frighten children with. Now I have seen a lich, a *trul*…Those things are awful, yet are apparently held small beside the Enemy's other servants. We might be glad enough of rocks to shelter behind."

"Well said, and very like my mother you sound." He cocked his dark head slightly; the wind's voice changed, its timbre shifting. The habit of watchfulness never left this man, hunted as he was—none guessed it then, but the Enemy knew his name and was already compassing his destruction. "Should you go to Dorael, I would ask you to befriend my sister Laleith. I have not seen her since she was in swaddling."

I could not imagine being separated from Astrid for so long. Even when Bjorn married out I would still see him at festivals, or on visits.

If, that was, I ever returned home. "It would be my honor, Lord Tarit."

He nodded, sharply. "I thank you for it. Would you care to witness a wonder?"

"As long as it is not..." I was about to say *like a lich, or other things we have seen*, and realized the rudeness just in time. "Forgive me, I speak unguarded."

For some reason, Tarit the grim smiled without reserve that once, and it was pleasant to see. Tiny bits of blown snow clung to his hair. "It is a relief to know someone might, even here. Come."

He trod firmly upon wind-cleared stone, and I followed, Arn at my side. We approached the carven throne, and as we did the wind mounted. Finally, Tarit paused, turning to regard us both with head held high, shaggy hair lifting as cold moving air combed it almost lovingly.

The dverger said that to stand near that seat upon Karat Vaerkil is to hear the world. It could be some manner of *seidhr*, though I did not feel it as I sense the unseen under warp and weft of the physical. Then again, the dvergers' own legends say they were crafted by the great smith of the Aesyr, not for arrogance but in loving imitation of the Allmother's gift of breath and life. That god made the very mountains, sowing veins of minerals and gems within them—not to mention the bedrock under hills, and the vast foundation the entire world-tree rests upon. Perhaps dverger *seidhr* is too subtle to be sensed, or perhaps it is of another kind, wedded firm and invisible to the substance of the physical in ways tallfolk cannot understand.

I closed my eyes, for the wind was speaking.

Rustles and rushing, the creak of frozen limbs and the whisper of sap buried deep to wait for spring. Small animals sleeping, burrowing, or hunting during daylight—snap of feathered wings, crunch of tiny teeth in leftover berry or bone—as well as the larger beasts eking out their winter existence. A bear slept in a deep cave, only dimly aware of the cold outside; wolves that were not of Naras howled many leagues away, singing their joy at finding meat while a lean haggard deer struggled in snow, knowing its time had come but attempting to break free of the pack's circling nonetheless.

Other deer sought through the white waste for food, finding it in bark, twig, or under hoof-scraped snow. Even the scattered boulders had a song all their own, low and grumbling at the very bottom of my hearing; the ice-locked streams sang slow crystalline notes.

"What do you hear?" the lord of Redhill asked, softly.

"Everything alive," I whispered. "Arneior?"

"Battle." My shieldmaid's voice was much quieter than usual. "Some few leagues east, and another north. There are foul things marching to the south; their boots have iron heels to crush the snow and everything underneath. More than one wolf pack is hunting today, and all will find what they seek."

I frowned, straining my ears, but I could not hear what she did. "A winter hawk, hunting as well." The scream of prey found and carried aloft on beating wings filled me with feather-brushes, as if the Wingéd Ones circled me instead of my shieldmaid. "I hear the wolves too, but not…"

"It has been long since I stood in this place and heard aught but the slither of the Enemy through these woods. Sometimes I wish I could." Tarit barely mouthed the words, but they were clear as a bell. "The Elder, though they may offer aid, do not rule here. I would advise you not to seek returning south if Nithraen is fallen."

I suppressed a shiver. The wind was rising; I could discern nothing in Tarit's voice but truth. Yet I longed to return home. The sickness filled me, toes to scalp, before draining to leave a cold, unsteady clarity in its wake. "I shall consider your counsel closely."

"I am gladdened to hear it, my lady." Tarit's tone did not shift, nor did his physical self. Soft and level, he continued. "When you leave, you will go to Dorael or to Taeron's kingdom, as you choose. This I promise you."

Those in the woods surrounding Redhill could not hear us; the wind brought tales, but did not spread them. Now I understood his invitation to see the hilltop. My eyelids rose, and the bright day was like a blow, a flood of impressions once a heavy stone-and-silver gate was battered wide. "It is more choice than I have been given so far, my lord, and I thank you for it."

A king could hardly have accepted my gratitude with more regal unconcern. "Listen as long as you please, my lady Solveig. I shall wait for you upon the edge of the stone."

Then did the son of Hajithe withdraw, either to find shelter from the cold or to let Arn and me pass what words we would in privacy.

No, I did not precisely like our stay at Redhill. Yet I liked Tarit the proud very much, and the songs of his fate grieve me still.

The Chair of Honor

*Aulm of the deep waters whispered into Taeron Goldspear
the High-helm's dreams, showing him a place of safety. Yet
the vision ever carried within it a warning—do not become
enamored of your own mighty works in the perishable
world. Laeliquaende's beauty was never meant to last.*
          —Daerith the Younger, *Floringaeld's Lament*

Deep in the hill was a hall of much higher vault than the others, and its walls ran with tangled carvings of dverger-runes. A round stone table was not placed but had been carved from the hill's heart, and its surface was polished to reflection. Mehem would not speak of *seidhr* or of how Redhill was constructed, but did look somewhat pleased when I let out a gasp of wonder upon seeing the rune-covered walls, reaching to touch the carvings and checking at the last moment, even as my fingertips burned with curiosity.

"My apologies." I snatched my hands back, letting them drop to my skirts. "May I?"

The bearded dverger sucked his cheeks in, his strange golden-flecked gaze depthless, and settled his thumbs in a wide leather belt. Inside the hill, he wore no mantle but a half-cloak lined with soft brown fur, and soft slippers with hide soles. "Your tall men have never noticed, nor remarked," he said, gruffly. "You are of the South, young one? I hear our writing is used there, or a form of it."

"Very close," I agreed. My heartsblood dress was fine enough for this occasion, at least, and I was glad of its weight. And of my father's bee-torc as well. " 'Tis not the carving calling to me, but what lies inside it. Is it history, or—"

"After a fashion." Mehem moved aside as Tarit entered, the tall Northerner glancing down briefly to avoid collision. The two seemed to share a cordial dislike, yet it was Mehem the son of Hajithe deferred to in most if not all questions of supplies or safety. If the dverger said *It is bad to leave the hill today*, no follower of Tarit would stir a step forth; if Mehem said *You should return by noon*, it was heeded as a father's edict. "Once there was peace in these lands, and my people came through with caravans of goods. We traded much with the Elder, and wrought many a treasure they still hold dear. News is written here, and genealogy, and things of note. But what is written is not what *is*. More must be added."

"Ai," Arn muttered, shaking her ruddy head; her woad-stripe was freshly applied and gleamed rich blue. "It is weirding-talk. I leave you to it." She followed Tarit; others appeared in the two other arched entrances set equidistant around the vault. Each group was brought by one of Mehem's sons, for the passages were tangled and even men who had arrived first with Tarit could still become lost in their labyrinth if not going to some memorized place.

"Pfft." Mehem gestured, brushing her words away. "You may look all you like, lady of the South, but do not touch. These are the things of my people; we share much, but I would not have these handled by the tall."

The curiosity in my fingertips was close to actual pain; still, I clasped my hands tightly and bent a knee, not a bow but the courtesy of a lord's daughter. "Forgive my rudeness, my lord dverger." I could almost feel the rough tweak Idra would have given one of my braids, reminding me not to be impolite in any matter, large or small.

The sharp ache of missing my teacher mixed with homesickness, a drink grown strong by the mixing of two liquors.

"At least you asked." He indicated my wrists with a short, sharp jab of his capable, callused hand. At first I had thought his fingertips discolored—or even inked as my *volva*-markings—but the dark veining and blackened nails were called *forgebless* among them, and the sign of a maker. "The marks, there. I would examine them, but would you let me touch?"

"No," I admitted. It was fair enough, and just besides. "Though you may look all you like, once this council is done. You may find our writing has not diverged far from yours."

"And you wear it upon your skin. How…" He glanced at the room, gauging its fullness, and despite the number of Elder and Secondborn present, there was no sense of crowding.

"Ink, forced under the skin with needles." I did not begrudge the explanation.

Still, he made a face, nose wrinkling with something close to distaste. He looked very much like old Flokin in that moment, though a third of that fellow's size. "Barbaric."

"Knowledge is ever paid for, my lord." I was somewhat nettled by the word *barbaric*, but as my mother said, even one's closest neighbors may oft seem strange. Such is the wide world, and every house is a country all its own. "I earned every one of my marks, and was glad to receive them."

"I suppose I cannot argue." Of all the men I met in the North, Mehem the dverger spoke our language best. I could not tell where he had learned it. "We say the same. All things have a price, whether or not one wishes to pay."

"Spoken like one of Ullwë's own." Aeredh drew close; he was no longer the smiling youth he had been in Dun Rithell or the first part of our journey north. His eyes had darkened, and his mouth was no longer merry. Elder do not age as Secondborn do, 'tis true, but sometimes a great grief may leave marks upon them which approximate it, and the fall of his city seemed to have done so. "My lady Solveig, we cannot have this council without you. Will you come, and listen?"

"Listen, but not speak?" I fought the urge to fold my arms or touch my torc. Either would show nervousness. "In the South, one does not dispose of a woman without her consent and counsel. Is it so different in the North?"

"Certainly not." He went still in the particular way of the Elder, as a granary feline will when something captures its entire regard, and the light in his gaze sharpened. "We began badly, though with the best of intent. Grant me the chance to make some amends, my lady, and say what you will. You are so quiet I oft think you disdain to speak."

"Perhaps she merely has some sense." Mehem moved away, soft-footed—dverger can be silent indeed when they choose, and remain unremarked by taller folk almost at will. He looked ready to leave us to our discussion, but Tarit motioned to him.

"Come, my lord Mehem," the son of Hajithe called, despite the looks exchanged by his lieutenants—bearded Kaedris, and Berehad called Bowman for his skill with placing shafts from a bow of Elder make and size to rival Daerith the harpist's. "I value your advice, as all should. Besides, the chair of honor is yours."

I would have passed Aeredh to join the others at the glass-glossy table, but he moved as if to catch my arm and I halted, my skirt swinging. Perhaps he mistook it for a flinch, since his hand fell to his side and his expression darkened still further. Once more I saw a flicker of his true age, and it was disconcerting against his usual humor.

I waited, but he said naught else, merely indicated the table and walked thence at my shoulder like a shieldmaid.

So it was I took my place at the Council of Redhill. One chair was stone, and shaped with steps for a dverger's shorter legs to climb into its embrace; the rest were a motley assortment of carven wood. Daerith the harpist of Nithraen was there, and four Elder from the wreck of their city; Tarit the Ill-Fated and his two chief lieutenants attended too, and the wolves of Naras except Soren and Elak, who were with many of Tarit's men and the other Elder hunting a group of *orukhar* between the hill and shattered Elder land, where a wyrm's stink was already blasting the trees and golden grass to sickly shadows.

Despite what they say of that discussion, Tarit and Eol of Naras did not come to blows, nor did Aeredh the Crownless sing a lament for lost Nithraen. It was more like an Althing where all speak their minds upon questions of import, though there was no ale and neither Aesyr nor Vanyr nor any other divinity were invoked at beginning or end. Nor was I treated with much false courtesy by rival groups eager to gain a sliver more than their neighbors, there was no question of a flyting—and there was not a single honorable bout of fisticuffs.

My father would have found it a dull affair indeed.

Arn disdained to sit, standing behind my chair with her spear a straight vertical bar and her dark eyes narrowed. In physical battle my place was where she set me, but here, I was the better warrior. Still, the men left a chair empty at my right should she change her mind, and Aeredh settled himself to my left. Apparently there was some honor in his position or mine, for those assembled looked to him to open the discussion.

It began, as such things do, with a recitation of what we knew: Nithraen was fallen, a large force marched toward Dorael—Daerith the harpist gestured to the shining tabletop, indicating the relative places and points between. There was some power in Aenarian Greycloak's land which would keep even an army of *orukhar* and other fell things at bay, but it did not leave those borders and might be overwhelmed in time, especially if the Seven rode forth together instead of singly.

Of the Seven of Kaer Angaran not much was said, since every Northerner knew of them. I gathered they were creatures like unto the lich we had seen, yet far more dread and deadly; the inference sent a chill down my spine.

The recent battles were discussed, and I learned summat of a grave insult which had driven Tarit from Dorael ere his sister Laleith arrived there for fostering—she had been loath to leave her mother before, and went only reluctantly. The son of Hajithe disdained to return to that Elder realm, though Daerith spoke of a pardon extended by the high king himself.

I could have told the harpist the idea of *pardon* for a wrong not of his making would only insult a man of Tarit's temper further, but I was not asked, and held my peace. Sometimes I wonder if I should have spoken. It was not my place…and yet.

There was talk of driving the huge wyrm from Nithraen; the thing was, according to some scouts, consuming even the Enemy's *orukhar* and a few mightier servants seeking parley or attempting to deliver their lord's directions to an errant creature. Aeredh found a grim amusement in this news, or at least the set of his mouth said so, and I could think of nothing to say. Imagining my own feelings had such a thing made its home in Dun Rithell among the shattered bodies of my kin was unpleasant at best.

In the end, no force large enough to retake the city could be raised without the Greycloak, and it was clear the great Elder king had his own troubles. Which brought the discussion to, of all things, me.

They had confined themselves to the southron tongue so far, but at that point Daerith fixed Aeredh with a steady look. "*I ask you to reconsider, my king.*" The Old Tongue in its most formal intonation turned the air expectant-tense, as if he had shouted. "*Whoever survived the city's fall will make for Dorael; once there, we may gain both reinforcement and the Greycloak's counsel.*"

"*I have asked you not to address me thus, old friend.*" Aeredh's mien was grave indeed, but he continued in the southron tongue. "You may lead what others you find to Dorael; my lord Tarit has graciously agreed to spare a few of his men as guides in that event. My own path is different, and those of Naras have sworn to accompany and protect the lady *alkuine* upon our journey."

"Hold a moment, my lord." Tarit spoke, forestalling me. "The lady has not given a single word yet, and I would know whence she desires to tread."

The blunt end of Arn's spear tapped dverger-crafted stone, a sharp counterpoint. The sleeves of my dress were folded back almost to the elbow, and my marks were—as is the custom at an Althing— upon full display as I rested my hands against cold mirror-gloss stone. "Many thanks, son of Hajithe. I am unwilling to be carted any further without my consent."

Eol shifted uneasily in his chair, but said nothing.

"*She considers herself our ally, my lord Aeredh.*" Efain gazed at the table as if he could see a map of the North upon its gleam, and his scars were pale as the rest of him. By then I knew those who have two skins rarely bear such marks unless they are given before the second form shows in them—or unless the wounds were near-mortal; I wondered which had happened to him. "*It would be good to ask her, instead of commanding.*"

"*And should she refuse?*" Aeredh exhaled heavily. "Lady Solveig, I cannot tell you our eventual—"

"A hidden city, wherein rests one of your Faevril's treasures." My gaze fixed itself over Eol's head; the shining stone table between us was easily the bodylengths of two tall men and the weight of the captain's own eyes settled upon me more often than not. I wondered what he discerned in my expression, for I could gain nothing from his. "I must tell you, son of Aerith, I cannot use the *seidhr*-weapon you would have me wield."

A silence greeted this assertion. The wolves of Naras did not glance at each other, but the Elder exchanged many a speaking look, and Tarit's head cocked slightly, a flash of puzzlement swiftly masked behind his usual expression. Eventually, the Elder seemed to concur in some silent way, and the harpist gathered himself.

"*Weapon?*" Daerith's eyebrows rose, and his tone, even in the Old Tongue, was both shocked and excessively careful. "*You mean to have a Secondborn—*"

"*Peace, my friend.*" Aeredh lifted a hand, and the harpist swallowed further words. "My lady, the end of our journey is hidden for good reason. The Enemy—"

"Caelgor the Fair knows the end, for it was he who told me of it while you demurred." It was time for these men to hear truths they preferred not to. It is a duty a *volva* must be cautious with, for nothing irritates a warrior like unpalatable, irrefutable honesty. "Which makes it not precisely *hidden*, and he has guessed your deeper aim as well. He offered me his protection upon the journey—and his brother's."

"*The cursèd oath still bears bitter fruit,*" one of the Elder—Yedras, one of the spearmen well-practiced in hunting *trul*—muttered darkly.

"The Hunter and the Subtle are no doubt in Dorael, blackening my name to the Cloak-Weaver despite the Greycloak's dislike of their line. I care little, for Melair will see past their purposes." Aeredh turned his attention to me, and I felt the full weight of an Elder's *seidhr*-glance then. It was akin to Curiaen's, but far more easily borne, since he did not seek to pry into my thoughts. "And I would not speak of aught else, be it plan or possibility, until we have reached our destination."

Dragging me, and my shieldmaid, yet farther from our homes. At the moment, I thought it quite likely his pride was touched, and Eol's too. Just like Bjorn, or even Eril—rare is the man who does not become stubborn when accused of misestimating some great matter.

Perhaps I was even comforted at that moment, for the eldest daughter of Dun Rithell had already handled more than one warrior or lord in that mood, and plenty afterward as well.

"You must listen to me, son of Aerith, no matter how it irks you." Now was the time for my most careful—and winning—toss of the bone-dice. "I cannot use your *seidhr* artifact, whatever it is. Caelgor gave me an Elder toy to open. You saw the result but did not truly understand its import. It almost killed me, and this thing you wish me to wield must be more powerful yet. I tell you, by the Aesyr and the Vanyr both, I cannot. And what is more, I do not want to."

Silence greeted this revelation. Daerith studied me as if I had suddenly grown another head, or a god had spoken brazen-trumpet through my mouth. Eol had paled, his eyes glittering, and Efain's gaze rested upon Arn.

It gave me little pleasure to have finally made my point.

Truth in Our Dealings

Yet by that time the third son of Mehem the Petty was dead, and though the Ill-Fated was wondrous wroth life could not be regained. Of this event's small seed much later grief flowered; the betrayal of Redhill began in that moment, though it took years to accomplish.
—Berehad Bowman, The Saga of Redhill

The quiet was of short duration, for Mehem laughed, his beard shaking and its decorations—leather braid-caps, a few beads carved from dull-finished gems, and more beads of bone—following likewise. Perhaps the look of open shock upon the faces of the Elder delighted him. Dverger find much about the Children of the Star risible, and the Secondborn only slightly less so.

Gelad inhaled as if to speak, but Eol won the race. "It nearly killed you?"

I could not tell whether he meant to express shock or disbelief. I lifted my hands from chill tabletop, my sleeves falling further back. The runes between my bands twitched but did not dance. "These mean I know my own strength, though I might attempt to surpass it at great need—as I have more than once upon our journey. If not for my shieldmaid's care and lord Aeredh's treatment, the *seidhr* in that silver ball would have boiled me from the inside."

"And yet you cleared the road to Nithraen, and we have seen you face not merely a *trul* but also a lich of Kaer Morgulis." Aeredh made a sharp gesture, somehow producing the *taivvanpallo*; I shuddered as he placed it upon the table with a tiny click. "And you unlocked one of Faevril's works, which only an *alkuine* may do."

Mehem eyed the silver orb with its shifting etched lines, all trace of his merriment gone. Naturally a dverger would be most interested in such a piece of crafting, for all their weirding is of a different type.

"Do you call my Solveig a coward or a liar?" Arn did not bother to contain herself, and I thought it best not to halt her at this point. "If she says she cannot, *Elder*, that is enough."

"*Do all women of the South speak so?*" Daerith the harpist had clearly never heard a shieldmaid administer a stinging reproof before; apparently he did not find it to his taste. "*And a Secondborn witch to wear Lithielle's Jewel, or even look upon it? My lord king, have you gone mad?*"

Yedras, seated upon his right, had a different question. "*The witchgirl opened a taivvanpallo?*"

Arn inhaled as if to speak once more, but I turned my head slightly, and she subsided. One lash from her was effective enough; more might prove a draught too strong. I thought Aeredh would speak again, but I was mistaken.

"*Name her witch again,*" Eol said quietly, "*and I shall answer, Yedras.*"

The Elder shook his dark head, subsiding. He leaned back in his chair, pressing his tented fingertips together, and examined me afresh like all his kin at the table were doing. My own *seidhr* was adequate to meet that weight calmly, though a prickle ran down my back, like tiny jeweled mouse-teeth gnawing.

"*I may be mad with grief, but my purpose remains firm.*" Aeredh's profile could have been carved with Elder skill in polished stone; he gazed at the far wall, his chin down and his blue eyes nearly incandescent. "*The Blessed have granted us aid, and that it comes from a Secondborn does not make it less welcome. Aenarian has troubles of his own; do we go to Dorael, the sons of Faevril will find our trail.*"

Tarit stirred slightly. "I still have not heard whither the lady means to travel."

It was upon the tip of my tongue to say *I will go home, to Dun Rithell*. It was, despite Tarit's advice, what I most longed for. Yet as I turned my head, my gaze fell across the son of Hajithe's, and his was heavy.

It is held the Elder granted his ancestors' line many a gift, including longevity and vitality behind that of the Southron, and nothing seen or endured since has disabused me of the notion.

"I am weregild no longer." The words stung my mouth with almost the same timbre as the voice speaking couplets through me in the great palace of Nithraen. Any *volva* knows the uneasy sensation of a throat being used by a passing spirit or god, and without that deep, irresistible discomfort such words must be held as merely spoken in anger or fear. I had no little of either at that moment, it is true—and yet, speech passed through me with a ring as of true metal upon the anvil. "I have pledged myself as an ally to the house of Naras instead. It is a poor ally who shows cowardice, even if brought to the battlefield under false pretenses."

A faint whisper came from the dverger-runes tangling over the walls, as of a mountainside whispering before it shifts. Mehem's eyes narrowed, and as he sat bolt upright in his great thronelike chair his callused, forge-blessed hands tensed.

"Ally?" Aeredh now chose to inquire of this openly. "*I have heard this said, though I do not know how it happened.*"

"*There seemed little harm in the swearing of such a vow.*" Efain moved uncomfortably in his wooden chair, his scars bearing a brief flush. "*I would have promised her anything to gain cooperation. The orukhar were hunting us; and besides, we did not treat her fairly, my lord Aeredh. You know it as well as I.*"

"Muttering in your foreign babble." Arn tapped her spear again, and even my imploring would not have restrained her. "Were it left to me I would take my Solveig home, and leave you to your falsity."

I could hardly reveal my understanding of the Old Tongue now; instead, I was finally forced to speak against my own deepest wishes. "It is unlikely we would reach Dun Rithell unless the Wingéd Ones consented to carry us. For better or worse, my shieldmaid, we are trapped in the North."

"*What is this talk of falsity?*" Daerith inquired, somewhat archly. "*And does that armed child mean to threaten my king?*"

"*You saw her face a trul alone, my friend.*" Aeredh clearly intended some moderation. "*The touch of the Blessed is upon both these women. And yes, I bear a shame and a heavy debt to the* alkuine, *for we brought her northward with a not-quite-lie.*"

"*Let their anger fall upon me.*" Eol shook his dark head, blue highlights running in his hair. "*It was my brother who—*"

Daerith did not like this turn of conversation; the harpist spoke sharp and peremptory. "*Do you forget what we face? Any means of fighting the Enemy is permissible, and—*"

"*By the Blessed,*" the heretofore-quiet blond Elder upon his other side interrupted. "*Do the Secondborn forget by whose grief and labors their soft southron lands are kept safe?*"

"Enough." Tarit's voice sliced the rising hubbub, and his eyes had kindled nearly as bright as an Elder's. His counselors remained silent, no doubt sensing their lord needed no aid upon this field. "If not for my sister in Dorael and thus my unwillingness to leave Aenarian's border unguarded, I would ask Lady Solveig to accept my aid upon her homeward journey. You shame not only yourselves but those slain by the Enemy, speaking thus."

"*I begin to think the son of Hajithe forgets his place,*" Yedras snapped.

"I forget nothing." Tarit's gaze was utterly level; I sensed a prickle in the air, as a storm descending the slopes of Mount Tarnarya to speak with Odynn's thunder-voice over Dun Rithell. "And I will not allow Elder to mistreat any Secondborn, much less a woman. You hold yourselves proudly, which I do not grudge—but we have our own pride, and are children of the Allmother as well."

"This Dorael is a refuge." I hurried to forestall more wrangling, as a herd-dog will dart among sheep when the shepherd whistles. So far, this was indeed very much like an Althing, or sitting in judgment between touchy smallholders and warlords. "And Aenarian Grey-cloak is the high king of the Elder, is he not? Perhaps he should be the one to judge what is to be done, and should I visit that place I may take kin-words to the daughter of Hajithe."

"*By the Blessed, these Secondborn are haughty.*" Yedras did not look away from Tarit, and I thought it quite likely the two of them would confine themselves to silence or icy formality after this discussion. "*It is for the son of Aerith to decide what to do with his witch.*"

Eol turned his head slightly, but the tension in him intensified. "Yedras," he said, quietly. "I will meet you, in whatever form you choose. Or you will offer an apology, though the lady *alkuine* may not understand the insult. That girl has faced the Enemy's servants with bravery unsurpassed, and ill deserves such language."

"And I would meet you as well, but for my lord Aeredh's regard." Yedras stiffened, though, as if he would rise.

"This is a holy place," Mehem barked. "No blood must be shed here."

Aesyr and Vanyr, give me strength. "My lord Eol, please." I flattened my palms upon the stone table again; strange, I would not have expected the captain of Naras so quick to anger. "I am not your weregild now."

"Nevertheless." That colorless ripple, not quite *seidhr* but not entirely unrelated to the great tree of wisdom, hung over him. The wolf in his skin was awake, and straining for release. "There has been enough of insult and to spare today. You are most forgiving, my lady Solveig. I am not."

"Let us not distress our hosts." I did not think my temper forgiving at all, and Arn might have concurred. Still, I had what I wished of this council, and surrounded by *orukhar* and even less wholesome things as we were, it seemed better to smooth the raised hackles than further brush against their grain. "If it pleases the lord Elder to insult me, let him. You and I shall confine ourselves to better behavior."

Arn tapped her spear again. No doubt she roundly enjoyed both the prospect of a brawl and the implication that an Elder could be ignored like a child yelling foul words at a feast.

"Yedras." Aeredh, for once, laid aside his refusal to command his fellow Elder. "The lady *alkuine* did something none since Faevril have accomplished, and a gleam from the West I thought never to see again was given to Nithraen for a few moments. I well remember your part in my father's departure, yet in this matter we are as allies, and Solveig daughter of Gwendelint a gift from those we turned our backs upon ere the Sun rose. My lord Tarit is right to be proud, for he has achieved deeds even one of our own might call mighty; the Secondborn are, after all, granted the Allmother's favor and greatest gifts though we know not whither such boons lead them beyond the world the Children of the Star are bound to." He paused, and even Mehem held silence, ready to hear more. "The Enemy warps all words, deceives at every pass, and treats all living things as his thralls. We have fought him so long, and at such great cost—yet as the son of Hajithe reminds us, we must not *become* as him." He inclined his head in Tarit's direction, and though he was crownless long before and after, Aeredh of Nithraen was regal that day. "We shall go to Aenarian's realm if our gift of the Blessed wills, and I entreat her pardon for the journey so far."

In truth I had not yet decided whether to chance Dorael or this Hidden City; my only purpose was to fix Arn's and my status as allies instead of mere baggage to be dragged hither and yon. I could have said the former, if not the latter, but Eol's gaze was fixed upon me and forestalled whatever I would have uttered.

"My lady." He was not nearly so grim now, though his black-clad shoulder was presented to Yedras in a manner no southron warrior would mistake. The glitter of the gem in his swordhilt was an ice-spear; he wrapped it before sallying forth, but would not inside these walls. "The risk of Faevril's sons doing some mischief should we go to Dorael is high indeed. I have little right to ask, yet I would not have their father's oath bring some harm to my lord Aeredh, or to you. Caelgor may have spoken fairly, but you are merely a means to an end for him."

"No more than for you, or for your Elder friends." I could not help but make the point. "I am your ally, Eol of Naras, and my mother raised me to act accordingly. I would accompany you for the asking, and for strict truth in our dealings henceforth."

"Better than Naras deserves," Tarit muttered.

Eol made no answer, studying me as if he suspected some hidden slight, or as if I had spoken in a tongue we did not share.

Daerith broke the resultant silence. "We go where you will send us, son of Aerith. And I offer any apology necessary to the Secondborn, with good grace." He did not look at his brethren, but something in his posture said he wished to and only refrained by an effort of will. "The life of an Elder is long, and I have been wrong more than once in the course of mine. Yedras?"

"It pains me to admit it." Now the spearman was cheerful, though the glitter in his pale blue eyes was less amusement and more banked coals. "But not as much as it pains me to give the Enemy any lee. I, too, offer my apology for any and all offense. If this is what you will have, my lord Aeredh, we will see it done."

"Then we await the lady's decision." Tarit glanced at Mehem. "There is no need to make it today, though. Our host deems it unwise to leave for some days more."

"The weather will turn soon." The dverger stared at the *taivvanpallo* almost hungrily, and his goatlike pupils had shrunk. "Better for travel. For a few moments of handling that bauble, though, I would take you to any point Redhill overlooks by hidden ways. Beyond that, I cannot say."

"*A dverger, touching one of Faevril's works?*" Yedras fell silent as Aeredh inhaled sharply, granting the spearman a warning look.

"*The taivvanpallo was gifted to the lady* alkuine, *and she placed it temporarily in my keeping.*" Once more the Crownless spoke as one well used to command. "*I will not seek to retract a gift I have not given, or indeed any that have left my own hand. To do so is beneath us as Children of the Star, and an act unworthy of any free creature. If she wishes to throw the thing into a fire-mountain's heart or play some Secondborn children's game with it, the matter shall rest as she pleases, and I will hear no more upon it.*" The silence was charged, and when he continued, his tone was no less sharp for the words being in the southron tongue. "My lady Solveig, the *taivvanpallo* is yours to do with as you will; I only hold it by your request. My lord dverger is welcome to examine it at leisure, if such is your pleasure."

"I cannot think of a reason to deny him." Indeed, I was surprised by Elder vehemence upon both sides. "It is not the way of my people, nor of a *volva*, to hoard craft or knowledge from those who seek with good grace and open hearts. I meant to give you the orb to do as you will with, my lord Aeredh; I do not want the thing."

So both greater and lesser matters were decided. It was some days before we left that place, and during that while the Elder except for Aeredh treated me with chill courtesy indeed—either because I did not bow to their will immediately, or because I did not want what they considered precious, though Caelgor called it a mere toy.

◼◻◼◻◼◻◼

The discussion turned to other matters—supplies for either journey I decided upon, the disposition of Redhill's forces over the next few days, whether it were better to meet some of the Enemy's slinking scouts with blades or let them attempt Dorael's well-held borders, impassable save by the will of Aenarian the high king.

I said little, for my purpose was achieved and I had much to think upon. Eol watched me closely and confined himself to responding when Aeredh asked his counsel upon travel-matters. Indeed, nothing about that meeting was as the songs or tales after describe, and sometimes I wonder if that is not the case with descriptions of other parleys of import or significance.

When the Council of Redhill ended, Mehem was given the silver orb for some short while despite Daerith's obvious discomfort, but the harpist need not have worried. Even a dverger's prying craft could not open it, and the *taivvanpallo* was given back into Aeredh's keeping.

I had what I wanted, and yet I did not know what to do.

Shieldmaid Dancing

The great liches arise from Kaer Morgulis, the lesser from battlefields where the servants of the Enemy brood over the slain. But the Seven come from the third tower of Agramar; burning and twisting they come, cold as the Unmaking itself, and they do not ever forget their chosen prey.
—Morgulis Morgaen, or, "The List of the Dread"

Arn stamped as she lunged, the spear-tip whistling just to the side of my ribs. I bent away, my breath coming tearing-hard; soft echoes bounced from stone walls and ribbed ceiling. "A bad choice," she said, hardly winded. "But you are right."

I could not tell if her refusal to commit to a course was merely because she did not care which way we went, or because the Wingéd were silent upon the matter. Stripped to a linen shift smelling of the resin packed in our trunk along with an old, cut-down pair of my shieldmaid's sleep-trousers, my hair braided without beads, I sweated freely. The spear flickered again; this time I spun, reading the intent of the strike and moving only enough to elude, barely giving ground. My shieldmaid followed, spearblade swinging laterally. I bent, supple as a reed, twisting at the same time with a hip-straining effort. Again, by the barest of fractions, a wicked-sharp edge avoided me, just barely whispering past my shift's fluttering edge.

We both liked this game, and played it often at home—ducking, dodging, *volva* dancing just a thread's width before her shieldmaid's attacks. While Arneior did not exert herself fully, she also did not dawdle, and the motion not only hardened my muscles and strengthened my physical self, but also helped me think.

It trained her against an opponent with *seidhr*, as well. *The strike,* she often said, *must be thoughtless—so my weirdling cannot read it.*

And if I could not, who else could hope to?

This windowless rectangular vault had plenty of space, and though its stone threatened to bruise bare feet I liked feeling dvergerwork against my soles. The new-winter freeze had descended upon the world and even the Elder did not set forth; Mehem and his two sons dared brave the broad stone hilltop for only a few moments each day to test a howling wind issuing from bruise-dark northern sky.

Bleak it smells, the dverger said, *and full of hate.*

Arn's hands moved, spear used as stave now, the distance between us halved and the strikes coming from both sides. I gave ground, yes—but slowly, and finally ducked under a lateral blow, my knees grating upon stone as I slid, chin tipped back and my belly tightening to bring me upright at the end of the motion. When I whirled to face her afresh I had the entire length of the room to retreat, and my shieldmaid looked pleased.

"*There* she is," Arneior purred; a thin sheen of sweat touched her brow, blurred the edges of her woad-stripe. "Very good indeed, my weirdling. You should sing to slow me."

"Not enough breath." The words rode a gasp from my throat. My heart pounded, throbbing in wrists and ankles as well as neck and chest; even my ears were full of its rushing. My shieldmaid was barely misted with saltwater; I was fair to dripping.

"Enough to complain is enough to move." She slid one booted foot forward, considering me. "You must train, Sol. It is the only way to strength."

Not the only way, small one. I had no chance or desire to say it, for she moved in again, harrying me down the room. Sidestep, twist, bending under the spearblade as it sought my throat, moving air kissing sweatslick skin with tiny puffs. Spinning on the forefoot, arm raised as the blade flickered underneath like a serpent's tongue—I danced before her, always just out of reach. Short huffs of effort, sour smell of stone, and I lost myself in the blessed relief of no worry, no thought, nothing but movement, *seidhr* flooding arms and legs.

The light from those strange veins of glowing rock brightened as I spun into her next strike, slapping aside the spear-haft with my elbow. It is not allowed for a *volva* to touch a physical weapon except to keep it from meeting her own flesh, and my hand jabbed forward, my arm giving a twinge as I flung a dart of gathered illumination for Arn's face.

It was like casting sun-dapples at the *trul*, and my shieldmaid's cheerfully surprised oath rang upon carved rock. I gasped in a lungful, attempting to gain enough breath for a battlesong, or a shield-shout, anything to keep her from me a moment longer. I did not often push this far—we had been at it for some time, and my legs were full of the trembling of a plucked bowstring.

The next time we faced *orukhar* or something similar, I was determined not to be a witless impedance.

She backed away, her weight balanced with each step, and Arneior's smile was just as wide and bright as it had been the day she was sworn to me, Idra binding our wrists together with a wide red riband and the knot most sacred to the Black-Wingéd Ones. "Not bad." She passed a critical glance from my tumbled braids to my bare toes, as I tried to quell the shaking. "We will halt now."

"No." A battle would not cease because I was tired, or had been wrung dry. "Again."

She shook her ruddy head. Her spear lifted slightly, considering the prospect before rising fully, its blunt end coming to rest upon the floor. "Save your strength. That's enough for today." My frustration must have been evident, for she laughed again.

An uncharacteristic wave of ill-feeling swept through me. "You're of more fishgutting use to the Northerners than I am. One more round, Arn."

"Ah." Her nose wrinkled, and she glanced at the doorway behind me, ever mindful of our surroundings. "So it's useful you want to be, hm? In that case, you should be practicing with that little ball of theirs."

"I would rather bathe in sheepshit." There was no use in whee-
dling, so I folded down to the floor, enjoying its steady coolth. Outside the wind would snap-freeze a breath as soon as it was exhaled,
but I was sweating and overheated here, glad of hill-heart's even chill.
"I hate this. I long to be home."

"Mh. Tedious legal arguments, your brother behaving badly,
everyone in sight asking you for a blessing—"

She had a point, but so did I. "At least there are no *orukhar*."

"Fair. But for how long?" She sobered, leaning upon her spear,
and regarded me closely.

"I know." It rankled to admit the Northerners still had advantage
despite all my maneuvering. I suspected we would do as Aeredh and
Eol wished, sallying forth for this Hidden City, and deep it irked me
indeed. "Where do you think we should go?"

"I think my *volva* knows, but she has not been in a stillroom to
mix concoctions or rambling along the riverbank to hear the Vanyr
speak." Her boots creaked slightly as she shifted. The storeroom was
bare and smelled of stonedust now, two breathing creatures disturbing its long slumber. "Difficult to find free air in this warren."

She was right, as usual. The deepwinter after solstice year-turn is
a time of rest, for huddling in the hall near good fires, telling sagas
and riddles. This year at Dun Rithell others would have to sing the
histories, and the story of Bjorn's strike and my leaving would be
set in verse as well. It would make my father glower, of course, but
once a song escapes its maker's mouth there is nothing to be done.

If Eril the Battle-Mad had known the Northerners' true purpose,
what might have happened? As it stood, he could take some pride in
his mighty son felling a two-shaped man with one blow—if he ever
realized that was what had happened. I could not decide how to feel
about *that*, either, especially with the murdered man's brother so
willing to hold an Elder to account for calling me a witch.

Yet Eol would not even accept a *volva*'s healing after a battle, and
he did not mention the curse upon him I was perhaps supposed to
mend. There was a deeper tangle than life-debt between me and the
eldest son of Naras, and I did not like the feeling.

Snarled thread is nothing to the mess the Three Kindly Ones, those weaving sisters of Fate, make in mortal lives. 'Tis said they even use Elder lives upon their loom, treating them just as cruelly as mortals when the mood strikes.

It was enough to make me wish the fishgutting Northerners had never come to Dun Rithell, had passed our small world upon the river-bank by. Perhaps the Enemy might have been satisfied warring with the Elder and left us in peace—except by all accounts the first son of the Allmother behaves much as a petty warlord for all his might, and those rarely have the sense to halt when they reach the limit of rea-sonable conquest. There are men for whom nothing is enough, ever, and the word for them bears a distinct resemblance to some of the Old Tongue's euphemisms describing the lord of the Black Land.

For all their silences, their grimness, and their levering me from my home, the Northerners did not seem... well, *bad*. Idra might even have liked them, and my mother held them in honor. Lady Hajithe and her son were somewhat forbidding, but also scrupulously just.

I had not been prepared to find the Elder of song, saga, story, and myth so grudging in certain aspects, though. A deep sigh worked up from my belly as I stretched upon the stone, taking comfort in its solidity. It remembered *dverger* shaping, but only distantly.

Redhill was delved very long ago indeed, even as the Elder count such things.

Arn, attending to her own stretching, peered at me. She was bent double, letting her legs speak of any soreness, her spear braced to provide readiness even at rest. Her hornbraids, their leather-wrapped dependents dangling, made her entire attitude into an inquisitive goatling's, and I laughed.

Her dark eyes gleamed. "Finally you are merry again. You look strange, too, my weirdling."

"Here we are, deep in a dverger hill with no sauna." Still, there was hot water for bathing, and that was luxury enough. "Perhaps we are in a comical tale after all."

"Unlikely." But her grin matched mine. "I am glad, though; soon my spear will have a name. I knew you were meant for great things, Solveig."

Of course a shieldmaid would consider this a grand adventure—at least, while there was no *trul* before us, or no ash-pale howling *orukhar*, I could even admit some part of me still felt the same. The rest longed to be home before a fire, with all this safely in the past and a lapful of sewing to attend to. I had not held a needle for some time save to repair our mantles; there is little better for hard thinking than pulling thread through fabric, making something new from flat panes of cloth. I could be listening to the thump-clack of Astrid's loom while she and Ulfrica told riddles, or the whirr of my mother's spinning wheel as she hummed the formless tune all her children know as well as their own breath.

I did not have further time to be homesick, for Mehem the dverger appeared in the storeroom's arched door. It was time to follow him through the passageways to our quarters and water-room. We readied ourselves early each day as if for travel, waiting for the weather to break.

Soon we would leave Redhill.

Venture into Winter

What might the world have been, if the Enemy had not marred it? Even Lokji's twisting serves the Allmother's end, for though he is a contrary child, he cannot bear to foul her work beyond redemption. The Blessed are silent upon this matter, even the Trickster himself. Once he fought at the Enemy's side; now he hates his eldest brother more than do those who never were misled...

—Naecil Nin-jaren of lost Gaeliquenden,
Saga of the Making

In a few full moons spring would bring thaw, if the gods pleased, and the Allmother's warmth breathe through the sun even unto the far reaches of the North. The season of the treecrack cold was almost over; we could not wait for the season of false ice, when any drift's surface or frozen skin over a stream may be hollowed from the bottom and break under an unwary foot.

Though there was no true melt yet, the killing cold was fractionally less.

We took our leave of Redhill upon a greying dawn. There was no parting cup, but Eol's men carried supplies—and my trunk, packed and corded, was to be carried as well, though I could not see how. The Elder grouped around Aeredh, who listened to Daerith with grave attention but no movement, his gaze resting somewhere over the harpist's shoulder.

Our farewells were said in a stone hall before a darkened archway, Mehem standing ready to take us through hidden passages to a place upon the periphery of the hill's view.

My mantle was heavy and dry; soon it would be crusted with ice, as would Arn's. I was not looking forward to the event, but we could not stay here forever. There was some talk of the Enemy's pressure forcing Tarit and his men away as well, for every trip outside the hill's safety now led to some clash and the skirmishes were growing in severity as well as number.

I did not ask where they would go upon leaving this fastness, since he would no doubt have a plan. But I did keep a red coral bead—large as my thumb from knuckle to tip—from my braids that morn, and pressed it into Tarit's hand as the gathered Northerners finished the last round of checking each man's equipage, burden, and weapons.

It is passing unwise to venture into winter without being absolutely certain of one's gear.

"This is red coral from the sea itself." My fingers were already cold, though it was merely cool as a summer cellar here in the hill's carven depths. "I wear all of Dun Rithell's supply; we often trade with river-travelers. It is a healthful thing, and keeps one from being led into a bog."

"Red coral." Tarit repeated the term carefully, paying great attention to the accent. "Very useful." He turned the bead over in his long callused fingers, giving it the sober attention due a *volva*'s gift. "I wondered at your wearing them. I have nothing fine enough to give in return."

"You gave me truth, son of Hajithe, and I would take nothing else." It was easy to treat him as a distinguished visitor, one my own mother had shown a distinct liking to. "Should I visit Dorael your sister will have all my care, and tidings from both you and your lady mother as well."

Eol was eager to be gone, for he left his men to draw a few steps closer to Arneior. Or perhaps he wished to hear what passed between his ally and the lord of Redhill; his expression was closed and distant as ever.

"I thank you for it." The slightest of smiles lit Tarit's stubbled face; his hair was windblown, for he and a few of the Elder had been out while the cold was at its late-night deepest, and from his low-voiced discussion with Aeredh, it seemed they had laid some manner of false trail south and east—and had slain an *orukhar* or two, even in the frigid darkness. "I will not ask whither you mean to wend, my lady *alkuine*. It is better we do not know, if even half of what Aeredh hopes is true."

"Many thanks for your restraint, my lord." I could well see his point, and it chilled me more than the weather ever could as I glanced unwillingly at the group of Elder. I had been granted no inner certainty even in the blessed moments of unthinking when Arn pursued me with her spear, nor had my dreams been anything other than ordinary, dark, and soon forgotten. "I could wish all Northerners like you."

"Could you?" His mouth twitched as if he meant to laugh, and a kindlier light was in his depthless gaze. In that moment he resembled his mother most, the dam peering through the foal's lines. "I fear the Elder would dislike the event. I pray the Blessed will watch over thee, Lady Solveig, and your shieldmaiden."

Arn did not reply—the Wingéd have little use for men, however doughty. But she did tap her spear against the floor, and nodded briskly besides to accept his good wishes.

He and Aeredh took their leave of each other shortly, yet with graciousness, and Eol clasped forearms with the lord of Redhill in the way of Northern warriors bidding both welcome and farewell. We followed Mehem down a passage veined with glowing rocks, and I never saw Hajithe's son again.

I did hear the tale of Karat Vaerkil's betrayal by one of its own inhabitants a very long time afterward, and later yet I heard of Tarit's sojourn in a hidden valley where a fair, nameless maiden had arrived grievously wounded and lacking her memory. The bulk of the tale is bound up in the death of Ugurthal upon the Ill-Fated's sword, and little does hearing it please me. Yet I do not leave any place where it is sung as my father always did during the sagas of certain battles, for listening to something grievous while remembering a better time is little enough tribute to the memory of an honorable man.

The tunnels were safe enough, and at least there was some light. But each step reminded me of the blackness under quaking, riven Nithraen, and my breath came a little faster than I liked even with Arn at my shoulder and the dverger's careful guidance. It did not help that each passageway looked the same, and each intersection was a tangle of confusion. I suspected some manner of *seidhr* in the turnings, and would have liked to touch the walls with ungloved fingers to see if they would tell me aught—how deep we were, which direction we would turn next, how much farther we had to walk.

I did not, for I suspected it would not be polite and in any case, we were wholly in Mehem's care. Dverger can be cunning, but they are not liars—at least, no more or less than mortal men.

Arn did not like the tunnels' confines either; there was not enough room to use her spear effectively. We walked for a long while through never-altering stone passageways and turnings fit to dizzy even those who have a lodestone or *seidhr*-needle in their heads, like Flokin or Albeig who despite lacking weirding are never lost and can point unerringly northward at any moment. With a moment's concentration I may do the same even underground, but there was no need.

The walls grew rougher, and the glowing rock-veins mere threads. It did not matter, for a low grey gleam hung in the near distance. Mehem halted, and pointed. "There is a hillside, and a thornbrake. The descending stairs will take you to the banks of the Yunek, which the Elder who lived here before the Sun called Nisael. South and west will take you through wilderness to the thinnest part of Dorael's skirts, north lies the Mistwood and the Glass. I would use caution in any direction; the trees of both Dorael and Mistwood are full of bewilderment and dark things."

"My thanks for your wisdom, Mehem of Redhill." Aeredh exchanged a glance with Eol, who drifted soundlessly toward the dawnlight filtering through the opening, followed by Soren and Efain. Yedras trailed in their wake, for he was accounted sharp of ear and nose even among the Elder. "We shall go quietly and quickly as possible, so as not to draw attention to this entrance."

"I doubt any will find it once you have left." The dverger settled with his back against stone, those glowing filaments brightening at his nearness, matching the flecks in his irises. "Spare me any speeches, my lord Elder. Once you are gone my home might return to some tranquility."

"May it be so; I lament the breaking of any peace." Aeredh next looked to Arn and me. "My lady *alkuine*? Will you consent to my aid, and your shieldmaid to Daerith's? The wolves of Naras may move without much trace, and I would not leave a trail."

"Your aid did us no harm upon the journey here." I did not think Arn would disagree. "And I would not repay our hosts with yet more of the Enemy's attention either."

"Mind you leave my spear arm loose." Arn fixed the harpist with a bright, unsettling smile. "Let us go, I long to breathe free air again."

I paused, though, to offer my gloved hand to Mehem. "My thanks for your hospitality, my lord dverger. Your halls are well-wrought."

He clasped my wrist gravely, surprising strength in his long, dark-nailed fingers. "My kin had their making, and I accept the praise only on their behalf." His voice, as always, was far more resonant than his chest should have produced despite its barrel shape. Yet he spoke softly, as if we were alone in the tunnel. "Be careful of the star-children, my lady. We of the Great Smith know their temper of old, and their pride oft leads younger folk to grief."

It was good advice, and despite everything which passed between him and the Ill-Fated, I still think he meant it kindly. Arn granted the dverger a nod of farewell, and we moved toward the light.

The cold was a blow, even with an Elder's steady warmth beside me. The thornbrakes were ancient, great tough vines with sharp spikes finger- to hand-long and dripping with icicles. Under their arching tangle a set of stone steps clung to hillside, oddly clear of snow but still treacherous footing. I managed well enough with my hand upon Aeredh's shoulder as we descended, and once we crossed a stream so deeply frozen it seemed likely to never shake itself free, we had left the view of distant Redhill. Even the closest inspection of the streambanks did not show our passage, nor the stairs themselves.

Some say the dverger may close the entrances to their homes at will, and I believe it.

I saw Karat Vaerkil once again in summer, with its top blasted open and the ruddy *vaer* clinging to its shattered slopes—but that was much later. At the time of our exit, I was merely glad as my shieldmaid to be breathing fresh air once more, though it was cold as a knife to the throat.

So we left Redhill, and ventured into lands even the Elder called *the Wild*.

Whistle, Bone

*Girt with shadow and hope, Lithielle left her home to find
her mortal husband; ever after that land mourned, having
lost what was dearest. Yet into the Wild she passed without
pause, for if even the Blessed bow before love, how can a
Child of the Star gainsay?*

—The Song of Wandering

Mornlight strengthened as we passed, dawn creeping between
snow-laden firs lightly as the Elder upon snow-crust. We
walked in silence, but swiftly enough. The Northerners spread out,
nearly vanishing among fir-pillars yet somehow keeping pace; my
own steps did not disturb the packed-tight white since Aeredh's arm
stayed light upon my shoulders, his fingers tense against my mantle.

I do not know what it cost him to keep my mortal weight from
leaving traces of our passage. None of the Elder sang; we simply moved
as ghosts among heavy-laden trees. The hush was absolute, save for an
occasional sharp creak or crack in the distance as a tree was caressed
by Lokji or kissed by black-ice sprites, shivering to pieces under that
painful pleasure. Oddly, the sound comforted me—sometimes in
hard winters, the slopes of Tarnarya the mother-mountain of my
home held such metallic cries, bouncing over the river.

There were tracks upon the snow's back. I saw the discolored
marks made by *orukhar* passing, and signs of animals venturing even

into this cold, from leaping fox fishing in the drifts for sleeping mice to the paired scoop-shoe shapes of great horned deer. Some of the latter bore traces of furred paws after them, and there were also strange signs like shod hooves, but blackened at the edges and with trailing tails, scorched and refrozen in the same moment.

Aeredh caught my interest in those and shook his head, his lips pursing.

We halted at midmorn, having come much farther than seemed possible in deep snow. The light was failing somewhat, for the clouds had thickened and it warmed enough for heavy wet flakes to fall in fitful spatters; the far reaches of the forest began to sough with rising wind.

It was not the deepfreeze, but this weather was not fit for travel either. We sheltered again near noon in a tiny dell, Eol's men melting out of daylight shadows to draw close. Snow lingered in their hair and upon their shoulders. Their eyes were bright indeed; Efain's scars were flushed, and Soren's sides heaved as if he had been running, though his breath was soundless and his mouth did not gape.

"Something ill has passed close by, keeping to the valleys," Eol murmured, his shoulder almost touching Aeredh's. They faced opposite directions, keeping watch upon each other's backs during rest. "At least one of the Seven, perhaps more. The stench is thick."

I had scented nothing but the forest, and thought my mounting anxiety merely the result of traveling in this manner. The mystery of those strange tracks was solved as I listened to them speak—the steeds of the Seven, those nightmares even the servants of the Enemy hold in caution, make such a pattern when they ride in haste. But Arn's nose was wrinkled too, and two spots of color stood high upon her cheeks as she and her woad-stripe glared at the day. The harpist did not hold her as close as Aeredh kept me, yet she did not protest at Daerith's grip upon her left arm.

So she was uneasy as well. I tried to find some comfort in the fact, but a sense of impending doom lingered over me, darkening the daylight.

"The snow will aid us," Aeredh replied. "Well, my lady *alkuine*? Do we go to Dorael, or will you trust me?"

Yes, I had told Arn I could not decide. Maybe her refusal to speak upon either course was because she knew I already had, down in the secret chambers of my heart, and simply could not voice it before that moment.

"I said I would go where Eol of Naras willed." I kept my voice as low as possible without whispering. "For the asking, and for his truth henceforth."

I had bound myself as his ally, after all. Not that it mattered; we were at the mercy of these men more thoroughly than ever, and though I dreaded the thing they wished me to attempt I could hardly back away from it.

Not after the Council. Certainly Eol had lied to my mother and father, and to me as well. He had also challenged Elder insults in my direction, and clearly believed in Aeredh's purpose enough to risk his own life—and the lives of his men—for it. Both he and the Elder agreed that Faevril's sons would do some harm to Aeredh if they could, and I suspected part of his eagerness to travel even in this weather was to deny the Hunter and the Subtle a chance at tracking us, or at least to slow their pursuit.

Then there was the matter of the curse upon him. Perhaps he was constrained from speaking of it openly; such things happened in the sagas about great maledictions I had myself memorized and sung. If I were fated to perform such a service, attempting to turn aside would do no good at all, and much ill besides.

I had merely been putting off admitting there was no other choice but to do as I was bid—though not as a weregild. At least I accomplished that much.

"North and west, then." The son of Tharos did not glance at me, hunching his black-clad shoulders as if struck. His mantle had been mended, though not with the care I might have shown; the wolves of Naras attended to such things as all without women nearby must. "I hate to mention it again, Aeredh, but have you thought of…"

"Fear not, my friend." Aeredh's arm over my shoulders did not alter, but he felt about in his own sable mantle with his free hand and produced a small glittering thing. "I had the chance to visit my old house well before the gates of my father's city were sieged, and to gather what might be useful."

It was a whistle of carved bone, with silver filigree like branching horns. He put it to his lips, but it made no true sound. Still, a thrill ran over me, hairs stiffening and attempting to rise, and I shivered, though snow-cold is not as fierce as the deep clear freeze.

Seidhr was in that high piercing unsound, invitation and enticement twined like ivy running up a tree's trunk.

It did not take long. A faint clicking arose like pebbles against each other in shallow, fast-flowing water, drawing nearer with each breath. Tall shaggy shapes melded from the strange yellow snow-light, and the Elder with us were all smiling like children upon a festival morn. The black-clad Northerners drew away, for the shadows were horned deer—large ones, their coats winter-rough and the females wearing proud antlers, their eyes turned blue as my mother's for the winter. The largest male stood slightly aside, eyeing the Elder askance until Yedras spoke to him in the Old Tongue.

"*We mean no harm, my brother.*" The words were full of pebble-clacks very like the walking-sound the beasts made, and the male—all the deer were taller than even the Northerners' white horses—turned his head to regard the harpist sidelong. "*We merely ask, if you're willing.*"

I let out a sharp breath of wonder. The nearest deer flicked her ears at the sound, her mild gaze very much like Farsight's for all it was winter-blue. My heart hurt, hoping the horses had escaped Nithraen's fate somehow; the pang is still with me today, fear and wonder and longing mixed together, a nail driven deep into seasoned wood with one swift blow.

The deer did not like the black-clad men of Naras, who withdrew even further, watching solemnly. "Much quicker this way, and the snow will cover us," Aeredh said, smoothing the long face of a large female while she investigated his mantle, her breath full of fir-scent and living warmth. I stood stock-still, afraid to move lest the creature take some exception to my presence. "Will you and my lady Minnow consent to ride?"

I do not think I could keep Arn from trying. "Arneior?" I met her dark gaze, and her freckles stood out against her paleness.

She nodded, beyond speaking, and once her spear was fastened to her back she even put her snow-caked, booted foot into Daerith's interlaced hands, gaining a winter-deer's back with a huff of effort; though a shieldmaid does not need to set aside her weapon for such an endeavor, a mount might take it ill if unused to such treatment. The deer, though, did not move beyond craning her neck, blinking at her new burden.

I was fairly tossed aboard another, Aeredh applying more force than strictly necessary—not to harm me, I think, but because Elder have a strength we do not. My fingers sank in deep mane-fur; I made a short, unwilling sound as if hurt, then shook my head at his bright blue inquiring look. The Elder mounted, all avoiding the largest male, and those of Naras disappeared between the firs. Though the two-skinned were out of view the deer did not relax, and a faint shiver went through the one I perched upon, my legs already aching.

And yet...a *winter-deer*, taller than a bullock and probably heavier too. And I was *atop* it, the creature not only willing but seeming to enjoy the sensation as I brushed tentatively at her ruff. Wiry, oily hair slightly speckled with snow yielded to my trembling, gloved fingers; the creature was full of hazy shimmering vitality to my inward sight. I could not stop smiling, and when I glanced to my right, Arneior wore a wide baffled grin.

Can you believe it? her gaze asked, and even though I am *volva*, I could hardly credit this wonder either.

Aeredh mounted last, springing lightly atop a long-legged deer whose antlers spread wide enough to scoop up and toss a hardy youth. The Elder made a chirruping, clicking sound and the small herd turned as one, like raindrops running down a pane of scraped horn during a hard summer shower. They set off, tentatively at first, and sometimes halted to strip a young tree or two of its bark, or pawed through the snow to graze. But they moved steadily otherwise, and I had no time to think of how the men of Naras would keep up.

For when the trees thinned, the deer lifted their heads, scenting change in the weather, and began to jog into curtains of steadily thickening, feathery-wet snow.

A Watchful Ride

A friend to all creatures save the Enemy's faithless,
We speak to the trees, and sing to the stars.
For we woke first in the gloaming, the dark before the Journey,
And found we could quicken even the stones.
                    —*The First Folk*, Anonymous

We rode far that day, though all landmarks were lost as the storm settled over us. Snow fell in whirling veils, and the beasts moved with surprising speed, the knee-clicking of their passage lost in the soft deadening of thick wet flakes. My mount stayed close to Arn's, the two browsing in tandem and jogging as a pair; though it was beautiful, the jolting and jarring of their ungainly canter threatened to shake me to bits. I clung to the broad back with more luck than skill or strength, and even now am certain the deer did not shake me from her shoulders only because she was charmed into taking great care with her frail burden by the presence of more than one Elder.

Arn's face shone with fierce glee and she looked very much like a Wingéd One herself, her spear rising and falling as her mount's back rocked. Snow gathered upon her shoulders and weighed down her dun mantle-hood, and once she laughed aloud, holding back a shield-maid's piercing victory cry only by sheer force of will.

The Elder rode gracefully, of course, and shadows appeared through the shifting white veils. The deer did not like them, but the dark shapes did not press too closely. They loped along, and I caught glimpses of black fur, lambent eyes, and strange shapes not quadruped or biped but sometimes one, then the other. They blurred between forms, never staying in one or the other too long, and the wolves of Naras ran in a loose ring around the herd—neither guiding as a dog will direct sheep nor harrying as their wild cousins will hunt, but simply keeping pace, guarding their friends.

I could not see much else, for Arn and I were ever in the center of the streaming flock. Aeredh's mount and the largest male set our pace and direction, following a deep inner urging I could almost-hear, a tingle of *seidhr* spilling through me each time an Elder loomed out of the white curtains on my left and glanced to make certain I was not in danger of falling or foundering.

They watched over us well, those who followed the Crownless from broken Nithraen. Their names are known to song and saga, but on that day they were simply travel companions, and though they may have thought little of two Secondborn women, they took every possible care for those more fragile than themselves.

I was too amazed to feel any fear or even much of the cold. In any case it was only snowing, not the soul-destroying, life-snuffing freeze. Mehem and his sons had scented the storm which would grant us cover; the Elder turned deliberately into it, and we rode through forest growing sparser and thickening in waves as the snow pursued its own thousandfold paths from the sky.

All things in our world must end, and so did that wonder. The antlered deer slowed, drawing near a ridge dark with thick woods shaking loads of fresh white from their branches as the wind teased and taunted. Behind us, a wide rolling plain vanished under whirling ice-feathers, and as we moved into the trees, the deer halted at odd moments, always just avoiding a heavy wet fall from overloaded branches.

The winged, hoofed, furred, and feathered have their own *seidhr*.

It took a few moments to realize the ride was at an end, and I half-fell from the beast's shaggy back with a faint groan of thanksgiving. Arn sprang down light as a leaf, not needing any aid, but I landed in Aeredh's arms with only a faint stab of embarrassment at my own gracelessness, immediately drowned by relief.

He rested upon the snow as lightly as ever, but my feet sank for a few fingerwidths before he righted me, and though I longed to untangle the *seidhr* I could not tell just how they walked so lightly. *"Forgive me,"* he murmured in the Old Tongue, then repeated it in the southron. "We will reach shelter soon."

I could hardly wait. The light was failing rapidly, and I could not even tell how long we had been riding. Shadows took shape at the edge of the herd, the wolves of Naras threading between uneasy deer; before the beasts moved away the Elder touched those they could, *seidhr* whispering through their fingers to strengthen and preserve.

It was only right to thank them for such signal aid, and I leaned away from Aeredh, my gloved fingertips almost brushing my erstwhile mount's side. "Fryja preserve thee," I whispered, letting what *seidhr* I could reach spark free. "And my thanks, hooved cousin. May you be blessed."

Arn appeared as the deer moved away, leaning upon Daerith's arm. Both shieldmaid and harpist bore a carapace of wet snow, but Arn's smile was incandescent with joy. "They will not believe this at home," she said, the words whisked away upon a cold breeze, falling like spent leaves amid the deadening snow. "I will have to sing it so they cannot doubt."

"I look forward to hearing you practice." My heart hurt as I said it, a sharp dart striking home as knowledge arrives unbidden to a *volva* when hunger or sleeplessness has cleared its path.

It was that moment I knew fully, without doubt or argument, I would never see Dun Rithell or my mother again. Nor Astrid, nor Bjorn, nor my father or Albeig or Ulrica or Hopfoot or any of the others I had spent my life among. The loneliness was colder than the freeze holding us immured in Redhill for days on end.

It should not have surprised me. Perhaps my face would have spoken, but 'twas shadowed by my mantle's great furred hood as Aeredh pulled me close again, his arm over my shoulders. Perhaps he mistook my flinch for uneasiness at the movement, for he stilled in the way of the Elder, the motionlessness of a breathless summer day when the heat hangs haze-heavy in any distance.

I could not explain, and in any case it did not matter. Let my shieldmaid think that we might after all return to Dun Rithell's familiar safety; it would do no harm and might even comfort her.

But I was not consoled, and in that moment—even amid the Elder and the Northerners pressing close to shield us from showering snow— I was lonely as if I traveled with no companion save my own thoughts.

Seidhr means solitude even amid a crowd. So does all knowledge, eventually.

The Northerners set off deeper into the forest, climbing the ridge like a herd, and we were borne among the men with little effort. It was good, for there was a rock in my throat, and I wished I could howl into the strengthening storm.

It is not fair, I thought over and over again, but each time the answer arrived in Idra's voice, woven between feather-falling flakes and whispering wind.

And what makes you think, Gwendelint's child, that anything ever will be?

Anything Unreasonable

Many times the Conjurer's wolf-beasts attacked, their eyes full of fire and their jaws dripping foam. Yet Lithielle sang, and the great hound leapt, and between them a fence was set. Mighty was she, child of the Cloak-Weaver; of shadow was her raiment, and bright the star upon her brow.
—Fragment of *The Battle of Kas-em-Aerim*

D eep among black-trunked trees, their branches creaking under loads of white rain, a clearing suddenly opened, swept bare as a greathall's floor when the rushes or sweet-straw are changed. Its borders were held by lumps of hunched grey stone akin to those at the borders of the Eastronmost, but no runes marred their surface; all were shaped vaguely like fat, squatting little men. If they had once been carved, the marks were long erased by the passage of time. Still, a humming passed through them and pervaded the expanse of yellowed grass, faint traces of green visible in its blades as if some small part of Nithraen lay trapped here.

The snow simply avoided this place. As soon as we stepped over the border a deep soft quiet fell, the storm's soundless mouthing retreating. Here, even in the dead of winter, tiny pale-blue flowers peered through long grass at the sky, shyly astonished by their own existence.

Daerith let go of Arn's arm and shook himself like a cat after an unwelcome showering of cold rain, melt spattering free; the other

Elder and Northerners followed suit. Soren shied as Gelad flicked a bit of ice at him, and the two exchanged mischievous looks like boys tossing stable-clods while mucking stalls. Arn and I attended to brushing each other's mantles, both of us hardly daring to look at this new miracle lest it prove some illusion.

"I did not think to ever see..." Daerith breathed, looking about. *"Is this place what I think, my lord?"*

"It is." Aerith studied the clearing, his blue gaze shadowed. "Here Hjorin the Faithful and Lithielle rested upon leaving Dorael, and she was granted a dream from the Blessed—or so it is said, though others say 'twas a sending from her mother, warning her of Bjornwulf's great need. It was here nine great direbeasts of the Enemy's own hall found them; between Hjorin's jaws and Lithielle's song they made a defense so mighty the ground became hallowed, and shall remain so until the world changes. I think that before you sing of it, though, we should build a fire for our friends."

The second spearman—Kaecil—approached Efain for some conference and the scarred Northerner listened, their dark heads bent close. Eol paced the circuit of the stones, examining each one in turn as if he suspected them likely to break or speak. I set myself to ridding Arn's back of snow while she gazed about in wonder, her spear gripped whiteknuckle-tight in her right hand. There was no danger in sight, yet her shoulders were stiff.

"Don't worry." The snow I shook free melted swiftly against yellow grass and tiny blue flowers. "This is a good place, small one. Nothing evil can tread here."

"That is very well," she half-whispered, as if we were in our shared bed after a long festival day. "But after we leave? And what if there is another freeze?"

Not to mention we have thrown our bone-dice, and are now bound to Aeredh's secret destination. I sensed what she did not say, and shared the concern. "We may as well rest while we can." It was a practical thought, one Albeig would have approved of.

Homesick longing caught me, settling afresh in my throat and filling my eyes with hot water. I sniffed heavily, using my mantle sleeve to rub at my face. Idra would have tugged at one of my braids before turning away sourly to let me compose myself, for she held it childish indeed to weep for anything less than a truly serious wound or the death of a loved one.

The world wavered before me for a few moments as saltwater trembled upon my snow-weighted eyelashes. Thankfully, Arn was occupied in scanning the clearing's edges, perhaps memorizing each tree in the way of shieldmaids.

Ever prepared are they, those the Wingéd breathe upon.

Daerith drew Aeredh aside for a whispered parley as Elder and Northerners vanished into the woods in pairs to bring back firewood and bedding-boughs. Eol finished his inspection of the stones and approached, not quite meeting my gaze. "A moment, lady *alkuine*?"

"Certainly." I took a deep breath, hoping my hood kept my expression shadowed. "What would you have of me, son of Tharos?"

"*Nothing, but be glad to give all.*" He shook his dark head, melt starring his hair and gleaming in the strange half-light. "Forgive me, 'tis merely a proverb. We are being tracked, my lady Solveig, and I must ask something of you."

If he meant to gain some *seidhr* that would throw foul things from our trail, I would do my best—though I thought the many Elder of far more use than myself upon that point.

To be useless is a bitter pill to swallow, for a *volva*. "I will do all I can."

"Were it clear, you would see the Black Wall in the distance, like a storm over plains." He tipped his head, likely northward, but did not point. "The Enemy raised the Marukhennor to guard his land, and these peaks are part of their chain. They are nigh impassable, so we may creep along their edge relatively unseen. But there are things upon our trail much worse than you have seen so far."

"You speak of the Seven." It was no great riddle to solve; for some reason, even saying the words in the southron language sent a shudder through my limbs, one I was hard-pressed to quell. "The tracks in the snow—melted, yet frozen again at the same time. And blackened, but not with ash nor with dirt."

"I should have known you would hear, or guess." His expression did not change, and though his swordhilt was wrapped once more I sensed the glitter of its gem longing to break free. "They are as riders in black with iron helms, and I hope you never witness one. There will also be the *belroch*—whip-monsters like the *trul*, but not nearly so easily dispatched, and other things as well. Some even appear fair at a distance, until you are too close to escape." He caught himself, glancing at Arn, who leaned upon her spear and regarded him somberly. "You are both brave almost to foolhardiness, so I will be blunt, and as commanding as I may. Should we meet anything dire, neither of you are to attempt anything unreasonable."

"What do you consider unreasonable?" Arn was not sarcastic for once, but genuinely curious. Her hair had darkened with the damp. "These sound like mighty foes, worthy of a Wingéd's chosen and a *volva*."

Naturally she would think so, but I almost flinched. The distance between my courage and hers seemed well-nigh endless, insurmountable as the peaks Eol spoke of.

"It is not for either of you to fight anything we are likely to meet upon this journey." He fixed her with the full force of his dark stare, and there was a light much like an Elder's in it. "This is our country, shield-maid, and we know its dangers well. Surely the Wingéd Ones must have taught you to study certain battles before attempting their like."

Arn looked to me, but I was too busy swallowing the lump in my throat to make any reply. "Fair enough," she said, finally. "In any case, my charge is to protect my weirdling, not to save your hide."

"In that we are agreed." Next he turned his imperious gaze to me, and the strange weight to it was neither *seidhr* nor an Elder's age and wisdom. I had little trouble meeting it, even if my heart did give an odd wringing motion, not quite a leap. "If we are attacked, you must stay close to Aeredh. He is the only one who knows our destination. We are prepared to give our lives to gain you its safety. I will have your word—*both* of you—that you will not attempt to interfere or to aid any of us, Elder or Secondborn."

"It seems ill to leave an ally upon the battlefield, my lord." I sounded much like my mother, for homesickness roughened my voice somewhat. "We have not done too badly so far, and could have done much worse."

"Oh, aye, we have been lucky enough to give me chills." He made a restless movement to accompany the admission, very like Bjorn when pressed to own some fault or mischief, and fresh sadness pierced me. "I give you bare honesty, daughter of Gwendelint. Everything depends upon you reaching our destination. So Aeredh says, and I believe him. I have little right to ask anything of one I have wronged, but if you would be an ally to me and my men this is what we must have of you. I will even beg, if you like."

I could have argued, but all I wished for was a few moments to collect myself. If this was his honesty, it deserved mine in return. "We will try," I said, slowly. "But I cannot promise more, for…" *For I am a coward*, I should have said, but mercifully, other words came. "For I have not much experience of battles, and they seem confusing things. I cannot say what I will do in another. Arn is of more use to you than I shall ever be, my lord."

"Then I will ask her to drag you bodily from the field, should it become necessary. You must reach Taeron's refuge, else all is for naught, and I would not have that." A muscle flickered in his stubbled cheek, and for a moment the wolf who shared his skin eyed me restlessly. How did he hide it, in the South? "Will you give your word to stay near Aeredh, and do as he asks with as much grace as you may? And you, shieldmaid, will you look only to our lady's escape, and not seek to aid us?"

"It is a reasonable request," Arn muttered, as if even admitting as much pained her, and she tapped her spear on cold but unfrozen ground once, thoughtfully.

"I will do my best." *I will probably flee screaming into the snow should another lich appear, and honor a promise by doing so.* Truly, I was beginning to suspect I had come to Lokji's attention in some way, and even my mother's beloved Fryja has a difficult time restraining her foster-son when he takes an interest in some affair or another. "I give my word as a *volva*, son of Tharos." To prove it, I offered my right hand.

He clasped my wrist in the way of Northern warriors, and for some reason my cheeks were scalding when we let go. Then he repeated the movement with Arn, who did not demur or flush, studying his expression with a faint puzzled line between her coppery eyebrows instead.

Aeredh approached, putting an end to further discussion. "Lady Solveig? May I trouble you to light the fire, as you did once before?"

I thought it likely he wished to prove some point to the harpist and the other Elder, so I agreed with good grace. The others were already returning with deadwood and damp kindling, and it was in that ring of stones Aeredh taught me the *seidhr* which, applied to wood, will make it burn with the blue tinge of *aelflame*.

'Tis strangely simple, like most Elder wonders. This time I was prepared for the lighting to take far less force than usual even if the fuel was damp, and when I shook out my fingers afterward there was no need to let unspent power echo away through my inner halls. I even smiled, satisfied that I had performed well for once, yet I found Daerith, Yedras, and every Nithraen Elder who followed Aeredh regarding me, wearing expressions I could not quite name.

I could distinguish a few threads in the tapestry—shock, longing, an uneasiness as if I had shouted something obscene or suddenly grown an unsightly appendage. Yet none spoke, and none quite met my gaze, especially after Aeredh gave a half-bow, thanking me with all the courtesy of an Elder king.

The flames burned blue and camp was made with little further ado, dinner attended to for Elder and Secondborn alike, Arn and I bedded upon sweet-smelling pine and fir boughs, snug within our mantles. A watch was kept, but such was the safety of that blessed place I slept better than I had in Nithraen *or* Redhill.

Yet for all the sense of security I did not dream, and woke only once to see Aeredh feeding damp fallwood into blue flames, singing quietly in the Old Language.

It was not quite a lullaby or a lament. He sang of an Elder princess whose glance was like a knife, of a Secondborn who loved her, and of a mighty strike they performed against the Enemy himself. I heard only a few lines before I drifted back into a deep well of rest, Arn's breath upon my braids and her arm around my waist, shieldmaid and *volva* surrounded by the smell of sap and soft springtime even amid the snow of winter just after the year's turning.

Mistwood's Shroud

Even up to the Cloak the dark things crept in those days,
for the Enemy sensed weakness in those he hated most.
— Ancilaen Gaeldflor, *The Alkuine's Tale*

The snow lingered, falling more or less swiftly as the mood took it. Yet a colder breath came from the North, a harsh exhalation soughing through laden tree limbs. We left the stone-ringed clearing just before dawn, Aeredh and Daerith holding Arn and me above the drifts while the other Elder moved in a loose guard-pattern at some distance, barely glimpsed among thickening trees. Slightly farther afield the wolves of Naras screened us, and occasionally wolfsong echoed through falling snow that day.

The forest swallowed us whole.

Perpetual twilight clotted under packed-together boughs, deepened with more than winter's long darkness. Eventually the canopy was so thick what snow reached the frozen ground fell in strange patterns occasionally starred with thorny leafless bushes, undergrowth dead or sleeping until thaw. Hard upon the southron side of our route was a deep gloom more than physical, a maze of bewilderment swallowing what little light could filter through. It was called Dorael's Cloak, a mighty *seidhr*-woven defense we skirted before turning more northerly. I gathered very little, from the whispers among our guardians, of the power in that Elder realm keeping the Enemy at bay—only that the wife of Aenarian Greycloak was mighty in her own way, and it was her invisible weaving netting the shadows between branch and bole. None passed that mantle save those given leave by the high king of the Elder who had left the far West, though kinsmen and those of certain houses of the Faithful were allowed to pierce it without much trouble.

But Dorael was not our destination. Not then.

To the north lay the bulk of the Wild, and an even thicker shadow. The land there was broken and reshaped, they say, during a long war fought between the Enemy and the gods themselves before any speaking or singing creature was awake to witness such mighty cataclysm.

Pressed against Dorael's Cloak was the Mistwood, and by the third day we were well within its grasp. Great greyish veils wrapped the branches, hanging in sticky, icy sheets. There are skittering sounds even in the depths of winter, though the mushroom-pale things who make Mistwood their home are sluggish in the cold. Even the relative lack of snow upon the forest floor is no boon, for the rasp-clinging veils draping each bough choke light and sound, and in the deep gloom that passed for noon one brushed my mantle-sleeve and stuck fast.

Arneior was ahead of me, her generous mouth set with distaste and her spearblade glimmering even in the dimness. She stepped over a large, twist-knobbled root, and I sought to follow—but my shoulder-sleeve was well and truly caught.

The tattered, pale fabric hanging from a low leafless oak branch was very much like linen, though finer-woven than any produced at Dun Rithell or brought upriver from the south. No warp or weft was visible, and when studied closely it looked akin to the membrane in a fresh snake-egg. I again sought to pull away, gaining only a soft nasty sound as the glaucous sheet stretched, clinging to heavy dark-green wool.

"Hold." Yedras the spearman, behind me as we moved single file, was suddenly at my untrapped left shoulder. "Be still, Secondborn."

I almost flinched from his nearness, and Arneior turned. Her dark eyes narrowed, and she hastened back. "Sol? What is it?"

"Sticky." I reached for the webbing, seeking to brush it free, but Yedras's hand arrived first, striking lightly to push mine away.

"Do not," he repeated, a tinge of exasperation sharpening each syllable. "And stand still, by the Blessed." A flickergleam of metal showed; he had produced an Elder knife, its blade leaf-shaped and bright even in the cavernous gloom.

Arn tensed. "Have a care where you cut." Her own dagger rested comfortably at her belt, though she did not lay hand to it as the spearman sawed at the strands.

He made no reply, working delicately at the ash-pale clinging stuff, his blade almost flat against my mantle. Aeredh returned from the head of the column, Eol behind him. Snow still clung to the captain's hair; though the force of the wind was broken, it was still too cold under the trees for any melt.

"Easy, my lady shieldmaid." Aeredh peered past Arn, and let out a soft breath. "It is best to move with caution here. The more speed, the tighter the trap."

"What is it?" My hood was pushed back, but the wolf-fur meant I could not see precisely what Yedras did, and he stood almost indecently close. Living heat brushed against my mantle, less a cessation of the chill than a fractional difference in its intensity. "Does it grow like lichen? How do the trees live, so covered?"

"I am not sure how, only that they do." Aeredh glanced at the oak looming over us. "And no, the veils do not grow. They are spun."

Eol slipped past, halting to speak with Gelad who walked behind Yedras, and a murmur went down our line. The men gathered close, Elder keeping outer watch while the wolves of Naras attended to what business was needful for a midday halt.

"Spun?" I held my breath as Yedras sheared the last bit of clinging from my sleeve. "I am sorry, my lord Elder. I should have taken more care."

"No need for sorrow." He scrubbed at the blade's flat with his fingertips, a flicker of *seidhr* giving a heatless spark. "But you are lucky the tree is dead, and this an old web fallen from its proper place." He tipped his chin up, and I followed the line of his gaze to the shrouded canopy. Thin blankets stretched tight or wound about branches, holes rent in no pattern I could discern, a faint powdery bloom upon each overlapping gossamer pane—I could not tell how such thread could be spun, let alone woven.

Waybread was produced, and a swallow of winterwine given to each Secondborn. Arneior settled into an easy crouch near Efain and Soren, the two men checking each other's gear while she examined the process, being very interested in Northern weapons and fasteners. Eol's gloved fingers brushed mine as he handed the wineskin over, and when I was done he drank, his throat moving as he swallowed a scant measure.

"Soon we shall need torches." He showed his teeth after swallowing as if the vintage tasted of strong mead, stinging while settling in the stomach.

"That is no hardship." I realized I was whispering despite the hush, and so were my companions. "Fuel aplenty here. And I may be useless in all else, but at least I can provide flame."

"Useless?" He stoppered the skin with a savage twist, looking down at me with what seemed honest surprise. "Hope is rarely so, my lady Question."

"Rarely so?" I could barely believe he was indeed speaking to me, instead of disdaining a *volva*'s aid; I counted it a pax-offering and essayed a smile. "Is that a riddle?"

"No." Eol looked past me as he did many times during our travels, his dark gaze moving from each member of our group to the next. He took much care with his men, for all they were so few. "The things which live here spin this fabric, and many are those who have been caught in it. We are fortunate winter makes them slow, but that bears its own danger."

What had changed, that he seemed so willing to grant some information? Yet I had other questions. "What manner of creature? Do they hibernate, or—"

"Sol?" Arneior uncoiled, and the word was a sharp bark. For a moment I thought her simply cautious of a man so close to her charge.

I had no time to wonder, for there was a skittering rush nearby; a cold breeze ruffled my braids. The oak's dead limbs thrashed, twigs festooned with rot-pale cloth shaking free. I might have cried out, startled, but *seidhr* thundered in my ears and Eol moved, blurring-quick.

My arm was nearly wrenched free of its socket. I flew, a short stomach-flipping journey ending on hard-frozen ground, a bare root digging painfully into my hip. There was little time to complain, for Eol of Naras landed squarely atop me, rolling us both aside with another wrenching effort as something large and glowing-pale lunged, sharp spear-legs burying themselves where we had rested a bare moment before.

"*Sol!*" Arn yelled, and one of the Northerners cursed in the Old Tongue—a term of surpassing vileness, almost scorching frozen air.

Dazed near-witless, I could only blink as the thing's bulk flickered aside, drumbeat-footsteps in pattering succession. It was unholy quick, and a rising growl shattered the stillness.

A shaggy ink-mass poured itself upward; Eol coalesced from its depths, his sword ringing free. Every blade had left its sheath, and there was a sharp twang as Daerith loosed, the arrow flicking to bury itself in a mass of weeping, fungal-glowing globes. Scabrous luminescence clung to a hairy hide, for in the gloom of Mistwood those long-legged predators carry what little light they need upon their abdomens and in their terrible, bulbous, many-faceted eyes.

Arneior skidded to a stop and bent, her hand closing about my wrist as I thrashed. She hauled me upright, looking over my shoulder, and her freckles glared no less than her woad-stripe.

By the time I could turn, my mantle all awry and my throat full of sour copper, all I witnessed was a whitish blur the size of a well-grown ram scuttle-diving into deep shadow. Branches thrashed afresh, snow pattered down, and I still had little idea what, by the bright gods and the dark, had happened.

"We must move." Bits of ashen clingcloth stuck to Aeredh's hair. His hand shot out, closing upon Eol's arm; the captain looked ready to dive into sparse undergrowth, and strained against his hold. "Gather torch-limbs, as many as you can carry."

My shieldmaid nearly dragged me along, and did not halt until we were surrounded by Northerners. "Fast," she said, softly. "By the Wingéd, I did not see it in time."

"They hunt by stealth." Gelad was pale too, but not nearly so much. "Are you hurt? Either of you?"

I felt almost transparent. My head still rang; had the thing attacked with *seidhr* or was I simply stunned? I could not tell, and patted at my skirts. I brushed my sleeves, tugged them into place, and a great wave of shuddering passed through me. "No." I was shaken, bruised, and dizzy, but it seemed little enough. "Not...by the gods, that... that thing..."

"'Tis gone now." Arneior held her spear aside and examined me for damage almost roughly, finally sliding her free arm around me for a brief, bruising hug. "Leaving only its stink."

So it was, a noisome odor lingering heavy at the back of the throat. A long streak of rotting ichor fringed with strange velvety patterns as it dried was the only evidence of the skirmish—that, and a few broken twigs wrapped with rotting, clotting not-cloth. The sticky, hanging veils moved slowly on soft invisible breezes, and each time I glimpsed one twitching I almost flinched.

It took me a few moments to kindle the first torch, but I accomplished it, and lit a few others besides. When I looked up from the task, shaking my bare fingers and pulling my glove back on with hurried tugs, I found Eol watching. Perhaps he was irritated at my stupidly needing rescue, for the wolf in him was visible again, a restless flicker under his skin, a savage brightness in his dark eyes.

In short order we set off again, most of the men carrying lit brands, Daerith with an arrow nocked, and every hand to hilt except mine.

We plunged deeper into the Mistwood.

Every Fire Loses

Swift as the falcon,
Fierce as the wolf,
Bright as the stars,
Cold as the North.
—Anonymous, *The Rede of All Things*

I did not see the creatures again, though their evidence was everywhere. They gathered as dark fell, strange multifaceted eyes reflecting firelight, but did not dare approach. That was one comforting thing—the wood's hanging shrouds crisp-cringe from flame, and fire is the greatest friend of those who must travel in that place.

Not many do. At least the long-limbed things living there hunt the servants of the Enemy as avidly as any other prey, and we traversed only the very barest edge of their territory.

Arn caught a clear look at the things once, during a moonless night full of relentless vigilance and stealthy shadow-sounds. She shuddered at the memory long after, and despite her desire for a good song she would not describe them beyond, *Like a long-legged weaver, and yet unlike, Sol. Twisted things. That sheep-monster must be kin to them.*

I spent a great deal of our time there lighting brands wrenched from the web-hung trees, blue *aelflame* casting radiance far beyond its small flickering. Perhaps that was the reason the Elder were now so polite.

Aeredh, of course, was only slightly more somber than usual. But Daerith the harpist gave Arn signal attention, asking many a question of southron habits and ways in a low tone. Yedras and the others—at Redhill I had learned their names, from golden-haired Hadril to the spearman Kieris Quickwit, from Gedron son of Maevras to Aeamiril the Knifemaster, and Kirilit called Two-Sword for the paired blades he carried, and the rest all familiar from songs of our journey—often made the curious Northern salute when our gazes met, a swift light touch to heart and lips before the forehead. It seemed akin to a shieldmaid's homage to a woman she respects, and of course the men of Naras used it occasionally, but I did not know what the Elder meant by the gesture.

I was merely glad to be of some use during sunless days of constant watch and chill misery broken with short, sharp battles I rarely saw. My only task was to light the torches for driving away many-legged creatures and the larger fires when we halted to rest, snatching sleep in brief spates until shaken awake by Arn at the approach of skittering feet and manifold eye-gleams. The calling of *aelflame* burnt itself deep into my fingers, for I performed it over and over again; had it been summer the fire might have escaped and given us yet another danger.

But in winter after the deepcrack freeze, every flame—wood-consuming or hidden in the depths of a living body—loses in the end. Even now I do not know how long we traveled in that terrible forest. 'Twas well past the solstice and the days were slowly lengthening, but the nights were still terrible and far, far too long.

Especially under those shroud-choked trees.

When the gloom of Mistwood faded there was little relief. Snow crept through unwrapped branches, thickening on hard-frozen ground littered with great clumps of granite boulders and dead or sleeping undergrowth; the thornbrakes and other bushes were filigreed with heavy clear frost. It was no longer so stifling-shadowed, but even at noon sunlight barely filtered through interlocked branches far above. The clearings were choked with drifts, and sometimes thin ice-hard streams glittered balefully amid their breathless shadows.

The near-constant sensation of being watched lessened somewhat once the trees drew away, and so it was we reached the Glass.

In thaw, summer, or autumn that vast shallow bowl is a swamp, the land depressed in great roundish pockets or branching sloughs, filled with melt or the mazed wandering of a thousand tiny watercourses. It was fortunate we crossed when we did, for it was slippery but solid, and did not swallow us whole.

Even in the deepest cold, though, strange lights burn over great branching rents in the ice, sickly colors having no name pulsing from twilight to dawn with nauseating randomness. They are not the dancing sky-lights of Fryja's veils but uncanny exhalations burning with heatless flame, as certain substances will emit noisome light when mixed. The denizens of Mistwood bear a different sickly, pale hue, so the change should have been a relief.

It was not.

I was glad of my felted overboots, for warriors' footgear is less sure upon the Glass. Nevertheless, the Elder passed without slipping, and shadows in the distance were the black-clad Northerners, moving with less grace but equal assurance in a wide guard-ring now that we were free of the trees.

We did not stop, for there was nothing to burn but great lumps of frozen, ice-hung thorn-tangle and the shrunken, twisted remnants of summer-succulent foliage dead and dormant in the cold season. The Elder gave Arn and me draughts from their flasks—winterwine, *sitheviel*, and other warming things. The Northerners... well, there were small animals suitable for hunting eking out a winter existence amid the crevasses and thorns, for life endures even on the Glass in that season.

Sometimes I can still feel Aeredh's arm over my shoulders, and the cold of that passage. When you walk with another for so long, so closely, it is impossible not to learn summat of their inner world, and it was there I glimpsed a fraction of the Crownless's true strength and thoughts. We spoke far less than Daerith and Arneior, yet we looked to each other often, and in agreement more often than not.

A terrible wind came from the North, raising whirls of stinging snow-pellets and doing its best to rob us of all warmth. And yet sometimes at night, the clear gemlike stars also bore veils of shimmering light in more wholesome colors than those exhaled from ice-crevasses, and I could not help murmuring a wondering prayer to Fryja whom my mother loved—for while it is Vardhra who lit the bright white fires hanging in the sky and scattered them in a river of milk, it is the green-robed, fruitful lady of the Vanyr who sends the shimmerveils on certain nights to remind us of joy's necessity.

Each time I did, Aeredh's arm tightened slightly, and he echoed my prayer in the Old Tongue. It seemed to help conserve a little heat.

The Glass, for all its name and seeming flatness, is relatively easy to hide upon even during the dead cold, for the freeze buckles and pleats the ground in strange ways. There are even tortured ice-shapes looming, where a spume tossed high at end of autumn snap-freezes in frigid wind. Yet each welcome obstruction to the fury of frigid, moving air also makes the swamp-bowl more difficult to traverse, for great rents and crevasses open in its floor, and none has plumbed their depths—nor will they, I think, except whatever god built that place. Or perhaps they will be emptied when the Allmother finally unmakes the world like a woman retwisting a skein.

On that day everything lost in those deep places may well return for a brief moment, all mysteries solved before the maelstrom of Unmaking swallows them afresh.

A long weary time of wandering, with Elder liquids burning in our limbs to grant some semblance of strength, passed under Arn's and my feet. The Elder shepherded us carefully, for we could not leap the ice-ravines, and often had to trudge along a crumbling edge before finding some slim thread of solid-ground safety. Yet a dark line of tree-robed hills approached in fits and starts as the Glass began to ravel at its edges, a wall of forbidding peaks topped with perpetual grey haze. Though none but Aeredh knew it, those hills meant we were ever closer to our goal.

We almost made it through without a battle.

Almost.

Hold, and Be Ready

So the Blessed directed him, and so did my father build his city. While fell things might go forth from Agramar and pass nearby, they long could not discover its fastness, and well 'twas so. Even the Enemy may be blind to the closest danger; long did he brood in his citadel, for of all the Children of the Star he hated Taeron not the least.
—Naciel Silverfoot, *The Rise of Laeliquaende*

Stormwind died between one step and the next as we edged wearily along yet another ice-ravine's southron lip. The Northerners had drawn close, for even a wolf's nose might well lose companions' scents in the driving, whirling white of ground-snow scrape-gathered and flung skyward. My mantle was heavy, ice building upon my shoulders, and at every stop Arn and I had to endure the Elder breaking frost from our clothes—quick, skimming hand-brushes laden with *seidhr* gauged just hard enough to shake the carapace free without damaging cloth or flesh underneath.

I saw how they performed that feat—Daerith let me stand close by while he attended to Arn, and did not bother to hide the technique—but I had little enough strength to try it myself. The warming breath and *seidhr* both barely sufficed to keep me from freezing solid.

The light was failing. All day something other than the cold had thickened around us, a steady invisible current dragging at our progress.

When the wind stilled, heavy vapor exhaled from the Glass's deep crevasses, giving the entire plain an eerie likeness to a steam-boiling pot.

I was almost too weary to shiver. Even the Elder cannot forever hold off a Secondborn's need for rest, and there is only so much sleep one may take while walking. When Aeredh halted that violet-dusky afternoon I could not even wonder at the event, for I was staring at my ice-capped overboots and the pebble-laced frost underneath, and at the edge of my vision the ragged edge of a ravine yawned. The crevasse was shaped like one of the spear-harbor shores far to the west; I had seen those only while my invisible selves traveled with the aid of herbal fumes from Idra's brass brazier.

Arn's sudden soft inhale brought my head up, my mantle-hood slipping slightly. I almost twisted to glance behind us—for we were once more in loose file, Daerith and my shieldmaid following, Elder before and behind us, and the Northerners upon our southron side suddenly appearing through rising icefog, drawing close. I caught sight of gaunt Eol slipping between two forms, and his dark gaze lingered upon me for a long moment before he turned, his snow-crusted back presented to us and his swordblade gleaming as he drew.

Aeredh muttered summat in the Old Tongue, and even had I not known that language I would have understood the curse. I still could not guess his true age, but he sounded as deeply unsurprised as Flokin, who could bring together scathing couplets capable of flaying a fellow warrior to bone, pride, *or* muscle, given strength by the sharp sheer depth of his experience in life and battle both.

"*Do not*," Daerith said, then cursed alike and used the southron tongue. "Do not, lady shieldmaid. This is beyond you. My king?"

"Hold, and be ready." For once, Aeredh did not take the harpist to task for addressing him with that particular honorific. "Stay close, Solveig."

I could not have moved, in any case. I was too tired.

A wolf-howl rose before us—Efain, I thought, for its modulation carried a *seidhr*-breath of his scars and his silences. It cut short, and there was a flurry of movement; Elder and perhaps Gelad and Karas, for they had been taking lead against the terrible stinging wind, relieving others who had endured its brunt most of the day.

Eol did not move, his broadsword's length catching a last ruddy gleam as the sun broke free of perpetual icefog, the golden flower of day reduced to a strengthless red coin as it sank to the westron horizon.

I shuddered, but not with the cold. At that moment it seemed there had never been anything other than journeying half-frozen through this nightmare, Arn and I simply fumbling strengthless in a trap. The Elder, especially the one holding me still as danger approached, had merely brought us here to die.

A great quiet ate every sound, even the clash of battle near the front of our line. Eol stood, sword still glowing, his shaggy, haggard head slightly cocked. He looked very small against the indistinct smear of ice-hummocks, icebreath fog rising in billows since the wind was now not knifing it to shreds, and jumbled, frozen thornbushes.

"Sol?" Arn whispered, as if from very far away. I had never heard her sound so...

Well, so *frightened*. And well she should be, for the certainty of death closed iron-frozen fingers around my throat. I gasped, and the tiny sound caught something's attention.

I see you, a foul rotting voice mumbled, yet I did not hear it with my physical ears. No, it lunged for my living warmth with a quick blind grasping of rot-clotted *seidhr* I had not noticed in my misery, for it had crept upon us in stealthy stages for days now. *Come, little thing. You are ours now.*

"Hold," Aeredh said quietly. His arm was an iron bar, his fingers digging into my mantle-clad shoulder. The eerie blue radiance of an Elder's *seidhr*-selves burned fitfully around him, coruscating like Fryja's shimmerveils—for, as I had discovered, they do not merely fight with hand or sword, the Children of the Star. "And be ready."

"*Nathlàs*," Yedras answered, and there was a terrible weight to the word. I tasted it, bitter forge-ash against the very back of my tongue, and there was another faint scuffling sound much nearer— Arn attempting to draw away from Daerith's grasp, to meet this foe the only way she could, with spear and warcry both.

That managed to loosen the thing's grip upon me. Not the presence of the Elder nor their collective might, not the copper taste of danger nor the sudden terrified pounding of my overburdened heart. But my fear for my shieldmaid, that she might somehow slip Daerith's hold and fling herself at this new terror—no, that broke the hypnotizing, blurring, buzzing invisible whisper of its preliminary attack. "Arn," I gasped, loud in the unnatural stillness. "No. *Stop.*"

The words held a snap of *seidhr*, a wild striking-out—not at her, but at the thing I could not see, the thing Eol faced, the thing stalking us.

It rose from the icefog, tall and dark, just as the sun slipped below the horizon. At first I thought a white-freighted thornbush had somehow been brought to life, for it was crowned with spikes and more sharp points rose from its shoulders. Its armor was iron, and over it a great sable mantle full of rents like the lich's spread in waves, faint unhealthy gleams showing as if its very being tore holes in thick dark fabric.

Now I understood, far too late, what manner of horror the North truly held. I cowered against Aeredh even as the thing let out a chilling, piercing cry, for my instinctive, invisible movement had snapped whatever hold it had gained upon us.

The howl was unearthly, and far colder than the Glass's frigid breath. It pierced me in a thousand places until I was tattered as its cloak, and my heart might have stopped but for Daerith's voice lifted in return, a mighty sound the likes of which I had never heard.

He was a harpist, true, and even a thrall may compose a saga. But there are those the Aesyr or Vanyr grant music more than earthly to; we call them *scvelling* or bards or even—when they are great indeed—songmasters, possessed of the *granr* itself, that holy echo of the Allmother's own making-voice.

Daerith of Nithraen was a songmaster of the Elder, one who had learned his craft before the rising of the Sun and practiced with diligence ever since. A welter of strummed strings lay under his words, mixing with brazen trumpets and the throb of man-sized drums pounding echoes against a greathall's walls. He used the Old Tongue, performing the oldest of *seidhr* like the Allmother herself before the world itself was made.

What is named is *known*, and may be fought or turned to some use; he addressed the thing before us by its proper word, and his song stripped some camouflage of dread and fear.

Some, but not all. The thing was still deadly, and it lifted a great spiked mace, the head dripping with foul tarry fluid. The weapon's anointed edges were razor-cruel, and I could well imagine the damage it would wreak in Elder flesh, let alone that of mortals.

We could not expect much aid, for the Elder before and behind us were occupied with other work. They, and the wolves of Naras accompanying each one, were faced with a pair of liches completing the trap—and summat else.

Eol shouted, a thin noise compared to the creature's malice and Daerith's song, and the heir of Naras drove forward. The gem in his swordhilt, though wrapped, gave a great white starlike glitter through the leather, and he met one of the Seven with a clash.

Nathlás they are named, those high servants of the Enemy. They draw the dead from well-earned rest to bind lesser liches in his service. The seven great captains of Agramar are terrifying creatures, brought by foul arts from some part of the Unmaking beyond the world and the Allmother's grace. They rebelled against Hel's rule as the *belroch* broke from Tyr's to follow a different master, one promising them an eternity of wreaking suffering upon existence itself. The greater liches take shapes taller than men or even Elder, with heavy spiked iron helms and armor full of sharp-rent edges. Over it all they wear the black mantles, but those are not woven by any seamstress or even the foul many-legged beasts—larger cousins to those infesting Mistwood—which linger in the Enemy's dungeons and spin noisome cloth from the agony of trapped thralls. The Seven's mantles are a *seidhr*-darkness so thick and foul it takes physical shape, and they spread like oily smoke during battle, to confuse and disorient their prey.

Do something, a voice inside me shrilled. But I was petrified, staring entranced at the thing, as Eol's cut was parried with a cold ringing clatter and the great mace descended.

The son of Tharos danced aside, handling the weight of his blade with more-than-mortal speed—for the wolves of Naras are granted great strength and quickness, and he used every fingerwidth of the gift upon that eve. From the left, there was a howl shading into a human cry at the end, and an Elder voice lifted as well.

Brought to bay by the Elder, a pair of lesser liches suffered dissolution that day; those who had fought the trap's jaws were now free to move to its center, granting aid to their companions—or dying with them, for the Seven are far mightier than the restless, corrupted dead they govern.

Soren, slipping between his two forms like a shaggy ink-smear upon an oiled plate, flung himself at the thing. Beside him, Yedras and the other spearmen harried it as well. For all its bulk, it was quick indeed, and the din of steel meeting steel mixed with another of its sharp, unholy cries. It now had a giant sword in its left hand to match the mace in its right. The blade was black, drinking in failing daylight as its mantle did.

"*Move!*" Aeredh shouted in my ear, and though an Elder's strength handily outmatched mine, I was so frozen with terror he had some difficulty lifting me bodily off my icebound feet.

But there was nowhere to run, unless we wished to leap into the deep, sheer-sided ravine we had been working along the edge of. For Gelad, Karas, and the Elder with them were driven back by the appearance of a fresh evil. It was a hungry floating thing, screaming as it burst upon us with a puff of freezing-foul breath, mouth gaping wide and its tattered feathery raiment flapping like giant wings, buffeting its prey.

Upon the Glass, a snow-hag might even be worse than one of the Enemy's greater captains.

Lich and Snow-Hag

Dark strength they are given, those who serve the Enemy, and foul cunning of hand and eye. Some may speak hon-eyed words, others entice with promises, yet in the end it all arrives at the same place; the disguise is dropped, the blade unsheathed, the corruption unveiled. All rots under their touch, swiftly or slowly, for swearing allegiance to evil is to court Unmaking itself.

—Aenarian Greycloak, *Aphorisms*

A skeletal yellowed face, serrated rows of clashing teeth, great staring swollen black eyes with foxfire sparking in their depths—if I were to describe a snow-hag I might halt there, for every Northerner knows of what I speak. But it does not express their deep dry unholy reek, or the sound when its multiple bone-veined wings clap, nor can it portray the utter wrongness of the creature. At least the great lich, *nathlàs* in the Old Tongue, is shaped like an Elder or Secondborn or even dverger: Two arms, two legs, a body, and a head.

But a snow-hag…it *shifts* as it floats upon a cushion of tinkling ice-shards ground so fine by whirlwind they can flay a great antlered deer to bone in moments. Through the cloud, stabbing insectile legs may be glimpsed, and its segmented hide is tough and hairy. It does not grow sluggish amid the cold like the weavers of Mistwood; only when sated does it slow. This one was hungry, having been leashed and brought on a hunt much as any man might bring a good hound, letting loose only when the quarry is in sight.

Gelad bled from a gash in his shoulder and another across his ribs, and even shifting between forms did not stopper the flow. He staggered away while an Elder—it was Kirilit, his paired blades flashing in a complicated pattern—darted at the hag, driving it back.

Aeredh halted, snapping a glance slightly to our left—but Arn cried out, a howl of baffled rage, and skidded to a stop before me; Daerith had loosed his hold. She leveled her spear at the hag, for though its bulbous eyes flickered with nictitating membranes, it stared unerringly at me.

I *felt* its attack, a great sticky-soft brush of *seidhr* so foul I can barely avoid a shudder at the memory. They are quick, those wintercloud hunters, and their many-jointed, clawed legs are dangerous.

But the chief way a snow-hag catches its prey is with its gaze, black as a pitch-pool and dangerous as a bog. Red coral in my hair turned to chips of burning ice, and there was a sharp twinge against my scalp—Astrid's fingers while she braided in great hurry, swift-sure and merciless in their love.

Two of the hag's legs flickered. Kirilit was flung toward the crevasse; Karas blurred into his second form, streaking for his fellow fighter. The wolf of Naras caught the Elder just at the crumbling edge, driving his sword into frozen ground as a woman will pin a fold to hold it in place for sewing, and my terror was such I almost did not notice. Aeredh hauled me aside, but there was Arn, and the hag was almost upon her despite all the Northerners' efforts.

My shieldmaid was going to die keeping this thing from me, and I was once again fishgutting, utterly useless.

Another sharp tug against my braids. This time 'twas Idra's fingers, an ungentle tweaking.

Then act, child. I almost…no, I *heard* my teacher, in an eerie moment of silence between another piercing cry from the great lich almost behind us, Daerith's song faltering as he fought for breath, a featherbrushing breeze as Arn's spear trembled upon the edge of swift movement, and Aeredh shouting something, I know not what.

I flung both hands out, and though Idra oft said *smaller is better*, the gout of *seidhr* I tossed was the entirety of the stock granted me that moment. A supreme effort, sparing nothing, and by chance it was the one thing that mattered. My mantle's hood was knocked back, the rest gale-whipped and almost torn from me.

Spending so long calling *aelflame* into being day after shadowed day in the Mistwood, both with Elder preparations for the fuel and later with will alone, meant the blue fire was what erupted through me now. My fear added force to the burning; well it was so, for a snow-hag is resistant fuel indeed. It was like trying to shift a boulder in a muddy field, my feet slipping as Aeredh's fingers bit into my mantle-sleeve and he sought to keep his grasp.

The very fabric of the hag's body fought my kindling touch. Its gaze was a great vat of rotten pitch attempting to suck down and drown me.

But I know pitch, as any daughter of a river steading must. Blackened tar or tree-dropped resin is sticky, and it *burns*.

I heard shouting in the Old Tongue, my voice high and silver-clear weaving a net of *seidhr*. *Aelflame* erupted from the hag's hairy skin, its tattered rotting vestments, its feather-rags. One of its great bulbous black eyes popped with a loud *crack* and the whirlwind underneath its abdomen exploded, a cloud of grit and sharp icicles flung in every direction. Arn's spear jerked, the leaf-tip smacking flying debris aside before it could touch her.

Chance saved us once again, for Aeredh had gained his balance and dragged me toward him with a convulsive effort. I still had a *seidhr*-grasp upon the hag, however, holding the flame as I had all through the solstice night. The bright blue-burning mass streaked past us, tumbling like a wheel and shedding razor ice-knives. It barely avoided Yedras, who lost a chunk of his dark hair to flying debris. Daerith scraped the dregs from his lungs, a last burst of song rising with terrible vein-popping triumph as Eol brought his blade down in one final, irresistible sweep. The leather wrapping at its hilt was burned away and the colorless stone sang too, a high crystalline note matching my scream. The eldest son of Tharos clove the great lich's mace-hand free even as the *nathlàs*'s sword-tip plunged into his shoulder, and the captain of the Enemy would have struck Eol down nonetheless...

...had not a burning wreck of maddened snow-hag crashed into the great lich with a titanic, world-ending noise. I fell, Aeredh's hand curling around the back of my head as he landed atop me with more grace than can be believed if not witnessed, meaning to shield me from both the great lich's next attack and the sudden explosion of debris. There was no recoil of expended force echoing through my inner hallways, for it had taken all my strength to hold the flame.

I was simply empty and dazed, sprawled under an Elder as the Glass shredded to pieces around us.

Love Latecomers So

We are not great lords, it is true. But we live in the shadow of Tarnarya called Haergaril in the Old Tongue. Her strength runs through our bones, as does that of the River-mother in our blood...
— Gwenlara the Golden, Lady of Aen Haergar

The lich and the hag tumbled away, and such was Daerith's mastery of song that he pressed the attack, managing to gain a full draft of breath as the flaming mass skidded across the Glass's icy floor. Another great crack-ravine yawned some distance from us, not terribly wide but riven deep, and the force of Daerith's singing aided the mad struggles of the hag as it roasted from the inside out.

It must have been a terrible death.

They tumbled over the lip as the edges of the ice-hole shuddered, great chunks breaking free to follow lich and burning thing down. A ripple spread through the frozen floor of the Glass, as if the earth itself cringed at violation. Aeredh rolled aside, lunging upright, his own blade suddenly free and twinkling in the foggy gloaming. *"Make for the trees!"* he cried, the words weaving into the last of Daerith's music, and almost before the sound died Arn was upon me, hauling me to my feet with no gentleness at all—the print of her fingers remained, dark-bruised, upon my arm for days afterward.

I did not care, for I was dazed and head-ringing, drained almost to transparency by the spending of vital force.

The Elder move swiftly when there is need, and my *seidhr*-bag jolted and banged against my hip as we ran along the rim of the ravine that had almost trapped us. Its deep cleft curved northward, tapering to a spear-point, and we could finally use a narrow bridge of solid land we had been aiming for, allowing some slim chance of escape.

Fog thickened, curds of freezing air clot-splashing in every direction. I do not know how the Northerners managed, but the Elder closed around Arn and me, bearing us along—Daerith staggered as he ran, his face twisted enough to show his great age for a few moments until he began to breathe in great bellows-gasps, the strain easing. A stitch sank vicious claws into my right side but my feet hardly touched the Glass all that last distance, for Aeredh had my right wrist and golden-haired Hadril was upon my other side, his arm about my waist, bearing me bodily at more-than-mortal speed.

We plunged out of mist and into powdery snowdrifts as black-bark firs rose upon either side, their embrace welcome after the endless swamp-bowl. Kieris and Kirilit bore Arn along, and she made no demur though a shieldmaid does not oft suffer a man to lay hands upon her in that fashion. Even in that state, however, she kept tight hold of her spear.

Behind us, the entire Glass reverberated with screaming. The hag's death-struggles were terrible, and though it would take much more than that to kill one of the Seven—given strength beyond even their great ken by the Enemy himself—we could at least hope to slip from that particular lich's notice while it dealt with an *aelflame*-maddened, dying hag and the collapse of an entire ice-ravine.

We had, albeit barely, survived the Glass.

Wild headlong flight sputtered to a halt amid tall columnar trunks; I collapsed to my knees in deep soft powder-snow and heaved. There was nothing but Elder draughts in my stomach to lose, and I did not manage to produce more than deep retching sounds as my body attempted to turn itself inside out. At least I retained enough control to keep from soiling myself at the other end.

It was a mercy I was grateful for, though only much later when I had time to truly think upon the battle.

Stragglers arrived around us—Daerith recovering quickly but propped half-bent against a tree while he did so, his elbows upon his knees as he struggled to breathe deeply enough, Kieris and Kirilit setting Arn upon her feet, their faces alight and their blue eyes blazing, Hadril and Yedras bearing a bleeding Soren, the Northerner cursing foully in a whispering monotone using both the southron speech and the Old Tongue by turns.

I heartily concurred.

Our remaining companions appeared one by one. Last of all, there were branch-snappings and thrashings; Efain appeared between the trees, hauling Eol. The Northern captain staggered, his sword-tip dragging and catching in undergrowth though he, like Arn, would never lose hold of his weapon even while unconscious; both men were covered with ice and Efain's face was bloody. Eol was almost limp, his breath coming in wheezes, and if he had looked ill during the escape from Nithraen he looked outright deathly now, his eyelids fluttering and a strange pasty greyish tint to his skin.

Aeredh gave a swift glance, counting our companions. "*How are we still alive?*" he muttered, and caught himself, glancing at Daerith.

"*The* alkuine *lit it on fire.*" The harpist coughed; his words were rough as a carpenter's scrapestone used to shred softwood. "*I begin to see why you love these latecomers so, my lord.*"

Arn went to her knees next to me, her spear-butt sinking deep into a drift. "Sol," she husked, and flung her free arm over my shoulders. "Are you…"

The heaving would not let me answer immediately. I finished my miserable cough-retching and gasped, my arms locked over my middle, swaying on my knees as melt trickled upward through mantle, my skirts, under-breeches, and woolen stockings to dab at my knees. "Arneior," I finally moaned, grateful for her shelter. We made a wall against the wind, my shieldmaid and I, our combined shape more stable than either could ever hope to be alone. "I hate…the fishgutting…North."

My shieldmaid let out a harsh, cawing chuckle. "On…on *fire*," she gasped.

"Don't…laugh." I longed to spit, to clear my mouth. All I could taste was thick copper fear; at least the Elder draughts meant I produced no burning bile. "I could…think of…nothing else."

We regained our breath in fits and starts, leaning against each other as if a riverboat had wrecked and cast us upon a sandbar. Soren's shoulder was swiftly bound, both that wound and the gash across his ribs already healing, but his gaze rested anxiously upon his captain. Eol's dark eyes glittered feverish under half-closed lids, and he was only semiconscious.

"*Always he does this,*" Efain muttered, holding his leader upright while pressing his palm hard against Eol's shoulder. "*He will not think of staying back.*"

Gelad resheathed his blade with a sudden, angry movement. "'*Tis his father's doing. Tharos wishes his eldest dead, and Eol is a good son. He obeys as far as he can.*"

"Cease." Karas attempted to shake snow and freezing fragments from his hair; the leather wrapping had been knocked free. All of us, even the Elder, were crusted with gravelly ice. "*Tharos is our lord too, my friend.*"

"*I swore my oath to one man, and it was not the Old Wolf.*" Gelad was not willing to be hushed; his eyes blazed like my mother's on those infrequent occasions when she is not merely irritated but outright angered.

I took the swallow of *sitheviel* Daerith pressed upon me, the drink's heat far softer than the echo of *aelflame* inside my veins. "My thanks," I murmured, trying not to look guilty of eavesdropping. "How fares my lord Eol?"

The harpist shook his snow-crowned head, rubbing at the flask-mouth politely before offering it to Arn. "He may be well enough in time, if the *nathlàs* did not leave a fragment in the wound. I begin to think the South able to withstand the Enemy well enough, if even its women are this brave."

"Arn is brave." I sagged against a handy tree-trunk while my shieldmaid drank. "I merely struck out in terror, my lord Daerith. There is no courage in that."

The harpist studied me for a few moments, thoughts moving in his bright Elder gaze.

"*We must move, and swiftly.*" Even golden-haired Hadril, usually neat as a well-combed cat, was sadly bedraggled. "*I no longer hear them screaming. Just the ice, grinding away.*"

I could hear it too, the low unhappy sound as of mountains rubbing their shoulders together. For once Arn needed my help to rise instead of the opposite, and by dint of cooperation we both reached a position approximating upright.

Aeredh had reached his friend. He pushed aside Efain's hand, then Eol's mantle, jerkin-shoulder, and the layers of cloth underneath, ripping leather and black fabric further in his haste. His fingertips dove into the bloody hole revealed underneath; Eol cried out—not even attempting to muffle the noise—and stiffened, his eyes rolling back into his head.

I stared, my stomach roiling despite *sitheviel*'s soothing. "What is he—"

The Crownless swore in the Old Tongue, foully enough even the cold air cringed. "*A splinter,*" he said grimly. "*I could just feel it; 'tis working deeper.*"

"*Leave him.*" Daerith nodded to Arn, capping his blue glass flask with a swift, savage twist. "*We can carry the women and the rest, but—*"

"I will stay with him." Gelad had gone pale. "Besides, I may halt them for some few moments, should they find us again. There is a blood trail now."

"Stay with him?" The cold pressed against every inch of me, crusted ice weighing heavy upon my mantle. My knees were damp, and the rest of me followed suit. I would freeze miserably soon, especially if we tarried talking. "What are you saying?"

"*You know what happens when it reaches his heart.*" Daerith's tone dropped, and he eyed the Northerners, who waded through snow to gather about their lord and Aeredh. "*We cannot risk it. The* alkuine *must reach Taeron; you were right, my king. I shall never doubt again.*"

Aeredh's expression was terrible. He gazed at Eol's sweating, chalk-pale face. "*I have known him all his life,*" he said, quietly.

"*Either we leave him, or we all die.*" Daerith's answer was soft, but ruthless.

I looked to my Arn. Grimed with snow and dirt-laced ice, my shieldmaid gazed back at me. She arrived at understanding much swifter than I, for all I could comprehend the Old Tongue. A bruise was flowering upon her cheek, and both of us would be stiff as stone posts come morning—if we gained any rest at all tonight.

They are right, her eyes said, *but I do not like it.*

Nor do I, mine replied. *Are you with me?*

I did not even need to ask. She was at my shoulder as I pushed through the snow, sinking and struggling since there was no Elder to ease my passage. Daerith moved as if to bar my way, but Arn's spear twitched and he halted, considering, his head tilted slightly and his lips thinning.

My hand closed over Aeredh's shoulder. "*Step aside,*" I said in the Old Tongue. At least I had the benefit of listening to their accent for a long while now; mine had become tolerably pure. "*We of the South do not leave our allies to die.*" I fixed Efain with my mother's most quelling look, the remains of a great weirding trickle-burning in my eyes. *Seidhr* may be spent swiftly, but every living thing slowly accumulates more simply by breathing—and I suspected I would need every iota I could gather soon. "*What ails him? A splinter, a fragment from the nathlàs's blade?*"

"*It will travel until it reaches his heart. Then, when it does—*" The scarred Northerner halted, staring at me with some astonishment. "*The whole time? You have known our language this entire time?*"

Suddenly, even through the terror and the ice and the devouring exhaustion from spending so much *seidhr* upon flame-calling, I felt a curious comfort. My mantle lay over my *seidhr*-bag, but there was no time to dig through folds of cloth to find what I needed. "Arn, your lodestone, quickly. You." I pointed at Gelad. "Something to clean the wound. Karas, take his other arm; Elak! Something to bind it with after I draw the thing free. Efain, you and Karas hold him, but tilt him back. *Move!*"

It was the same as when Ysderas the Fisher had the harrow accident, or Nifa's daughter Kevryn fell through rotten ice and near-drowned, or Flokin's hunting mishap the year I gained my first inked band upon both wrists, or the ague that swept from the river when I was fourteen winters high. The same as difficult births when the baby wishes to come feet-first and must be coaxed otherwise—or worse, torn quickly free so the mother may be saved. I had the benefit of watching Idra bind many a wound and concoct many a cure; later, Dun Rithell and neighboring settlements turned not just to her but to us both. As the saying goes, a warrior may kill but the *volva* is mightier, for it takes far more skill to heal than to wound.

This, I knew how to do, and Eol would not gainsay my aid now.

I shoved Aeredh aside, not gently, and perhaps the Elder was stunned, for he did not resist.

"Arn, watch his feet; he may thrash." I stripped my gloves off, my knuckles aching with cold. My shieldmaid had already dug in her belt-pouch, and her lodestone dropped chill into my palm, sending a faint thrill up my wrist. The Northerners moved with alacrity too, following my direction.

The only impediment was Daerith. "*We do not have time for this,*" he hissed. "*The nathlàs will climb free of that hole and hunt us through the night, and—*"

"*Cease thy yapping.*" I felt no qualm at my rudeness. The *volva* says what she pleases at the sickbed's side, for swift action means survival instead of agonizing death, and hers is the will that accomplishes it. "*If you would be useful, watch the treeline and tell us if that foul thing approaches.*"

"*She knew all along,*" Efain repeated, in a mutter. "*Canny girl.*"

I could not hesitate. I pushed aside cloth, my fingers slipping in hot blood, and slapped the lodestone against Eol's wound.

Lodestone and Splinter

Three ways there are to make a lich. By corpse-dream and miasma they are raised, but by splinter they are born into darkness. Even kinbonds shatter when a fragment pierces the pulse; yea, even love is set aside when the heart is nathlàs-riven.
—*The Saga of Dragulein*

The eldest son of Tharos cried out again, seeking to thrash; it took much strength to hold him. The only good thing about cold and fatigue was that it made slipping the chain of my physical self easier; the draughts of the Elder helped too, for they strengthen more than flesh.

"Do not touch her!" Arn snapped. "Or I shall strike thee, and to kill."

The wound pulsed under my touch, swelling with fever-fire. The body knew it had been invaded and was burning with a wolf's vitality, attempting to evict the intruder.

And it told me, in its own silent way, of its ailment—a single sliver of thin blackened metal, colder than the Glass and malignant as well.

It strained from my grasp, even with the lodestone's aid. Such stones attract certain things, and *seidhr* may magnify the pull. I made a low frustrated sound, weak from the spending of my vital force upon calling a vast gout of *aelflame*.

The thing lost in the wound had a baleful intelligence all its own, burrowing through Eol's flesh like a drilling insect in rotten wood.

It fought my grasp, a bleak chill *absence* like unto that between stars. Any *seidhr* I could summon vanished into its hunger, though I could well see its path with inner vision, black against the glow of a living body. My wrists twinged, ink-marks flaming with pain, and the runes danced between the bands.

The splinter worked unerringly upon its heartward path with sickening, twitch-serpent wriggles, dodging my *seidhr*-grasp. I should not have been aware of anything around me, but my concentration fragmented, and I hissed out an obscenity a warrior at axe-practice would have found eminently understandable.

Arn's voice, raised. Aeredh, seeking to reason and restore calm. Daerith hissing that we had to flee *now*, there was no use in wasting time for a Secondborn stabbed by a heartseeker. And Efain, saying *I will not leave him*, quietly but with great force as the wind rose whirling over the Glass. The keening in the weather's rising song could have been a snow-hag breathing its last, or...summat else.

I was too weary and had lost too much strength; even another reckless spending of my inner reserves achieved little. I cursed again, my voice breaking—I had done nothing right since leaving Dun Rithell, and this failure would crown all the others.

No. I will do this. By all the gods, you shall not take this man from me.

The splinter squirted free of my grasp again. I sobbed out a breath, a prayer to Baldyr the Wounded losing strength as my lungs halted, my heart stuttering under a too-heavy burden.

Just as hope left me, tears standing behind my eyelids and my teeth clenched fit to shatter, a warm spot dilated upon my back. A flood of strength filled me, crown to soles. It was not the fitful sharing Idra and I could perform for each other, nor the simple warming Aeredh had done upon the road to Nithraen.

This was a deeper gift, life offered without reserve, and I took it without question. The splinter fought further, its cold cresting triumph turning at the last moment into a screech of cheated ire, but with the lodestone's pull and that deluge of heat and bright blue light, I wrenched a thin shard of blackened metal free of Eol's flesh, further tearing the wound.

He screamed as it left his shoulder. I did too.

Our paired cries were lost in the Glass's fresh howling, for a storm had descended over that vast bowl. Blood pumped hot against my skin; the splinter stung my fingers and I tossed it away, then clapped my palm over the wound, attempting to dam the flow.

The hole in Eol's shoulder resisted. I could not close it wholly, but with Elak helping to apply pressure and the hot flood of *seidhr* passing through my own flesh we managed to stanch somewhat, and bind. Daerith plucked the cold steel splinter from the snow where it lay steaming, wrapping it in a scrap of black cloth torn from his own mantle. I found myself blinking and headsore, my knees quaking and Aeredh's left hand flattened against the small of my back, pressing hard enough I could feel his fingers through mantle, dress, and shift alike.

His right hand clasped the leaf-blade of Arn's spear, and now I knew how the Elder bled, for gold-tinged crimson welled against the sharpness. He stared at my shieldmaid, his blue eyes half-closed and his entire body tense as a stone statue as he held her attack in quivering quiescence.

He had touched me during *seidhr*, and she had struck. Arn surged forward, her boots digging in powdery snow; Aeredh's hand left me, and I staggered.

The Elder's palm and fingers were badly cut, and I could only distract Arneior by calling her name, for I needed her aid to stand. Eol still bled, though sluggishly. Most of the Northerners were wounded in one way or another; the remaining Elder regarded Arn as they might a viper and me as something even less natural, perhaps.

But the son of Tharos, heir to the House of Naras, was still alive.

At least, for the moment.

There are songs of our passage along the Maraekhos—that particular spur of the Black Land's shield-wall, part of the Marukhennor's greater chain—to the Ice Door. Though Elder may move swiftly at great need they were also carrying Arn and me, and the sagas are true when they say even Aeredh the Crownless was near the end of his great strength. It is also sung how the wolves of Naras bore their wounded captain; though free of the *nathlàs*'s poisoned sword-shard, he could not shift to the other form sharing his skin or call upon the wolf's burning ability to fully heal.

What no saga may truly describe is the weariness, the cold, the stinging wind against our cheeks, and the fear as howls both wind-made and otherwise echoed from the Glass's crevasse-depths to the black peaks of Agramar's skirts. For we were upon the very feet of mountains the Enemy raised during his great war with the Vanyr and Aesyr, just where they curve as if to scoop up Dorael, like a healing root grubbed by a crescent blade into a *volva*'s waiting hand.

I saw the borders of the Black Land for the first time then, and the darkness which hung upon them.

The forests there are grim, massive thick-clustered and oddly twist-shaped trees rising behind tortured, pleated foothills. Above, sharp sheer pinnacles are draped with a shadow made of neither tree-crowding nor weather haze, but a thickening of air itself. Sometimes during ill winters or damp summers the darkness creeps down those gorges and drops, questing blindly amid the lowlands; we were lucky to go no closer.

I *felt* it, though. In those forests even an Elder's wound might not properly heal, and the undergrowth is full of creeping, slinking things half-seen even in the depths of treecrack freeze. They poured the last of the *sitheviel* down my throat amid that shadow, and something else into Arn; she submitted resentfully, glaring at Aeredh whenever he passed too near.

I could not smooth her temper. I was numb from insensate toes to my slipping braids, snow collecting upon my mantle-hood and every space inside me bare-frozen as the Glass's flooded mirror. Night cast a cloak over the soughing forest, and with it came soft whispers.

Such a fine volva, you cannot even heal a man, the wind snickered, shaking a load of heavy frost onto my bowed head. *Can't use their Elder toys, either,* the trees responded, diseased sap ice-bubbling with hurtful, frozen glee. *Useless, witless, worthless,* the snow chanted, each flake a single voice in great whispered chorus listing my failures, my inadequacies, my sins, and my unfitness for the bands I wore.

I staggered under Aeredh's arm, the steady warmth of an Elder body beside me finally failing. Even the usual brief cloud-clearing past midnight in that season, starlight filtering through ice-hung, tossing branches, brought no hope. I watched the freeze-clogged toes of my felt overboots brush granular snow, and thought longingly of lying down in a drift.

Snow-death is quiet, and brings with it a great warm stillness.

Each dawn was a stinging lash, and each early dusk a progressively greater torment. The Black Land's mountains hung over us as we followed the treeline west, step by painful staggering step. We were so close to our goal, though I did not know it. The air was knives; I could not summon the strength to warm it as I breathed. Even Arn dry-coughed with increasing frequency, and I hoped she was not developing ague or any other winter ailment.

Such things do not often trouble shieldmaids, but the thought would not leave me. I flinched every time I heard her clear her throat, or Eol infrequently make half-swallowed, grit-tooth sounds of pain. He held to twilit consciousness by a thinning thread, and hung between Gelad and Efain like a damp black rag.

"*They are fading,*" Daerith said in the deep cold quiet long after one particularly hellish midnight, just as the cold had turned not only my toes but my arms and legs to dumb meat. "*Should we build a fire?*"

Aeredh shook his head; dark hair clung to his glisten-damp forehead. Even his steps had slowed, and sometimes our feet sank a finger-width or so into the snow. More was falling to erase our tracks, yet I thought of the great lich somewhere behind us, passing through the cringing forest with rapid ease, and a great wave of shudders coursed through me.

The mental image was so strong I thought it a sending for a moment, a warning granted by grace of a passing god or spirit. It faded reluctantly, my teeth chattering hard enough to rob me of speech.

"We are close." Short, sharp words, by far the least gentle I ever heard Aeredh utter. "*I will burn every lamp remaining to me, and should I fall you must—*"

"*You will not.*" At least the harpist sounded as if he meant it, as if he believed without question in the one he followed. In fact, his tone bore a great similarity to Efain's on certain occasions, though Daerith might or might not take that as a compliment. "*It is merely the Shadow upon the mountain speaking. Take heart.*"

"*It is not my own despair I fear, but theirs.*" Aeredh sucked in a pained breath, and his arm tightened across my shoulders. "We are close, Lady Solveig. Stay with me."

Perhaps he had forgotten I knew the Old Tongue, or perhaps he was merely being polite. In any case, I raised my chin with a supreme effort, and found dull iron-grey light had crept upon us while we suffered.

Another dawn had come.

The Ice Door

Into the North did he fly, and settled amid icy peaks. Deep
he did delve, riven earth groaning under his will. Dark
plans did he set into motion, upon which he had brooded
during his long punishment. And many terrible fires did
he light to create a shield of noisome smoke—for above all
things, the Enemy fears light.
      Yet within that fear lies a deep craving…
                              —*The God-Tale of Dun Mirit,*
                        attributed to Bjornvalt the Younger

Some little strength returned that blessed morn. The Elder were
slightly more cheerful and even Eol rallied a bit, every step away
from the sheer peaks and their foul icy shadow granting some manner of relief. We sore needed it, for another series of jagged hills rising
to high crests cut across our path, falling west and south. Though
forbidding, they were cleaner than the dark mountains, their plain
white caps bearing no gloom. In fact, as dawn rose they turned gold
for a short while, and I thought I glimpsed tiny specks riding a freezing wind above them.

I had seen the ravens of the Blessed, those great birds who take
news to Odynn and to Manhrweh the Judge. A great good omen
indeed, though I did not know it then.

Each flask was drained and all the waybread gone; the Elder had no more to give us. My feet would not work quite properly; I almost slithered from Aeredh's grasp when my knees failed. He halted only long enough to bend, exhaling softly as he straightened. I curled in his arms like an overtired child on a river-festival night, too cold to feel any shame at being carried thus.

Arn suffered it just as she suffered Daerith and the Quickwit at either arm, bearing her over frozen ground even as she still grasped her spear. The remainder of the Elder and the wolves of Naras spread out to screen our passage as much as possible—except for Gelad and Soren, who had taken over the duty of supporting Eol. There were no skittering, malformed creatures in the shadows, though I could not even feel relieved at the absence. The wind fell off after the sun rose, bringing in a sparkling, crystalline winter day.

I would have endured this weather with good grace at Dun Rithell. I could have walked along the frozen riverside, well-wrapped and thoughtful; returning to the hall would mean a hot cup and a good fire. Arn would enjoy practicing in the ice-crusted yard, not to mention the ale Albeig would pour when she returned. Bjorn would be anywhere and everywhere, into mischief or using his ox-strength to aid our neighbors with repairs and winter chores; Mother would be in the stillroom or at her loom and spinning wheel; Astrid would dance while she carried and fetched, singing the winter songs in her clear light voice. My father would be hearing cases in the hall, or stamping through the snow with a group of warriors to make certain no outlying settlements were in distress.

Were we at home, as the sun fell there would be more singing in the hall and I would be called upon for a saga or two, making the fire shift and crackle with colored pictures while I intoned stories of heroes, history, or the Blessed. I might even have sung of the wars against the Black Land, not knowing the awful truth—I had many a time during my training, after all.

Songs do not even approach the reality; that is a lesson only time and life may grant.

I fell into a fitful doze as Aeredh moved briskly on, seeming to take no notice of my weight. Dun Rithell rose inside my head, an image clear and detailed as I had seen the *nagàth* striding through the woods. Later, I found the Seven have a captain as well, as dire to them by comparison as they are to other liches.

At that moment I was still blissfully unaware of so much.

Again I could not tell whether the vision was a true sending, a possible future, or a foul lie from the gloom-wrapped peaks of the Enemy's borders. My home showed itself to me as a blackened shell, the great timbers transformed to bare flame-chewed ribs and the roof's gilding melted into frozen puddles. Strange shapes crouched or lay motionless amid the charring, and for a moment I thought them children.

Yet I soon realized otherwise. The heat had simply been so furious the corpses of my home's inhabitants shrank, curling around themselves like tired small ones at the end of a long day just as I lay half-coiled in an Elder's arms, lacking even the strength to stand.

Near nooning the cold fastened its teeth upon my marrow, and sharp ague-pains speared me. Had there been anything resembling proper food in my middle I might have vomited upon myself and Aeredh, who began to sing once more. Gaps lingered between the notes, for he could not quite gather his breath. Still, some small warmth crept back into my limbs, stinging terribly as I sank my teeth in my bottom lip to keep from making a sound.

Daerith intoned another Elder song quietly in Arn's ear, but I do not know if it was meant to strengthen a shieldmaid or soothe her rage. Her lips, bleached with cold, moved slightly as she was borne along, no doubt swearing; the woad was gone from her face and even its yellowed ghost was pale. Eol sought even in extremity to keep from making any noise at all—unsuccessfully, but sometimes a wolf-howl rose nearby and any of our small cries or mutters were lost in that music.

There was no melt as the sun began to fall from its apex. Soon it would be night again, and all I felt was relief at the prospect. It is a strange thing, to know you will not survive the coming darkness and to feel not quite resigned but almost grateful to halt all painful striving. The image of Dun Rithell—burned, blackened, broken, the outbuildings shattered and the steadings or halls along the river still sending up curls of steam-smoke from some unimaginable catastrophe—was a torment, and would not leave me.

Aeredh's voice faltered; he came to a halt amid snow-speckled trees. He sucked in a pained breath; I tried to clear my dry throat, to say, *Turn me loose, let me lie down to die in peace.* The Elder tucked his chin slightly, gazing thoughtfully about us, and his face seen through my welling tears was suddenly a warped, bloated nightmare.

I was not weeping. The saltwater came unbidden as my body protested, helpless and otherwise mute. Perhaps I would have struck out in fear one final time during that terrible passage, but I was empty. No *seidhr* remained to me, though sheer weariness might have freed my subtle selves to the cold wind had I decided to step outside my wretched mortal frame. Nothing remained save silent, beastlike endurance, and even that was dregs.

The Old Tongue slipped from Aeredh's mouth, slow and unsteady. "*I was sure it was…*" He trailed off, raising his head to look about him as one just waking from a dream.

"*Don't tell me you've forgotten the way.*" Daerith's laugh held a ragged edge; Arneior's dun hood rested against his shoulder, her coppery hair masked underneath. She kept a whiteknuckle grip upon her spear—it takes much more than winter-death to steal a shieldmaid's weapon from her grasp—but in this extremity she also permitted the Quickwit upon her right side to wrap his fingers about it as well. His own weapon rode his back, its blade glittering no less fiercely than hers.

Eol coughed, a soft, hopeless sound. His dark head hung, and his boot-toes dragged in snow.

"*No.*" Aeredh looked down again, this time peering past my hood's edge at my face. I was no help at all. Even my shivering had lost its strength. "*It was summer when last I stood here, that is all.*" He shifted to the southron language. "Have no fear, my lady." His voice was a dry husk, and unutterably weary. "A short while more, and we shall be safe enough. We must climb this hill, and in the next valley—"

"Are you certain?" Gelad's brow was furrowed, and he was gaunt. The cold strips even wolves down to bone, and they had not time to hunt. "I smell nothing but snow, my lord Elder."

"If even a wolf could scent it, the place would not be safe." Aeredh's voice gained a slight measure of fresh strength, and the

Crownless straightened, shifting my weight more comfortably. "How fares Eol?"

"Another night will kill him." Efain's tone was quiet, and sharp as a curse. The swordhilt rising over his shoulder bobbed as he shifted, taking a firmer grip upon his captain. "We should have gone to Dorael."

"Take heart." Aeredh set his shoulders. The strength humming through him mounted yet another notch, then still more; his eyes burned a deeper blue than the patch of cloud-feathered sky visible overhead. *"We are upon the last league, my friends."*

Even so, the final hill almost defeated us all. Aeredh sang in broken snatches, or spoke in the Old Tongue; I no longer listened except to the mere sound of his voice meaning I was not alone. Once Gelad all but dropped Eol and Efain hissed a warrior's obscenity, hauling his captain upright. The men of Naras drew into a close knot. Even the surefooted Elder slipped upon the steep snowy pitch, and each one had to help another at some point.

At the top of the slope, Aeredh counted the survivors. We had lost none in Mistwood or the Glass, which would have seemed near-miraculous to me had I been warm enough to care. Nothing seemed particularly important at that moment, my cheek resting against an Elder's thin, snow-damp mantle. I no longer heard his voice, simply the slow powerful thumping of a heart caged in an ageless chest.

The valley below us was thickly wooded, thornvines and bushes packed between tall frowning firs and other conifers. Its far side was mostly sheer, studded with great grey boulder-warts under a carapace of ice and dusting snow. The wall rose in folds before breaking into two separate mountains, each easily twice as tall as Tarnarya of my birthplace.

Aeredh moved carefully, and so slowly it took most of the short afternoon before we reached the valley floor. But no thorn caught my mantle, and each Elder again took charge of a Secondborn to ensure no trace was left—except Arn, who was between two. Eol went over Yedras's shoulder, and the Elder spearman did not look sour at the burden, merely resigned.

A wave of icy vine-spikes met us, but Aeredh did not halt. He moved among them, carrying me. The sun touched the westron edge of the valley, dusk thickening along its stony bottom; I realized it was an ancient watercourse. Perhaps in spring it would be flooded to the knees of thick undergrowth bushes, but now it was merely a forgotten scrap of the winter-choked Wild.

A blank stone face met us, overgrown with yet more ice-blasted vines. Melt from above had cascaded over it as autumn turned into the season of cold sleep; the successive liquid layers spread an iron-white lacework over hard granite.

"*Congratulations,*" Daerith said, softly. "*It's…a wall.*"

A slight murmur went through the group. Aeredh smiled grimly, and his arms tightened upon me. "*I do not begrudge your lack of faith in me, Loremaster. But you should trust the Blessed more.*"

"*By the Blessed,*" Soren breathed. "*Is it…a cave-crack, there. See?*"

"*Aye.*" Aeredh now sounded satisfied. "*'Tis larger than it looks. Through the Ice Door, my friends, and at long last our journey is done.*"

It was not quite so simple. There were eyes upon us even then, though they were not the Enemy's.

The Passage Guards

The folk of Nithraen would have called him king, and asked him to take up his father's crown. Yet the son of Aerith turned to them, not in fury but with deep pain, and swore that he would not lead so faithless a crowd. "My father did what he must for love instead of for gain," he said, "and I shall do the same. May your new rulers bring you joy." Then he left his home, and never returned until the coming of doom…

—The Ballad of Aerith's Son

The crack in the hillside had been made by running water uncounted ages ago, and though it was so thin only one person could pass at a time, the chamber beyond was spacious and full of soft echoes. Aeredh turned and managed to draw us both through the aperture, though he could have easily handed me to someone upon the other side had he suffered any but himself to go first.

The floor was a great plain of river-washed stones, round and satiny; it was dim, but not the bleak darkness under Nithraen or even the gold-veined shadow of Redhill. High above another fissure, made by mountains' slow movement instead of water, let in a gleam of failing, snowy bluish dusk. It was still cold, but not so bad as outside, and I revived a bit as Aeredh waited for our companions.

Arn drove her spear-butt hard against the stones, pushing her helpers away and nearly buckling; instead of an Elder, Soren caught her arm.

"Easy, my lady Minnow." The once-stocky Northerner's black mantle hung upon him as a blanket upon a scarecrow, but a wolf's vitality still shone in his gaze. "Do me the honor of granting some aid; my legs are not quite steady."

It was perhaps a polite fiction, but she accepted it and in any case they both swayed as she leaned upon him, almost staggering. There seemed little call for silence now, and even the Elder had some small difficulty moving over the shifting, clacking tide of smooth pebbles.

On the far side was a sandy strip, a shore when water still flowed but now merely a dry scallop-lapping against sheer stone wall. We could move a little more swiftly having gained that fringe, and Kaecil the spearman unlimbered a blue-glowing Elder lantern from its hiding place amid what little gear they carried. Its light glittered in his fair hair; he walked just behind Aeredh while the glow painted shadows upon worn cavern walls.

The steady motion and cessation of the killing cold felt glorious. I stirred, but Aeredh's hold did not loosen. "*Stay with me,*" he repeated in the Old Tongue, or sometimes in southron. "*Just a little longer, my lady. Stay with me.*"

In truth I could not have fled, and I could make no answer either. My throat was dry as the stones to our left, polished by a foaming long-gone river. I was so thirsty I could almost hear echoes of its chuckling as it carved, the stone walls remembering a merry once-companion.

I do not know how long we walked. Eventually Aeredh must have decided there was no danger, for—softly at first—he began to sing.

Other Elder joined in, tentative music swelling the longer they moved. The Old Tongue had a different shape in their mouths, and the first quiver of *seidhr* renewing itself pervaded my limbs. Even the thought of numbness from the black kisses of frostbite failed to rouse or alarm me.

The Elder sang of the stars named before the sun rose, of their making by the lady of the Blessed they love the most. Wrought with care and hung upon the face of night, Vardhra's lamps were the first light the Elder saw from the shore of a mere long since forgotten, but they have ever remembered the one who did not wish for them to wake in darkness. Hope she sought to grant them, and a promise that she, at least, would never abandon the first-awakened children of the Allmother.

Sorrow there was in the song as well, for the West was closed to the Children of the Star since they had left at Faevril's urging. Still, a soft hope threaded through the names; the sky-fires still burned, did they not? And the promise, once given, might be delayed but never left wholly unfulfilled.

So the Elder say. Or, at least, those who trust in the Blessed of the uttermost West.

I drifted upon that music, though the warmth stealing through my limbs was not of its making. Rather, it was the languor of shock. I came close to snowsleep even while clasped to an Elder in the Hidden Passage, and the vision of blackened, blasted Dun Rithell was no longer a torment. Instead, I simply longed to stop breathing so I could join those who had died in the flames.

The passage narrowed, its roof rising to an indeterminate point high above. The blue lantern's glow touched the edge of another light, for there was illumination in the distance, growing steadily closer.

A great booming word sliced across the Elder-song, bounced from the walls, and caromed down the cave-throat. "*Hold!*"

Arneior swore softly in the sudden silence, and I twitched. My shieldmaid was near; I could not slide into snow-death while she was still alive and possibly needed me. My cracked lips parted; I meant to ask to be placed upon my feet if we were called upon to fight.

I did not have the chance. The Guards of the Passage had found us.

"*By rights we should slay them all,*" an Elder in a tall helm with a white feather adorning its single spike said resentfully, casting a sharp gaze over our bedraggled group. "*Such is the Law, Floringaeld.*"

"*Our task is to guard the Passage, not murder refugees.*" The leader of our rescuers had freed his golden head from another single-spiked helm, and regarded Aeredh with bright blue-eyed interest as he tucked the head-armor under his arm. A gauntlet gleamed upon his left hand, dull silvery metal with a single cloudy green gem upon its back. "*Aeredh? Is that you?*"

Rescue might be too strong a term for the way they ringed us, swords and spears to the ready. Hidden galleries had been carved in the stone sides of the Passage; now they were full of bowmen, arrows nocked and unerringly trained upon intruders.

"I am Aeredh son of Aerith," our leader answered in the southron tongue. "If Taeron Goldspear wishes to slay me for returning to his doorstep, 'tis his right as king in his own land. But you should first tell him I have arrived, bearing a hope of the Blessed."

"And wolves." Blond Floringaeld—for that was the name of the Elder captain—cast a dark glance at the black-clad men of Naras as he spoke, and his handling of my language was heavily accented. "You I will take to visit the king and hear his judgment, son of Aerith. And you, Loremaster, I know your voice as well. The rest may wait at my lord Taeron's pleasure in our dungeons."

"The Secondborn require some care." Daerith moved forward cautiously, his hands loose and relaxed but not raised. There was no need to cry pax, apparently. "Especially the women. Has hospitality grown so cold here as to turn away half-dead kinsmen?"

"*The Secondborn are no kin of ours,*" the spike-helmed lieutenant answered, somewhat coldly. "*But we will offer no unkindness. And if we are forced to slay them for our lord, it shall be quick and painless.*"

"*You may find us unwilling to be slaughtered,*" Efain muttered, but subsided when Aeredh glanced at him. Eol was not even semiconscious now, though he still breathed as he hung between Gelad and Karas.

And I? I listened without any great interest, my skull full of emptiness. All I cared about was Arn, who had regained some use of her legs and was at Aeredh's shoulder.

"I would see the women given some care," the Crownless said. "Then I will go to Taeron, and glad I am of your restraint, Floringaeld. This one needs summat stronger than *sitheviel*; she is barely alive. And Eol of Naras was grievously wounded facing one of the Seven. Much bravery has been shown by these Secondborn."

"Be that as it may, they have entered the Passage and may not leave save by my lord Taeron's permission." Floringaeld examined our disrepair with no little interest. "Still, we may make some shift for their comfort before stowing them safely."

"They are not robes to be folded in a closet, my lord Heavyhand." Daerith cocked his dark head. "And my lord Aeredh is right; these latecomers have shown so much bravery those who hide in corners might well be ashamed to hear of it."

"No doubt." Floringaeld now sounded a little less welcoming. "I never thought to hear *you* defend Secondborn, my lord Loremaster. Perhaps you should stay with them."

"Taeron will want to see the son of Tharos." Aeredh sounded more as if he were in command than this Floringaeld, but I did not care. It seemed he would set me down soon, and I was occupied with the question of whether or not I could stand.

It did not seem likely.

In the end, we were carried or hurried into a long low room behind a hidden door, for there were such chambers tunneled alongside the Passage for the guards standing in unceasing vigilance. *Aelflame* gleamed blue in a great hearth; the sudden cheerful warmth was like a blow. I tried to swallow small pained sounds as my gloves and mantle were stripped by Elder hands and the blood returned to my extremities, Aeredh's grasp upon me shifting but not loosening. A tiny, marvelously carved flask of smooth white stone was produced and held to my unresisting lips. The cordial it contained burned all the way down. It was red as summer sunlight through tight-closed eyelids, and tasted of small bitter herbs growing upon sunny slopes when the heat is as deep-cloying as oil, winter only a distant dream.

I choked upon it the first few times, my body refusing even so healthful a potion. But Aeredh patiently held the flask to my lips, and finally I was able to drink. Melting ice streamed from my mantle as well as Arn's; we dripped upon the floor as if the river had returned. One of the point-helmed Elder had some skill as a healer; he bent to aid Eol, who had been laid upon a beautifully carven stone bench near a table crowded with implements, jars, and other things.

We had surprised them at a meal, perhaps. I could not tell.

I was placed upon a graceful wooden chair near the fireside, my *seidhr*-bag a sodden lump in my lap, Arneior lowering herself with a sigh onto a stool set nearby. She had no difficulty drinking and indeed took down quite a few flagons of Elder winterwine, each draught returning a bit more of her strength. She was pale, her freckles glaring no less than her dark eyes, and kept her spear closed in a hard grip. Any Elder who approached as if to take it from her met with a level look and the unheard sound of brushing feathers as the Wingéd Ones shone in her gaze.

It is always best not to try a shieldmaid's temper.

Aeredh argued politely with Floringaeld and his lieutenant for what seemed an age. Finally, the Elder attempting to aid Eol gave orders for him to be propped up, and another small whitestone flask was produced. Efain massaged his captain's throat to help the drink go down, and the healer Gaercis announced the heir of Naras was in no danger of dying.

"*Strong, this one,*" he added. "*What made the wound? His kind should heal more swiftly.*"

"*A nagàth's blade, broken in the flesh.*" Daerith produced the shard from the lich's sword for examination, and when the tale of it drawn free was told in swift words many of the Elder looked solemnly at Arneior and me.

Aeredh's hand had healed, of course, but there were still thin white lines upon his palm and fingers where Arn's spearblade had bit. "*My own fault,*" he admitted, mildly enough. "*'Tis dangerous to touch a miracle while it is wrought, and the shieldmaiden is the lady alkuine's sworn protection.*"

Arneior's spear-haft bumped my knee. I was occupied in staying upright, but our gazes met.

My voice scraped like the bottom of a cask during a hard winter. "Are you…"

"Well enough," she husked in return. "*You* look draggled and half-dead. What say they?"

There was no need to pretend incomprehension now. "Eol will live." A great hot feeling poured through me as I gave voice to the news. I had, finally and at long last during our journey, succeeded at something. Or at least I had not failed completely, though the credit no doubt belonged more to the care of the Elder after my treatment of the wound, or to whatever restorative they had dosed him with. "And they are impressed by your temper."

"As every man should be." Her grin was a shadow of itself, but a scalding passed through me.

It was pure relief. My fingers and toes burned with fresh blood, the pain slightly ameliorated by the red drink. I was beginning to believe we had survived, and might not even be frost-kissed upon some numb extremity or another.

The vision of burned, shattered Dun Rithell rose before me again. I gripped the chair-arms, wishing I had enough strength to send one of my subtle selves flying to truly see. I hoped we would be left alone someplace warm and quiet to rest so I could perhaps dream of my mother; I was selfish enough to wish for comfort, though dreaming of others is to reassure *them* upon waking.

Some further discussion waxed and waned; I simply sat where I was, breathing as deeply as possible. There were no *orukhar* or liches trying to murder us, no monsters threatening life and sanity both, there was no snow or ice or wailing wind, and the light, while blue, was also powerful and clear like moonglow upon Tarnarya's white hood.

I am no stranger to the cold paleness of winter, but at that moment I longed never to see ice again.

Finally, it was decided. Aeredh, Daerith, and scarred Efain—for it seemed ill to the Elder to decide the fate of Secondborn without at least one present to hear doom pronounced, and Eol was in no fit condition to attend royalty—were to be taken to this king Taeron, and the rest of us would be held awaiting the result of that meeting.

I might have insisted upon accompanying Efain, for I was the ally to the house of Naras, was I not? But I was too weary, the world a moving tapestry hung before my senseless, blinking gaze. There was some small excitement when a Guard of the Passage loomed nearby and gestured, as if to take Arn's spear.

"*Cease,*" I heard myself say in the Old Tongue, sounding much like my mother when tired of her children's wrangling. "*She needs it, for she is sworn to my defense. And you are all men.*"

"*I had half forgotten you speak our tongue,*" Soren said, and though he had unbuckled his sword-belt, he had not yet placed the blade in an Elder's keeping. *"She speaks truth, my lord Aeredh, though it may well pain our pride."*

A short silence followed, during which Aeredh gazed steadily at Floringaeld, Arn stiffened, and the feather-brushing of the Wingéd lingered close about us both. I would not have put it past my shield-maid to brawl, even in her condition. And I would have aided her all I could—which was not much from a chair, true.

Yet I would have tried.

Floringaeld studied us both for a long moment. "Leave the women their single weapon, then. It does no harm—though if you seek to strike one of my guards, Flame-hair, it will go ill for you."

"Not half so ill as for any who seek to injure my Solveig." Though she slumped upon a stool, one hand grasping her spear and the other clasped about a silver Elder goblet, Arneior managed to look near-regal. "Are you finished talking every matter to death, my lords? My *volva* needs rest; we do not complain of hospitable poverty, but ill greetings by great lords well able to care for travelers is another matter entirely."

"Sharp tongues have the women of the South." The corners of Floringaeld's mouth twitched upward.

Aeredh laughed, and though the sound was weary, it was also full of grudging amusement. *"That is a truth indeed."* Faint smiles were evident upon the wolves of Naras, and even the Elder of our group who would not accompany Aeredh handed over their weapons without demur.

Waterstone

Who can tell from whence doom springs? Did it have its source in the Crownless's burdened return, or earlier with the son of Hrasimir? Did it come from the arrival of Maedroth, or of the sojourn of his mother with Ganaetir the Silent? Further back the woe may be traced, to the Enemy's great theft, or to his betrayal of the Allmother before the world was made. Who, then, shall we blame? Even the Wise cannot say.

—Naciel Silverfoot

I could not walk properly, swaying like a drunken warrior, my bag bumping my hip. Arneior was hardly better; though she managed without aid she could not brace me. She needed to use her spear as a walking-stave at intervals. Afterward she would not speak upon it, for the act galled her.

It fell to Aeredh, having given his sword to Floringaeld, to put his arm over my shoulders once more. "It is as it must be," he said softly. "Their secrecy is necessary, for the Enemy would dearly love to destroy this place even as Nithraen. As much as he hated my father, he fears Taeron more."

It meant little to me at the moment, for I was braced for a return to the killing cold and consequently loath to leave the fire. The guards did not take us through the door into the Passage but alongside its flow, through a tunnel much airier than Redhill's many passages and lit with blue-burning lamps nestled in holders of carven stone.

I said nothing, and we walked for some time parallel to our former course, Eol still hanging between two of his men but sometimes attempting to move his wet boots. Aeredh glanced at me often, but the red drink was doing its work, and I could at least raise my chin— though I frequently staggered. A sweet breath streamed past us, full of green scent.

"It is not like an ordinary dungeon," Aeredh continued. Perhaps relief was working upon him like mead as well. "And in any case it will not be long."

He seemed to expect some answer. I wet my cracked lips, coughed, and managed to clear my throat. "As long as there are no liches," I husked.

"Not here, no." He did not laugh, though, and grew grave. "I pray you will never see another, my lady."

So do I. "It seems unlikely, if you wish me to wield this *seidhr*-thing." I could find no more breath for banter, wholly occupied with my faltering feet. A thin, forge-hot wire of strength ran through my bones, but it had to pull the rest of me along; I was a reluctant puppet at best.

Finally, there was a tall, broad iron door flanked by more hidden galleries, and a great iron key was produced. The lock did not grind, simply gave a soft sound of well-oiled parts. Golden mornlight burst through the widening aperture, bathing Arneior, Aeredh, and my own blinking, sodden self.

We had spent the night in the Hidden Passage, and a new day was come.

On the other side were easy stone steps descending from a platform cut into sheer mountainside—but even here, there were slits carved in the rock we had so recently been under, and behind them archers ready to pincushion any enemy so foolish as to attempt this narrow entry.

And it was not cold. Oh, it was not summer, nor was it spring, but it seemed a mild autumn day instead of the frozen wastes of the Wild. Arn gasped, I let out a harsh disbelieving breath, and Aeredh all but carried me over the threshold.

A vast green valley-bowl starred with shady copses and bright glitterthreads of running water lay amid high white peaks. The sun had not yet crowned the rim of the mountains, but enough winter dawnglow had risen to light Laeliquaende—such is Waterstone's name in the language of its inhabitants, a dialect of the Old Tongue changed by degrees in their long solitude. Music there was from the vast valley's streams, for it was carved by great cascades which retreated in the long peace after the Enemy was bound the first time, before he sued for pardon and used the Allmother's forgiveness to wreak yet more havoc.

In the valley's palm, the city lay. Shimmering amid the meadows, white spires rose—not just white, but every shade of paleness, from glistening pearls brought from the mouth of my own home's river to the snow of high places, from bone fresh or old to the inside of sea-gathered shells, from bleached linen to the evanescent glitter of rainless clouds. The immensity of the vale made the city a distant dream, a toylike shimmer—yet Waterstone's very size meant it was clearly visible instead of a mere glimmering speck.

A star—visible and steady both at morn and eve—burned through the rising dawn, peering just over the shoulder of a mighty mountain holding back a smear of deeper darkness. *Maedroth* they named the star, meaning *the Watchful*, and *Aeredhe-il* the mountain, meaning *guardian*.

"Behold Laeliquaende," Floringaeld said, with soft reverence. "Here the Enemy does not trouble us. You are lucky to see this sight, Secondborn; not many of your kind have, and even fewer have left while living. You will be held in safety while our king Taeron judges your case."

I could find no answer. To go from winter's heart to this was a shock greater than the red cordial, an *orukhar*'s blow, or the snow-hag's scream. There was movement upon the meadows—Elder, dancing or walking as the light strengthened—and from far away as the cool breeze shifted there was a sound as of many bells rung in melody as well as lifted voices.

Everything in Waterstone sings. The sun chose that moment to crown the mountains' eastron rim, and the entire valley filled with gold, green, and white.

I did not stumble upon the stairs, but only because Aeredh was there. My weariness was too great for words, or even for much surprise when a stone bailey swallowed us, and the men now made prisoner—both Elder and Secondborn—were led away through one door of a vast white building. Soren and Karas both turned back in the dark archway, whether to take one last look at Arneior and me or to grant us some comfort I could not guess. Eol made no sound as the shadow swallowed him.

At least the Elder would not let a wounded prisoner die. Or so I hoped, in the thick mud-soup my head had become.

My shieldmaid and I were led through another doorway, this one carved with two graceful trees bearing interlocking bough-crowns. Aeredh steadied me down another flight of easy stairs carved from porous bleached stone, and there was a hallway with a procession of vertical bars upon either side. Strengthening light filtered through high windows, and one of the cells accepted us. It was larger than our closet at Dun Rithell, though not so spacious as the apartments in Nithraen, and its water-room was not so private as it could be.

I could not even blush. There was a flat stone shelf along one wall, and though Floringaeld said bedding would be brought I stepped away from Aeredh and tacked unevenly for its shelter. Bare rock or not, all I wished for in the world was to gain some harbor.

Aeredh's arm dropped to his side. He watched as Arneior followed me, my shieldmaid turned sideways and moving with terrible slowness, an exhausted warrior covering her army's retreat.

When I stretched out upon the cold white shelf, I sighed. My grey travel-dress dripped, and I would probably take the ague or lung-blight from resting thus upon bare rock.

I did not care. Barred doors slid upon grooves in the floor, and when the slight sound of movement finished, Aeredh, Efain, and Daerith were upon the other side.

Free, while Arn and I were caged.

"I will return," Aeredh said quietly, blue gaze burning through the bars. The metal looked powdery, thinly carved and entirely too frail to hold even a sparrow, let alone a *volva* and her shieldmaid. But the doors were of Elder make, and likely far stronger than they seemed. "As soon as possible."

"And I," Efain added darkly. He nodded to Arn, who returned a grudging movement of her own. She lowered herself onto the stone shelf near my knees, leaning upon her spear, and since her mantle had been taken wet ring-and-scale made a soft grating sound as her weight settled.

I turned away from the cell, from the white city and the green sward. I turned from the Glass, the Wild, the terror of the journey, the Mistwood's choking silence. I turned from Redhill and the breaking of Nithraen, and everything in me longed for Dun Rithell. I did not feel my wet dress or the aching in every muscle; I curled around my useless bag and stared at the wall for a few moments, unable to believe we could at last cease moving.

I closed my eyes, and blackness took me. Arn leaned upon her spear as she slept sitting next to me, the picture of a weary shieldmaid.

⬚⬚⬚⬚⬚

Thus did we arrive in Waterstone, the hidden city of Taeron Gold-spear, the High-helm. We did not leave for a long while, and though we did not know it our coming was as doom to the white towers and singing fountains.

That day, all we knew was imprisonment, and finally, my shield-maid and I could rest.

The story continues in...

The Fall of Waterstone

Book TWO of Black Land's Bane

Keep reading for a sneak peek!

Acknowledgments

This is a difficult undertaking, and thanks are due to several: to Mel Sterling, whose support never wavers; to Lucienne Diver, the best agent a weary writer could hope for; to Jennifer Parrack, pocket friend and beta reader par excellence; to Skyla Dawn Cameron, who listens with good grace and better advice; to my children, who love to put the quarter in; to Nivia Evans, Angelica Chong, and Bryn A. McDonald, for their weary patience; to Deangelo, who knows what he did.

And, last but never least, to you, my very dearest readers. As always, I will thank you in the way we both like best, by telling you another story...

...soon.

extras

orbit

meet the author

LILITH SAINTCROW was born in New Mexico, bounced around the world as an Air Force brat, and fell in love with writing when she was ten years old. She currently lives in Vancouver, Washington.

Find out more about Lilith Saintcrow and other Orbit authors by registering for the free monthly newsletter at orbitbooks.net.

if you enjoyed
A FLAME IN THE NORTH

look out for

THE FALL OF WATERSTONE
BLACK LAND'S BANE: BOOK 2

by

Lilith Saintcrow

*Solveig and her shieldmaiden have finally made it to
Waterstone, a fabled city hidden in a world of frost by ancient
magic. Shrouded from the Enemy's gaze, they are safe to rest
and regroup—or so they think.*

*Sol suspects their hosts are not as benevolent as they seem.
Whispers race through the halls, hinting at self-serving agendas
and secret plots. So, as Sol attempts to harness her awakened
magic, she must fight for her voice to be heard or risk being used
like a pawn in the greater game.*

*But the Enemy is always watching and nowhere is truly safe.
Before the darkness finds a way in, Sol must decide if she will
take up the mantle of power to save not just the home she's left
behind, but the future of the world.*

A Brazen Voice

Arneior set me upon my feet with more care than usual, studying my expression. Her freckles glowed, and a healthy flush mounted in her cheeks. The stripe of blue woad upon the left side of her face nearly leapt into thin air, so vivid was it in the noontide. "What a place, Sol. Such gardens. But they live so close—'tis a warren."

Better than Nithraen. The cave-city had been beautiful indeed, but I preferred open sky, no matter the weather's fury, to so much rock overhead. "At least we are not underground." A dry cough clawed at the last word; I denied it.

At the center of Waterstone a great shining palace the color of fresh cream basked in wintry sunshine. Perhaps my anxiety was simply the jarring difference between that light and the temperature, for when the great lamp of day looks pale in a drained sky it should be cold. Yet I did not need my great green mantle, its hood and back lined with fur from a shieldmaid-hunted wolf, nor did I need my sturdy felted overboots.

It was utterly, simply *wrong*. At least the hideous discordance was somewhat muted here.

The palace was of much grander form than Nithraen's, and its great silver-chased doors stood open at the head of marble stairs veined with gold. I held fast to Arneior's arm as we climbed, securely contained in a knot of black-clad Northerners, velvet-wrapped Elder, and the armored guards.

Did they fear us—two lone women, levered from their home and brought here all but unwilling? Eol and Aeredh exchanged meaningful glances as another group of armored Elder appeared, taking charge of visitors with precise movements. Floringaeld did not leave, however—the captain simply slowed, and when he drew level he examined us with much interest, as if he had not seen me and my shieldmaid enough the past few days.

I did not return his gaze, being wholly occupied with placing

one foot before the other. Halls folded away upon either side, pillared or lined with bright tapestries and murals I might have been
interested in had my head not throbbed so awfully. Arneior glanced
down at me several times, especially when we passed gardens and
courtyards open to the sky, each with its own plashing, jangling
fountain.

"Sol?" Her mouth barely moved; it was the whisper we used in
our closet at home, away from prying ears. "You're pale."

"So many people." I had thought the folk of Nithraen beautiful
with their shining eyes and bright hair, but every Elder I now saw
looked furtive or outright haughty, viewing us with secret disdain
and more than a hint of malice. "I can barely breathe."

"Do you require rest?" Floringaeld stepped nearer; I almost
blundered into Arn's side, flinching from his presence. "Our king
gave orders that you be brought, yet at your own pace."

"I am well enough." My throat was almost too parched to grant
passage to the words; I pushed my shoulders back and set my chin.
"This is only the second Elder city I have seen, my lord. Our settlement is small by comparison." *Though fine enough, for it is full of
honest folk.*

I kept that thought trapped behind gritted teeth, and wished my
stomach would cease its rolling.

"Our journey was long, and few our companions." Blue-eyed Gelad
moved forward, almost as if to step between the Elder and me. The
Old Tongue, familiar though of archaic Northern accent, pierced
my head like an awl forced through heavy leather. *"No doubt this is
a great change."*

I could have been grateful for his intercession, but there were
yet more stairs to climb. I almost wished to be on horseback again;
my knees were soft as Albeig's sops for ill children or the toothless
elderly.

At last another set of glittering doors fit for giants swung open,
quiet as a whisper, and we were ushered into a vast space full of
trees.

Spreading branches met overhead, bearing broad yellow leaves veined with green. I recognized the foliage—the Northerners' dense sweetish waybread had been wrapped in them, and the forest above Nithraen populated by these smooth greyish trunks as well. In this hall the trees were far more ancient, for even if Arn and I clasped hands their boles would be too large for us to encircle. They grew from a mirrorlike stone floor which imperceptibly turned to soft grass-clad earth where their roots delved, and small pale-blue flowers peeked over their gnarled feet.

I had seen those blossoms before, too—after leaving Redhill and traveling far upon the backs of winter-deep, we had reached a stone-ringed clearing full of them. I strained to remember their name in the Old Tongue, and could not.

That was another wrongness; a *volva*'s memory does not misplace such small details. My unease turned sharp as a good blade. So did the nausea. Something dire approached, yet I could neither halt nor evade it. A whisper of *seidhr* trickled into my bones, easing some of the discomfort—but not nearly enough.

"Sol?" Arn, whispering again. I had no attention to spare for her concern.

The center of the space held a slight, natural rise, and upon it stood a simple bench of white stone. Such was the throne of Laeliquaende, and Taeron Goldspear chose no further decoration for his seat. The music here was muted, which was a distinct relief.

Or it might have been, were I not sweating and trembling like a frightened horse.

He was tall and dark-haired, the king of this place, with piercing sky-blue eyes very much like my mother's. He sat with one leg drawn up, resting an elbow upon it as casually as my brother Bjorn when taking his ease upon a fallen log between practice-ring bouts, and rested his chin upon his hand as he regarded our group. A silver fillet like Aeredh's clasped his brow, and nearby a bright-haired Elder girl—Naciel his daughter, the treasure of Laeliquaende— with skirts of pale new green like soft early fir-tips set aside a graceful harp. She rested in a nest of pillows, all covered with muted jewel-color velvet. Next to her was a Northerner in the garb of the Elder inhabitants though black as Eol's cloth, dark of hair and proud of nose, his gaze bearing the same weight as Tarit of Redhill's.

Not quite *seidhr*, but very close.

At the king's left hand stood an Elder man appearing of Aeredh's age, though that is little indication among their folk. He was another black blot, as if he wished to dress as the wolves of Naras— armor of matte finish, engraved with flowing, near-invisible lines. His eyes showed little difference between pupil and iris, and he wore an air of pronounced vigilance; Maedroth was he, called *the Watchful* after a star well-beloved by the Elder, and he was Taeron's nephew.

Their names I learned later. At that moment, I saw only their physical forms as if through a sheet of clear rippling water, distorted as the so-called music. I swayed, pulling upon Arneior's arm, and the whisper of *seidhr* became a thunder.

No, please. I cannot.

But fighting this flood was a doomed battle; Idra my teacher would have tweaked one of my braids with ruthless precision. *Ride the power, child. Don't fight it.*

But I was so tired, and everything hurt.

"My friend." Aeredh's voice should have been comforting—after all, he had carried me upon the last leg of our journey, as if I were a youngling sleepy after a great feast—but it near tore at my cringing nerves. "I bring you Solveig daughter of Gwendelint, *alkuine* of Dun Rithell, and her shieldmaid Arneior, taken by the Black-Wingéd Ones."

It was a great honor to be announced thus, presented to an Elder king by the equally royal Crownless himself. I might even have enjoyed it, had my stomach not suddenly plunged and a red-hot wire of pain run through me from scalp to heels.

The black-eyed Elder at the king's side cocked his dark head, and a shadow lay over him. *No,* I pleaded silently. *I don't want to see. Stop.* My wrists flamed too, as if every bit of ink forced under the skin pinprick-by-pinprick was suddenly full of molten lead.

It was no use. In the great thronehall of Nithraen I had spoken in couplets helpfully provided by a passing spirit, but this was different. Perhaps something about an Elder throne was inimical to me, or provoked *seidhr* in those who carry the weirding? I could not guess, I knew only the pain.

"Welcome are your friends in my demesnes, son of Aerith." Taeron's tone was pleasant, and he used the southron tongue instead of the Old—another signal mark of honor, especially for mortal guests. "So, this is another *alkuine*? Great indeed is the—"

Agony roared through me, not merely a wire but a heavy sword-blade. The *seidhr* drew me from Arneior's side, my hand sliding nerveless from her arm, and I took three staggering steps as if mead-drunk upon a festival day.

My head tipped back, my mouth opened. Even submitting to the prophecy-speech granted no relief, for I was ill indeed and had hidden it much as a dog or caged bird will, unwilling to show any vulnerability.

A great brazen voice rose from my lungs, scorched my swell-aching throat, rattled my teeth, and tore past my lips. I was vaguely surprised no blood sprayed forth with it, for it *felt* as if I bled, a great gout of force rammed through a channel far too narrow.

"**Taeron**," it boomed, and the entire hall rattled, darkening. A salt-smelling wind loomed over the trees; their ancient pillars groaned, branch and twig thrash-dancing. A great soughing as of a summer storm in the forest swept the name high, tossing it back into the hall's cup like dice into a leather container before the gambling begins. "**Taeron, my child, I told thee once, and sent one fated to tell thee twice. Now arriveth my final warning.**"

The Old Tongue it spoke in, that terrible tone, and the sky over Waterstone turned the color of a fresh bruise. Salt and fish the wind smelled of as it whistled through the white city; I sought to collapse, but the *seidhr* would not let me. My spine arched, my head thrown back, and Arneior sprang for me, attempting to reach her charge.

She was pushed back, not ungently but clumsily, as if the invisible force inhabiting me for that brief moment did not wish her ill but would brook no interference. Again the voice was drawn forth, this time from my heels as they touched the earth.

"**Love not the work of thy hands too much,**" it intoned. "**Be not so proud of thy House that thou scruple'st to join it to another. Thou know'st my voice, and know'st the truth in thy inmost heart.**"

The king had risen, and for a moment I glimpsed a cold blue brilliance about him—for the Elder have *seidhr* too, though not of our mortal kind, and their subtle selves burn bright-hot. My eyes squeezed shut, tears slicking my cheeks, and for the last time, the voice wrung me like a rag in our housekeeper Albeig's capable, callused fingers.

"**Hope has been offered thee, Taeron. The hour is late; let it not grow later.**"

The thing speaking through me—certainly some divinity instead of a mere passing spirit, though at the moment I could not even wonder which—perhaps also tried to be gentle as it lifted up and away like a white bird upon chill salt-freighted breeze. I had only seen the sea with my inner eye, subtle selves freed from my physical body by drugging fumes from Idra's brass brazier, but its smell was everywhere in that city. For that brief tearing instant I was free of all pain, gliding over the deep cold spear-harbors of the westron shore so far from Dun Rithell.

"Sol! *Solveig!*" Arn was calling, but I could not answer. Does a pipe feel exhausted when the breath forced through it ceases? I had been used as an instrument, and collapsed at last. A vast soft darkness enfolded me, welcome because it was painless, and the last thing I heard was Aeredh's voice, the Old Tongue ragged and breathless.

"*We passed too close by the Marukhennor; she is in the despair. Fool that I was to not see it.*"

For a brief interval I knew nothing, not even to be grateful at the cessation of discomfort. Such was my greeting to Taeron, and little did I guess he knew that voice, having heard it before the Sun rose and a few times thereafter as well.

But I? I landed upon stone floor with bruising force, saved only from skullsplit by Arneior reaching me at last, her spear clattering free as she thrust her hand between my cheek and cool, hard, mirror-glossy stone to cushion the blow.

if you enjoyed
A FLAME IN THE NORTH

look out for

SHIELD MAIDEN

by

Sharon Emmerichs

Fryda has grown up hearing tales of her uncle, King Beowulf, and his spectacular defeat of the monstrous Grendel. Her one desire is to become a shield maiden in her own right, but a terrible accident during her childhood has thwarted this dream. Yet still, somehow, she feels an uncontrollable power begin to rise within herself.

The last thing Fryda wants is to be forced into a political marriage, especially as her heart belongs to her lifelong friend, Theow. However, as foreign kings and chieftains descend upon her home to celebrate Beowulf's fifty years as the king of Geatland, the partnership begins to seem inevitable.

That is, until, amid the lavish gifts and drunken revelry, a discovery is made that threatens the safety of Fryda's entire clan—and her own life. Incensed by this betrayal, Fryda resolves to fight for her people no matter the cost. As a queen should. As a shield maiden would.

And as the perilous situation worsens, Fryda's powers seem to grow only stronger. But she is not the only one to feel the effects of her newfound battle-magic. For, buried deep in her gilded lair, a dragon is drawn to Fryda's untamed power and is slowly awakening from a long, cursed sleep....

Prologue

Geatland, in the year 987 CE

On the morning of her thirteenth birthday, Fryda of Clan Waegmunding—daughter of Weohstan and jewel of King Beowulf's eye—wanted only one good kill. She wished for a sturdy arrow shot straight and true, the rending of flesh under her knife, and the tang of hot blood sending curls of steam into the chill air.

In the pre-dawn darkness, she wriggled her way into trousers pilfered from the laundry the day before. The icy glimmer of stars peeped through the smoke-hole cut into the roof as she pulled on a roughspun tunic and fastened a leather belt around her childishly slim waist. *Good*, she thought. No one else in the household would stir for another hour at least.

She gathered her wild, butter-coloured curls into thick braids and wound them around her head, hoping the pins would hold, and slid a short *seax*—a sharp, tapered hunting dagger—under her belt. For a moment she considered fetching Theow from his pallet in the kitchens and asking if he wanted to come with her.

As Theow's name hovered in her mind, she felt a small frisson shimmer up her spine. Her breath quickened, the hairs on her arms stood up, and her young body woke in ways she did not entirely understand. She nearly surrendered to the rush of temptation that

426

tugged her towards the kitchens, but did not want to risk Theow receiving credit for her hunt. A warrior gets credit for his kills.

Her kills, she thought. Or at least, one kill to prove her prowess at the hunt. One wolf pelt to hang in the mead-hall and call her own.

She grabbed her bow and a quiver of arrows from her wooden chest and crept from the building, trying to be as silent as possible. In the early morning hush, every step, every breath sounded unnaturally loud, and she startled at each rustle and distant birdcall. Her breath misted in the late autumn air, but the nights were not yet cold enough to freeze the dew that pearled on the grass, making everything smell fresh and green.

Fryda made her way towards the western wall, stealing through the *burh* as quietly as she could. In the hovering darkness of the far-northern autumn, the structures resembled a sprawling village rather than a walled estate. Warm, reddish earthen walls rose in square and rectangular blocks, adorned by thatched, timbered roofs and arched windows set with real glass, sparkling like gemstones. Wooden structures hunkered in rows around an ancient standing stone. The air smelled like salt and brine, and she could hear the distant thunder of waves crashing against the rocky shore.

She nodded to the guards stationed at the gate and they let her pass without question. She had no doubt they would report her early morning exit from the *burh* to her father, but by that time—she hoped—she would have a fine wolf pelt to placate him.

Fryda padded through a wooded grove outside the stronghold wall, avoiding rustling leaves and noisy twigs. Soon her boots were soaked through and a chill pebbled her skin, but she did not think about turning back. Shield maidens did not stop fighting because of damp feet.

She scanned the ground as she moved, alert for any sign of the beast that had plagued the *burh*'s hunters since summer's end. After several cold, breathless moments she spotted the paw prints of an enormous wolf in some soft mud and steadily tracked them westward. They led her out of the woods to the bare, wind-ravaged meadows along the edge of the cliff. Elation filled her, making her

extras

feel as if she floated above the ground. She was going to find the wolf. She would find it and kill it and her father would finally see her as a worthy shield maiden. He would finally let her...

Her thoughts rattled out of her head as the earth beneath her shuddered and jerked. Fryda gasped as she staggered, trying to keep her feet. A terrifying roar filled her ears—a sound so monumental she thought Woden himself must have made it. Certainly no wolf could produce such a clamour.

The ground shifted sideways and violently flung her into the grass. A sharp report echoed across the sky, as if the very fabric of the air cracked and tore. The meadow undulated beneath her as though suddenly turned to water, and Fryda clutched the long grass in her fists. The coarse blades tore in her grip as the earth tried to shake her off, like a flea in a dog's fur.

The great cracks and rumblings became deafening, and Fryda sobbed in terror. The ground lurched, and then...disappeared.

For one breath she lay on solid, if tumultuous, ground and the next she plummeted downwards. A scream tore from her throat and she clawed with frantic hands for anything to break her fall.

Something grabbed her by the wrist, and for one breathless moment she thought Woden had indeed stretched out a hand to save her. But when a lightning bolt of pain shot from her hand down to her shoulder, Fryda understood why the clan revered the All-Father as the god of madness as well as death. She screamed again as her hand became fire and flames licked through her arm, her shoulder, and into her chest. She blinked against the sparks dancing across her vision and wondered if disobedience to her father had truly brought about the end of the world.

The violence of the earthquake had hollowed out a deep, deep chasm in the earth and she'd managed to jam her hand into a narrow crack in the wall. Fryda stared at the shards of white bone jutting from her ruined skin, the wells of shocking red blood running down her arm. It dripped from her fingers onto her neck, her face, into her clothing, and fear rushed to fill the spaces of her body left empty by leaking blood and protruding bone. She clutched the wall with her good hand while her feet scrabbled against the rock, trying to find purchase. But every movement caused great flowers of pain to bloom in her hand and chest, and she realized the fall had separated the bones of her arm completely from her shoulder.

Time began acting strangely. She had no idea how long she hung there, drowning in agony and hoping she would soon die. Eventually the darkness of night crept into her bones. Her throat burned with thirst and screams. Her eyes grew dim; her body shook with cold and weakness. Her arm and shoulder had gone numb hours before, but her hand seethed with pain from the bones piercing her skin and from the rock that kept her trapped like a rabbit in a snare. She screamed again, her voice feeble and wounded, and heard an answering music rise from the bottom of the chasm, a tinkling like bells or chimes.

It wasn't real, of course. She knew that now. Once night had claimed the land, she had fallen into a kind of delirium wherein she heard and saw things from the wrong side of reality. Strange phantasms from her life that could not possibly exist in this place and time hovered around her, like the scent of Hild's delicious mushroom soup, or the tang of the ground galls the hunters used for tanning skins. Perhaps the visions, the scents, the music were heralds of her death. If so, she welcomed them.

The torment from her trapped hand writhed through her body like a living thing. The hours since the earthquake had not acted as a balm for her pain. She thought, as she had a thousand times since she fell, about the hunting knife tucked in her belt.

She whimpered. Her hand, with all its torn flesh and broken bones, had swollen so rapidly she could not budge it from its rocky prison. But she could wrap her belt around her arm; tighten it. Take the knife and...

A gust of wind from the sea snaked through the chasm and buffeted her against the cliff wall.

Fryda screamed in earnest as her broken wrist twisted and the bones ground together. She fumbled for the *seax* at her waist, but her fingers faltered as the darkness closed in on her, and she gratefully succumbed to her fate.

orbit

Follow us:

f **/orbitbooksUS**

X **/orbitbooks**

▶ **/orbitbooks**

Join our mailing list
to receive alerts on our
latest releases and deals.

orbitbooks.net

Enter our monthly
giveaway for the chance
to win some epic prizes.

orbitloot.com